End Game

David Baldacci is one of the world's bestselling and favourite thriller writers. With over 130 million copies in print, his books are published in over 80 territories and 45 languages, and have been adapted for both feature-film and television. He has established links to government sources, giving his books added authenticity. David is also the co-founder, along with his wife, of the Wish You Well Foundation®, a non-profit organization dedicated to supporting literacy efforts across the US. Still a resident of his native Virginia, he invites you to visit him at DavidBaldacci.com and his foundation at WishYouWellFoundation.org.

Trust him to take you to the action.

ALSO BY DAVID BALDACCI

The Camel Club series
The Camel Club • The Collectors • Stone Cold
Divine Justice • Hell's Corner

King and Maxwell series
Split Second • Hour Game • Simple Genius • First Family
The Sixth Man • King and Maxwell

Shaw series
The Whole Truth • Deliver Us From Evil

John Puller series
Zero Day • The Forgotten • The Escape
No Man's Land

Will Robbie series
The Innocent • The Hit • The Target • The Guilty

Amos Decker series
Memory Man • The Last Mile • The Fix

Vega Jane series
The Finisher • The Keeper • The Width of the World

Other novels
True Blue • Absolute Power • Total Control
The Winner • The Simple Truth • Saving Faith
Wish You Well • Last Man Standing
The Christmas Train • One Summer

Short Stories
No Time Left • Bullseye

DAVID BALDACCI

End Game

MACMILLAN

First published 2017 by Grand Central Publishing, USA

First published in the UK 2017 by Macmillan
an imprint of Pan Macmillan
20 New Wharf Road, London N1 9RR
Associated companies throughout the world
www.panmacmillan.com

ISBN 978-1-4472-7784-2

A CIP catalogue record for this book is available from the British Library.

Printed and bound by CPI Group (UK) Ltd, Croydon, CR0 4YY

To Bob Holsworth, a mentor and friend

End Game

CHAPTER

I

As WILL ROBIE STARED out the plane window, he knew the next twenty-four hours could possibly be his last ones on earth.

Yet that was simply another day on the job for him.

The undercarriage of multiple reinforced wheels touched down and grabbed the tarmac, and the thrust reversers engaged. The world's largest commercial airliner taxied to a stop at the gate. The doors, both forward and aft, on the upper and lower cabins opened. The passengers trooped down the Jetways and into Terminal Five at Heathrow Airport.

The English skies were slicked with fat, darkened clouds and the rain was falling. It was weather familiar to any Brit.

Robie, wearing a navy blue two-piece tailored suit and fitted white collared shirt, was among hundreds of passengers deplaning the British Airways jumbo A380 just landed from Washington, DC.

The flight had become a little bumpy midway over the Atlantic. However, Robie hadn't noticed. With his flat business-class seat, he'd slept pretty much the whole ride.

He cleared Customs, informing the border officer that he was there solely on business of an academic nature. He had carried on his single small bag and thus had no reason afterward to go to Baggage Claim. Everything he would need was already in London. And none of it was anything he could reasonably have carried on a plane.

It was seven thirty a.m. local time when he finally exited the airport.

Robie rode in a multicolored taxi into the city, which, with traffic and the rainy weather, took well over an hour. He was dropped off at an address near Marylebone Road. It wasn't a hotel, but rather a nondescript private row house near the juncture of Marylebone and Baker Street. Robie punched in a code on the electronic box set next to the front door, and the fortified portal unlocked. He walked in, secured the door behind him, and headed upstairs.

He exchanged his two-piece suit and dress shirt for more casual wear. He popped open a wall safe in the closet and took out the flash drive. His Agency used cloud computing, but the leadership didn't fully trust that it couldn't be hacked, since clearly anything *could* be hacked. He pulled out his laptop and inserted the drive in the USB port. He tapped some keys and up on the screen appeared the only reason he had come to London.

It was a read-only document, and it was *not* remotely business of an academic nature.

He absorbed the information on the screen. It ended with a note from Robie's superior, Blue Man. His real name was Roger Walton. The term *Blue Man* came from his exalted position at their Agency. The note, written more than a week earlier, was brief and to the point, just like Blue Man always was.

You can do this for one simple reason: You're Will Robie. I'll see you when we both get back. Onward.

Robie understood that in those few words was a volume's worth of meaning.

I am Will Robie and I've been through hell and back. And I will survive this.

Onward.

He next performed an NSA-level wipe of the flash drive, tantamount to smashing it flat with a brick then setting it afire. The ones and zeroes were permanently gone, now existing only in his memory.

He stretched out on the bed and stared up at the ceiling.

Mississippi seemed a long time ago.

His father seemed a long time ago.

Everything seemed a long time ago.

He was back in harness and glad for it, because all other elements of his life sucked.

Stop the bullshit. This is your life.

Like the NSA cleanse on the flash drive, he shed these thoughts and closed his eyes. Despite his rest on the plane, he needed sleep. He would not be getting any later tonight.

He rose in the early evening and checked the sky. Still cloudy, but no more rain. Since this was London, that could change at any moment.

He ate at a nearby pub and walked the pavements. His swift gait carried him past many buildings and hundreds of people walking along in what he knew was a blissful ignorance of another possible attack on London. Then again, full knowledge might have started a panic. And they couldn't have that, could they? Londoners had endured several recent terrorist attacks. Evil driving in cars had smashed into innocent pedestrians on both Westminster and London Bridges. Yet with enviable courage and calm, the town's citizenry were carrying on with their lives. But something else was up now and it had to be dealt with.

So they had sent Will Robie.

He returned to his row house, made some calls on a secure line that bounced off one particular bird in the sky, and was told that everything was a go for the moment. As with the weather, he knew that could always change.

It was like a false start in the hundred-meter dash. Cocked and locked and fired and then called off. It could be unsettling.

It was a wonder he wasn't messed up from it.

Well, maybe he was.

Robie sat by the window for two hours, like a sentry on watch, missing nothing. This place was heavily — though discreetly — fortified and monitored 24/7 by eyes on another continent. Still, his stone-cold rule was to rely on himself and no one else. He was the one who would die if everything went to shit. The eyes on the other continent might simply get a memo on how to fix the mess in the future.

A little too late to do him any good.

Darkness had come as the globe spun on its axis, and another part of the world got to see the light.

He checked his phone. The solitary bird in the sky told him that his mission was still a go.

Later, Big Ben chimed midnight. It was a soothing, familiar melody to most Brits. To Robie, it was like the sound of a time card being punched.

He donned a customized, lightweight, black one-piece waterproof motorcycle suit and left by the back door. He opened the locked door of a garage in the mews and climbed astride the black Ducati XDiavel parked there and key-started it. The big engine bled noise and power through its stacked twin oval exit pipes. He slipped on his helmet, popped the kickstand, gunned the throttle, and blew out of the garage riding a power plant that displaced more than twelve hundred ccs cranking at a max rpm of 9,500. Its Bosch fuel injection system was a full ride-by-wire package.

For most, this was an expensive toy that, fully racked out, would set you back about twenty grand.

Tonight, it was simply Robie's ride to work.

He headed northwest.

The bike's tires gripped the asphalt firmly and threw up rainwater as he flashed through nearly empty streets. A bit later his destination was up ahead. Well, it was the *first* of his destinations tonight. He thundered into an alley and quickly slowed.

He cut the power to the bike, hopped off, and used a tool hidden behind a dustbin to lift the manhole cover located there. This was Destination #1. He used the metal rungs to clamber down about a hundred feet.

He kept his helmet on for one reason only.

He hit a switch at the back of the headpiece, and his helmet became the latest-generation panoramic night-vision optics, the same platform used by American combat pilots. It enhanced the visuals in the darkened utility tunnel to such a degree that it was almost like he was on the surface of the sun, minus the heat. Researchers were now working on contact lenses utilizing a thin layer of graphene between slender layers of glass that could take the place of the current bulky devices. The percentage of light pickup was not yet where it needed to be to make the innovation viable, so for now, Robie wore a bulky helmet to see in the dark.

High-tech to kill.

But it wasn't like the other side came to the battle with six-shooters and WWII-era optics.

He looked at his watch. He was one minute ahead of schedule. He slowed his pace. Early in his line of work was never a good thing.

He was forty-one years old, six one, a buck-eighty, and physically ripped because his job required it. His endurance levels and pain tolerances were off the chart—again, because they had to be. He had been selected for this line of work with the basic requirements already in place: He had a body, he had a mind, and he feared basically nothing.

Then over the years they had ground into him a whole other being, still possessing the basics plus a spectrum of skills that most people could never imagine, much less achieve.

Some days it was hard for Robie to see where the machine ended and the human began. If the human was in fact still there. In Mississippi it had shown itself. Now? It had receded.

Maybe forever.

His face was lean and weathered, and his eyes deep-set and alert. His hair was always cut short because he had no time to bother with it. He had old wounds and scars over his torso and limbs; each told a story of near-fatal results he would rather forget.

As he walked along he moved his right arm in a slow circular motion. All surgically repaired, scar tissue removed, tendons and ligaments all *tidied up*, as the Brits would say. It was 99 percent of what it used to be, the docs had assured him. That was really good. But really good rarely cut it in Robie's world.

They rebuilt me. But am I as good as I was? Or am I a slightly lesser version?

He would find out tonight if the missing one percent made the key difference between his walking away from this or remaining behind as a corpse.

Destination #2 was just up ahead.

If the Ducati had gotten him to Destination #1, what was coming up would get him back.

Alive.

He used a key to unlock a door set in the wall of the tunnel he was in.

Inside the small storage room revealed behind the door, he gunned up and put on his protective gear, which included the newest generation of personal armor.

His main arsenal consisted of an H&K UMP chambered in .45 ACP with a thirty-round box mag. He checked all working parts of the weapon and slung it over his shoulder. He slipped two extra mags into long pockets on his one-piece designed for just this purpose.

He figured if he couldn't do the job with ninety rounds he didn't deserve to come back. But just in case, there were twin M11s, each chambered in ten-millimeter with a laser sight built under the barrel. Where the dot hit so did the round.

He slipped the gun belt around his waist. Both pistols rode on the left side so he could pull with his dominant right hand, though if it came to it, he could kill ambidextrously with great efficiency.

A German-made KM2000 combat knife in its holder was attached to his belt.

Two M84 stun grenades were cradled in pockets on the rear of his belt.

Robie closed the door behind him and walked on.

Destination #3 was a quarter mile away.

In a fairly short time, Will Robie would know if he would get to see another sunrise or not.

CHAPTER

2

OXFORD CIRCUS.

It was one of the busiest stations on the London Underground, vying with both Waterloo and King's Cross in a back-and-forth annual battle for the statistical title. It was in an upscale part of London with pricey and fashionable shops and buildings resting above it. The Underground carried nearly a billion and a half passengers per year and nearly a hundred million of them came through the Oxford Circus station annually.

The Underground had suffered a terrorist attack on July 7, 2005, when terrorists had blown themselves up on three separate train cars. A fourth device had been detonated on a London bus. In all, fifty-two victims were killed.

The explosive devices used that infamous day were powerful, but not nearly so powerful as what was currently being planned.

A cobalt bomb was at the center of this. One had never been detonated before. Also known as a salted bomb, it was a thermonuclear device designed to maximize the radiation fallout, leaving a large area contaminated for a hundred or more years.

Fortunately, it was a very difficult thing to accomplish.

Unfortunately, it was not impossible.

Even more unfortunately, one was now in London.

The speaker in Robie's helmet relayed information to him as he walked along.

His final destination was just up ahead.

As he walked along he spun a suppressor onto the barrel of the UMP, then did the same for the twin M11s.

Stealth was called for tonight.

Until it wasn't.

He reholstered the military-grade pistols and touched his chest. What was underneath there might end up saving his life tonight. He had the same protection on both thighs. Right below these shields were his femoral arteries, twin pipelines of massive blood flow. If those got pierced, he was a dead man. The bleed-out from a punctured femoral was almost never survivable.

Four people had given their lives in order for the intel leading up to the mission tonight to make its way to the Americans. The intelligence agencies had then shared it with the British, who remained one of the United States' closest allies, regardless of who was in charge of the government at any given time. That had been the case ever since the English redcoats had burned down the American White House, which showed that strong friendship could indeed bloom from previously infertile ground. According to the information, the planned London op was merely a dress rehearsal for what would come later, in the United States.

Just like a manufacturer did in trying to commercialize a new product, terrorists needed to work the kinks out, too.

The kink was why Robie was now ascending a hundred feet to the surface.

His final destination was not another alley. It was a basement.

Of the four people to die in this operation so far, the third person had sacrificed her life to maneuver the target to stay in this building. Situated on the outskirts of London on a lonely street of a few modest residences, the structure had been used during World War II as a safe house and an operations center for senior government personnel. An escape tunnel and a bomb shelter had been paramount, and so they had been added. Over the last seven decades a floor had been put over the basement concrete and the trapdoor covered.

And forgotten.

It was no longer covered. And it was no longer forgotten.

London was an ancient city, and no one truly knew or understood all the passages and tunnels and labyrinths that lay underneath it, or how they all connected. A series of tunnels beneath that basement eventually intersected with a concrete pipeline that, with some minimal wall piercing, would allow one eventually to reach an equipment storage room under Oxford Circus Station. In that room the cobalt bomb was to be planted and detonated at the busiest hour of the day for the tube stop, when over a hundred thousand passengers would be in the station, with at least another hundred thousand pedestrians and vehicles immediately above. In all, over two million persons would be affected by the detonation as well as over a thousand buildings.

The place would be uninhabitable, for a century or two, at least.

Some dress rehearsal, thought Robie.

He didn't want to see a far larger encore on American soil.

The terror cell he was targeting tonight planned to use the tunnel to their advantage.

Robie planned to use it to their supreme disadvantage.

The reasons that an army of police and special forces was not descending on this terrorist plot instead of one man were complicated but, distilled to bare essentials, easily understood.

Panic.

When an army moved, it could not be kept a secret.

But when one man moved, a secret could be maintained.

And to avoid revealing what had been planned to the world and causing just such a panic that the terrorists no doubt would have rejoiced over, they had sent Robie in to have a shot at taking the terrorists down. Alone.

The Brits had special-ops people who could have performed this mission. But the higher-ups had concluded that if things went sideways, having a non-Brit involved gave the home team the best grounds for plausible deniability.

However, nothing was being left to chance. There *was* a hidden army surrounding the home. If Robie failed, the army wouldn't, panic be damned.

There were two homes on either side of the target. The residents in them had been prevented from returning home that night, so Robie had a bit of a buffer in which to operate and try to keep the mission out of the morning news broadcasts.

Hence the trio of suppressors on his gun barrels.

He finished climbing the rungs to the trapdoor. Though the people inside had no idea their mission had been compromised, they had taken standard protection procedures. The trapdoor was securely locked and also alarmed. But using three different tools provided to him, Robie ensured that it no longer was locked or alarmed.

He received one more communication in his headset.

"Vee-one."

It was the same call-out used by the aviation industry. *Vee-one* meant the aircraft had reached sufficient takeoff speed and there was no going back.

Robie acknowledged that command and turned his comm pack off. From now until either he or his opponents were dead, there would be nothing more said.

His helmet *was* fitted with a wireless camera so that his handlers could see everything that he could. They would either watch Robie win, or else see the bullets coming that would kill him.

An M11 in his right hand, he opened the trapdoor and looked around.

Nothing.

He climbed up and quietly set the trapdoor back into place. The basement was what one would expect in an old, crappy house in a tattered neighborhood—it was dirty and smelled of mold.

But there was one element of interest. In a far corner was a metal box about six feet in length. He slipped over to it, squatted down, pulled an instrument from his belt, and ran it over the box. He looked at the readout meter.

Cobalt bomb confirmed. It wasn't armed yet. They wouldn't do so until they moved it to Oxford Circus.

And Robie also knew that he would keep himself between them and the bomb at all times.

He holstered his M11 and readied his UMP.

He rose and moved to the wooden stairs. From his intelligence briefing on the house he knew that the fourth riser up squeaked, so he went from the third to the fifth.

In addition to him, there were currently seventeen people inside this place.

Robie's goal was to kill sixteen of them.

The fire selector on his UMP was set to two shots. One shot was enough to kill any man if placed properly, but Robie had left no room for chance.

The basement door was partially open.

He peered through it into the kitchen.

Two men sat at a table drinking what looked to be cups of coffee. They apparently needed a stimulant at this late hour.

He looked at his watch through his panoramic goggles.

The second hand was just sweeping to twelve.

Four…three…two…

On cue, the lights in the house went out as the power was cut.

Through his helmet Robie saw the two men clear as day jerk forward and then stand.

Then he watched them fall from suppressed UMP bursts delivered to their chests.

Two down, fourteen to go.

Robie was through the kitchen in three seconds and then hit the hallway.

His finger nudged the shot selector to full auto.

He did so because darkness tended to make people congregate closer.

Sure enough, coming down the narrow hall were three men, all with guns.

They opened fire. With pistols.

Robie pulled the UMP's trigger, and two seconds and twenty-six rounds of concentrated fire later there were three more dead men on the floor of this humble abode. The UMP's ejector sent the spent casings tumbling to the floor, where they sounded like metal pearls cascading from a broken necklace.

Five down, eleven to go.

He ejected the mag, slapped in a fresh one, and turned and rolled to his right as more gunfire came at him.

He counted two heads through his goggles.

He emptied half his UMP mag at them.

Seven down, nine to go.

Two more men appeared at the head of the stairs and fired down at Robie.

He could see that they had on NVGs as well, so his tactical advantage had lessened.

He pulled a stun grenade, released the pin, and threw it up the stairs at the same time he looked away.

The stunning flash of light did not blind him, nor did the concussive sound paralyze him, since his helmet cushioned him from this effect.

The two men at the top of the stairs could not claim the same.

One tumbled down and landed at the bottom of the stairs.

One slash across the neck from the KM2000 severed two critical arteries, and Robie added another to his tally.

He reholstered the bloody blade.

Eight down, an equal number to go.

The other man slowly rose at the top of the stairs, but was obviously concussed. He then fell back down and lay unconscious. That was the only thing that saved his life.

That and two men attacking Robie from his right and left flanks.

The M11s came out, one in each hand. Robie aimed an M11 in each direction simultaneously and then trigger-pulled ten shots from each gun, sweeping up and down from chest to thigh, the arc of fire evenly spaced over a ten-foot radius. A kill zone field of fire delivered with max efficiency.

Jacketed rounds tore through flesh. These sounds were followed by two thumps, as corpses hit carpet.

Ten down, six to go.

Since the cat was definitely out of the bag, he sprayed the stairwell using the rest of his second mag on the UMP. He then raced up the steps, after reloading his M11s.

A bullet, fired from above, struck him in the abdomen.

The liquid armor vest he had on hardened within a millisecond, catching the round and wringing out virtually all of its kinetic energy by forcing it to be displaced along the breadth of the vest.

The armor then lost its rigidity and became flexible once more.

Robie had no idea who had invented this stuff, but if he survived tonight, he would buy the person a drink.

His second stun grenade flushed out the shooter. Robie shot him once in the knee with an M11 to incapacitate, then performed the kill shot to the head on the upper stairwell.

Eleven down, five to go.

He reached the upper hall, reholstered the M11, and reloaded the UMP with his final mag just as someone blindsided him. They tumbled back down the stairs. His attacker had a gutting knife and he managed to strike Robie in the thigh. His liquid armor once more seized up, and the knife didn't even penetrate to the skin.

Robie's right hand clamped down on the wrist with the knife. He torqued himself around so that he was on top when they slammed into the floor at the bottom of the stairs. The man beneath him was stunned by the impact but for only a second.

That was still a moment too long for survival.

Robie had used the man's own knife to slit his throat. Arterial spray danced across his visor.

He hoped the handlers back in their safe space were enjoying the show.

It wasn't nearly as much fun on his end.

Twelve down, four to go.

He rose, turned, and rolled out of the way as a volley of machine-gun fire blew down the stairs, ripping off part of the handrail, shredding the wall, and exploding a slew of the risers.

With his night vision, Robie could see where it was coming from.

Instead of trying to attack back up the stairs, he moved to his left, where the upper part of the stairway was partially covered by the wall rising from the lower floor.

He pointed the UMP at a forty-five-degree angle up and five clicks to the left. He pressed the trigger and fired half his mag. The ACP rounds blasted through the cheap drywall. Robie counted to three and watched as the shooter's body rolled down the stairs and landed at the bottom and on top of the gent who'd had his throat slit by Robie.

Robie made sure the shooter was dead with an M11 round dotting the man's forehead.

Thirteen down, three to go.

And those three were upstairs.

Now it became purely a tactical game. A chess match played with guns and battlefield strategy instead of molded pieces on a square board.

The enemy had the high ground and Robie the low. For him to attack, he would have to move through a funnel where they could concentrate their fire, and he couldn't count on the liquid armor to see him through.

What Robie wanted was the high ground, and as he looked to his left, he saw a way to take it.

He popped open the window, climbed out, and found hand-holds in the uneven brick surface. On past missions he'd scaled what appeared to be sheer rock walls, so this was not a stretch for him.

The window was just above. The floor plan of the house told him exactly where this opening would take him. He spent three seconds calculating, which was his allotted time to think at any interval during a mission such as this.

Holding on to the windowsill with one hand, he jimmied the window with his knife. He did a controlled tumble through the opening and rolled up to a defensive position.

Having seized the tactical advantage, Robie charged into the upstairs hall and saw one man peering cautiously down the stairs, unaware that his rear flank was fully exposed.

His life ended with a pair of M11 rounds in his back.

Fourteen down, two to go.

The next man came out of another bedroom holding the exact same type of weapon that Robie held.

It was UMP versus UMP.

But not really. It wasn't just about the hardware. A gun was a gun. The same models worked pretty much the same.

What really mattered was the software.

And the shooter was always the software.

Robie threw himself through a doorway as the muzzle of the opposing UMP took aim at him.

He transferred his UMP fully to his right hand, making sure by touch that his selector was still on full auto. The only part of him exposed was his gun and his hand. He used the lower part of the doorjamb as his fulcrum because the recoil kick on an UMP was not always kind if the collapsible stock was not firmly against one's shoulder. That might foul the shot and Robie didn't have the time for that.

The UMPs fired at the same time.

The man's UMP managed to take a chunk of polymer off Robie's weapon.

Robie's UMP managed to blow the head off the man.

Robie dropped the UMP, his ammo exhausted.

Fifteen down, one to go.

But what a one it would turn out to be.

The young woman stepped out of a room and into the upstairs hall.

In her hand was not a weapon, at least not a conventional one.

Clenched in her fingers was a dead man's—or in this case a dead *woman's*—trigger wired to the vest around her torso. Strapped there were six packs of connected Semtex. More than enough to collapse the house and kill her and Robie, and maybe crack the belly of the cobalt bomb in the basement and radiate the neighborhood until the twenty-second century.

He understood at once. She was the designated fail-safe.

She smiled at him.

He didn't return it.

The bloodstained KM2000 flashed through the air.

It severed the wire from the trigger to the suicide vest before lodging in the wall.

The woman looked down at the useless trigger, then back up at Robie. She screamed at him even as her hand went to the vest.

Robie did not wait for her to blow them up another way.

He shot her in the head and she fell to the floor wrapped in her unexploded bombs.

Sixteen down.
None to go.
Time clock punched.
Sunrise coming.
Ninety-nine percent was apparently good enough.

3

THE CLEANUP WAS quick and efficient.

To keep things as secret as possible, they made use of the same tunnel that Robie had. The house was going to be leveled in the next week and the debris buried forever. The tunnel was being permanently plugged. Any complaints about the sounds of explosions or gunfire that night would be referred to the appropriate agency with instructions to bury it as deeply as the remains of the house.

The concussed survivor was revived and would be interrogated until he gave up every secret he would ever have. Then he would disappear into the permanent shadows with no ability to harm anyone again.

The cobalt bomb was removed and disarmed, and it would be reverse-engineered to see how the terror cell had done it. Neither the Brits nor the Americans were under the illusion that a terrorist cell alone had had the wherewithal to pull this off. This operation smacked of a serious institutional backer. Whether it was the Russians or the Iranians or even the North Koreans, they would trace this op back to its source.

Then the diplomats would have their shot at de-escalating this sucker.

If the statesmen failed, it would be the generals' turn.

And no one wanted that scenario.

When the British tactical team had entered the house, Robie had taken off his helmet and was calmly sitting on the couch in the living room.

The team took its time viewing all the carnage, including the suicide bomber, as Robie filled them in on how he had disarmed her. *Bloody hells* resonated from all corners of the house as the team saw firsthand the American's handiwork.

One armored assaulter had sat down next to Robie and asked him if he needed anything, politely addressing Robie as "sir."

Robie had shaken his head and said, "I'm good."

"You're far better than good. In fact, you're the bloody best I've ever seen, mate."

Robie appreciated the sentiment, but he had exited the house with no positive feelings, despite having defeated a maniacal attempt to throw the world off its axis.

He was now wheels up on a private ride back to the United States.

He rubbed his gut and then his thigh where the rounds and the knife had struck, respectively.

Either one would have disabled him. And then he would have been fresh meat to kill. Just another corpse on the floor.

And that made a person think.

Robie closed his eyes and tried to sleep. But while slumber had come easily on the flight over, it was not so easy on the way back. He had killed sixteen people the previous night. And nearly been killed himself about a half-dozen times.

It was all in a day's work for him, on one level.

On another level, part of him couldn't process it.

It wasn't like an endorphin high after winning a Super Bowl or a World Series, chiefly because nobody died in those events. However, it *was* clearly a contest, of sorts. There *were* winners and losers in Robie's world, only the losers left the field of battle in body bags.

He opened his eyes, and his thoughts reached back to Mississippi.

The reunion with his father. A reunion from hell. But the ending was what mattered. And it had ended better than it had begun.

And he and Jessica Reel had been together, battered but together.

Now nearly six months had passed and Robie hadn't seen Reel in all that time. He had called, e-mailed, and texted. Nothing. She was still working for the Agency, that he knew, but he had no idea where. He had asked. And received not a single answer.

After returning from Robie's hometown of Cantrell, Reel—then in a wheelchair because of injuries sustained during their time there — had told Robie that they would always have each other. That they might fall, but together they were unbeatable.

That had been the only thing keeping him going through his rehabilitation.

Yet when he'd been released from rehab, Jessica Reel had not been there. No calls. No e-mails. No texts. Nothing.

So much for being unbeatable together.

They'd obviously been meaningless words.

He landed back in DC and went immediately to his apartment, a nondescript space in an unremarkable building near Dupont Circle.

Robie had nothing of a personal nature in his apartment.

And that was when he saw it.

The envelope on his bed.

There was no writing on it.

It had not been there when he had left for London.

Robie's first instincts were defensive. He slipped the gun from its holster and held it at the ready.

He gripped the envelope with his free hand and shook the letter out.

It was one page folded over.

The handwriting was one he was familiar with.

The words were few and still managed to cut through him like the KM2000 had through neck arteries back in London.

It's complicated. I'm sorry. JR

Robie put his gun away and folded the letter back over and placed it in his pocket.

He walked over to the window.

It was dark now and the rain had started. With the inclement weather he could be back in London.

Yet this was a perfect time for Robie to take a walk. He didn't like crowds. And right now he was in no mood for sunny and fair weather.

He made his way along his favorite route, which led him to Memorial Bridge. Arlington National Cemetery was across the bridge, and the Lincoln Memorial was behind him. He stood by the rampart and looked down at the waters of the Potomac.

The river was flowing far more freely than his thoughts.

What exactly did she mean by "It's complicated"? They both knew everything about their lives was complicated. So what had changed between Mississippi and the note being left on his bed?

He looked around.

The last time he had been here, Blue Man had appeared out of the darkness and given him some much-needed advice. Robie could always count on Blue Man. He always told him not what he wanted to hear, but what he needed to hear.

As if on cue a figure appeared out of the darkness.

Only this time it wasn't Blue Man.

Robie's gun came out and he pointed it at the approaching figure. The person stopped.

"They told me you might be here."

"Who are you?" asked Robie.

Drawing closer, the person was illuminated by the lights on the bridge.

It was a woman.

But it was not Jessica Reel.

"I know you," said Robie, peering at her.

She nodded. "I work with Blue Man."

Robie looked around. "Where is he? Why did he send you?"

"He didn't. I mean, he *couldn't*."

"Why not?"

"Because Blue Man has disappeared."

4

S<small>AND.</small>

And not from a fun day at the beach.

It was in your mouth, your lungs, and your nose.

And possibly in your dreams.

Or here, more likely, in your nightmares.

Gritty, omnipresent, there was no way to avoid it.

Jessica Reel was using a tactical scout sniper periscope to safely get eyes on those she would later try to kill.

Iraq looked like Iraq had ten years ago, at least to her. Buildings were reduced to rubble, people were dying violently. Armies massed and attacked, and terrorists counterattacked, deploying an array of weapons either stolen or bought from countries around the world.

Everything was for shit here, although the politicians tried to put a positive spin on it all. Or blame others after the spin no longer worked.

Right now, the fighting was divided neatly into urban and desert.

Reel wasn't sure which she preferred. Urban was more complicated and potentially more lethal. One wrong step and a hidden IED takes you away from life in a millisecond. Or someone you thought was an ally confronts you with a C4 suicide pack strapped around his waist. Or a kid hiding a gun under his shirt walks up to you asking for candy, and you have a single moment to decide whether to kill him or not.

In the desert there was nothing between you and them except sand either flat or with some height. And killing from long range could come at any moment. Reel knew this for a fact, currently being a major source of her country's long-range kills.

She lowered the periscope and made some notes in her DOPE (data of previous engagements) book. In it she had made references and notes on every shot she had fired during this deployment. All the hits and the rare misses.

She learned the most from the misses.

She was part of a fifteen-person team that had only two snipers, of which she was one. She was also the only female in the group. They didn't care that she could run three miles in under eighteen minutes or that she could do twenty or more dead-hang pull-ups or perform two hundred crunches in four minutes. That was what the Marines required at their sniper school. Years ago Reel had passed every test there and been the first female candidate to complete the course successfully.

They only cared whether she could do her job, which meant pulling the trigger and eliminating someone on the other team whose only goal was to kill Reel and her team.

Still, there had been some grumbling about her from some of the men, mostly the younger ones. Younger ones these days were those barely freed from their teens. After the first two days when Reel had laid down nine out of nine targets, the grumbling had mysteriously vanished. And she was suddenly one of the guys.

Every member of the team was only about one thing: the mission.

The second unspoken goal, but of no less importance to all of them, was survival. None of them wanted to die in the desert. All of them wanted to get back home.

Reel included, though she really had no home to go back to.

And a sniper who could consistently kill people trying to kill you was a valuable friend indeed.

Tikrit, Ramadi, Fallujah, and finally Mosul had been taken back from the enemy. Although, like putting Humpty Dumpty back together again, it was proving nearly impossible to make the situation right. The terrorists had had a long time to inflict maximum destruction on these cities and the people living there. Most of the places were simply uninhabitable, because basic things like water and sewage lines were no longer operating and electrical power was spotty at best. And added to that the cities were still filled with hidden explosives and other death traps.

But rebuilding was not Reel's job. Her mission was to kill as many of the enemy as she could. That could be her only focus.

Her group consisted of Americans, Brits, French, Australians, and two Iraqi force members who still looked at her with unfriendly eyes, even though she could outshoot and outwork both of them. And maybe that was why they looked at her the way they did, other than her being a woman—which in this part of the world was disqualifying for most occupations, and certainly one that required wielding a gun.

The boom of mortar fire and RPGs constantly filled the air along with gunfire and IEDs sending the unwary or the unlucky to early graves. Overhead, called-in air strikes happened with great frequency, with the U.S. providing most of the muscle in the sky.

Reel had been here nearly six months, a loan-out from a civilian agency that provided military support. The other members of her team had been assigned to this duty.

Reel had volunteered for it.

She sniped during the day for the most part unless there was a particular mission on. At night, she was still on duty, but would alternate with her co-sniper. Each often acted as a spotter for the other, and sometimes, due to the dictates of combat, they went solo.

She knew one thing clearly: She was the single most lethal person on this battlefield, able to precisely and consistently kill at over twelve hundred meters. The other side knew this as well. Thus, the bull's-eye on her was a large one.

And if she were ever captured?

Well, in addition to being an American and a woman, snipers historically were not known for receiving a kind reception from their captors.

If she were about to be captured, Reel had long since decided to eat a round instead.

The time came and she readied her rifle.

Years ago her head had been turned into a ballistic computer, analyzing the key physical forces on a bullet fired long-range: altitude, temperature, humidity, and wind, particularly wind two-thirds of the way to the target. But now, with second- and third-generation long-range sniper systems, these calculations were done faster and more accurately by machine than a human ever could. Automation was even hitting the ranks of the elite snipers, not just working joes on assembly lines in Detroit. Thus devices like a ballistic computer, projected reticle display, digital compass, and meteorological and in-clination and related sensors traveled everywhere she did. She had ballistic software downloaded on her iPhone. It was all fed into her optics, which had cost twice as much as her gun.

As the old saying among long-range shooters went: Buy once, cry once.

Now covered with a ghillie suit the color of sand, she lay on the ground and went to work.

The key attribute for any sniper was patience. You worked in a bubble of focus, staying sharp and alert despite exhaustion. And you didn't move. For this reason, she wore a diaper under her clothing so she wouldn't have to get up to relieve herself.

She'd already zeroed her weapon at the range she would be shoot-ing. Her computer had allowed Reel to laze her target, and a ballistic-solution crosshair had been spit out.

When holding her weapon Reel never *gripped* anything, because muscular exertion caused the limbs to do something no sniper could tolerate: It caused appendages to shake, however imperceptibly. It was also called the death grip in sniping circles; if you missed be-cause you were shaking, the other side would get a chance to take you out.

Thus, her left forearm ran straight and true along her weapon's stock. Angled right or left you used muscle to hold the gun. Vertical on vertical meant gravity was doing the job for you. Her toes were pointed out, the sides of her feet flat to the sand. She looked like she was about to do some yoga move. She could and had held such a po-sition for hours, because virtually no strength was required.

Her main snipe rifle was based on the tried-and-true Remington 700 platform with some customization. Her spare was a Barrett M82. For this tour of duty she had switched over her ammo from the legendary .338 Lapua magnum rounds to the .300 Winchester Magnum rounds. Her rifle barrel held a right-hand twist, which meant the bullet coming out of it would cheat a bit in that direction, a phenomenon known as spindrift, which she had accounted for. And she was shooting over such a long distance that the earth's rotation also came into play; it was known as the Coriolis effect. It really only mattered if you were shooting pretty much straight north or south. The bullet would fudge slightly to the left if the target was north and to the right if the target pointed south. If you didn't compensate for it, the earth's constant movement would rotate your target right out of the kill zone. A millimeter error of calculation on this end would result in the shot's being a foot off on the other end.

Ballistics confirmed, her spotter satisfied, all data dialed into her optics, she was ready to execute.

Her finger went to the trigger. She would press with the soft part of the finger midway between the tip and the first joint. This was the area of the finger that moved the least sideways.

She slowly squeezed the trigger on the down breath right at the point where she no longer needed to exhale or to start inhaling again. This respiratory phase was the stillest your lungs would be without duress or discomfort and that meant it was the most calmly immobile your body would be. When you inhaled, the muzzle dropped, when you exhaled, the muzzle rose. But the sweet spot was on the exhale breath, and in between a heartbeat; that was what every good sniper strived for.

Reel kept a smooth, consistent trigger-press pressure all the way through the shot and then led the trigger back to its forward position.

The bullet blasted out of her barrel and was immediately subject to the rules of drag, and also of gravity, meaning it had begun to fall back to earth. The Win Mag round covered 30 percent of its max flight in a heartbeat. Two-thirds of the way to the target, drag was minimized and gravity became the biggest obstacle to a clean shot.

And that was why Reel had fired at an angle equal to the target being nearly sixty feet tall. By the time it got to the end of its flight path, it would impact the target at fifty-four inches off the ground, meaning directly into the brain of the five-foot-ten-inch man seated at a rough wooden table on the other end.

Before the ISIS field commander that had caused her side endless grief even fell dead, Reel's scope had come directly back to her such that after recoil she saw the same image through her optics. If this had been on the range for practice she would have received high marks.

Since it was combat for real, someone's life had just ended.

Her shot had covered nearly fifteen hundred meters, or a little under a mile. A superior distance, it still would not have put her in the top ten of longest kill shots. The current number ten on that list was a Marine sniper who had done the deed from over sixteen hundred meters. For many years number one on that list had been a Brit who had killed two Afghans from nearly twenty-five hundred meters with a single bullet. But that shot had recently been bested by a Canadian elite special forces fighter who had recorded a kill shot in Iraq at more than thirty-five hundred meters.

After Reel's shot killed the man, things got interesting.

There were few events that got the adrenaline going faster than knowing that a sniper was in town. Seconds after the dead man slumped forward on the tabletop, his comrades were running and ducking and throwing themselves behind whatever they could find that would stop their fate from being the same as their deceased commander's.

And with her spotter constantly feeding her data and Reel inputting that data into her optics, she kept firing.

Six trigger pulls later her rounds had found five fleshy entry points. The only one that hadn't was the one that had impacted the rifle barrel of the targeted man, who had moved his rifle to the front of his chest *after* Reel had already fired. The round glanced off the barrel and buried itself in the sand.

That was the major problem with sniping at this great distance. The targets had to be stationary. If they moved right after you fired, the round would miss, because it would take the bullet a few seconds to get there. The bullet fired by the Canadian elite special forces member had taken nearly *ten seconds* to reach its target.

Yet being only a hundred yards away from an enemy carried another set of complications. Reel and her team would be subject to a variety of counterattacks and the threat of being physically overrun. Right now Reel had her spotter and four other soldiers with her. The target they were attacking held a hundred ISIS fighters and an assortment of hand-me-down armored vehicles in which they could counterattack.

Being nearly a mile away gave Reel and her team a lot more latitude. And time for exfiltration, which was a fancy military term for getting the hell out of Dodge.

Her work finished for now, Reel filled out her DOPE and put away her weapon. They drove back to their base, only to be told that they would be heading out on another mission that night. They would support a SEAL team attack on a compound where it was rumored the number two man in ISIS would be, along with three hostages, one of whom was a U.S. Marine captured two weeks prior.

Reel and her team attended the briefing. She snatched some shut-eye, and then they geared up and moved out.

Just another night in the neighborhood.

Only it wouldn't be like any other night for Jessica Reel, ever.

CHAPTER

5

SEAL TEAMS DID everything in the fast lane.

The stealth chopper came low and fast over a rise in the sand, its engine and prop wash as quiet as the best and brightest of American engineering could make them.

Ten SEAL Team Six members fast-roped down to the interior of the compound. Moving as one unit, they hit the sole entrance of the building and disappeared inside.

A football field's length away, Reel, her spotter, and other team members watched the proceedings closely.

Reel lay in the sand behind her sniper rifle. Her optics held on the interior of the courtyard, which could be seen through an opening that had once held a gate.

Four of the other team members had optics on the target zone. They were also commed together and following over their headsets what was happening inside the compound.

A minute later the all clear was given. The mission was a bust. There was no one inside.

As quickly as they had come the SEALs departed. The stealth chopper disappeared over a sandy ridge and was gone.

Reel and her team were packing their gear and about to board two Humvees when explosive rounds hit both vehicles. Secondary explosions came when the hardened fuel tanks were punctured and the gas vapor inside was combusted.

The twin explosions cremated the driver and the grunt riding next to him in one vehicle and burned alive the driver in the second Humvee. The concussive blast ripped limbs off another team member, and he bled out seconds later.

Reel and her spotter rolled to the left and sighted their weapons in the direction from where the rounds had come.

Another explosive hit behind them, sending three more team members to the hereafter, in pieces.

"We're fucked," screamed the spotter as incoming fire poured in from *behind* them as well. "This was a setup!"

Reel already knew this. She spun her weapon around and crab-walked over so it was pointed at their rear flank.

That was when she saw what was coming.

Into her headset she said, "Get air support in here. Now!"

There were three lightly armored Toyota pickup trucks carrying maybe twenty-five fighters in total. Another dozen armed men were hustling behind the cover of the trucks. Mounted in the beds of the Toyotas were .50-cal machine guns.

Fifty-calibers didn't wound when they hit you; they pretty much vaporized whatever they touched.

Reel looked behind her as another round struck. Two more of her team were dismembered, their helmets spinning through the air before coming to rest as mangled composite a hundred feet away.

And one of them was their communications person.

Reel turned to her spotter. "Use your phone. Call in our coordinates. And we need some—"

The .50s opened up again and the decibel-shattering barrage canceled out whatever else Reel was going to say.

Two rounds hit her spotter, and Reel was instantly covered in blood, brains, and guts. The spotter's right arm flew through the sky in a long arc before plummeting back to the sand.

Now, with less than a minute having passed, there was just Reel and one other man left alive, a Brit named Hugh Barkley.

Reel waited until the .50s ceased firing to reload and then she sighted through her optics.

Three quick trigger pulls, and each ISIS member manning the machine guns toppled off the back of the trucks.

Reel had bullets and she had enemies, and she set out to merge the two forevermore.

Three men tried to take the place of the machine gunners. And three men caught Win Mag rounds in their heads for the trouble.

Then the ISIS force wised up and the trucks went into evasive maneuvers, with the lead truck providing cover for the other two.

Reel grabbed her spotter's weapon, and without taking her eyes off the targets, her fingers snagged the ordnance she wanted to deploy next.

She fed the rounds into the rifle, took aim, and fired.

The incendiary round found its mark, and the gas tank of the lead truck was pierced. A split second later the ordnance ignited and so did the vapor in the tank.

The concussive force lifted the Toyota pickup straight off the ground, like a rocket taking off. Then gravity took over and the truck flipped and came to rest on top of the second truck, crushing it.

Reel sent another incendiary round into the third truck. The gas vapor detonated and also caused the .50-cal ammo stacked on the truck beds to explode, turning the night sky bright as day. Bodies and weapons and pieces of Toyotas hurtled across the sand, some landing as far as a half mile away.

When the smoke cleared, Reel could not see one living person in front of her. Just wreckage, flaming objects, and burned corpses.

She had not a second longer to dwell on this, because firing came from behind her. She saw Barkley strafing the ground in front of him with rounds from his MP5.

Reel sprinted that way, planted her weapon on the sand, slid into firing position, and sighted through her scope and fired. And kept firing.

But bullets were coming at them far faster. And then grenades landed and started exploding all around them.

Barkley moved to his left, which was a mistake. The heavy round sliced right through his body armor and blew out his back. He moaned once, gurgled twice, and fell facedown in the sand.

Now it was only Reel left.

She sighted through her scope looking for targets, when it emerged out of the smoke, dust, and darkness.

"Shit!"

It was an *American* M1117 armored security vehicle. A bunch of them had been captured by ISIS from the Iraqi army. It was heavily armored, weighed thirty thousand pounds, and had a top speed of seventy mph. It had a grenade launcher and a .50-cal machine gun in addition to a second machine gun, all mounted on the rotating turret. That was what had been firing at them. That was what had rained grenades on them, and a round from the .50 had just killed Barkley.

Reel grabbed the other rifle she always brought to battle, the Barrett M82. It was already chambered with the most powerful ordnance Reel had to combat the armored rhino coming for her. She would only use it if everything had gone to shit.

Now seemed the perfect time.

The round she was about to fire was technically known as the Raufoss Mk211, developed by a manufacturer in Scandinavia. It was so devastating that, under the Geneva Conventions, it was not supposed to be used against humans.

Right now Reel knew it was her last chance to survive. She didn't try to change locations. If she got up and ran, they would simply mow her down with the .50-cal like they had Barkley. She didn't move a muscle. They might assume she was already dead.

Reel aimed her weapon, centered her breathing, and let her finger slip to the trigger. The M1117 had good armor, but armor needed to be maintained. And she had spotted some missing plates on the front underbelly of the vehicle, probably from a previous run-in with an IED when the metal beast was still working for America.

Yet Reel didn't aim there. Her muzzle was pointed at the front window of the ASV. The glass was multi-layered ballistic glass, but the Raufoss's tungsten core could punch a hole in eight inches of concrete at four hundred meters or an inch of steel at two thousand yards. Well, she was a helluva lot closer than that. And glass, even ballistic glass, was not steel or concrete.

"Do it, baby, do it," she murmured as she slowly pressed the trigger.

The round blew right through the glass, probably killing one of the crew on contact. And she followed that up with two more rounds where the missing armored plates had been.

Its ability to pierce armor was not the reason she'd selected the Raufoss. Like the rounds she'd used to take out the Toyotas, the Raufoss had an incendiary component. But the Raufoss also had a *high explosive* charge built in. It could take out aircraft, choppers, and ships.

And, as it turned out, M1117s.

The trio of explosives detonated and the ammo and the fuel in the vehicle ignited a millisecond later.

Reel had to look away and bury herself in the sand to escape from being blinded by the flash. Debris, flaming objects, and body parts rained down all around.

She finally leapt up, sprinted away, and threw herself under one of the destroyed and still smoldering Humvees as large objects struck it and the ground all around.

After a minute things stopped falling and it grew quiet.

Another minute passed, and Reel dragged herself out from under the Humvee.

She looked around at her destroyed team.

She looked at the body parts of her attackers.

She looked at all the burning vehicles.

She was still sitting there when a chopper flew over and swept a light over the area.

When the SEALs fast-roped down to her she didn't acknowledge them, though she did let them attach a harness to her. The winch was engaged and she was swept into the air and hauled aboard the chopper.

A minute later they were heading back to base, and to safety.

Jessica Reel didn't say a word the whole way.

6

"TRAITOR IN THE ranks, I'm afraid."

The dour-faced colonel looked across the desk at Reel.

"One of the Iraqis. We traced some communications. False intel on the ISIS leader at that compound. They were going to hit the SEAL team, too, but apparently they were in and out too fast. That left your team as the sole target. They obviously wanted to take you out as our primary sniper. It was amazing that we didn't pick up their presence on the earlier recon. They were quite well hidden. But it was night and that area is hardly secure, not that any place here really is."

The man fidgeted with a pen on his desk as he shot glances at Reel, who had said nothing the whole time.

"We never received a distress signal from your team. I imagine you hardly had the chance. But the battle was seen and reported. And the SEAL team that had deployed to attack the compound was sent back to help. I'm sorry it came too late to help your team."

He glanced at Reel to see if these words had dented the invisible armor that seemed to surround her.

They hadn't.

He had been fully briefed on Jessica Reel, to the extent that he was cleared for it.

He knew some of what she had done in the past. He well knew what her lethal capabilities were. The colonel had a ballpark understanding of how many people she had killed over the course of her career. And he knew what she meant to a certain intelligence agency whose sole mission was to keep America safe.

But what he didn't know, what he could never know…was Jessica Reel. And what made her tick. Here, clearances didn't matter, because there was no file and no briefing that could fill in those blanks.

He cleared his throat. "I have to say, your performance was truly remarkable, Agent Reel. You single-handedly took out three attack vehicles, *and* an M1117 and about forty enemy fighters. I've never seen anything like it. Frankly, I'm not sure we have enough commendations to award you," he added with a nervous chuckle. "If you were military they'd be talking about the Medal of Honor. I'm certain of that."

Finally, Reel stirred and looking directly at him said, "I would have thought, since I failed to save a single member of my team, that any talk of commendations or medals would be complete *horseshit*. And the Medal of Honor is not given out for saving your own ass, *sir*."

The dour face now turned red. "That was hardly your fault, Agent Reel. What you did was indisputably heroic."

"We'll have to agree to disagree on that." Reel stood. "Is that all, sir?"

"What? Oh, um, yes."

As she headed to the door he added, "You're heading back stateside. Not my call. Above my pay grade."

She didn't turn or answer him. Reel just shut the door behind her and kept walking.

* * *

Reel had boarded a jet in Iraq, flown to London, and boarded another jet there. The plane she was on now quickly shed altitude as it passed over New York City en route to its final destination right outside of DC.

Jessica was not the only passenger on the government wings, but she was the only one to look out the window at this point. Though she really couldn't make it out clearly at this altitude, in her mind's eye she took in lower Manhattan where the Twin Towers had once stood. Now One World Trade Center soared 1,776 gloriously symbolic feet into the air like a defiant fist upraised to the clear sky. Fittingly, it was the tallest building in the city, and also in North America. Indeed, there were only three other buildings taller in the world. And none of them carried the gravitas of the one she was visualizing now.

Horrible memories tagged to hopes for a better future were represented down there.

Yet right now Reel did not hold out much hope for a better future. War kind of did that to you.

It messed with you in a way that not much else ever could.

Later, on final approach into Dulles, the jet passed by the airport and banked to the east so it could land into the wind.

Reel was the last passenger off. The rest were a mixture of uniforms and civilian contractors all deployed or employed in the fight against terror.

It was a war Reel had finally realized halfway over the Atlantic her side could never really win.

We kill ten and twenty more take their place.

It was an even more insidious version of Medusa that had leapt from the pages of mythology and landed squarely in the twenty-first century.

It was the works of George Orwell and Franz Kafka smashed together and then spun out into the worst nightmare of all time.

She carried her small bag and took a cab to a hotel in DC. She checked in and went to her room.

She tossed her bag in the corner and fell back on the bed. She felt like she hadn't slept in a month. And in a sense, she hadn't. Snipers didn't really sleep, even off duty. You just…*existed*…until the next shot.

She rose, popped open the minibar, chugged a ten-dollar bottle of Fiji water, ate a six-dollar candy bar followed by four Advil, and lay back on the bed.

She closed her eyes.

And the whole damn thing was replayed in her mind. And the outcome was always the same.

Everybody dies except me.

Enemy and ally.

She went through each step, wondering what she could have done differently to change what had ended up being a slaughter.

For both sides.

Sole survivor. She didn't wear that label well.

She thought of her spotter, a man two months away from being a father for the first time. She thought of Hugh Barkley, married with three children back in Birmingham, England. She thought of all the rest, including the man who had betrayed them.

What could I have done better? How could I have prevented this?

She had no answers to these questions. She would never have answers to these questions for the simple fact that there were none to be had.

Humans were imperfect beings operating in a world over which they had diminishing control.

Particularly in the parts that were at war.

Giving up the possibility of sleep, she opted for a shower instead, letting the hot water pour over her, while her forehead was pressed to the tiles.

She wanted to cleanse Iraq from her being. Reel wanted every molecule of sand lurking on her skin to vanish.

Like finding answers to her questions, it was really an impossible task. The mission that night would be with her always, joining a legion of others where things did not always turn out right.

She dried off, wrapped a towel around her, went to the window, and peered out. It was cloudy in DC. The seasons were in flux, warm giving way to less warm, and then eventually ceding to quite cold.

The knock on the door brought her back.

Her hand automatically pulled the Beretta from her bag. Her finger disengaged the safety without her even having to look because the Beretta was as much a part of Reel as was her hand.

Holding the pistol behind her, she padded to the door and looked through the peephole.

She sucked in a breath and then let it go.

Her nightmare had just ratcheted up a notch.

She opened the door and looked up at him.

"What the hell are you doing here?"

Will Robie looked down at her and said, "We need to find Blue Man."

CHAPTER

7

T<small>ICK-TOCK</small> OF the clock.

Robie and Reel sat on opposite sides of the table in the small conference room at Langley. It was a room they had sat in many times before.

Only this time was different. For a variety of reasons, and none of them good.

Robie glanced down at Reel's oblique. In Mississippi, a bullet had struck her there.

"Healed?" he asked.

"Apparently" was her reply.

She glanced at his right arm, which had been torn apart and then surgically repaired. "How about your arm?"

"*Apparently* good enough."

Robie fiddled with something in his pocket. It was the note that he had found on his bed. He wanted to pull it out and ask her what the hell it meant.

Then the door opened and they both sat up straighter.

The woman entering the room was Blue Man's boss, the director of Central Intelligence. Blue Man's *new* boss. The old one had resigned due to stress and an inability to manage it as one professional crisis after another slammed into his Agency.

The new DCI was Rachel Cassidy. She was in her late forties. She'd been an intelligence officer in the Army, then in politics for a short while. She'd worked a few years in the financial world on Wall Street, then returned to her roots where she'd held positions in the Defense Department and the NSC before being named deputy director of the CIA.

Now she held the top spot, and she looked up to the task.

She was petite and wiry with shoulder-length brown hair. She was dressed in a dark pantsuit with a white blouse. She wore no jewelry and only the barest of makeup. Her eyes were wide and hazel and held on you like a laser. By her demeanor the term *wasting time* did not appear to be in her lexicon.

Cassidy was regarded as a thorough professional who saw no obstacles, only solutions, and whose bullshit meter was among the best in the business. That last attribute was an absolute necessity in this field, mainly because she had to deal with elected officials, who could spew crap like an untended fire hose did water.

She sat down and looked first at Robie and then at Reel.

"You've had a preliminary briefing."

It was not really a question, yet both of them nodded.

Cassidy leaned forward and looked at Robie. "London."

Robie glanced at her.

"Are you fully recovered?" asked Cassidy.

"Nothing to recover from," replied Robie.

Cassidy looked at Reel. "And you?"

Now Reel looked directly at Robie. "Same answer, Director."

"Good. Roger left here six days ago on vacation."

"I didn't think Blue Man took vacations," said Robie.

"Everyone takes vacations, Robie, even Blue Man," Cassidy said briskly. "He flew to Denver and then drove to his final destination. He did this every year about this time. He was going fly-fishing for a week."

Both Robie and Reel looked surprised by this. Neither knew much if anything about Blue Man's personal life. That was just the way their world worked. Need to know extended to all corners, both professional and personal.

"Why there?" asked Reel.

"He was from the area. Born there, raised there. And he went back there pretty much every year."

Again, the pair registered surprise at this.

"Did he go alone?" asked Robie.

"Yes. Sometimes he went with some old friends, but not this year. He went alone and a few days ago he vanished."

"The place is called Grand," noted Robie. "Was it a mining town or something?"

"They thought it was, apparently, until they realized the gold and silver were mostly on the other side of the state."

"I assume the police have been called in," said Reel.

"The local police force, as you can imagine, is quite small. The state police were called in, but they've found no trace. They've officially departed the situation."

"What were they told?" asked Reel.

"That a man was missing. They know nothing of his background. And that won't change."

"We're not investigators, Director," said Robie.

She swiveled her laser gaze around to him. "That's not what Blue Man told me after your trip to Mississippi. He said you were actually quite good at it."

"We made mistakes along the way," said Reel.

"Just don't repeat them here."

"Wouldn't it be more prudent to enlist the FBI on something like this?" asked Robie. "We're not a law enforcement agency. We have no arresting authority."

"The Bureau has been notified and is monitoring the situation. But we like to look after our own, Robie." She stared hard at him as she said this. "I think you got a dose of that in Mississippi, didn't you?"

Robie glanced away. "Yes."

"Blue Man's disappearance may be unrelated to who he is and what he does. But I still consider this a national security issue, and I have asked for and received backing on this position from the highest levels. That brings it directly into our jurisdiction. And the last thing we need to reveal is that a high-ranking intelligence officer has gone missing. The world is a tinderbox right now. This would add enough fuel to that fire that I'm not sure any of us can accurately predict the downside. You will have the assistance and cooperation of all relevant federal agencies, but you and Reel know him best. That's why you're here. He covered your backs many a time. Now you can return the favor." She rose. "So find him. And bring him back safely, if at all possible. You'll receive fuller particulars and all logistical details before you leave here."

Then she was gone.

On to the next crisis, no doubt.

Robie looked at Reel. "I guess we're working together again."

She nodded curtly.

"Whether we want to or not," he added.

She didn't nod at this comment.

He said, "We need to put aside any personal issues and get this job done."

Reel glanced over at him. Her gaze was reminiscent of Cassidy's, and it was not the first time that Robie had felt the burn of it.

"I have no personal issues about anything, Robie," said Reel.

"Good, glad we got that straightened out."

"We find Blue Man," she said. "Then we go our separate ways." She rose and walked out.

Robie took out the note that she'd left him, balled it up, and tossed it into the trash can.

8

ROBIE AND REEL rode government wings to Denver, landed, and retrieved a large, hard-sided case that was waiting for them at the airport. They had reserved a big Yukon, and they loaded in their stuff and set off heading northeast.

They had not spoken on the three-hour flight and had passed the town of Fort Morgan on Interstate 76 before Robie broke the silence.

"Eastern Plains. Westernmost section of the Great Plains where it notches into Nebraska. Not much out here. Pawnee Buttes, Comanche National Grassland. Rolling hills, flat farmland, one-room schoolhouses, forests, canyons, rivers, and lakes. Not much rain. Small towns. Yuma and Sterling are big cities out here. Dwindling populations. People heading to somewhere else. Never really recovered from the Dust Bowl in the thirties."

Reel glanced at him. "Thanks for the guided tour," she said drily.

"Just making small talk."

"Since when?"

"Since now, apparently. You know, to fill in the gaps that appeared out of nowhere."

She made no reply to this, but stared back out the window at the stark, rugged landscape as they got off the interstate and kept going more east than north. As they drove on, the conditions of the roads deteriorated from paved to gravel, and Reel saw some roads that were only dirt.

They'd passed one farmhouse in the last four miles. The rest of the land was just empty.

"I guess Blue Man liked his privacy," she said.

"Didn't know he was from here. Or that he was a fly fisherman."

"It wasn't that sort of a relationship," replied Reel. "It was just work."

"Maybe for you."

She shot him a glance. "I want to find him too, Robie."

"Never doubted it."

The "town" of Grand seemed a misnomer, as there were only about sixty structures total on the macadam street that constituted the main downtown area. A few streets bled off the main one on either side. The buildings there were a mixture of businesses and private residences. It seemed that most people did not live in town, preferring the wide-open spaces that surrounded Grand.

Robie pulled the Yukon to a stop in front of one of the buildings with a sign proclaiming it to be the Town of Grand's sheriff's office. A dusty cop cruiser, a Ford Mustang, was parked out front.

Robie and Reel got out of the Yukon and stood in front of the station.

"What were their names again?" asked Reel.

"Valerie Malloy and Derrick Bender. Sheriffs and detectives all rolled into one."

"Which one is the boss?"

"She is. He's the deputy sheriff."

"Well at least they got that right," noted Reel.

She stepped forward and opened the door, while Robie shot her a glance.

The front room was small and warm, and the glare of sunlight coming through the single window made it hard on the eyes.

The door of an interior room opened, and a woman in her midthirties appeared there. She was in uniform, which rode well on her lanky, athletic frame. Her hair was dark and hung straight to her shoulders. Her face held sharp angles, and the overall effect was quite pretty. However, these features were flexed into a scowl, which was not attractive at all. The dark hair was paired with icy blue eyes. Her gun belt encircled her narrow waist. She placed one hand on top of her service pistol as she looked across the width of the room at them.

"Sheriff Malloy?" said Reel.

"Yes?"

"We're here about Roger Walton? I assume you got a call?"

Malloy stepped forward after giving first Reel and then Robie a long, scrutinizing look.

"I did. They said someone would be coming. You have ID? I like to know who I'm dealing with."

Reel and Robie pulled their IDs and held them up. They weren't their real creds, but these would pass any check that Malloy could run.

"Who exactly is this Walton guy that two Feds show up here?"

"He exactly is someone we want to find," said Robie crisply.

"So he's important to the Feds or something?"

"Or something."

"He's not a criminal you're looking for?"

"What makes you say that?" asked Reel.

"I like to cover my bases. Is he?"

"No. He's one of the good guys."

"Were those your real creds?" she asked.

"Why wouldn't they be?" asked Reel.

"I haven't always worked out here. I used to be a cop back in New York. We dealt a lot with the Feds back there. They weren't always straight with us. I doubt things have changed."

"I doubt they have, too" was all Robie would volunteer.

"What made you trade New York for…this?" asked Reel.

"Life." She turned and motioned for them to follow her into her office.

She closed the door behind them and indicated two straight-backed wooden chairs fronting a gunmetal-gray desk with two large dents and what looked to be a bullet hole in the right side.

Perched on a wooden file cabinet was a fan that looked about sixty years old. It halfheartedly moved warm air from one side of the room to the other.

There was a wall air conditioner unit, but its unplugged power cord dangled against the wall like a limp snake.

On another wall was a large duty roster with only two names on it, hers and Bender's. His status was shown as "on patrol."

Her chair squeaking, Malloy sat down and looked at them over the neatly arranged items on her desk.

"Roger Walton."

"That's the man," said Reel.

"I Googled him. Didn't find anything other than some distant Walmart heirs that had nothing to do with your guy."

"Our guy's not in retail."

"State cops were here for a bit. Then they left. I wonder if they were called off?"

"I wonder," said Reel curtly.

"And then you guys show up. I thought it would be more than two. I thought maybe some private jet would wing it in here and a whole team of people dressed in black with MP5s might ride a motorcade into our humble town."

"Nope, just us," said Robie.

Reel said, "You have a file on this? We'd like to see it."

"I have a file and I've been told to share it."

"Okay," said Reel expectantly.

"But I'm not looking to get pushed off an investigation on my turf. We work this, we work it together."

Robie glanced at Reel. She kept her eyes on Malloy.

"Where in New York?"

"NYPD, first the Bronx, then Queens. Then I moved out to Westchester."

"Tired of getting shot at?"

"No, my boyfriend at the time thought it would improve my mood at home. It didn't."

"You ever work any cases beyond uniform?"

"I had my papers in for detective before I left. I've got my forensics certifications. I notice stuff. I sweat the details. And this is my town," she added. "I know everybody here. And I mean *everybody*, because there aren't that many of us."

"I can see that," said Reel. "What do you say, Robie? In or out?"

"If she can help us, I don't have a problem."

Reel turned back to Malloy. "The file?"

The door opened.

Standing there was a tall, uniformed man in his thirties with wide shoulders and hips so narrow his pants seemed in danger of sliding off him. His blond hair was short on top and longish in back, as though the hair was sliding off his head. He held a sweat-stained Stetson in his hand. His face looked like it had been out in the sun and wind since his birth. His facial features were long and slender, like narrow gullies cut through hard rock by water.

"Thought you were on patrol," said Malloy, frowning slightly.

The man took a long step forward. "I was. Finished. And heard they were in town."

"And how'd you hear that?" asked Reel.

The man glanced at her. "Folks saw your Yukon."

"Is that so unusual?"

"It is if we don't know who's driving it. Know every Yukon round here. Hell, there's only five. And none of 'em are black. Or new, like yours. With Florida plates. Rental, most likely," he added knowledgably.

He pulled up a chair, sat down next to Robie, and put out a big, weathered hand.

"Deputy Sheriff Derrick Bender. Pleased to meet you. We don't get many Feds out here."

Robie shook his hand. "Will Robie. My partner here is Jessica Reel."

Bender offered his hand to her. After they shook he glanced at Malloy.

"We were just going to go over the file on Mr. Walton," said Malloy.

Bender grunted and sat up a little straighter, his holstered gun smacking lightly against the wood of the chair. "Damnedest thing. Man comes into town and then disappears."

"He came out here every year," said Reel. "So I suppose you've run into him before?"

"I haven't," said Malloy. "Because I've only been here about a year. In my official capacity. Before that I would come and visit my sister, Holly, who lives here. But I never ran into your Mr. Walton."

Bender rubbed his face and then tossed his Stetson across the room, where it neatly settled on a hook on the wall.

"I met him before. Lots of times. Like you said, he came out here most every year. Fishing up in the rivers, lakes, and streams. Watched him a few times. Man knew what he was doing. People think fly-fishing is easy. Well, it ain't. Takes skill. And patience."

"Did you ever speak to him?" asked Robie.

"Oh yeah. Nothing in particular. Just chitchat."

"He was from this area," said Reel.

Bender nodded. "My momma knew Mr. Walton pretty well. They went to high school here together. Long before I was born, he'd gone. Headed east. Guess he wanted to get the hell out of here."

"He ever do anything besides fish?" asked Reel. "Did he mingle? Catch up with old friends?"

"Sometimes. There's the Walleye Bar. He'd go there. Most visits he'd have dinner with my momma at her house. I was there for a few of them. Once he brought some fancy French wine." Bender shook his head. "Just give me a good old American beer."

"Did he visit your mother this time?" asked Reel.

"Not that I know of."

"We'll have to confirm that," said Reel.

"Did *you* see him this trip?" asked Robie.

Bender nodded. "He was staying at the same place he usually did. Little cabin up on the north face of Kiowa Butte. One road up and down. About a half mile from the cabin is the river he'd fish in. A trib runs off the North Platte. It's tailwater fishing."

When they looked at him quizzically he said, "Meaning downriver from a dam. In this case the Jedediah Smith Dam. Water releases from the bottom of the dam so it keeps the temperature stable. Good for fishing. You can catch brown and rainbow trout, some perch, walleye, smallmouth. Now, the South Platte over near Denver is better fishing. Lots of tourists go there to fish. But we get some here, too." He paused. "The Platte's where we get most of our water. We don't get too much rain here. Only way we can farm is to irrigate the crops. The North and South Platte Rivers hook up to form the Platte River in Nebraska. Then it connects with the Missouri and the Missouri to the Mississippi, and that sucker flows all the way to the Gulf of Mexico. Quite something when you think about it."

Reel and Robie exchanged a puzzled glance at this long tangent, then Reel said, "Did you *talk* to Walton this time?"

Bender waggled his head. "No, I sure didn't."

"When was the last time anyone actually saw him?" asked Robie.

Malloy opened her file. "Three days ago. He came into town to get some more fishing line. He ate at the restaurant across the street. I've spoken to the waitress and she said he seemed perfectly normal. Same for the fishing gear shop. Then he drove back up to his cabin and that's the last anyone saw of him."

Robie said, "Any signs of something unusual at the cabin? Our notes say his rental car was still there."

"No signs of a break-in or a struggle, if that's what you mean," replied Malloy. She closed the file. "Now maybe we should head up there and look around. Might find something that strikes you. After all, I assume you knew the man."

Did we? thought Robie as they headed out.

CHAPTER

9

THE DIRT ROAD to Blue Man's cabin snaked upward, with switchbacks and narrow straightaways intersected with hairpin curves making up most of the journey. Though the elevation wasn't that great, the sun seemed more intense and the air thin enough to be noticeable to your lungs.

They finally pulled to a stop in front of a rustic cabin about nine hundred square feet in total. It had weathered cedar siding, a planked front porch with an overhang, a shingled roof, a stone chimney, one front door, one rear door, and four windows all on one floor.

A dark blue Chevy Colorado pickup truck was parked in front.

Robie and Reel had followed Malloy's Mustang. Bender had ridden shotgun with his superior.

They all got out and congregated in front of the cabin.

Reel and Robie took in the surroundings, each gazing at angles and flanks from where trouble could have come. There weren't many of them. As Malloy had said, this was the only road up here.

"Any other people living around here?" asked Robie.

Malloy shook her head. "Just this cabin."

"Who owns it?" asked Reel.

"Roark Lambert. He lives in Denver. He owns about a dozen cabins and houses around here. Rents 'em out to tourists."

"All fishing?" asked Reel.

Bender answered. "No. Some are here to photograph wildlife. Others to hunt wildlife. Some come to just get away. Go hiking, camping. Smoke pot without being hassled."

"I take it the house and truck have been searched?" said Robie.

Malloy nodded. "Didn't find much of anything. But we can take another look. You might notice something we missed."

Reel looked at the truck. "Colorado? Seems appropriate."

"Nice set of wheels," said Bender. "You got rear seats plus the truck bed. Pretty popular here. Can handle the terrain real well."

Malloy pulled out the truck keys. "We found these in the cabin." She popped the locks and opened the driver's-side door. "We swept it for prints and other forensic residue. Came up empty. State police did, too."

It didn't take long to search the truck. It was pretty much empty of anything.

There was a Georgetown Hoyas ball cap on the rear seat.

Bender said, "I thought he went off to Stanford. That's what my mom told me."

"He had multiple degrees," said Reel, picking up the cap. "Georgetown was where he got his master's."

"Good school," said Malloy. "In *Washington, DC*. You never did mention what Mr. Walton did for a living."

Bender stared at his boss for a second before looking at Robie.

"No, I never did," said Robie. "Ready to hit the house?"

Malloy lifted the yellow police tape stretched across the front door and unlocked a police padlock that had been installed there.

"We don't have the manpower to station someone here twenty-four seven," explained Malloy. "We do the best we can."

"Who reported him missing?" asked Reel.

"He'd hired JC Parry, a local guide," said Malloy. "JC said they were supposed to meet here at six in the morning. JC drove here to pick up Walton. The Colorado was here but no Walton. The front door was unlocked. JC went in, and when there was no sign of Walton, he called us in."

"I thought you had to wait for a certain period of time before someone could call in a missing persons report," said Robie.

"That's true under normal circumstances. But the man's truck was still here. He couldn't walk down to town. The truck started up just fine, so there were no problems with it. The cabin was empty, and Walton wasn't here for his appointment with JC. We searched all around the cabin and even went down to the stream where he fished, even though his pole and tackle and the rest of his fishing gear were in the cabin. We found zip. We looked at all the places he might have fallen or gotten into trouble. There aren't too many of them. Nothing."

"Any animals up here that could be the cause?" asked Reel. "Bear, mountain lions?"

Bender said, "Mountain lions very rarely go after an adult. Same for coyotes, lynx, and bobcats. Now, we got bears. Black bears. But unless you get between a momma and its cubs or surprise it, you ain't going to have problems with them. Now some people claim we still got grizzlies in Colorado, but I ain't never seen one. And I don't know anybody who has."

Malloy added, "And an animal attack would have left traces. There were none."

Reel pointed to the cabin. "Then let's see what we can find inside here."

The cabin had only three rooms. An open front space that held the kitchen and a sitting area in front of the stone fireplace, a bathroom, and a single bedroom. They found Blue Man's luggage, clothes on hangers in the bedroom closet, a toiletry bag in the bathroom, and some food and drinks in the fridge. His fishing gear was neatly stacked on a side table in the front room.

"Bed was slept in," said Malloy, pointing to the covers in disarray. "Don't know if he went off in his pajamas or some other clothes. We did find a gun. Glock ten-mil. It hadn't been fired. It was in the nightstand next to the bed. We bagged and tagged it as evidence. It's back at the station." She looked at both Robie and Reel to see if they wanted to comment on this news.

Robie said, "How about his phone? Laptop?"

"We didn't find either. And we couldn't find his phone number, so we couldn't check to see if the phone is on. We can trace it that way, unless someone's taken out the chip."

"It's not on," answered Reel.

"So you already checked on that?" said Malloy. Her voice held a bit of an accusatory tone.

"Yes," said Reel, as she glanced around the room. "So the state police were called in?"

"And then the FBI, in case it was a kidnapping. Funny, when the Feds were called in, that's when we heard from some folks in DC. Maybe *your* folks."

"Nothing funny about it," replied Robie, though he didn't elaborate. "No sightings? No other strangers around here?"

"Not that we could connect to Mr. Walton," said Malloy.

"So he just vanished," said Reel. "From a place this isolated. Unless he went somewhere on his own, we have to assume that someone came and took him away." She looked at Malloy. "Any ideas on that? You have any criminal elements around here?"

"Every place in America has criminal elements."

"You have any that are unique or obvious?"

She glanced at Bender before answering. "This place is isolated. Some folks like that isolation for good reasons, you know, get off the beaten path, off the grid."

"And other folks?" asked Robie.

Bender said, "They come here because they can more or less do what they want. I don't mean break the law necessarily, you know, but live their lives how they want."

"What exactly does that mean?" asked Reel.

Malloy said, "That means they can build communities with like-minded people."

"And what sort of communities would those be?" asked Reel.

"Most are innocuous. Some not so much."

Robie said, "Care to elaborate?"

"I'm talking about people who don't want to live in the mainstream. They have their own rules, don't get in trouble, and they keep to themselves," said Malloy.

"I'm more interested in the ones that *don't* keep to themselves, that get in trouble and maybe kidnap people," said Reel.

Bender shot a glance at Malloy.

She said quietly, "I can't say we don't have any of those."

10

"I DON'T LIKE getting played," said Reel.

Robie sat across from Reel in the front seat of their Yukon. She had pulled off the road after they had left Malloy and Bender.

He looked at her. "Meaning?"

"Meaning Malloy was being less than forthcoming about bad elements being here. She gave no specifics."

"It was clear she was fudging her answer."

"So why'd you ask what I meant?" she barked, staring at him.

"Because I like things to be absolutely *precise*, so there's no *misunderstanding*," he shot back.

She put the truck in gear and drove on into town.

They had reservations at the only hotel in Grand. It was at the end of the main street, a surprisingly modern-looking structure with clean lines and an inviting entrance.

As they hauled their bags in Robie commented on this incongruity in the poor, isolated town.

Reel said, "Tourism. It's all about dollars. I can't imagine they have much more to live on."

The young woman at the front desk kept giving them curious glances.

"I see that you don't have a departure date," the woman said.

"When we know, you'll know," said Reel.

"Will you need help with your bags?" she asked.

"No," said Reel curtly.

"And just to confirm, it's *two* rooms?"

"Absolutely," said Reel, just as curtly.

They went to their rooms on the second floor, which were next to each other, with one interconnecting door. The rooms were nicely if a bit fussily furnished, like the designer wanted to see how much stuff could be crammed into each. Robie and Reel unpacked and met back down in the lobby.

"What now?" asked Reel.

"You hungry?"

"No."

"Then maybe we look around and find people to ask questions about Blue Man."

She looked uncomfortable with this suggestion.

"What's the problem?" asked Robie.

"I work much better behind a scope than a badge."

"Well, now we work behind both, apparently. Actually I hope it's more badge than scope."

They walked outside. Reel noticed the group of people staring at them from down the street.

Four men and one woman. They all looked as rugged as the Eastern Plains.

And they each carried guns in holsters. One of the men also had a long gun on a strap over his shoulder. It was a Remington 700 with a scope on the Picatinny rail.

"Forgot Colorado was an open-carry state," said Reel.

Robie said, "Legal pot and lots of guns. Like chocolate and peanut butter."

"You mean oil and water."

"You think they might know anything?"

"We won't know until we ask."

They moved in that direction and both watched as the group stiffened on their approach. Hands flicked closer to weapons.

Robie's and Reel's pistols were concealed under their jackets. They kept their hands at their sides. Yet if the time came, their gun pulls still would be faster than the opposition's. Practicing the motion thousands of times tended to give one the edge on deploying and firing one's weapons.

They stopped in front of the group. Two of the men were tall and lanky, and two were shorter and barrel-chested, with guts that drooped over their too-small waistbands. The men all wore dirty cammie pants, dusty work boots, and ball caps. The woman was in her late thirties and of average height. She was wearing faded jeans and a tank top that showed her arms and shoulders to be sinewy and well developed. Her hair was pulled back in a ponytail. Her expression was suspicious, and in that it neatly matched her colleagues'.

Robie slipped a picture of Blue Man out of his pocket and held it up. "We're looking for this man. He rented a cabin up on Kiowa Butte. He's gone missing. Have you seen him? Did you ever talk to him?"

The men shuffled their feet and eyed one another. The woman stepped forward.

"That's Roger Walton."

"That's right, it is."

"He was engaged to my mother way back till she broke it off."

"And you are...?" asked Reel, her eyes widening at this piece of information.

"Patti Bender."

"Are you related—"

"Derrick's my brother," she interjected.

"We just met with him and Sheriff Malloy," said Robie.

"Why do you want to find Walton?" asked Patti.

"Because he's missing and he shouldn't be," replied Reel.

"I hear you're from Washington, DC."

"And who did you hear that from?" asked Robie.

"Everybody, basically."

The men all nodded.

"News travels fast here, I take it," noted Reel.

Patti said, "It doesn't have far to go."

Reel nodded. "Still, it's nice to know you folks are observant. With your help we should be able to find Mr. Walton in no time."

"He works for the government, doesn't he?" asked Patti. "Something high up?"

"Do you have any idea where he might be?" asked Robie, ignoring her query.

She shook her head. "I didn't see him this trip."

"I understand from Derrick that he had dinner with your mother when he came to visit."

"He did sometimes. They were still good friends, even after all these years." She paused. "And even after what happened."

"Her breaking up with him," said Robie.

"That's right."

"Can you give us her address?"

"Drive out of town to the west. Second road take a right. Go about three miles and she's the only one down there."

Reel ran her gaze over their weapons. "You look loaded for bear."

One of the men laughed. "Actually, we're going light today."

"And what is it that you do?"

He said, "People come here to hunt and fish, and we act as guides. Or they want to do some rafting, or bird watching or rock climbing or hiking. Pays pretty well, though it's not regular work. Lots of stuff to do out here. But you can't be no couch potato."

Reel eyed the two men with guts. "Yeah, I can see that." She settled her gaze on Patti. "And is that what you do as well?"

"I do what I need to do to get by."

"You live with your mom?" asked Robie.

"Not for a long time."

"So why do you think she broke off the engagement with Walton?" asked Robie.

Patti considered this for a moment. "I think he didn't want to stay here but she did. It was her home. But he apparently didn't think of it as his home anymore."

Robie looked around the area. "I can see why that might be a problem."

Reel looked at the men. "Any of you see Walton on this trip?"

They all shook their heads. One of Patti's friends said, "He was here to fish. He knew where to fish, and he knew what he was doing. Didn't need us to show him."

"But he came into town from time to time," pointed out Reel.

"Yeah, but we didn't see him."

Patti said, "I hope you find him."

"We will," said Reel.

11

On the drive to Bender's house, Robie read through the copy of
the file that Malloy had provided them.

"Not much in here," he said.

"Not much *out* here," replied Reel as she turned down the road
that Patti Bender had indicated.

"People like their privacy around here, I guess," noted Robie.

"Well, I think you're going to get privacy out here whether you
want it or not."

They rounded a bend. The house that appeared in front of them
was large and modern looking, and surrounded by landscaping that
mostly involved rock and pebble gravel.

"You don't have to water rock," observed Reel.

There were two stone pillars with a gate blocking the entrance
into the property.

"I didn't expect this," said Reel. "I was thinking a shack on cinderblock."

She pulled the truck up to the gate and punched a button on the
black box mounted on a pole set in the ground.

"Hello?" said the female voice. "Are you Roger's people?"

Reel glanced at Robie. "Well, there goes our cover for sure." She
said to the box, "Yes, we are."

The gates opened and she pulled the Yukon toward the front of
the house.

As they climbed out of the truck one of the wooden double doors
to the house opened and revealed a woman standing there. She was
in her sixties, tall and lean, with long, silvery blonde hair that fell

loosely to her shoulders. She had on jeans, black boots, a white shirt, and turquoise jewelry on her wrists and around her neck.

"Come on in," she said pleasantly.

They trooped up onto the porch. Robie held out his hand. "I'm Will Robie, this is Jessica Reel."

"And I'm Claire Bender. You thirsty?"

"Some water, maybe?" said Robie.

"Coming up."

They followed her into a large foyer with timbers soaring overhead and forming a cathedral-like dome. The floors were slate; the walls were a combination of wood, stone, and brick. The furnishings were large, looked custom-made, were colorful, and appeared to be relatively new. Original artwork hung on the walls along with some framed family photos.

They trooped to a spacious kitchen with granite counters, stainless steel Viking appliances, and walls of windows giving a view of the rear of her property, which was fenced.

"Beautiful place," said Reel.

"Thank you. I had it all redone about eighteen months ago. Before that, it didn't look like this, trust me. It was basically a knockdown."

She poured them out glasses of water from a freestanding dispenser, then they settled in chairs next to a gas fireplace off the kitchen area.

"We met your daughter and your son," began Robie.

"Patti already called me. Said you'd be coming by."

Up close her features were finely wrought, the nose slender and straight, the cheekbones high and hard, the jaw square, and the chin shapely. The eyes were a delicate blue. Based on her being a contemporary of Blue Man, Robie pegged her age at closer to seventy than sixty, yet she could pass for being in her early fifties. She looked like she would be equally at home in a boardroom or astride a horse.

"I guess news of any strangers in town gets around fast," noted Reel.

She smiled. "Well, it doesn't have far to go."

Robie smiled. "Your daughter said pretty much the same thing."

Claire replied, "I guess I taught her well."

"And what is it that you do?" asked Reel, looking around the interior.

"I used to do some farming: chickens, turkeys, and crops like soybean, wheat, and oats. But that just kept me out of the poor house, really. No, it was only later on that I hit the mother lode."

"The lottery?" asked Robie.

"No, medical marijuana. I have six dispensaries across the state and two more opening next year."

"I take it that's pretty lucrative?" said Robie.

"It paid for this place. Now, the business is competitive, but it's not insane like on the recreational side. Prices per pound on the rec side are plunging because of a glut of supply. You can grow as much as you want. And we can't export from Colorado, of course, and there aren't enough marijuana users here to make up the difference. Now, on the medical side the law requires that you have to own a dispensary and you have to grow seventy percent of what the dispensary sells. It keeps the production supply side from getting out of whack. And the growth in farmers is on the rec side, not the medical side. So because of that, prices per pound on the medical side are holding up well. And our output is really premium, so we can command about $2,400 per pound, pretty top of the market."

"You sound like you really know the business," remarked Robie.

"When I take on something I throw myself into it. So, yes, I've educated myself a lot."

"Do you grow it here?" asked Reel.

"I started out here on this patch of land with a little greenhouse and some cheap lights and not really knowing what I was doing. But I learned quickly, saw where the markets were going, got out of personal-use farming and into the medical side, and expanded from there. We have first-rate equipment, and professional staff, we're always looking for ways to expand our yield more efficiently, and we have built up a great customer base. And we've also expanded into marijuana edibles and cannabis-infused products, too."

"How'd you get into growing pot?" asked Robie.

"Wasn't for the money, I can tell you that. At least not initially. I got thrown off a horse, broke a bunch of bones, including my skull, and was in terrible pain for a long time. Only thing that worked was pot. Back then it was illegal, but you could find what you needed. And I started growing some myself. Now, legalization of marijuana in Colorado is a pretty convoluted tale with lots of fits and starts. Used to be if you were a caregiver to someone with chronic pain or illness you could get marijuana with a doctor's prescription, but you were limited to five patients. Then the courts kicked out that limitation and also left it fuzzy about what the term *dispensing* actually meant, so medical marijuana dispensers started popping up here, like what was happening in California. Then the Feds announced that enforcement of a state's medical marijuana programs would be a very low priority, that is, 'We're not going to prosecute you.' Then it was off to the races, at least on the medical side. Later, growing and selling pot recreationally was legalized and the boom was on. But I started doing it because I know how it helped me." She looked around at her beautiful home. "And it has, in more ways than one."

Robie and Reel took sips of their water as Claire watched them.

"But you didn't come to see me to learn about pot in Colorado. This is about Roger."

"We understand you know him," said Robie.

"Yes. We go way back."

"And you're worried?"

"I wasn't initially. I just thought he'd gotten called back to DC or something."

"Why would you think that?" asked Reel.

"Look, I don't know exactly what Roger does, but I suspect he isn't selling bananas from a street cart. Even way back we all knew he was going places. And I've seen him a lot over the years when he'd come back here. He never talked about work with me. When I asked what he did, he just said he pushed paper across his desk. Once he mentioned having a midlevel job at the State Department or some such."

"And you didn't believe him?" asked Reel.

"Roger Walton was the golden boy from Grand, Colorado, small as it is. Football and baseball star. Accepted at half a dozen Ivy

League schools. Smartest person I've ever been around. And one of the kindest. He could've been an insufferable jock type, but he was the exact opposite. Ask anyone who knew him. He helped everybody when he lived here. Even those that didn't deserve it."

"Did you know his parents?" asked Reel.

"Of course. What happened was so tragic."

"What happened to them?" asked Reel.

"Oh, I thought you knew."

"Knew what?" said Reel.

"They apparently had a suicide pact. They were found in their car in their garage. They'd turned on the engine and stuffed the tailpipe."

"When was this? Recently?"

"Oh, no. It was while Roger still lived here. He was the one to find them. He'd been away at some regional debate championship in Nebraska his senior year of high school. When he got back, well…it was awful."

"Damn," said Robie. "Pretty tough situation for a teenager."

"Pretty tough for any age," said Reel.

Claire said, "Well, the town rallied around Roger, of course. In fact, he came to live with my family for the rest of the school year."

"Does anyone know why they killed themselves?" asked Robie.

"Dorothy, Roger's mom, had ovarian cancer. Late stage. Back then there was nothing to combat it. She was going to die. I don't think Roger's dad could live without her."

Reel frowned. "So he kills himself and leaves his kid alone. If you ask me, that's kind of selfish."

"That's what I thought, too. But Roger didn't see it that way. He loved his parents. And he survived. He always survived." She paused. "I'm counting on that right now. For him to survive." She paused again. "He kept the house. He's never been back there, as far as I know, but he never sold it, either. I drive by it every once in a while and think about Roger. All he went through at such a young age."

"That's very sad," said Reel wistfully.

"You said you were initially not worried when he disappeared," prompted Robie with a quick glance at Reel. "What changed?"

Claire said, "When I heard that he'd left everything at the cabin, including his rental. That wasn't like Roger. He was organized and efficient. If he got called back to DC suddenly he would've taken care of all that, or had someone do it for him."

"Did you see him while he was here this time?"

"Yes. We usually have dinner. And we did. Here. We both cooked."

"So you have a good relationship?" said Robie.

Claire smiled. "Look, I'm sure one of my kids told you that Roger and I were engaged to be married. Only I didn't want to leave here and he wanted to get the hell out. Am I right?"

"We did hear that from Patti," conceded Robie.

"So it wasn't a question of love. I loved him and he loved me. We just had a difference of opinion on where that love should be located." She paused and frowned. "Looking back, I can see now why I didn't want to leave. Back then I was a simple girl with simple ambitions. Roger wanted to see the world, do everything, which scared the crap out of me. Now, look, I'm no dummy. I've held my own with some pretty smart people who come through here from time to time, and I have managed to build a pretty successful business. But Roger was on another plane. He was flat-out brilliant. I…I guess I was afraid if I moved with him, I would end up not measuring up and we'd get divorced. And then where would I be? Stuck in a place that would seem like another planet to me."

Reel studied her. "And do you still think that?"

"Doesn't matter, does it?"

"But now?" persisted Reel, drawing a curious look from Robie.

Claire said quietly, "I can't say I don't have regrets, because I do. But I think we're past the do-over stage in life."

Reel said, "But he came back here. And spent time with you. That probably tells you something."

"What, that maybe *he* had regrets?"

"He never married, at least to my knowledge," said Robie.

"I know. Well, water under the bridge." She looked squarely at them. "Now you need to find out what the hell happened to him."

Reel said, "We asked your son and Sheriff Malloy if there were any people around here that might be responsible for his disappearance. Malloy was vague on that. What do you say?"

"Every place on earth has bad people, and Grand is no exception to that."

"Care to be more specific?" asked Robie.

"This is wide-open space, a long way from Denver. You've seen the size of the police force. So folks have become accustomed to taking care of themselves."

"We've seen the open-carry lifestyle here," said Robie. "Including your daughter."

"She's very responsible with her weapons," said Claire defensively. "Now, that's one side of the equation. The other side is being out in the middle of nowhere attracts some folks who want to live off the radar. And not be, well, constrained by societal norms."

"What exactly are we talking about?" asked Robie.

"We've got some skinheads and white supremacists, though some would say I'm repeating myself. But they more or less keep to themselves."

"Okay," said Robie. "What else?"

"Well, we've got others who practice their own type of religion. If you want to call it that."

"What do you call it?"

"You remember the Branch Davidians in Waco? Well, that's what I would call it. They've got their own compound and everything."

"So why wouldn't your son and the sheriff tell us about them?"

"Practical reasons. There're two of them and a whole lot more of the others. Nobody wants a riot. Nobody wants those awful people to take over the town. So it's an uneasy peace, I'd guess you'd say."

"You still have the state police if things go sideways," said Reel.

"Yeah, well, I don't think the state police want to mess with it, either. Colorado is a big state and there aren't that many cops to go around, really, especially in a place like Grand."

"Sounds like a bomb waiting to go off," said Reel.

"You could say that about a lot of places," Claire retorted.

"Did Walton know about all of them being here?"

"Oh sure. You come here often enough, they're pretty hard to miss."

"Did he ever have any run-ins with them?" asked Reel. "Because he's not the sort of person who would turn a blind eye if they did something criminal."

Claire stared down at the floor. "Anything's possible. So you might have to just go ask them yourself."

12

ON THE DRIVE back to town Robie glanced over at Reel. "Why all the questions back there about Blue Man's relationship with her?"

Reel kept her eyes on the road. "Why not? We were there to gather information. So I was gathering information. I'm not an experienced investigator, so I just sort of went with the scattergun approach."

Robie did not seem convinced by this but looked away.

She said, "He kept the house all this time. But never goes there. Why do you think that is?"

"Blue Man is a complicated guy. I doubt we're going to figure that out, nor do we have to in order to do our job." Robie paused. "So there's an abundance of skinheads, white supremacists, and religious wackos here. Nice if Malloy had told us."

"And any one of them might have taken Blue Man," noted Reel.

"So why not just have the Feds come in here and bring the hammer down on those assholes?"

"I think it's called civil liberties and being presumed innocent."

"Disciples of Hitler and people wearing hoods are *presumed* innocent?" snapped Robie.

"Under the law they are, until they break it." She glanced at him. "Remember, badge not scope."

"Scope is simpler."

"Yes, it is."

They pulled in front of the hotel and Reel slid the Yukon into park.

"I heard about Iraq," said Robie.

"Did you?" said Reel, not looking at him. Her hands gripped the steering wheel.

"You did everything you could."

She turned her head slightly. "You weren't there, so how the fuck do you know that?"

"Because I've been there before."

"Yeah, right."

She slammed the truck door behind her as she headed into the hotel.

Robie caught up to her halfway across the lobby.

"This is not helping the investigation," he said.

She whirled on him. "*You* brought it up, not me. And if you think you need to perform some sort of psychological voodoo on me, you don't. And you're not!"

Robie could have said something—anything, really—but he chose simply to turn and walk away from her.

In his room he sat on the bed, laid out his pistol, and field-stripped it blind. He wasn't focusing his mind on the familiar elements of the weapon. That required only tactile senses. His mind was overloaded on Reel.

When it should have been fully engaged on finding Blue Man.

They were screwing up this investigation by their very presence here together. And they'd just started the damn mission!

He slammed in his mag and then slapped himself in the face.

"Get it right, get it clear, Robie. Or Blue Man won't be coming back. Your personal shit is just that, shit. Your scope sight is black. You can't see a damn thing because you keep jumping around. Get your crap together. Now!"

He went to the window and looked out onto the main street of Grand.

Bad elements. They needed to see if any of those elements and Blue Man had run into each other somehow. Robie as yet did not have a good feel for the lay of the land here. He needed to better understand all the parts and how they interconnected. Claire Bender had given them some info on that, the cops some more, and Patti Bender and her group still more. But it wasn't nearly enough.

There was no sign of a struggle at Blue Man's cabin. Nothing really missing except for him. But that didn't mean he hadn't been taken against his will. One man with a gun would have been enough, with the element of surprise on his side.

As he continued to look out the window, a surplus Army truck with a canopied bed came barreling into town. It pulled up to a stop in front of the bar across the street.

Eight men clambered out of the back. They were all armed.

And they all walked into the bar with their weapons.

Guns and liquor, what could go wrong? thought Robie.

But then it might also hold some opportunities.

He slid his gun into his holster along with a couple of other items and headed out to do some digging. And he was going to start with these guys.

Because on one side of the truck was painted a symbol he'd never seen before. It was a *K* and an *A* set at forty-five-degree angles from one another.

Robie paused on the street to eyeball the truck. The driver was still sitting in the front cab. It looked like he was reading a book.

Maybe *Mein Kampf*, thought Robie. Brushing up on his hatred and intolerance.

Robie passed by the truck and let his peripheral vision do a screen shot of the driver. He was young, maybe early twenties. He was lean with a shaved head, on which Robie could see tats of the same *K* and *A* set at angles. All the other men had shaved heads as well. And they probably had similar tats.

He looked to his left and saw Valerie Malloy leaning against a column holding up the porch in front of the police station. He nodded to her. She inclined her head back at him. Derrick Bender was nowhere to be seen.

With one last glance at her, Robie walked into the Walleye Bar.

The space was large and half full. Low tables with chairs were in the center of the room; high tables with seating for two or four ringed this main area. The bar was set against the far wall and had seating, too. It was about twenty feet long and made of mahogany. Two bartenders were manning it. Behind them were multiple rows of liquor bottles stacked on shelves.

The young men from the truck had pushed two tables together and were ordering from a tawny-haired, slim waitress around forty who seemed to know them, and she looked like she would rather be any other place on earth than in the same room with them.

Robie walked over to the bar, sat on a stool, and ordered a beer.

He could see the group without turning around due to the large mirror behind the bar.

They were loud, annoying, and they acted like they owned the place.

So in addition to being possible skinheads they were *dick*heads.

Well, then again, you probably couldn't have one without the other.

When the bartender, a man in his fifties with a crown of graying hair around a dome of skin, brought him his beer, Robie said, "The freak show over there? Where do they call home?"

"What's it to you?"

"I'm sorry if they're friends of yours."

The man snorted. "The day I call them friends is the day they can lock me up in the loony bin."

Robie reached into his pocket and showed the man his badge. "That's my interest," he said.

The man quickly glanced over at the men and then back at Robie. "I don't think even the Feds want to mess with those guys. They're badasses."

"We have our share of badasses with the good guys," Robie pointed out.

"Well, I'm just seeing one of you and eight of them."

"I consider that an even fight."

The man grinned until he saw that Robie was serious.

Robie said, "What's the *K* and *A* stand for?"

"King's Apostles."

"Okay. And are they the ones with some sort of compound?"

The bartender nodded and said, "Fifteen miles east of town, straight line on the main road. Can't miss it."

"So in the same direction as the cabin owned by Roark Lambert?"

The bartender took a rag and started wiping the bar. "So you're here about that Walton fellow gone missing."

"I am. You think the skinheads could have done that?"

"I can't tell you they didn't. And we got neo-Nazis in the area, but just so you know, this bunch here don't consider themselves skinheads."

"So what do they consider themselves?"

"Enlightened. And they don't cause any trouble, really. They just don't like anything about the government. They can get pretty vocal about it. They're their own law. But they keep to themselves, thank God."

"How long have they been around here?"

The bartender wrung out the rag over the sink. "About three years."

"Who started it?"

"Dude named Doctor King. He's the letter *K* in the *K* and *A*, in case you're wondering."

"So is he a doctor?"

"No, you don't understand, his first name, he says, is Doctor. He rolled into town, set up camp a few miles out. He started making his rounds, doing some preaching, or so he called it. Then he started up a little business. Mentoring, he said it was. Printed up pamphlets and fliers and kept talking away, mostly to the young men around here who got nothing in their future 'cept the next beer, chick, or bong. Well, before anybody could really see what was happening, he'd built this big outpost and eventually all them men went to live and work there."

"How do they get by? Where's the money come from? Drinks for that crew don't come cheap."

The bartender pointed a finger at him. "Now there's the sixty-four-thousand-dollar question, man."

"Drugs, guns? Human trafficking?"

"Maybe your Mr. Walton?"

"That industry pretty much sticks with young and female. And you just said they don't cause any trouble."

"Well, they don't. I mean not for the likes of me. I can't speak for others."

"Interesting group."

The man wiped the bar some more. "Good luck on finding out anything from them. Think you're going to need it."

The man left to attend to another customer while Robie nursed his beer and thought about all this.

He heard him coming before he saw him.

"You a Fed?"

Robie put down his beer. He didn't turn to look at the man. He watched him in the mirror.

"Right now, I'm just a thirsty guy having a beer," replied Robie.

The man looked to be in his late twenties, about Robie's height. His muscled delts and veiny arms were exposed by his tank top. He had tats down both arms. *Doctor* was tatted on his right and *King* on his left.

"Hear you're looking for somebody."

Now Robie glanced at him. "I am. You know anything about it?"

The man leaned in, a twisted grin on his features. "Maybe, maybe not. But I'm not telling you shit. We don't talk to Feds. We are not under your control. We are a sovereign power. We are *first* among all others," he said in a loud voice.

Robie turned and looked at him fully. "Based on what?"

The man looked down at him, his mouth curved into a cruel smile. "Based on superiority. Based on nature."

Robie noted the sidearm the man had.

"Glock 26?"

"Damn straight."

"What's your ammo?"

The man told him.

"Ever have trouble with stove-piping?"

The man looked confused.

Robie explained, "The cartridge doesn't fully eject. It gets stuck halfway and sticks up out of the gun like a stovepipe, hence the term. The ammo you're using has a history of doing that."

The man looked down at his gun. "Yeah, it does do that sometimes. Weird shit."

"Glocks run best wet. Lube the rails. On a new gun the slide can be stiff. Lock it in the rear position for a couple days. Only need to do that once. If that doesn't work, your ammo is underpowered. Go for a heavier load. That should fix the problem. You don't want your gun jamming on you when you need it, right?"

"No, you don't," the man said slowly.

He kept staring at his gun for a moment and then looked up at Robie. "Okay, thanks," he said quietly.

"You're welcome."

The man glanced nervously at the two tables where his mates were watching him, then looked back at Robie. "Look, I don't know nothing 'bout the dude that disappeared. I mean we didn't…"

"He's a friend of mine, so thanks, I appreciate the info. I really do. What's your name?"

"Apostle Matthew."

"No, I mean the one your parents gave you."

He said hesitantly, as though he hadn't spoken the name in a long time, "Bruce."

"Okay, Bruce, I'm Will Robie."

Bruce looked back over his shoulder and the men were now staring hostilely at *him*.

When he turned back to look at Robie, Bruce swallowed nervously. "I…I better get back…"

Under his breath Robie said, "Before you do, tell me to go screw myself and that I'll get jack shit from you, and I'll look sufficiently intimidated."

The men stared at each other for a moment.

"Go screw yourself, Fed, you'll get jack shit from me," Bruce screamed.

Robie put up his hands in mock surrender and turned back to his beer.

Bruce walked back to his friends and high-fived several of them.

But when he sat down he glanced over at Robie, and his stare lingered for a few moments.

Robie finished his beer, rose, and left, the eyes of the "apostles" on him every second of the way. But at least one of them now might not want to kill him if it came to it.

And, as Robie knew better than most, *one* could be a very powerful number.

13

JESSICA REEL WALKED into the hotel lobby just as she did any space: with her eyes open and her gaze taking in all possible threats.

She stopped on one possibility.

The man sat in a chair near the double front doors. He was in his forties, with salt-and-pepper hair and a face that was more youthful than the graying hair would suggest. His build was lean but wiry. He wore wire-rimmed glasses and a navy two-piece pinstripe suit. His starched white shirt was buttoned all the way to the collar. Polished cowboy boots were on his feet.

When Reel came into the lobby he rose and put out a hand.

"Agent Reel?"

She stared at him, her hand remaining at her side. "And you are?"

"Doctor King."

"What kind of doctor?"

"No kind. Doctor is my given name. My parents' idea. They never told me the reasons."

"How do you know I'm an agent?"

King smiled. "Small town. Just the way it works."

"And what do you do here?"

King took a few moments before answering. "I'm trying to implement change. I'm trying to show people who were born and grew up in a bubble that there are options in life."

"And you have a compound outside of town?"

"I see you've been talking to some of the locals."

"Roger Walton, you know him?"

"No, but I do know that he went missing."

"Do you know anything about that?"

"It's one reason I'm here. I don't know anything about it."

"What's the other reason you're here?"

"To ask if you needed any help."

"Unless you've got Walton tied up somewhere, the answer to that would be no."

"I could give you insights on the people here."

Reel sat down in a chair opposite and stared across at King. "Let's start with Sheriff Malloy."

King looked surprised. "Why her? She's on your side."

"Nobody's on my side until they prove they are. She wasn't all that forthcoming when we met with her. If we're going to be working the case with her, I need to know if she's the real deal or not."

King nodded. "Okay, that makes sense. She came here because of her sister."

"She mentioned that. Holly. Do you know her?"

"I've met her on occasion. I understand she had a drug problem and went into rehab for it. I encouraged her to become one of my apostles, in fact. I thought it would help her."

"Apostle. So you're a religious organization?"

"I didn't say that."

"The term *apostle* sort of implies that."

"Perhaps in your narrow definition, not mine. But you're certainly entitled to your interpretation."

"You choose your words carefully," noted Reel.

"I've found that to be a good practice."

"Are you from this area?"

"I am now."

"What else can you tell me?"

"If you want my two cents, Malloy is the real deal. She's been a good, fair sheriff here. People respect her, and that's not an easy thing to come by out here. So if you're worried whether she'll have your back or not, I'd say you could trust her."

He rose.

"Is that it?" asked Reel. "I have a lot more questions."

"I'm sure you do, but I have some things to take care of."

"Why did you come here? To see me, or my partner?"

"I wanted to make your acquaintance. Your partner is in the bar across the street. Some of my apostles are there as well."

"Your apostles like their liquor?"

"They're young men. You have to be flexible. But they work hard."

"Doing what?"

"I wish you luck in finding your friend."

She watched him walk out of the lobby.

She waited a minute and then followed. She met Robie in the middle of the street. They each brought the other up to speed.

"This King guy reminded me of a lawyer or something," said Reel. "But he said he knows nothing about Blue Man."

"Yeah, they all seem to say that. But this place is small enough that it seems everyone knows everything that goes on here."

"He did say that Malloy is the real deal. That we can trust her."

"Well, we don't know if we can trust *him*," retorted Robie.

"True. So no guess as to how King and his court make a living?"

"The bartender didn't seem to know. "

"King told me that Holly was in rehab for drugs. He said Holly was the reason Malloy came out here in the first place."

Robie threw up his hands. "So what? And I don't think we've made a jot of progress."

Reel shrugged. "I still don't get why they don't just flood this place with FBI agents."

"You heard the DCI. That's not how they want to play this."

"You know the probability is that Blue Man is dead, don't you?"

"No, I don't know that. My money's on Blue Man surviving."

"Well, then what's our next move?" replied Reel curtly.

"We've checked out where he was staying. We've talked to his ex-flame. So let's go check out the house where he grew up. I got the address from Claire."

Reel said, "Why is that relevant?"

"I don't know that it's not, so that means it's relevant."

He walked toward their Yukon and she reluctantly followed.

Twenty minutes outside of Grand, a pair of bullets cracked the Yukon's windshield.

CHAPTER

14

"Now that's more like it," said Reel, as Robie guided the Yukon to a stop off the road. They took up position behind the SUV and Robie sighted through a pair of binoculars in the direction of the shot.

"Rounds hit dead center of the middle row," Reel said. "Optics shot, so the shooter didn't want to kill us, just send us a message. If he could hit the windshield he could hit us."

Robie nodded but said nothing. He knew all of this, and she knew he knew it.

Reel gazed out at the bleak landscape. She pointed to some higher ground about six hundred yards away. "I'm thinking there."

Robie nodded again and lowered the optics. "So do we keep going? The next shots might not hit the seats."

In answer Reel popped the rear cargo door and unlocked the aluminum case that was in there. In less than a minute she had assembled her rifle and attached the scope. She climbed into the cargo area, used the rear seat as her fulcrum, and sighted through her scope.

Twenty seconds went by and she said, "Got 'em. Two guys, one rifle."

"So a spotter?"

"Looks to be."

"So maybe professional then."

"Most people out here probably know how to use a gun. At least most people we've seen have them."

"Right."

"Dodge Ram truck. Can't see the plate." She turned back to look at Robie. "What do you want to do?"

"Send them a message back," instructed Robie.

Reel smiled at this, climbed out, stood on the rear bumper, placed her rifle on the roof of the Yukon, manipulated her scope, made her sighting, locked them in, settled down, took aim, and fired once. She took another aim and fired again.

Six hundred yards away each bullet slammed into a tire sidewall, exploding it.

The two men were so startled that they threw themselves down on the dirt and then scrambled like mad for cover behind the truck.

"Now let's go have a chat," said Robie. "Keep eyes on them."

He took the driver's slot while Reel slipped her scope off the rifle's rail and climbed in on the passenger side. She kept eyes on the pair as Robie wound the Yukon up to eighty. He slipped his pistol from its holster and cradled it between his knees.

"Movement?" he asked.

"They're still hunkered down wondering what the hell just happened. Now they're climbing into the truck. Started up and…they just found out they have two flat tires. Idiots. They should have checked that first."

"So maybe not professionals then."

"*Probably* not."

The Yukon had rounded a bend, moved up the high ground, and Robie slammed it to a stop twenty feet from the disabled pickup.

He and Reel climbed out, their pistols trained on the front cab where the two men sat, looking stunned. They slowly raised their hands.

Robie motioned with his weapon for the men to get out of the truck.

The doors squeaked open and the men nearly fell out.

One was older, in his fifties, with a full beard and a sunburned face. He wore faded dungarees, dusty boots, and a leather vest over a flannel shirt.

The other man was in his twenties, lean and wiry, about five nine. He was dressed like his companion. His beard was bushy and dark. His eyes were small and resembled gray, moistened pebbles.

They each had holstered weapons. Robie told them to drop their gun belts and kick them away. They did so without saying a word. Lying next to the truck was a rifle with a scope.

Robie pointed to the Yukon's punctured windshield. "I think you owe us some new glass."

Reel looked the younger man up and down and said, "You dropped your rifle on the ground. No way to respect your equipment. And what, you were just going to drive off without it?" She went over and nudged it with her foot. "Nice optics. Too bad they got damaged." She stomped twice on the device with her boot and the scope broke in half.

"What the hell are you doing?" screamed the younger man.

Reel looked up at him. "It's pretty simple. I'm making sure you can't ever shoot me through that scope."

Robie said, "Who are you and why are you firing at us?"

The younger man looked toward his elder. The older man said, "Just saying hello. It's a local custom."

Reel pointed to his truck's flattened tires. "Well, we returned the greeting. But since you fired on two federal agents, the only hellos you're going to be saying for the next twenty years are to people from the federal correctional force, your lawyers, and fellow inmates who want to get to know you better."

The young man's features fell. "You talking prison?" He shot his colleague a look of stark betrayal.

The older man said, "Now let's just hold on here. We didn't mean no harm. Boy could've hurt you if he wanted to. He's a damn fine shot. I don't think we need to involve the law on this. Just a misunderstanding."

"Who are you and why did you fire on us?" asked Robie again. "We can talk about misunderstandings and the law later. And you bullshit me again with this is your way of saying hello, your ass is gone."

The older man considered this. "My name's Zeke Donovan. Russell here is my nephew. We got us a place about two miles from here. Do some guide work. Miscellaneous stuff. Whatever we need to do to get by."

"Why did you fire on us?"

"Well, somebody asked us to put the fear'a God in you."

"And who would this *somebody* be?"

Donovan stroked his beard. "I can't say without breaking a confidence."

"Is that confidence worth twenty years in a federal pen?" asked Reel.

"Probably not," admitted Donovan.

"Well then?"

"His name's Roger Walton."

15

ROBIE STARED AT the pair through the width of the cell bars.

Valerie Malloy stood next to him.

"Zeke, do you know how stupid that was?" she said to the older man.

He looked up at her. "Well, hell, I do *now*."

Russell sat next to him looking at the concrete floor.

"How do you know it was Walton that told you to warn them off?" Malloy asked.

Zeke pointed at Robie. "Like I done told him, he left a note at my place."

"Yeah, I get that, but—"

Robie interjected, "How do you know it was Walton then? If you didn't see him?"

Zeke spread his hands. "Well, who else would'a told me to do it if not Mr. Walton?"

Robie looked at Malloy. She shook her head and closed her eyes for a moment. When she reopened them she said, "Well, Zeke, since these people work with Walton it's highly doubtful he would've wanted you to scare them off. And when did you get the note?"

"Well, I seen it early this afternoon, but I'd been gone for a few days so it could've been there a while. Or it could've been delivered today."

"Well, since we just got here this morning I doubt somebody would have sent you a note that said scare off people who weren't even here yet," said Robie.

Zeke's face brightened. "Hey, I bet you're right about that. Yeah, that's a good point, son."

"Did it mention the two people by name?" asked Malloy.

"No, just said a couple of strangers looking for Walton. Well, I guess according to you maybe it wasn't Walton what sent the note after all."

"And why would you do something like that just because Walton told you to?"

"'Cause he also included five hundred dollars cash along with the note."

"And did he say why he wanted you to do it?"

"Said it was a joke, sort of."

"So you didn't know that Walton had gone missing then?" asked Malloy.

"No. I mean, like I said, I just got back and saw the note. You say he's missing? Where'd he get off to?"

"If we knew that he wouldn't be missing!"

Reel walked in and joined them in the holding cell area. "Did you know Walton?" she asked Zeke.

Zeke shrugged. "I knew him. Couldn't say I really *knew* him, you know. He kept things close to the vest."

"Did you ever act as a fishing guide for him?" asked Robie.

Zeke shook his head. "Nah, he didn't need that. He grew up here. Knew the area real well. But we'd see each other from time to time. He fished some of the same streams we do. Had some beers together at the Walleye. Stuff like that."

"Did you know him back when he lived here?"

"No. He was quite a bit older'n me. Heck of an athlete."

"Did you know his parents?" asked Reel.

Zeke shook his head. "I was just a little kid when they killed themselves."

"We heard his mom was dying. You think that was the reason?"

Zeke thought about this, glanced over at Russell, whose gaze was still planted on the floor, and shook his head. "Hell, I don't know. Like I said, I was just a little kid when they did it." His face brightened. "Hey, maybe Walton really killed 'em and somebody knew it and they took him to make him pay for what he done. "

Reel said in an exasperated tone, "Okay, I think we're done here." She turned to Malloy. "Robie and I were going to check out the house when these idiots opened fire. We'll go there now."

Malloy looked surprised by her comment. "But I thought you were here to find Walton?"

"I'll take any lead I can get," replied Reel. "Because right now we don't have a single one."

Robie said, "Sheriff, what's your take on this Doctor King guy and his apostles?"

Before she could answer, Russell said, "My brother's an apostle."

They turned to look at him. Reel said, "And what does he think about it?"

Russell shrugged. "I don't know. He don't come home anymore."

Robie eyed Malloy. "And your opinion?"

"They don't break any laws and they don't cause trouble, so that's a good thing."

"I heard that no one knows where the money comes from to fuel their operation. Feeding and clothing the apostles. I saw them come into town in an Army surplus truck. They've got guns. They live in a compound, you said. That all costs money."

"I think they get donations from folks," said Zeke.

"How much can that amount to?" scoffed Reel.

"Just saying."

"They grow pot," said Russell. "And they sell it to folks."

"And you know this how?" asked Reel.

"Seen 'em doing it."

Reel said to Malloy, "Let's keep this pair on ice for a while." She drew close to the bars. "You two ever take a shot at us again, it'll be the last thing you ever do. Are we clear on that?"

Zeke eyed her with trepidation. "Are you the one what shot out the tires?"

"I am. And I could have done the same thing at twice the distance.

Only next time I won't be aiming at rubber." She put her hand through the bars and stabbed her finger into his forehead. "It'll hit right here."

"Then I understand you loud and clear, ma'am."

* * *

"It's so flat out here it's hard to believe the Rockies are right behind us," said Reel as they drove to Blue Man's childhood home.

"It's hard to believe lots of things," replied Robie. "Who would have gotten those two idiots to try to scare us off?"

"Half the people we've already met," answered Reel. "Doctor King and his minions for one. Then the white supremacists that we haven't met yet. Or the skinheads. Hell, Malloy and her deputy for all we know. The point is, Robie, we don't understand this place or what went on before here. And we probably never will. Blue Man could have disappeared because of some shit that took place when he was growing up here."

"Don't tell me you're buying that crap Donovan was spinning about Blue Man killing his parents and then somebody here coming after him for it?"

"Of course not!"

"Well then?"

"I just mean we don't know this place. We're flying blind. That's never a good thing."

"Still doesn't excuse us from finding him," said Robie.

"Never said it did. I just mean we need more intelligence."

"We're gathering intelligence every time we talk to someone."

"But we have no way of knowing if they're telling us the truth or not. When I'm prepping a shot I can do my wind call and my distance read and all the other factors that go into determining whether the shot will be successful or not. But my tools don't lie to me. They give me the facts. This is different. Way different."

"Still not an excuse. We have our mission. We have our orders. We just need to adapt and execute."

Reel shot him a glance. "Okay, how do we adapt?"

"We're both good observers, Jess. We listen and we hear everything, not just the bullshit. We can read body language, because our job requires us to be able to do that. So we employ all of that while we're here."

Reel turned her attention back to the road. "Okay, what's your take on Malloy and Bender?"

He glanced at her. "Still distrusting the local constabulary? Didn't your good 'Doctor' King give them a clean bill?"

"Like you said, we don't know him."

"Okay. Malloy hasn't been here long enough to really be part of this place. Bender on the other hand has. And so have his sister and their mother. I'm not saying they had anything to do with Blue Man vanishing. But I'm also not saying that everything they told us was the truth. The guy that confronted me in the bar, Bruce? I take him as someone with no future who found one with this Doctor King. And what's your take on *him*? You said he struck you more as a lawyer type."

Reel didn't answer right away. She gripped the steering wheel, her face lined in deliberation.

"He's smooth but not psycho smooth. The guy appears to be leading some wacko cult, but he didn't come across as that sort. Tough one to figure out. He said he had nothing to do with Blue Man disappearing. Same as what his 'apostle' told you. And I think I believe him. Just my gut."

"Sure you're not just falling under his spell?" asked Robie in a joking manner.

She shot him another glance. "Hook, line, and sinker of course," she replied with an eye roll tacked on.

He looked away. "There's something that somebody said that didn't make sense."

"Like what?"

"I don't know. But it's like grit in your barrel. It's throwing everything off."

"Well, think hard and come up with it."

He closed his eyes and leaned back in his seat.

Reel looked at him once, and her features softened and a look of uncertainty came into her eyes. Then she glanced away and concentrated on her driving. As she eyed the twin holes in the windshield, she had no idea if another pair of rounds might be heading toward them. And this time they might not strike simply leather.

16

IT WAS SMALL, squat, and devoid of any architectural detail of interest.

The inauspicious childhood home of Blue Man.

Robie and Reel stood next to their truck and stared at the structure.

"Oh, how the lowly have risen," said Robie.

"I just always assumed Blue Man was born into a family of academics on an Ivy League campus," offered Reel.

"Well, like you said before, we don't really know the man that well."

"Who really knows anybody these days?" countered Reel.

"You got that right," retorted Robie, drawing a quick stare from Reel. But he wasn't looking at her.

He walked over to the single-car garage and peered through the window. The garage was now empty. "I would imagine they took the car away when they investigated the deaths." He shook his head. "I can't imagine coming home and finding my parents dead by their own hand."

"It might explain why Blue Man never married."

"He wanted to marry Claire," Robie pointed out.

"True."

The front door was locked. Robie took out her pick tools and it no longer was.

"He left the furniture," noted Robie.

The front room had a couch, two chairs, and a battered coffee table.

They passed through into the kitchen. Plates and glasses were still in cabinets. A framed picture of the Rocky Mountains was on one wall.

Robie tried the kitchen faucet and water came out. "They have to be on a well. No water lines out here. Septic, too. Looks fresh and clean. He's probably paid someone to maintain it all."

He tried a light switch. It came on. "Place has juice, too."

"So he must be paying the utility bill."

Robie opened the door to the garage, and both gazed at the spot where the car would have been with the two dead people inside it.

Robie glanced at Reel, but she didn't look at him.

They took the stairs up and encountered one bathroom. The fixtures were all from decades ago but the sink and toilet worked.

One bedroom they entered had a bed and an empty closet.

"He obviously cleaned out their closets," observed Robie.

"And no pictures on the walls or furniture. He must have taken those, too."

There was only one other bedroom up here. The bed was still in this one, too. And under the bed was a large wooden box.

Robie slid it out, put it on the bed, and opened it. He took out a number of faded athletic trophies and frayed first-place ribbons.

They all had Roger Walton's name on them.

"He was a high school sports star," noted Robie.

Reel looked over the items with amazement. "I just thought he was this big brain. I never saw him as an athlete."

There was a scrapbook in the box. Reel lifted it out and opened it.

On the yellowed pages was basically a chronicle of a youthful Roger Walton's achievements in Grand, Colorado.

"He made the local paper a lot," noted Robie. "For sports. And he was high school valedictorian and the damn prom king. He captained the debate team. And this clip is about him accepting a full ride to Stanford."

"It's a wonder he had time to sleep," observed Reel.

"I don't think he sleeps as an adult," replied Robie.

"Why do you think he left all this stuff behind?"

"I'm no shrink, but maybe it has something to do with preserving his life here. I mean, the one he has in DC couldn't be more different from what he has here. Maybe he uses it to balance his life out. Probably why he keeps coming back. To his roots."

"Robie, he never talked about his life here. Even the DCI didn't know about this stuff. It would have been in the briefing book."

"Did you ever talk about your life to him?" he asked. "I never talked about mine."

"That's true. But he obviously worked his ass off for all this. Why not be proud of it?"

"Maybe he had a reason. Blue Man always has a reason for everything."

Reel pointed a finger at a picture on the page in the scrapbook. "And she was the prom queen. I can still make out the names at the bottom."

They both stared at a decades-old photo of Claire.

"She was a knockout," observed Robie. "I could definitely see why Blue Man would have fallen for her."

"Well, there were limits to their feelings for each other. She wouldn't leave and he wouldn't stay. Game over."

Robie looked at her curiously. "Just like that?"

"Just like that," replied Reel, staring at him.

For some reason Robie felt like they were no longer talking about Blue Man.

The next moment they heard the front door open, and footsteps followed as someone came into the house.

Reel and Robie pulled their guns. Robie pointed to the window while he edged over to the door.

Reel peered out the window. "It's a cop car. Malloy's."

A moment later they heard the sheriff call out to them. They headed down the stairs and met her at the bottom.

"Find anything?" she asked, looking around.

Robie said, "An old scrapbook, a bunch of trophies."

"And no Roger Walton," added Reel.

"He owns the place and keeps it up, but Claire Bender said she doesn't think he ever comes here. He must pay someone local to keep it clean."

"But I don't see what all this has to do with what happened to Roger Walton. He was obviously not here when he was taken."

Robie shrugged. "We're just collecting intelligence. And we can't rule out the possibility that his disappearance is tied to something in his past."

Malloy said, "You're not believing what Zeke Donovan said—"

Robie cut her off. "No, I'm not," he said, glancing at Reel because she had raised this same point earlier. "But it could be something else. He was the local town hero and then went off to college and then on to DC. Maybe somebody here was jealous of him. And decades later decided to do something about it. Wouldn't be the first time."

Malloy thought about this for a few moments. "I can check into that. See if anyone here was holding a grudge."

He handed her the scrapbook. "You might want to start with this. Maybe somebody from high school?"

Malloy took the scrapbook and then looked at Reel. "Where'd you learn to shoot?"

"Wherever I could," said Reel curtly. "And keep those two morons locked up. For *their* safety."

She walked out the front door.

Malloy glanced at Robie. "She always so friendly?"

"You should catch her on a bad day."

Then Robie walked out, too.

17

IT WAS NIGHT and Robie couldn't sleep.

It was getting to be a frustrating pattern.

He sat up in his bed, then got out and padded over to the window in his skivvies. He touched the scars on his arm and his shoulder. Both had been repaired to the Agency's satisfaction, though Robie figured that within another few decades they wouldn't feel all that "satisfactory."

He parted the curtain and looked down upon the darkened main street of Grand, Colorado. It reminded him some of Cantrell, Mississippi, his hometown on the Gulf Coast. Actually, Cantrell was a bit bigger than Grand, though it had never been more than a traffic light stop on the way to somewhere else. His father was there with Robie's half brother, Tyler. It was just his father and the young boy now, after what had happened back then.

When Robie had finally gone back to his hometown, he had discovered secrets that perhaps would have been better left buried in the past.

Blue Man, on the other hand, had come back to his childhood home often. And on this last trip back, the man had vanished.

There were more dissimilarities there than parallels, Robie noted. But had something from Blue Man's past come back to cause his disappearance? Did it have something to do with the suicide of his parents nearly fifty years ago? But how could it? There was nothing criminal about that.

Or was there?

Earlier, he had sent an encrypted e-mail with their first-day report to the DCI. Her response had been terse but direct.

Dig deeper. And pick up the pace.

Right. Easier said than done in a place like this.

Cantrell had kept its secrets for a long time. Small towns just seemed to be able to do that, though one would think with fewer people the truths would stand out.

Well, those who thought that would be wrong.

Robie knew that each day that went by would make it more unlikely that he would ever see Blue Man again, at least alive.

Robie had few friends.

Blue Man had been one of them.

Is one of them.

Blue Man had never given up on Robie, not even when Robie had perhaps given up on himself. And for that sole reason, Robie could never give up on the man.

His attention turned back to the street.

The growl of a motorcycle.

Robie squinted out into the poor light coming from a few streetlamps.

The rider looked big, his bulk seemingly dwarfing his bike.

He had on no helmet, and as he passed under a disc of thrown light Robie could see that his head was bald. The rider pulled into a slot in front of a building across the street and two doors down from the Walleye Bar. Robie had noticed the building before. There was a large NO TRESPASSING sign on the front door. The windows were all dark.

Robie moved over to his bag, pulled out his night-vision scope, and returned to the window.

Sighting through it, he watched as the man strode up to the door and knocked.

Two beats passed and the door opened. A shaft of light from inside was freed, and Robie got a better look at the man. He was dressed all in black. There were creases where his head met the back of his neck. Tatted on one side of his head was a large swastika.

The skinheads, Robie assumed. He wondered if they were all as large as this gent, who Robie estimated was about six four and three hundred pounds, with not much of it fat.

The person opening the door was also revealed. She was petite, and looked to be in her twenties with soft brown hair and pretty features that looked familiar to Robie, though he couldn't place them. She had on jeans and a sweater.

She stepped aside, the man passed through, and the door closed behind him.

Robie lowered his scope and tapped it against the palm of his hand.

Did the woman live there? What was the place? It might be abandoned for all he knew.

He looked at his watch. It was nearly one in the morning. Was this just a late date? But they hadn't acted like a couple. They hadn't hugged or kissed upon seeing each other.

Robie quickly dressed, left the hotel by a side door, bypassing the sleepy front desk clerk, and stepped into an alleyway. He got his bearings, listened and watched for anyone coming, then stole across the street.

He reached the bike, saw that it was a highway Harley, and snapped a picture of the license plate with his phone. The door the biker had entered was just ahead. But Robie decided on another entry.

Robie hung a left, skittered down a side street, cut a right, and came up on the back side of the building.

It was three stories tall with windows riding up the brick on each floor. There was a back door. Robie assumed it was locked, and when he checked, his assumption was proved correct.

He stepped back and gazed up at the building's façade. He couldn't see one light on in the place. When the woman had opened the door an interior light had been revealed. But no light had come through the windows.

He walked over to one and examined it.

They had been blacked out with paint.

Okay, that was definitely interesting.

Robie stepped back and again looked up at the façade.

This might or might not be connected to Blue Man's disappearance, but it was certainly out of the ordinary, if not downright suspicious.

He flipped out his pick tools and attacked the back door. If the place was alarmed he could always run for it.

But he was faced with another dilemma when he tried to pick the lock but failed. The knob turned but the door wouldn't open. Was it nailed shut? But the front door had been operational.

What the hell was this place?

He used a knife in an attempt to open the lower window. Again, he got the clasp to turn but the window did not rise.

Clenching his knife between his teeth he put a foot on a window ledge and boosted himself up. Finding nearly invisible handholds among the uneven bricks, he made his way to the second floor and then to the third. He figured the second-floor windows might be nailed down, but not the top floor.

He reached the window and used his knife to lever open the clasp. Then he pushed up on the window and was relieved when it slid cleanly open.

He was inside in a moment and squatted down, letting his eyes adjust to the deeper darkness in the room and listening for any sounds. He heard nothing. He straightened and placed one foot carefully on a spot on the floor and then put his weight fully on it.

There was no squeak.

He put away his knife and pulled his gun. Technically he was trespassing, and whoever lived here could lawfully shoot him.

Technically.

It was a calculated risk, but one he figured was worth taking if for no other reason than Robie was most comfortable doing inherently dangerous things. It was only the normalcy of life that tended to bother him.

He reached the door and opened it slowly, testing the quietness of the hinges.

He slipped into the hall and took a few moments to study the long passage. There were doors leading off it, but they were all closed.

He reached the top of the stairs. They were carpeted, which was good, since they would absorb sound better.

He walked down them to the second floor. It was a mirror image of the third floor.

He looked down the flight of steps to the first floor.

Lights were on there.

Harley Man and the woman were down there. Whether anyone else was Robie didn't know.

But he decided to find out.

And that was when all hell broke loose in Grand, Colorado.

CHAPTER

18

HARLEY MAN RAN out into the hallway. He had an NFL lineman's huge, blocky build. He had a gun in one hand. He scooted over to a front window and tried to see out.

The woman sat frozen on the bed inside the room he had just left. She had on a bra and underwear and nothing else. Her clothes were lying on the floor.

Shots rang out and one bullet pierced the front door, zipped past Harley Man, and lodged in the wall behind him. He dropped his suitcase, ducked down, and retreated. He called out over his shoulder and the woman appeared at the doorway, squatting down.

He pointed up the stairs.

She nodded and fled toward them even as more bullets pierced the doorway and thudded into the walls. Her bare feet pounded up the risers and she hit the second-floor landing.

And ran right into Will Robie.

She started to scream, but he showed her his badge and put a finger to his lips.

"What's going on down there?" asked Robie, even as bullets continued to fly with Harley Man now returning fire through a cracked window.

"I don't know. I just heard the shots."

"Who are you? What is this place?"

"I'm...I'm Sheila."

"Who's the guy down there?"

"Luke."

"And who is Luke?"

"Just a guy I know."

"Luke with a swastika on his head is just a guy you know?" He looked at her state of undress. "And what's with that? Is this some kind of brothel?"

"We—I am not a hooker!"

The firing picked up.

Footsteps pounded up the stairs and there was Luke.

"Who the hell are you?" roared the man upon seeing Robie.

He started to point his gun at Robie, who disarmed Luke with a kick to the hand.

"You son of a bitch!" screamed Luke.

He dropped into a crouch, his arms at his sides.

A brawler, thought Robie. *Okay, here we go.*

He hurtled at Robie, who easily sidestepped the charging man. He delivered a bent elbow strike directly against the back of Luke's neck, rotating his hips as he struck to give the blow the entire force of his weight and thrust. Robie could feel the tip of his elbow impact the tip of the spine, and the big man moaned and dropped to his knees. Robie followed that with a knee kick to the chin, which chipped two teeth and toppled Luke onto his back. Robie bent over the fallen man and delivered a short punch directly to the man's nose, bouncing the back of his head off the floor. Luke groaned and lay still.

"You bastard!"

The woman jumped on Robie's back. It took exactly two seconds for Robie to pull her off, lay her on the floor, and keep her there with his boot.

"Let me up! Damn it, let me up! Luke!"

Robie ignored her cries, calmly took out his phone, and punched one key.

Reel picked up on the first ring. "You hear the gunfire?" she said.

"I'm in the middle of it." He explained the situation in two brief sentences.

"On it," was Reel's curt reply.

Next, Robie called Malloy, woke her up, and explained the situation.

"I'll be there as fast as I can," she said. Robie could hear her feet hit the floor and a drawer open. "But it's going to be about twenty minutes."

"It's going to be over before then," said Robie.

Robie put away his phone and looked down at Sheila. "Stop screaming. I'm trying to save your ass."

"Get your foot off me," she shouted.

Robie pointed his gun at her. "Stop screaming."

She froze.

"Stay down," he ordered.

Robie removed his foot, stepped to a cracked second floor window, and saw a half-dozen men congregating in front of the building. They all had either handguns or shotguns. They were obviously preparing to storm the building.

He called out, "I'm with the authorities. You have one minute to leave town. After that, I can't vouch for your safety."

One man, larger and older than the others, looked up. "You ain't no authority in this town."

"The sheriff is on her way."

"Who the hell cares?" replied the man, a comment that drew laughter from his companions.

Robie took out his night scope and drew a bead on the man. He was momentarily taken aback. This man also had a swastika on his head.

Was this a turf battle between skinheads?

"You've now got thirty-six seconds," announced Robie.

"Yeah? Well, now you got fuckin' zero, prick."

The man aimed his gun and fired at the window. So did the others.

Robie had already stepped well back and the bullets did no damage.

He counted down the seconds in his head.

He hadn't just been talking to the skinheads. He'd been communicating with Reel, who was right now lining up her shots from the window in the hotel.

Robie moved past the unconscious Luke and strode into a bedroom while Sheila cowered on the floor. He ripped sheets off the bed, tore them into lengths with his knife, and used some strips to bind Luke.

He used the others to form a rope. He went to the top floor, opened the window he had come in from, tied one end of the sheets to a bedpost, and ran the other end out the window. Then he brought Sheila to the top floor.

"Let's go."

She looked terrified. "I don't like heights. I might fall."

"Do you like bullets better than heights?"

She appeared to get his meaning. She looked down at her nearly naked body. "Can I get something to cover myself?"

Robie took off his jacket and handed it to her. "Use this. Hurry up."

She slipped on the jacket and zipped it up. "I don't think I'm strong enough to climb down there."

"I'll give you a piggyback ride."

"What?"

He grabbed her arm and pulled her behind him. "Jump up. Arms around my shoulders, legs around my waist. Do it!"

"But what about the guys outside?"

"They're going to be preoccupied in about five seconds."

Robie counted down in his head until he heard the first report of Reel's rifle.

"Let's go."

She climbed up on his back, grabbed his shoulders, and locked her thighs around his waist.

He moved to the window. "You ready?"

She nodded, but looked scared.

"So long as you hold on you'll be fine," he said. "I can do this and so can you, okay, Sheila?"

She finally nodded.

"Don't look down, and don't close your eyes, understand?"

She nodded again.

Robie ducked down, gripped the sheet rope with both hands, and climbed out the window. He could feel Sheila's heart pounding against his back.

He made his way down, hand over hand, keeping his feet planted against the side of the building as both a guide and a brake on his downward momentum.

His feet finally touched down and he said, "Okay, we're here. You can get off."

Sheila gingerly lowered her feet down to the ground.

Shots were still coming from the front.

Robie pointed behind him. "You run that way and keep going for about a minute, okay. Then just hunker down and stay there. I'll come get you when it's done."

"Mister, there're a lot more of them than there is of you."

"Not anymore. Now go!"

She turned and ran off.

Robie hustled to the right and came up around the building adjacent to the one he had just been in.

He peered around the corner to see the men taking cover behind the two trucks. Robie figured that was how the group had arrived in town.

They were firing back at the hotel.

Robie phoned Reel.

"You good?" she asked.

"I'm good." He told her his position. "I'm the brush beater. You're the cleanup. Aim low, no use killing any of these assholes. Too much paperwork."

"Roger that."

"And take out the wheels."

"Roger that too."

Robie put away his phone, pulled his M11, and attached his night scope to the rail. He sighted through it and opened fire. His bullets pinged off the truck metal.

The result of this was instant chaos on the skinheads' side. They were obviously not seasoned soldiers, because seasoned soldiers did not panic when caught in a crossfire.

They started firing wildly around and running in all directions.

And Reel mowed them down as soon as she had even the narrowest of firing lanes.

All six men went down grabbing their ankles and calves where she had shot them, and screaming bloody murder.

Then Reel turned her attention to the trucks and shredded two tires on each. For good measure she drilled holes right through the radiators, and next the windshields, where her shots tore off the steering wheels of both vehicles.

Robie, keeping to the shadows, called out, "The state police are on their way. If you put down your weapons, lie on the ground, fingers interlocked behind your head, you'll get triaged. Keep your weapons and we let you bleed out."

Weapons were tossed aside as men groaned and collapsed fully on the ground, hands behind their heads.

Robie stepped out, and under cover of Reel's rifle made his way to the fallen men.

As he bound their hands with zip ties he received a steady stream of invectives.

The older man who had bantered with him before swore to Robie, "I'm gonna see you dead, asshole!"

"I think you got that backwards," replied Robie.

CHAPTER

19

IT MIGHT HAVE been the most excitement Grand had seen in decades.

Malloy had shown up with her uniform shirt untucked and her boots unlaced, but her service weapon was out and her features were grim.

Reel and Robie had triaged each of the men, stanched the bleeding, and bandaged the wounds using a kit Reel had gotten from the hotel. Ambulances were on the way to take the men to a hospital that was about an hour away.

Derrick Bender showed up five minutes behind his boss.

Luke had been revived and came outside to confront the men who had tried their best to kill him.

After screaming matches back and forth, Malloy had cuffed Luke and stuck him in Bender's cruiser.

But both Robie and Reel saw Malloy say something to Luke, and she didn't look remotely happy.

When the state police showed up in the form of four troopers in a Humvee, things started to get interesting.

The skinheads claimed that Robie and Reel had opened fire on them first and they had fired back to defend themselves.

When Luke was questioned, all he would volunteer was that Robie had sucker punched him when he'd confronted him after Robie had broken into the building.

While the troopers were interviewing the men, Robie and Reel pulled Malloy and Bender aside.

"What is that building?" asked Robie.

Malloy said, "It was a B and B, or it was planned to be one. Then the hotel came to town and the B and B plans got torpedoed and the owners ran out of money and the project went bankrupt. The bank owns it now, but people, from time to time, were using it for a certain, specific purpose."

"You mean as a hookup place," said Reel.

"Among other things." said Malloy. "Until I put a stop to it. I locked it up tight and put up the NO TRESPASSING sign."

"Well you didn't lock it up tight enough. There was a woman named Sheila in there with Luke. She climbed out the window with me. I gave her my jacket because she was half naked. I told her to hoof it a few blocks over and wait for me to come get her. But all I found was my jacket on the ground behind the B and B and no Sheila."

Reel looked at Malloy. "Who's Sheila?"

"I don't know a Sheila. Describe the woman to me."

Robie did.

Malloy let out a long sigh while Bender frowned and said, "Damn, Valerie, that sounds like your sister."

Robie and Reel stared at Malloy. "Your sister?" said Reel. "You said her name was Holly. Why would she call herself Sheila?"

"I don't know. Maybe she didn't want you to know her real identity because of all the crap going down."

Reel said, "We were told your sister had a drug problem and was in rehab. And that maybe she was the reason you came out here. Is that true?"

Malloy leaned against the front fender of her cruiser and rubbed her eyes.

"Holly was the baby of the family. She came out here five years ago because she said she wanted to live in the outdoors and just get away from civilization. And family expectations."

"And what were those expectations?" asked Robie.

"Holly graduated magna cum laude from MIT. She was a brilliant student. She was offered a position at NASA and another one at Google. She turned them both down and moved out to this godforsaken place."

Robie glanced at Bender to see his reaction to the harsh words about his hometown, but his expression didn't change. Maybe he'd heard this before from his boss.

"Burnout?" said Reel.

"I guess, although she never showed any indications of it while she was in school. But as soon as she got the sheepskin it was good-bye."

"But you said she'd been here five years. And you came just recently."

"I had a life in New York and a career. And we all thought Holly was just going through a phase. That she'd get this out of her system and come back to reality. But as time went by we realized that was not happening. So I decided to come out here and find out what the hell was going on."

"And did you?" asked Reel.

"It's not exactly a new story. Holly was book brilliant and street stupid. She got in with the wrong crowd, got hooked on drugs, did some dumb things to get money to buy drugs, and did some time in jail. That's where she was when I got to town. I visited her, got her sentence reduced, and she was finally released on parole three months ago. She went into rehab, got clean, and was released three days ago. I was in the process of getting her the hell out of here when she just vanished on me."

"When was this?"

"I picked her up from rehab, dropped her at my place, went to work, and when I got back she was gone and so was her suitcase."

"So vanished, like Walton?" said Robie.

"No, not like that. She left a note in her handwriting, so I knew it was from her. She thanked me for all I'd done but said she couldn't go back to New York. She said she was too embarrassed. She said she was okay and would be moving on with her life."

"And she hooks up with a skinhead a few doors down from where her sister works?" said Reel.

"Did she know this guy Luke before this?" queried Robie.

"Why do you ask that?" said Malloy suspiciously.

"Two reasons. She was half naked and having or about to have sex with the guy. Second, I saw you talking to Luke when you put him in the squad car. From the looks of things it seemed this was not the first time you two had met."

Malloy sighed again. "When I saw Luke tonight I thought he might know where Holly was. But he wouldn't tell me anything." She paused. "I really thought she'd left the area. I was praying that she had." She looked at Robie. "Did she…did she look strung out on drugs to you?"

"No. She was in full possession of her faculties tonight. Which means she was sleeping with the skinhead voluntarily. I don't know which is worse, quite frankly."

"Shit," muttered Malloy. "When she was staying with me, she must have taken the key I keep to the B and B. That's how she got in, I bet."

"Why would she need to do that?" asked Robie.

"Because she was obviously going to leave and probably thought she might need a place to hide out for a bit. I've got to find her."

"Well, like I said, she was half naked. I don't think she could have gone far."

Malloy looked at Bender. "Can you finish up here?"

"Yeah, sure."

Malloy jumped into her car, started it, and drove off fast in the direction of the last place her sister had been seen.

As the dust from her exit settled down, one of the state troopers came over to Robie and Reel.

"Okay, we got a little bit of a 'he said, she said' here," said the trooper. He was in his forties with a wiry physique and long sideburns.

Robie said, "Well, what I say is they came here to kill the guy in that police cruiser. I was in the building at the time because I'd seen suspicious activity and went to investigate. The skinheads opened fire. The other guy returned it. I got out a window with the woman. And then my partner and I got into a gun battle with the skins. We identified ourselves and gave them multiple chances to stand down and they ignored every one."

"But their version is different. They said they were driving through town when you opened fire."

"And if you do an analysis of the gunshots, particularly in that door and building, you'll see that they're lying their asses off," barked Reel. "And we're Feds. They're scum. Who are you going to believe?"

The trooper looked offended by this comment. "I'm not going to get into that with you. We're going to escort them to the hospital for treatment. But we may have to release them if we can't get any more proof of wrongdoing."

"Did you talk to that Luke guy? They were coming to kill him."

"He won't talk to us."

"What a surprise," snapped Reel.

"I'm just telling you how I see it," the trooper snapped back. "And you just better watch yourselves, Feds or not."

"You're really taking their side over us?" said Robie.

The trooper lowered his voice. "In case you didn't notice, there are a lot more of those pricks than there are of us. The guys I brought with me tonight—that's it. It's the full on-duty crew for this part of the state."

Robie looked over at the three other troopers. "I see your dilemma."

The trooper nodded, glared at Reel, and stalked off.

Robie looked at Reel. "Nice shooting."

"From what, twenty yards? The day comes I can't make that shot ten times out of ten, then just shoot *me*."

She walked off, leaving Robie alone in the middle of downtown Grand.

He put on his jacket and placed his hands in his pockets.

His fingers touched the paper there.

He pulled it out.

It was a note. And it got Robie's full attention.

I'm sorry about Mr. Walton.

20

MALLOY SAID, "I don't know what to tell you, Robie. I didn't even know my sister was acquainted with Walton."

It was the next morning and Robie and Reel were sitting across the desk from Malloy in her office.

Malloy continued, "And the note is sort of ambiguous anyway. Everyone in town knew that Walton had disappeared. And that you were here to check on him. She might just literally mean what her note said, that she was sorry."

"*If* she wrote the note," said Robie.

"What do you mean?"

Reel answered. "She was wearing basically nothing when she ran away. Robie didn't have paper or a pen in his jacket. She obviously met up with someone to get it, and it had to be fast, because Robie went to check on her and found his jacket not that long after she ran off. That person might have written the note. It's in block letters. You can't confirm that that's your sister's handwriting."

"No, I can't. But who would she have hooked up with?"

Reel said tightly, "It's your town and your sister, you tell us."

"I don't know what to tell you because I don't have the answers you want."

Robie shifted in his seat. "The trooper last night said he might not be able to hold the skinheads. 'He said, she said' issue. But really I think they're intimidated by those guys."

"Look, the state troopers are good cops and they're as brave as anyone in uniform. But they're vastly outnumbered and outgunned. And Luke Miller is already out. There was nothing to hold him on.

They were trying to kill him, like you said. He was just defending himself."

"And do we know why they were trying to kill one of their own?" asked Reel.

"I can't say I know their inner workings, but sometimes the shit hits the fan with these guys and they want to do a purge. I guess Luke was on the outs."

Reel said, "And why did he come into town to hook up with your sister? That must have been prearranged."

Malloy shrugged. "Well, I can't ask Holly. And Luke will say nothing."

"Did they ever go to that place before?"

"Not to my knowledge, no."

"Why is she with Luke?"

"They had a thing a while back."

"Was Holly part of the skinheads?"

"No. She's not like that. But she's screwed up, and apparently Luke showed her some kindness. And they sort of fell in love, if a guy like Luke can do that. I don't really know him."

Robie said, "Someone knew he was coming into town last night to see her."

"What were you even doing there? You never said."

"I saw something suspicious and I went to investigate."

Reel spoke up. "This is all very interesting and totally irrelevant to why we're here. I don't give a crap about your sister's romantic entanglements. We're here to find Walton. That note from your sister indicates she may know something about what happened to him. So that means we need to find Holly. Do you have any idea where she is?"

Malloy bristled. "If I did, I would have told you. I went looking for her last night and found exactly zip. I talked to the people she knew. I went to the places she's stayed before. Nothing."

"So she vanished, reappeared, and vanished again. All in the middle of nowhere," said Robie.

"Seems so," snapped Malloy. "And just so you know, I want to find her as much as you do!"

Reel stared at her. "I hope that's the truth. Because if it isn't, you're in a shitload of trouble."

"Don't try to intimidate me, Agent Reel. I don't break easily."

"So I've heard so many say."

Robie broke in. "You said you had gotten her help. Where was that?"

"There's a rehab facility about an hour from here."

"Give us the address."

"Why? She's not there anymore."

"Just give us the address. And the names of the people in charge of her care."

Ten minutes later Robie and Reel were on the road.

"What are you thinking?" asked Reel as Robie drove.

"I'm thinking we have to get traction on this case. You're right, all the other crap we've stumbled on here has nothing to do with why we're here." He paused. "Until it *does* have something to do with it."

"I don't think I understand what you mean."

"Someone put that note in my jacket pocket. Maybe it was Holly or maybe whoever she hooked up with put it there. But it seems to me that those words could be interpreted as her having known what happened to Blue Man, and that was why she was sorry. And that means it's a lead we have to explore."

"Do you think Blue Man is dead then?"

He glanced at her. "Like I told you before, no, but you knew that was always a possibility with this."

"Yeah, I knew."

"He told me it was never about luck."

She shot him a look. "What?"

"My mission in London. He sent an e-mail. He told me he would have wished me good luck, but he wasn't going to because it was never about luck."

Reel did a quick intake of breath.

"What?" asked Robie.

"He wrote me the same e-mail before I deployed to Iraq."

Robie nodded. "Two peas in a pod. Well, he was there for us in Mississippi."

"There for *you*, Robie. And I was there because Blue Man ordered me down to clean up your mess."

"I thought you came down on your own volition."

"Well, you thought wrong. I was just following orders. Just like we've both been trained to do."

"You haven't always followed orders, Jess. Not that long ago you pulled the triggers on people you were never authorized to kill. And I had to come in and clean up *that* mess."

"So I guess that makes us even."

"I guess it does," replied Robie.

21

"SHE LEFT HERE about a week ago," said Brenda Fishbaugh. "Her sister came and picked her up. She'd completed her treatment here. That's the last I saw of her."

They were seated in the office of the director of the rehab facility where Holly Malloy had gone to address her addiction issues.

"When I asked her name, she said it was Sheila," said Robie.

"She would occasionally tell people her name was Sheila," admitted Fishbaugh. "Sort of like a defense mechanism. That was when she first came here and was pretty suspicious of everyone here. She was a bit paranoid, actually," she added quickly. "She was here for about three months. As I said, she went through our program. And successfully completed it. Or so we thought."

"She might have stayed clean. When I saw her she wasn't strung out on drugs, but she was with a skinhead."

Fishbaugh nodded sadly. "Luke Miller. He came to visit her here often."

"We understand that they knew each other," said Reel.

"Yes. Holly was here voluntarily, although rehab was part of her parole. We couldn't stop her from talking to Miller. Her sister actually got her into our program."

"But it seems that fraternizing with a skinhead would run afoul of her parole," observed Robie.

"Miller didn't have a criminal record."

"We know that," said Robie. "I took a picture of his license plate. We ran a check on him. He's clean. Except for the fact that he's running around with some pretty bad people."

"To tell the truth, I don't think he really was ever a neo-Nazi. He just liked tattoos and riding around on motorcycles and belonging to something."

"Well, since they were coming to kill him last night you might be right about that," said Reel.

"I do think he loves Holly," said Fishbaugh slowly. "I mean, he showed her great tenderness, and he would inquire as to how her treatment was coming."

"Sounds like a real sweetheart," said Reel sarcastically.

Fishbaugh looked at her. "This is a very tough place to live in. People like their independence, and they tend to rely on themselves and not the government. They join groups that represent what they believe in. Sometimes that's a good thing and sometimes it's not, with the skinheads being a case in point. But if you want my critical opinion on Luke and Holly, it's that they were two lost souls looking for something. And maybe they had found it in each other."

"So why not get married and live happily ever after?" said Reel, shooting Robie a quick glance that he did not notice.

"Maybe that was their plan. But Luke could never do that while he was with the skinheads. They wouldn't have allowed it. And I doubt Luke would have wanted Holly anywhere near those people. They *are* bad news."

Robie said, "Maybe that's why they came for him. Because he told them he was leaving the group so he could start a new life with Holly."

Reel said, "That actually makes sense. Too bad we don't know where either one is so we can ask them. The police let Luke go and he's disappeared."

"Did Holly have any other visitors?" asked Robie.

"Her sister, Valerie, on a regular basis. A couple of young women she knew. Her parole officer also visited regularly, of course. But Luke came more often than anyone else. Now, let me see if there were any others. We keep records of all of them."

She turned to her computer and clicked some keys.

"Yes, there was another person." She glanced at the name on the screen. "Roger Walton."

Both Reel and Robie tensed.

"When did he come by?" asked Reel.

Fishbaugh clicked some more keys. "He came by only once."

"When was that?"

"Five days ago."

"So, shortly before he disappeared. Did you talk to him?"

"Briefly. He seemed to know this area well. When I asked him he said he had been born in eastern Colorado."

"Did he say why he wanted to talk to Holly?" asked Robie.

"He said he was a friend and just wanted to see how she was doing. Holly voiced no objections to seeing him."

"Were their conversations monitored?"

"Well, we had someone in the visitor's room, because that's part of our procedures, but we don't record conversations, if that's what you mean."

"Did anyone else here have interactions with him?"

Fishbaugh thought about this for a few moments. "Probably the nurse on duty." She clicked some keys. "Laura Boyd. She might have spoken with him."

"Can we talk to her?" asked Reel.

"She's on duty now. I can get her for you."

They met with Boyd in an empty office. She was in her fifties with brown hair streaked with silver, a compact build, and alert green eyes.

"Brenda said this was about Holly Malloy?"

Robie nodded. "That's right. She had a visitor, Roger Walton?"

"Yes. He came once recently. I escorted him back, and he and Holly spoke."

"Did he talk to you at all?" asked Reel.

"We chitchatted while I walked him back and waited for Holly. He was an interesting man. Just from our brief conversation you could tell he was highly educated and had traveled extensively. I had mentioned wanting to take a trip to South Africa and he told me places to stay and things to do while I was there."

"Did he ever say why he wanted to talk to Holly?" said Robie.

"He was a friend, I think he said. I can't remember if he said he was her friend or a friend of a friend."

"But let's say he was a friend of a friend," said Robie. "Why would Holly have agreed to talk to him if she didn't know him personally?"

"Oh, I see what you mean. He would have had to say what the connection was, or else why would Holly want to see him?"

"Right," said Robie.

"Well, come to think of it, he did say he was a friend of a friend."

"And did he name the friend?" asked Reel.

"Just give me a second, it'll come to me."

They watched as she thought it over.

"That's right, I remember now. He said that he and Holly had a mutual friend. When I told Holly the name she said that she'd meet with Walton."

"Don't keep us in suspense," said Reel sharply.

"His name was JC Parry."

22

"We should have known that from the start," said Robie angrily as they drove back to Grand.

"Known what?" asked Reel.

"That there was something fishy with this Parry guy."

"Why?"

"Because he told Malloy that he was at Blue Man's cabin to act as a guide when he found him missing."

It took Reel a second to get his meaning. "And at least two people have told us that Blue Man didn't need a guide because he knew the area so well."

"And Zeke Donovan was one of them, and since he's a guide you'd think he'd know. That's the inconsistency I was talking about before. So why did Parry lie about being Blue Man's guide and why did he want him to visit Holly Malloy."

"We need to find Parry and ask him."

Robie picked up his phone and called Malloy. "We need to talk to JC Parry. Where does he live?"

"But did you find out anything at the rehab facility?"

"Can you just give me the address?"

She did so and Robie clicked off.

Reel looked at him. "I sense you want to wall off the good sheriff from our investigation."

"Right now, I want to wall off everyone except you and me. Things are way too convoluted to know whom to trust."

"Let's hope that Parry can enlighten us. But I doubt we can trust him, either. Why do you think he was at Blue Man's cabin?"

"Maybe to check on him."

"So if he discovered that Blue Man had gone missing?" said Reel.

"He's going to be scared for himself."

They reached Parry's home about forty-five minutes later. It was, like all the homes around there, isolated and hard to get to.

As they cleared a slight rise in the ground the house came into view. It looked like it had been built from odds and ends and scraps of secondhand wood. There were several outbuildings, some chickens clucking behind fencing, and they were greeted by a mutt of a dog that came out from a crevice underneath the front porch.

A dusty pickup truck sat under a lean-to.

Robie put the Yukon in park and they climbed out.

The dog started to growl menacingly.

Robie put a hand on his gun but Reel dropped to one knee and beckoned the dog to her. It approached cautiously, and then, sensing that Reel was showing neither aggression nor fear, it ambled over and let her scratch its ear and stroke its head.

"What's your name, cutie? Huh? Does that feel good?"

Robie watched in amazement as arguably the most lethal person of his acquaintance gently made friends with the beast.

She stroked its flanks and looked at its muzzle.

Then she looked up at Robie. "This dog hasn't eaten in a while, Robie. You see its ribs showing. And you see how it's swallowing and panting like that? No water."

She looked around, spotted a dog bowl next to an outdoor tap, and filled the bowl up and put it down for the dog, which instantly started gulping water. Reel picked the bowl up before the dog was finished. "Don't want it to get sick. We need to find its food."

"We *need* to find JC Parry," he reminded her.

"That's sort of my point. The dog's fur is well maintained and it otherwise looks healthy. I don't think Parry is the sort to mistreat animals. He's got water bowls for it and you see that dog bed over on the porch."

Robie looked around. "So you're saying Parry hasn't been around to take care of his dog."

"Right."

"Didn't know you were such an animal lover."

She glared at him. "I had dogs growing up. They were my only friends. You know the rest of that story."

"Let's hit the outbuildings first and then the house."

He touched the hood of the pickup truck perched under the lean-to. "Cold. You think he has another vehicle?"

"I think it unlikely. This doesn't look like a two-vehicle sort of residence."

They searched the three outbuildings and found lots of junk, hunting and fishing gear, and no sign of Parry.

They entered the front door of the house, which was unlocked.

Now they both had their weapons out.

Reel had left the dog outside.

The house was only one story. The front room was cluttered but the furniture, while worn, was in good shape. There was a blackened-face fireplace. Beyond that was a small kitchen that was neat and clean.

"No plates or cups in the sink," said Robie.

The bathroom was tiny.

"No used towels, toothpaste, wet washcloths," noted Reel.

"That leaves the bedroom," observed Robie.

They approached the door down the short hall. Robie motioned to his left and Reel took up position there and crouched with her gun pointed at the door. She nodded.

Robie touched the doorknob with his hand and then withdrew it.

He nodded at Reel, slammed his foot against the door, and it flew open.

They swarmed into the room, with Reel clearing the area left and Robie the right and their guns meeting up in the center.

The room was empty and the bed made.

They checked the closet for clothes and/or a body.

They found the former but not the latter.

They holstered their weapons and looked at each other.

"Vanished," said Reel.

"Seems to be a lot of that going around," added Robie.

23

THEY WERE STANDING in front of the abandoned B&B where Luke Miller and Holly Malloy had hooked up the previous night.

They had taken Parry's dog and dropped it off at the sheriff's office, where it was being fed and watered.

"Why are we back here?" asked Reel.

"I want to see if anything was left behind."

"But wasn't the place searched after the gun battle with the skin-heads?"

"I never saw anyone do it. Malloy left to look for her sister. The 'undermanned' state troopers had their hands full with the skin-heads. And look, they don't even have police tape over the front door. So I doubt there's an investigation ongoing. Now, I'm not a lawyer, but they've already royally screwed up any legal case by not securing the place and putting a cop on premises to guard it. Now it's contaminated."

"The Wild Wild West all over again," commented Reel.

Robie opened the bullet-pocked door and they went inside.

They found it on the second floor in a closet.

A single suitcase. The nametag on it read "Holly Malloy," with a phone number printed under it.

Robie pulled it out of the closet, laid it on the bed, and opened it.

Inside were clothes, toiletries, a passport, and apparently all of Holly's other worldly possessions.

Robie checked out the passport. "This was issued to her seven years ago, before she came out here. No stamps inside. I doubt she's been out of the country."

He looked at the passport photo. "Holly Malloy. She's obviously younger in this picture, but it's the woman I was with last night."

"So it looks like she was planning to leave Grand. Maybe with Luke Miller last night."

"This suitcase is small enough to be carried on his Harley, so maybe they *were* getting the hell out."

"But then his fellow skinheads came to town to stop that from happening."

"Appears to be."

"Well, Luke Miller owes us big-time. But for you and me he's a dead man."

"I don't think he sees it that way."

Robie looked at the phone number on the luggage tag, pulled out his phone, and punched in the number. "Worth a shot," he said to Reel.

Three rings later a voice answered.

"Who is this?"

"Holly, this is Will Robie, the guy you piggybacked on out of the window. One question: Where were you carrying the phone? In your underwear or your bra?"

The line went dead.

"Was that her?"

"Sounded like her. Maybe I shouldn't have been so flippant in my query. I'll take another whack at it from a different angle."

He thumbed in a text and sent it to the phone number.

"What'd you say to her?"

"If she wants her stuff, she needs to call me back."

Two minutes later his phone buzzed.

"Hello, Holly."

"What do you want?" she said in a strident tone.

"First, we've talked to your sister and she explained your situation. You got a second shot and I wish you nothing but the best. And I have no desire to get in your way of leaving this hellhole, but I saw the note you left in my jacket. Roger Walton? You know we're here to find him. Or else you wouldn't have left the note. So what do you know about what happened to him?"

"I...I don't know anything."

"Come on, Holly. I've got all your stuff right here. Including your passport. The cops missed it, but I didn't. You're not going to be able to get another passport, and at some point you're going to need an ID. So this is your only ticket out. You want it, you can have it, in exchange for answers to my questions about Walton. That's all I want."

Holly didn't say anything for a few moments. "I...I can't."

"The cops let Luke go, but you probably already know that. Are you with him now? His skinhead buddies are royally pissed at him and us and the cops let them go, too. They're not going to make it easy for you two to get out of here. Maybe we can help with that. In exchange for information. That's my offer and you'd be stupid not to take it, because the way I see it you've got zero better options."

She sighed. "Where and when?"

"How about Walton's cabin in an hour?"

"I can make it in two hours."

"Okay. By the way, who did you hook up with last night after Luke Miller? We know somebody picked you up, and it wasn't Luke, because he was with the cops."

"That has nothing to do with Walton."

"Fair enough. See you there."

Robie clicked off, closed up the suitcase, and lifted it off the bed.

"You really think she's going to show?" asked Reel.

"Yeah. I just don't think she's going to show up alone."

24

THEY PARKED THEIR Yukon well behind Walton's cabin and entered the house from the rear. After searching it and making sure it was empty, they took up surveillance on high ground away from the cabin, but where they could keep eyes on the road leading up to it.

Reel had her scope out and was looking through it.

Robie did his surveillance with the naked eye. Then he checked his watch. "We've got some time."

"Who do you think she'll show up with?"

"Either Luke Miller or whoever helped her last night."

Reel made a slight adjustment on her scope calibration and then shot him a glance. "I heard about London. Sixteen for sixteen with a spare for interrogation."

He shrugged. "That was the assignment. I heard you did all you could and more in Iraq."

She frowned and said, "Well, just goes to show that scuttlebutt is inherently flawed."

"Outnumbered and outgunned and facing armor with a rifle? What options did you have that you didn't employ?"

She shot him another glance, this one suspicious. "That sounds like you got *debriefed* on the mission."

"Why did you volunteer for Iraq, Jess?"

"They needed a sniper and I fit the bill."

"The Army has a lot of snipers who fit the bill."

"Okay, maybe I just missed Iraq."

"I'm glad you missed something."

She sat back on her haunches and looked over at him. "We're up to our asses in another mission right now, so why don't we just focus? How's that for a plan?"

"So just to clarify, all the things you said on the tarmac when we got back to DC were what? Just stuff to make me feel better?"

"Robie, this is not the time or the place for this!"

"Apparently, it's *complicated*."

She shot him a glance.

"You could have just sent a text, Jess," he said quietly. "You didn't have to break into my place."

Reel looked away, started to sight through her scope but then slowly lowered it. "It *is* complicated, Robie. And I'm not prepared to talk about it right now."

He looked out onto the road. "Well, that's good, because here they come. An hour earlier than Holly said."

It wasn't a Harley coming their way.

It was a van with no side windows.

"How many people you think they can stuff in there?" asked Reel.

"About a dozen. From how far down the chassis is riding on the rear wheels, I'd say it's pretty full of something."

"You know, I was really hoping it would just be her."

"Shows how much hope is worth," replied Robie drily.

She slid her rifle out of its pack and attached the scope on its rail.

Robie watched her load the Remington. "Why did you switch from Lapua rounds to Win Mags?"

"Just wanted something new, I guess."

When she caught the rigid look on his face at this comment, she added, in a more contrite tone, "Someone I respect recommended them. That's the only reason."

"Yeah," said Robie tersely before looking back at the van. "How do you want to do this?"

"On the off chance it's just her and the weight in the van is due to something innocuous, let's not open fire until it's confirmed that she tried to double-cross us."

Robie examined one of his M11s and then burnished the blade of his knife with his coat sleeve. "Works for me."

She said, "If we keep this up, we're not going to be too popular here."

"We were never popular here."

The van pulled up to the cabin and the doors opened.

"You ready to fight?" said Reel.

"It's what I do," answered Robie.

25

"THAT'S DOCTOR KING," said Reel.

"And his apostles," added Robie.

It was indeed Doctor King climbing out of the van's passenger seat. Five young men clambered out of the back, and one emerged from the driver's side.

"And there's Holly," said Robie.

She was dressed far more modestly than the night before, in jeans and a long-sleeved shirt with hiking boots. Her hair was tied up in a bun at the back.

"I don't see that they're armed," Reel observed.

Robie took out his phone and punched in the number.

They watched as Holly reached into her back pocket and pulled out her phone.

"Yes?"

"Why all the friends?" asked Robie.

Holly started to look all around as King watched her closely.

"Where are you?" she demanded.

"In a place where I obviously can see you and you can't see me. Why did you bring all those people, Holly?"

"Because I don't really know you, that's why."

"Okay. But why King and his apostles?"

"Because they found me last night and helped me. I was with them when you called. Doctor offered to come with me, just in case I needed any help."

"Well, you don't need any help, so you can ask them to leave. We'll drive you where you need to go."

"How do I know I can trust you?"

"I could have easily hurt or killed you last night, right? But I saved your life and then I let you go. Didn't I, Holly? And we saved your boyfriend's life, too. But for us, Luke's dead."

"That's true, I guess," she conceded.

"All we want is information. In exchange for that you get your stuff. But we're not doing it with all these people here. So either ask them to leave or we're out of here. And we're going to take your stuff with us."

"You promise you won't do anything to me?"

"We're Feds, Holly. We won't do anything to you for lots of reasons, including the hassle of paperwork. I wouldn't be doing any of this except for the note you left in my jacket."

She pondered this for a moment. "Okay," she said. "Give me a minute."

She kept the line open and walked over to King. They could see her talking with him and then he said something back. She shook her head. He nodded, looked around the surrounding area, and called to his men. They climbed back into the van and slowly drove away.

Reel watched them leave through her scope. When they were far enough away she nodded to Robie.

They made their way down to lower ground and then took the path to the cabin. Holly was waiting near the front door and turned quickly to stare at them when they rounded a bend and came into view.

"Who's she?" asked Holly, pointing to Reel as they drew nearer.

"She's the one who saved your boyfriend's life last night by taking out his fellow *skinheads*."

She dismissively waved this comment off. "Luke's not like that. He just joined those assholes to have something to do. He was bored."

"He has a swastika tatted on his head."

"It's not a real tattoo. He did it with some temporary ink so he could take it off when he wanted to. He has it just to fit in. They have rules and crap. He's going to take it off when we leave here."

They stopped a few feet from her. "Okay," said Robie. "About

Roger Walton? We know that he came by to visit you at the rehab facility. Why was that?"

Holly said, "Where's my suitcase?"

In answer Reel went inside the cabin and came out a few moments later carrying it. She handed Holly her passport.

"Signed, sealed, and delivered," said Robie. "Now it's your turn."

Holly sat down on the porch of the cabin and glanced at Walton's rental, which was still parked in front. She let out a long breath and looked nervously at each of them.

"I don't want to get into trouble over this. I'm on parole."

"Which means you probably can't leave the area," said Robie.

"I thought of that. I checked in with my parole officer and talked to him about my plans. They're allowing me to transfer to another location where I'll be checking in regularly with a new parole officer. I just can't stay here anymore."

"Your sister has been telling you that for some time, hasn't she?" pointed out Reel. "She came out here because of you. She's worried about you. She went looking for you last night but couldn't find you."

"My sister has been trying to run my life since we were little" was Holly's surprising reply, her features hardening. "Did she tell you I was the brainy one? The golden girl?"

"She did. Are you saying you're not?" asked Robie.

"Oh, I'm smart. I've got a head for math and science. I proved that. I graduated from MIT. I got offers from NASA and others."

"But you turned them all down and came out here, why?" asked Reel.

"Because I wanted to get away from my family. I wanted to live my life."

"Pretty drastic move. If you worked for NASA you would have moved from New York, surely."

"It wasn't just geographic. It was everything to do with that part of me. I was tired of all the expectations. Of making the family proud."

Reel stared her down. "So your family is so bad that you came out here, got in with the wrong crowd, did drugs, got arrested, did some prison time, and now you're hooked up with a guy with a temporary hate symbol on his head. Nice work. And your sister puts on a uniform and risks her life protecting people like you," she added quietly. "I know she's proud of you. Maybe you should be proud of her."

Holly stood and snapped, "I didn't come here to be lectured. Do you want my help or not?"

"We do," said Robie with a sharp glance at Reel. "Walton?"

Holly sat back down. "When I was in rehab I heard some things."

"What things? And from who?" asked Robie.

"Another patient. A guy named Clément. He was in for drugs like me."

"What did he tell you?"

"That he thought people were being brought here against their will."

"Brought here to Grand, you mean?" said Robie.

She nodded.

"Why?"

"He saw it. He saw the people in a van. They were tied up with hoods over their heads."

"Where?"

"He wouldn't say exactly. But he said there were people with guns guarding them."

"And you believed him? Even though he was a drug addict? He could have just been making shit up. Either delusional or maybe trying to impress you."

"No, I think he was telling the truth. There were too many details. He couldn't have made it all up. And he was really scared. I could tell."

"Did he tell anyone else?"

"I don't think so."

"So why confide in you?"

"We were sort of thrown together. They have a buddy system at the facility, and he was my buddy and I was his. We were supposed to look out for each other. And Clément was really fragile. He needed a friend and I was it. We had just finished up a counseling session when he pulled me aside and told me about it."

"Did you ask him any questions?"

"Some. I was more concerned with doing my time there and getting out, but he talked to me about it on a couple of other occasions and I became more focused."

"Where's Clément now?"

"I don't know. He left the facility before I did."

"What's his last name?"

"Lamarre. Clément Lamarre. He wasn't from around here. I think he mentioned Boulder. But he's originally from Canada. He's French Canadian, or so he told me."

"What was his issue that he was in rehab?" asked Reel after she wrote this information down.

"Like I said, same as me, drug use. Opioids, coke, and heroin. He'd done some prison time too."

"And how does this tie into Roger Walton visiting you?"

"He just showed up one day. I had heard of him. I knew that he visited the area. Over the years I'd also heard that he was high up in DC in some way."

"And you heard this from who?" asked Reel.

"Lots of people."

"A nurse at the rehab said that Walton used JC Parry's name when he came to see you. Why would that be? What's the connection?"

"JC was my friend. I called him from rehab and told him about what Clément had said. Next thing I know, this Walton guy shows up."

"So presumably Parry talked to Walton and asked him to come and talk to you about it?" said Robie.

"Yeah, I guess so. I didn't know who else to call."

"What about your sister?" pointed out Robie. "She's the law out here."

"I...I didn't think she'd believe me."

Robie studied her and decided she was telling the truth. "Did you tell Walton what Clément had told you?"

"Yes, everything."

"And what did he say to that?"

"That he would look into it."

"We know he only visited you once while you were in rehab. Did you talk to him again by phone?"

"No. And then I got out of rehab and then, I guess, Mr. Walton had disappeared."

Robie looked at Reel.

"Parry has disappeared too," he told Holly.

"Oh shit. Do you, I mean, do you think I'm…?" She couldn't seem to finish.

"In danger? If I had to hazard a guess, I'd say, yeah, you are."

"Where do you plan to go with Luke Miller?" asked Reel.

"California. Start over. I know I've screwed up big-time, but I graduated from college early, and I'm still only twenty-five. I want to get my master's and Ph.D. at Stanford, prove myself again. I want to teach."

"Where's Luke now?"

"The police released him this morning. We're supposed to hook up tonight and then head out."

"Hook up where?"

"There's this place we used to go to. We're the only ones who know about it."

"Like last night, you mean?" said Robie.

Holly looked indecisive. "You're really scaring me."

"Then I'm really doing my job," countered Robie.

Reel said, "And if you really want to start over, do you want to take Luke with you for the ride?"

"I told you, he's not a bad guy. Hell, he has marketing and computer science degrees from Northwestern and has designed mobile phone apps. He just got kind of burned out like me, came out to the middle of nowhere, and basically wasted years of his life. He's going to get on with a really successful company out in Silicon Valley when we get to California. He's already interviewed and everything and they made him an offer. He didn't tell them what he's been doing out here, of course. He's only been hanging out with those idiots for a few months anyway. He's never even been arrested. He's going to support us while I go to school and get back on my feet. We're going to get married and we want to have kids."

Robie said, "Well, that sounds like a plan. I never would have guessed he was like that just by looking at him. But, like a book cover, you shouldn't judge."

Holly said pleadingly, "I have to get to Luke. And I have to get the hell out of here. Can you help me do that? We just want to have a life together."

Robie looked at Reel. "Hey, people in love, right? They deserve a shot."

Reel said nothing to this. She just stared stonily at Robie.

He returned his gaze to Holly.

She said tearfully, "So you can help me?"

"Yeah, I think we can," he answered.

CHAPTER

26

THE NIGHT WAS as dark as it was going to get. There was no ambient light here, which meant it should have been an amazing night for stargazing. However, a storm system had moved in over the Rockies and marched its way to eastern Colorado. The rain had not started yet, but it was not far off.

Robie, Reel, and Holly Malloy sat in their Yukon, its lights off, and watched the road. There was a shack up here, long abandoned, that Luke and Holly had used as a meeting place. It was remote, just like everything was remote here. One road in and one road out.

Robie, in the driver's seat, looked back at Holly in the second row of seats. Just beyond that, in the rear cargo area was their hard-sided case with the weaponry they had picked up after landing in Colorado.

"I hope he's not coming on the motorcycle, or else you two are going to be drowned before you get to Denver."

"He rented a car. He sold his bike."

Robie nodded, but something was nagging at him. They had gotten here a couple hours early just in case.

But still.

"Were you two planning to leave that night at the B and B?"

"Yes."

"But you took time out to have sex? How stupid was that? You should have just hit the road. Then they never would have been able to find you."

"I'm not sure about that. We would have for sure run into them on the way out of town."

"It was still stupid," said Robie.

"But we'd never been to that place before. And Luke said no one knew that he was leaving. We met up at the B and B because no one would expect us to go there. It's been shut down for over a year now."

"But still," persisted Robie.

Holly looked sheepish. "Shit, Luke got horny, okay? He's a guy, what can I say? And he was insistent that they had no idea where he was. So I thought it was okay. It wasn't like it was going to take long," she added, her gaze averted from Robie.

Robie looked at Reel. Her gaze moved back and forth across the landscape in front of them. It was mostly flat, only occasionally obscured by some higher, rocky ground. There were patches of trees scattered here and there, but the sight lines were still excellent. They could see anyone coming.

But still.

He moved a bit in his seat and his hand reached out and automatically touched the butt of his M11.

Reel must have noticed this because she glanced at him. Their gazes met, and in a wordless display of communication everything that needed to be said was said.

Robie looked into the rearview. Though there was little light he could still make out Holly's strained features.

Now what had been bothering Robie finally percolated to the surface.

"Holly, how did you arrange to meet with Luke at the B and B in town?"

She glanced at him, one hand clinging tightly to the handle of her suitcase.

"I texted him. He texted me back. That's how we usually do it. The cell reception out here isn't the best, so you can't always hear the person if you call. But the texts seem to work okay."

Now Reel stirred in her seat. Next to her was her sniper rifle, the stock of it resting on the floorboard and the muzzle pointed to the ceiling.

She said, "Where did Luke get his phone?"

This was just the question Robie was about to ask.

"His phone?"

"Yeah. They're not cheap. You have to get a call plan with it. Did he do all that himself?"

"I...I don't know."

Robie glanced out the windshield again. "Well, try to remember."

Holly thought for a few more seconds. "Come to think, I do recall Luke telling me that the skinheads gave him the phone. If you can believe it they had some type of business plan set up for all—"

Reel cut in. "Did you and Luke text about meeting tonight?"

"Well, yeah. Why?"

"How did they know you were meeting with Luke at the B and B?" said Robie. "They had to know because they came roaring into town and went right there a few minutes after he got there."

"I...are you saying—?"

"They give out the phones with malware on them," said Robie.

"So they can listen in or read every communication," added Reel. Her hand slipped down to her rifle even as they heard a car approaching. Two dabs of light could be seen coming along the road toward them.

"What kind of car will Luke be driving?" asked Robie.

"He didn't tell me."

Robie glanced at Reel, again silently communicating.

She slipped on a headset, powered up the comm pack clipped to her belt, slid out of the car with her rifle, and flitted away into the darkness.

"Where's she going?" asked Holly.

"I'm going to hit the button for the rear cargo door, Holly. I want you to climb over the seats and exit the vehicle that way. Then, keeping the truck between you and the road, I want you to keep moving away from here. That direction will take you back to town."

"Mr. Robie, what's hap—"

"Just do it, Holly," he said firmly. "We'll find you later."

"But Luke."

"Go, now, before it's too late," he barked.

A shaky Holly climbed over the backseat as the cargo door lifted.

She got out and, keeping behind the truck and carrying her suitcase, Holly moved away into the darkness.

The Yukon was on a slight incline. Without turning the truck on, Robie shifted into neutral, and the GMC rolled backward. Even with the engine off Robie managed to maneuver the steering wheel just enough to turn the truck to the left.

Like Holly, he climbed out the back, keeping the truck between him and the approaching car. He put on a headset and turned on his comm pack.

Into the headset he said, "Talk to me."

"Bogie's a half mile away, coming at a slow speed. I can't see how many are in it. It might be Luke and it might not."

"Anything else?"

"Hold on a sec."

A few moments went by and Reel said, "I've got movement at three and nine o'clock, directly in front of me." She paused another moment. "They're ATVs, Robie. You should be able to hear them by now."

"I do," he affirmed. "How many?"

"I count…eight altogether."

"And the car, evasive maneuvers?"

"No, coming on straight and true."

"So it's not Luke driving."

"No, it's not. I guess they weren't smart enough to think of that."

"You got high ground?"

"High enough. Where's Holly?"

"On the retreat behind us. Let me know when you can confirm who's on the ATVs."

"They're coming fast. But they're blowing up a shitload of dirt. It's going to make it hard to get a sight line."

"Roger that. Let me give you an assist."

He hustled to the back of the Yukon and unlocked the hard-sided case. He gripped the launcher and hefted two RPGs. He slung the launcher over his shoulder after loading the grenades into a belt carrier attached to the launcher's frame.

He ran to a spot behind a thick tree, knelt down, took out a pair of night optics, and peered through them. He could clearly see the car on the road and the ATVs on the dirt. Reel was right, they were creating quite a dust storm out there. They were now only about three hundred yards away. He would wait until they cut that distance down by half.

He knew it wasn't the cops or the state police. They didn't have enough bodies to fill all those vehicles. He was certain it was the skinheads.

He loaded in an RPG and said into his headset, "Fireworks are coming in ten. I'm aiming to make them stop to let the air clear so you can get a lock."

"Roger that."

Robie aimed the launcher at a spot in front of the wave of ATVs.

Four-three-two-one.

He hit the trigger and the RPG left the launcher, arced upward, and then came down within a foot of where Robie had been aiming.

The explosion rocked the still air, sounding like thunder from the storm bearing down on them.

The car and the ATVs did what Robie had expected. They stopped and through his optics he saw figures jumping out of the vehicles and taking cover.

Reel spoke into his ear. "Nice touch."

"See if you can get a look in the car now."

He could hear Reel's steady breaths in his ear until she said, "The driver has exited. He and another man have taken up cover behind the vehicle."

"Anyone else in the car now?"

A few seconds went by. "There's something in the backseat, Robie. It could be a person. It could be Luke Miller."

"That's what I'm figuring. They brought him along alive to witness the fun before they put a bullet in his head. I need the guys outside the car to leave that immediate area but leave the car operable."

"On it in five."

Robie loaded his last round into the launcher and moved forward, keeping low, but also keeping his night optics on the car that was less than half a football field from his position.

He counted off the five seconds and on the fifth beat Reel's sniper rifle thundered. Two rounds hit right next to the car. The third passed right over the trunk. The fourth kicked up dirt a foot to the left.

The two men hiding there did the only sane thing. They ran for it.

Robie was now in a full sprint.

"Robie, they're on the move."

"Burn 'em right after I fire. Move them all away from the vicinity of the car." Robie stopped, knelt down, hefted the launcher to his shoulder, took aim, and fired.

The RPG flew a short distance and then hit the dirt about sixty yards to his right.

An instant later Reel's rifle opened up and she rained bullets down on the men from right to left and left to right. Dirt, grass, and rocks flew up in the air near the men. Reel was not aiming to kill them, just to get them to move. Her rifle was her cattle prod.

Robie was sprinting once more and reached the car five seconds later.

He ripped open the door and checked the backseat.

Luke was back there, trussed up, gagged and unconscious, but Robie could find no visible wounds.

Robie checked the man's pulse, found it, slid into the driver's seat, turned the key, and the engine came to life.

He said into his headset, "I'm taking him to the Yukon. Disable the ATVs. Then meet me there."

He hit the gas and the car jumped forward. Immediately, shots rang out and several pinged off the skin of the car. Robie ducked as one blew out the rear glass, with a shard of it slicing across the back of his neck. The blood dripped onto the seat.

Then Reel opened fire, and this time her rounds connected with rubber.

Eight shots later every one of the ATVs was rendered inoperable with an incendiary round smack in its gut that had ignited the fuel tanks. Explosions rang out over the darkness even as the rain started

to pour. And then came the lightning, which lit the sky like detona-
tions in the clouds, and the following booms of thunder were very
nearly deafening.

And then came the hail, and the burning ATVs were quickly
doused, but still unable to move.

Robie reached the Yukon at the same time Reel raced into view.
Together they lifted the still-unconscious Miller into the back of the
Yukon. They jumped into the front seat and Robie took the wheel.

Reel eyed up ahead. "You going to run the gauntlet?"

Robie shook his head and looked behind him. "I'm going to make
a new road. We'll pick up Holly on the way."

He slammed the Yukon into reverse and the four-wheel-drive vehicle hurtled backward until Robie spun it into a J-turn, and with
the truck pointed the other way, he hit the gas and the Yukon leapt
forward.

They had gone a quarter of a mile when Reel said, "There she is."

Sure enough, Holly was struggling along in the darkness over the
uneven ground. She was now drenched with rain. She heard them
coming but apparently couldn't see it was them, because she started
to run away.

Robie sped up, and once they were beside her Reel rolled down
the window and called out to her. Holly immediately stopped running.

"Get in!" called out Reel.

Holly grabbed the door handle, threw her suitcase in, and followed right behind it.

She slammed the door behind her and Robie accelerated.

"Luke, oh my God! Luke!"

She put her arms around him and started sobbing. "Oh, please tell
me he's not dead. Please."

"Probably drugged." said Robie. "Nearest bus station?"

"But what about Luke's car?"

"Not happening. The bus station?"

"There's a Greyhound station sixty miles to the west on the main
road."

They raced on with the storm chasing them the whole way. Ten minutes later Robie worked his way over to an asphalt road, while Reel checked the GPS.

She directed him to the town with the bus station, and they arrived there over an hour later.

By this time Miller had woken up, and he and Holly were hugging in the backseat.

As they slowed to a stop at the bus station, Reel checked her phone.

She said, "A bus is leaving for Denver in thirty minutes. You can get there and then make plans to get to LA. Bus, car, train, or plane. Do you have money?"

Miller nodded. "I got credit cards. Luckily, those dumb shits didn't think to take my wallet."

"They were tapping your phone," said Robie. "That's how they knew where you were meeting both times. And if they're tapping your phone they may be able to trace your credit cards. Do you have cash?"

"Probably not enough," conceded Luke.

Robie and Reel took out their wallets and gave them what they had.

"This should be enough to get you out of the state," said Robie.

"Thank you so much," said Holly. "And we will repay you. I swear."

Luke put out his hand for Robie and Reel to shake, "I want to thank you both. You saved my ass and Holly's."

After they shook hands, Robie said, "You can clean up in the restroom. How did they get a hold of you? An ambush somewhere?"

"Exactly. Then they shot me up with some drug."

As they climbed out of the truck Reel asked Miller, "Were you really that bored that you had to join those guys?"

"It was beyond stupid," said Miller sheepishly. "But they talked a good game, at least initially. I pretty quickly figured it out and just wanted to escape."

"Remember to take the swastika off," said Reel. "Hard to make the right kind of new friends with that on your head."

"Right," said Miller.

"And get rid of your phone," added Robie. "They can track it even when you're not using it."

Miller reached into his pocket, pulled it out, and chucked it into a nearby trash can.

Holly hugged both Robie and Reel and said, "Thank you so much."

"Call your sister," said Robie.

"I will. Look, I know all that stuff I said about my family and all. The truth is, I was jealous of Valerie. You're right, she wears the uniform. She was out there fighting the good fight. Risking her life. I thought no matter what I did that I could never measure up to that. So that was my problem, not hers. She's been nothing but supportive of me, no matter how many mistakes I made. I know she loves me and I love her."

"Sounds like something you should tell her yourself, at your first opportunity. You don't want to squander chances with your family," added Robie, drawing a quick glance from Reel. "You never know if you'll get a second shot to make it right."

Holly smiled. "Good advice. I'll take it. And I hope you find Mr. Walton."

"We will," said Reel. "Guaranteed."

As they drove back to Grand, Robie said, "Think they'll be okay?"

"I think they have a far better shot of surviving than we do. They're getting out of the storm. We're heading right back in."

27

"I CAN'T GUARANTEE your protection," said Valerie Malloy. "I don't have enough resources, and the state police aren't going to come up with any."

Robie and Reel were sitting opposite Malloy in her office. Deputy Bender was standing next to her.

"We can look after ourselves," said Reel curtly.

"Did my sister tell you anything else about this Clément Lamarre?"

"No, just what we told you," said Robie. "Do you know him?'

She shook her head. "Missing people. Hoods. Armed guards. I don't know what that's supposed to mean."

"It means people are being held against their will," interjected Reel.

"That I get. But is it the skinheads?"

Bender said, "What about Doctor King and his group?"

"That's a possibility," said Malloy. "Although they were helping Holly." She turned to Robie. "She really was okay?"

"She was fine when she left us. We dropped her and Luke at the bus station. It was leaving shortly after we left."

"And you really think he's a good guy?"

"I do, for what it's worth. It was a plus in my book that the skinheads were trying to kill him."

"Maybe they discovered what Clément told her somehow. Maybe through JC Parry. Maybe they're the ones involved in that."

"And you say JC Parry has also vanished?" said Bender.

"As far as we could tell. We saw no sign of him and he left his dog behind, as you know."

"I found a temporary home for it," said Malloy. "I hope JC gets back to reclaim it."

Robie said, "And it's clear now that he was the go-between with Walton and Holly. He wasn't acting as Walton's guide. He didn't need one."

"That was a good catch on your part," conceded Malloy. "I should have seen that one."

"If the skinheads are the ones with prisoners, where would they be holding them?" asked Robie.

"They have a compound about twenty miles east of here," said Bender. "It's a fortified camp. Nobody goes near there unless they have business with them."

"Sort of like the King's Apostles folks?" said Reel.

"I've been out to Doctor King's," said Bender.

"So have I," added Malloy. "The skins are a whole other story. And you've shot up a bunch of them and now you've wrecked their ATVs. They're going to want blood."

"Well, they kidnapped Luke and were trying to kill him and Holly. Would you rather we just left them to fend for themselves?" snapped Reel.

"I didn't mean it that way. I'm incredibly grateful that you helped Holly. I'll never be able to repay you for that. I wish she had told me what she was planning to do. I could have helped her."

"You ever been there?" asked Reel. "To the skinheads' compound?"

"Once. To serve a warrant to appear."

"What happened?"

"I served the warrant and they never appeared."

"And you let that slide?"

"I had no choice. The witness against them disappeared, and the case fell apart and was dismissed."

"Tell us about the compound."

"There's nothing for miles around it, which means they can see anyone coming from a long way away."

Bender added, "It's got a perimeter wall, with concertina wire on top of it. There's only one road in and out. There are guard towers all along the perimeter. They have their own water source and a generator for electricity."

"How many people are there?" asked Robie.

"About a hundred or more," replied Malloy. "At least there were when I went out there. There're probably even more now. They've got lots of firepower."

"Any idea how they generate the cash to pay for all that? When I asked the bartender how the Apostles make a living he suggested drugs or guns or human trafficking. But he said he really didn't know."

"I don't believe that Doctor King and the Apostles are involved in any of that," said Bender. "But the skinheads sure could be. They definitely got money. They come to town every so often and buy whatever they need and pay in cash. So they're getting it from somewhere."

"They're like a cancer," added Malloy. "I'd love to cut it out but I've got nothing on them, so my hands are tied. Any time they do something wrong, people vanish or clam up or get paid off. You saw what happened after they shot up the town. The state police dropped their investigation. I argued with them until I was blue in the face, but they're not following up. I think palms are getting greased high up. Or maybe people are just afraid."

"Who's the leader over there?" asked Reel. "The equivalent of Doctor King?"

"You're going to think this is funny, but it's not," said Malloy. "He calls himself Dolph."

"As in Adolph?" commented Reel. "Wow, how creative."

"Yeah. I guess he doesn't feel he even needs a last name. He sometimes wears an old Nazi uniform with medals and everything."

"Have you had interactions with him?" asked Robie.

"A few times. He's an older guy and slick. Comes off as more of a college professor than a hatemonger. But he runs that group with an iron hand."

Reel glanced at Robie.

Malloy noted this and said, "What?"

Robie replied, "We know a little bit about the neo-Nazi movement. We spent some quality time with them a while back. And it didn't end well for them. But we had firepower on our side that we're apparently going to lack here."

"How do the Apostles and the neos get along?" asked Reel.

Bender said, "They don't. Simple answer is they hate each other."

Malloy nodded in agreement.

Reel said, "Well, that might be useful down the road."

"Could be," said Malloy.

"We need to find out about this Clément Lamarre person," said Reel. "He's got to be the key to this."

"How so?" asked Malloy.

Robie answered, "He told Holly about the prisoners. She told Parry, who told Walton. Walton visited her at the rehab, and shortly thereafter he was taken. So was Parry. That's the connection. We thought maybe this might have something to do with his past, but Walton has been coming out here for years and nothing has ever happened to him. But then he finds out about these prisoners, starts poking around, and boom, he goes missing."

Reel added, "If Lamarre saw the prisoners, we need to figure out how. Maybe he worked near the place where they're being held, or was passing by where it was happening."

Malloy said, "I started digging into the scrapbook you left me. Ran down some leads. But I found nothing. Most of the people associated with Walton are either dead or they've moved from the area. Claire Bender is one of the few left."

"This is all about his present, not his past, I'm convinced of that," said Reel. "We need to find Lamarre."

"Which means we go back to the rehab facility," said Robie.

Malloy said, "The skinheads are going to know it was you two last night. And they're going to want revenge. I can have Bender ride along with you for protection."

"That won't be necessary," said Reel.

"There are a lot more of them than you," pointed out Malloy.

Reel shrugged. "Well, so far we've held our own. And their numbers keep dwindling, don't they?"

28

"CLÉMENT LAMARRE?"

"Yes. Holly said he was a patient here."

Robie and Reel were sitting across from Brenda Fishbaugh, the facility director.

Fishbaugh clicked on some computer keys. "This information is really confidential," she noted. "We're not supposed to reveal who is or was a patient here."

"And this is a federal investigation," replied Robie. "You spoke to us about Holly and now she's on her way to a new life with Luke Miller. All good. That wouldn't be happening without us."

Fishbaugh nodded slowly. "All right. So long as it goes no further." She pulled up the screen she was looking for and swung the computer monitor around so they could see.

"I remember Clément. He was here for an addiction to methadone. Very common in this area. He's thirty-six."

"He looks a lot older," noted Reel.

"Methadone will do that to you," replied Fishbaugh. "He was a very quiet type. He and Holly were buddies here—that's the term we use."

"She told us about that."

"Why are you interested in Clément?"

"He told Holly something that we need to follow up on."

"Can you tell me?"

"I'm afraid not," answered Reel. "What's his background? Where did he come from?"

Fishbaugh swung the monitor back around and scrolled through more screens. "FYI, he was a voluntary admission here, meaning he checked himself in. It wasn't because of any court-imposed order. He was born in Quebec and emigrated to America and became a citizen. He came to Colorado five years ago. He had family here."

"Where did he work?"

Fishbaugh hit another key. "He worked on an oil rig for two years. And then when the bottom dropped out of the industry, he became an assistant manager at a convenience store about forty miles from here. That's where he was working when he got hooked on meth and came here."

"What's the name of the store?" asked Reel.

Fishbaugh told her and Reel made a note of it on her phone.

"Where did he live?" asked Reel.

"When he came to us he gave no address. I believed that he was homeless."

Robie said, "But you mentioned that he had family in the area?"

Fishbaugh nodded. "His sister and her family live in Boulder."

"Did she ever visit him here?" asked Robie.

"Yes, twice. I think after he left here she thought he was going to move in with her until he got back on his feet."

"Do you have her contact info?" asked Reel.

Fishbaugh provided this. "What will you do now?" she asked.

Robie and Reel stood. "Keep digging," he said.

Outside Robie's phone buzzed. The woman on the other end told him to access his laptop in two minutes.

Robie and Reel climbed into their truck and Robie popped open his computer, placing it on the dashboard so they both could see.

A few moments later the screen came to life, and DCI Rachel Cassidy appeared there.

"Report," she tersely instructed them.

Robie and Reel took turns filling her in on what had happened. Cassidy did not look pleased.

"Your job is not to screw around with local issues and start a war with a bunch of psychopaths," she admonished them. "You're no closer to finding Blue Man than when you got there."

"We haven't been here all that long," Robie reminded her.

She did not take this comment well, either. "You both know how much is riding on this. Blue Man is indispensable to the operation of this Agency. The world is more full of threats right now than I've ever seen it. And every day we get new threats coming in. There is something building that I don't like. And if enemies of this country have him and are trying to extract information from him, well, I don't have to tell you how catastrophic that could be."

Robie said, "We think his disappearance is tied to something local, not some grand plan by the Russians or Iranians to kidnap him. So I'm not sure we have to worry about someone interrogating him for secrets."

"I don't have the luxury of assuming that, and neither do you," the DCI snapped back.

"We're trying to approach this logically," pointed out Reel. "And if it walks like a duck and quacks like a duck, it must be a duck. So what we have is Blue Man found out about some prisoners, started asking questions, and then he disappeared. I'm not an experienced investigator, but it doesn't take a Sherlock Holmes to see a possible connection there."

"Just find him," ordered Cassidy. The screen went dead.

Robie looked at Reel. "You're right."

"About what?"

"It's a lot easier just killing people." He put the truck in gear.

"Where to now?" asked Reel.

"Clément Lamarre's last place of employment."

"Do you think that's where he might have seen the things he described to Holly?"

"You have a better idea?"

"Not even close."

The drive took nearly an hour with nary a highway in sight. Their travel was over a two-lane road that oftentimes, when over-the-road semis were blowing past the other way, seemed more like the eye of a needle.

On the way, Reel called Lamarre's sister and explained who she was and what she was interested in. The woman quickly told Reel that her brother had never spoken to her about anything other than their family and his treatment at the rehab facility. She confirmed that Clément was supposed to come and live with her and her family in Boulder. She had volunteered to come and get him or send him bus fare, but he said he would get there on his own. At the last minute he had called and said his plans had changed.

"That really pissed me off. And I've got four kids under the age of ten so, frankly, brother or not, I didn't have the time or energy to follow up on him. I tried to help him, but Clément made his bed and he has to lie in it," she told Reel.

"So that leaves the convenience store as our last shot," said Reel, after putting her phone away.

"Well, let's hope they can tell us something. The DCI is not going to like it if we have nothing to report next time."

"What do you think happened to Blue Man, Robie, really?"

"I think he was being very typically Blue Man."

"Meaning?"

"Meaning he was trying to help people who needed it and that got him into danger."

"If he was taken, do you think they know who he is? I mean, *really* know who he is?"

"Doubtful, or they might not have kidnapped him. Now they're caught between a rock and a hard place, especially if they've since found out who he is."

"So we're sort of like Blue Man then."

"How do you mean?'

"Well, we played the good Samaritans, helped Holly and Luke, and look where it got us. A bunch of neo-Nazis gunning for us."

"I see your point."

"They're going to come at us, Robie."

"They absolutely are."

"There are a lot more of them than us."

"There clearly are."

"And yet I sort of feel sorry for them," she said sardonically.

"You'll get over it."

They drove on.

CHAPTER

29

"CLYDE'S STOP-IN," said Reel, reading the sign as they drove into the parking lot in front of the convenience store. It had gas pumps out front, a pay phone against one wall with the phone receiver missing, a freezer box with ice inside and a padlock on the door, and dirty windows, along with a general air of a place barely staying alive. There were no other cars in the parking lot, and the store was off a winding road with the nearest town ten miles away.

"I wonder how you wake up one day and decide to build a store in the middle of nowhere," said Reel.

"This whole place is the middle of nowhere," noted Robie. "I've seen more population density in an Iraqi desert."

They climbed out of the Yukon and pushed open the door, causing a bell to tinkle. The interior of the space was as dilapidated as the outside. The shelves were only half full, and what was on them looked like it had been there since the seventies. An ATM machine was set against one wall with an OUT OF ORDER sign taped across its front. A door marked RESTROOM was on the back wall next to a refrigerated unit full of beer. A rack of newspapers was against another wall; a modern-looking soda dispenser stood against the far wall, and a shelf with automotive products, condoms, and packaged foodstuffs was next to it. On the front counter was a warming machine containing rows of hot dogs and slices of pepperoni pizza; the commingled smells permeated the place. The cash register was fronted by bulletproof glass, and entry was gained via a thick door with a deadbolt lock on it. Like in a bank, one had to slip the cash or credit card into a slot under the glass.

With the tinkle of the bell a tall, lean older man in a stained cowboy hat emerged from a back room. He had long, scraggly gray hair and a bushy beard.

"Can I help you folks?" he said.

"Are you Clyde?" asked Robie.

The man shook his head. In addition to the hat, he was dressed in faded dungarees, worn leather boots with silver toe caps, a jean shirt, and a hand-tooled belt with an Anheuser-Busch buckle cinched tightly around his narrow waist.

"Clyde's been dead, oh, twenty years now. I'm his son."

"How long has this place been open?" asked Reel.

"Sixty years. Nearly as long as I've been alive. Name's Sonny Driscoll. Not too complicated the reason why. My old man didn't have the best imagination when it came to names."

He grinned and held out a big, weathered hand. They took turns shaking it.

"That's a long time to be in business," said Robie.

Sonny looked around his store. "I know it don't look like much, but we get by. Mostly truckers gassing up. We got truck diesel here. Or them needing to take a leak or wanting something to eat. People who are lost—there are a lot of those—and they usually buy something just so they don't feel bad asking me for directions for free. And some folks from Newton, the little town back down the road there. And on Fridays during high school football season folks come in here and clean the place out. Keeps me going through the winter. I don't need much to get by. Now, what do you folks need? Gas? I got the credit card reader on the pumps. Or you can just pay in here after you finish up."

"Ever have any trouble here?" asked Robie.

In answer Sonny pointed to the fortified counter. "What does that tell you? Get some strange dudes coming through here. Late at night, you can't be too careful. You got trouble and call 911, they'll get here in the morning to take your body away."

"We're actually here for some information on one of your former employees," said Reel. She took out her ID and so did Robie.

Sonny studied them with a frown. "Which employee?"

"Clément Lamarre."

"Shit, is he in trouble again?"

"Why would you think that?" asked Reel.

"Because Clément was always in trouble. Meth head. Stole from me. I didn't press charges 'cause he must've been out of his damn mind when he did it. He stole some beer, a can of motor oil, and a box of Ho Hos. And he knew how to open the damn cash register and didn't take a single cent from there. I mean how stupid is that?"

"Pretty stupid," agreed Robie.

"Serves me right for hiring somebody with a name like that. I think he was French or something. I'm not into foreigners, don't care who knows it."

Robie said, "He was from Canada. That's not really so much of a foreign country. Right on our border."

Sonny shrugged. "I guess Canadians are okay. Weird name, though."

Robie said, "When Lamarre was in rehab he told someone about something he'd seen, maybe while he worked here."

Sonny's tufts of eyebrows knitted together. "What'd he say he saw?"

Robie studied him for a moment. "People in distress."

"Hell, half the people who live round here could be said to be in distress," scoffed Sonny.

"I meant people being held against their will. Tied up and with hoods on."

"What?" snapped Sonny. "You mean like they were prisoners?"

Robie nodded. "That's what he said."

"And you believe a meth head?" Sonny's look turned suspicious. "Your IDs say you're Feds. Why are you interested in this?"

"If people are being held against their will, it's a crime," pointed out Reel.

"Well, yeah, I get that."

"Can you think of anything that Lamarre might have meant? Even if he was mistaken about it? The person he told said he had a great many details about it. And he wasn't on meth at the time. He was clean."

Sonny took this all in, leaned against the counter, and rubbed at his beard.

"Look, we got some seriously effed-up people hereabouts," he said slowly.

"Neo-Nazis, we know about them," said Reel.

"Not just them. You keep going along this road for another twenty miles you're going to see an encampment of white supremacists. They got the sheets and the hoods and a big-ass Confederate flag you can see from fifty miles away." He paused and stroked his beard. "About six years ago two black fellows were found hanging from trees about ten miles from here. They had the N-word carved on their foreheads. Everybody around here knew who'd done it, but the law couldn't prove nothing, so there you go. Them pricks are still around. And then you got assorted pockets of antigovernment types, vigilante groups, religious zealots, motorcycle gangs, and folks just generally pissed off that their lives suck or that in their minds the country's going to hell. And they all got guns, lots and lots of guns. And some of them traffic drugs, stolen guns, and other shit, anything that'll make 'em a buck. If you want to get out of the mainstream, this is a good place to come. We apparently welcome any and all nutcases equally."

"And what about you? You belong to any of these groups?" asked Reel.

Sonny cracked a grin. "Nah. I'm just a businessman. You see, if I hooked up with one of them groups, the other groups would come here and burn down my store and shoot my ass. I keep a shotgun under the counter and I got a Dirty Harry Smith and Wesson forty-five at the small of my back, but I couldn't fight those guys off night after night. So I call myself Switzerland, see, neutral. All them bad boys come here to get their gas, beer, hot dogs, and condoms. And because I don't swear allegiance to any of 'em, none of 'em touch the place. I mean where else they gonna get their fuel, alcohol, and rubbers? And it was pretty bad when my daddy was running this place, so he had the same philosophy and passed it along to me."

Reel said appreciatively, "So I guess that's the other reason you've stayed in business so long. Pretty smart."

Sonny grinned, swept off his hat, and gave a mock bow. "Thank you, ma'am."

"Back to Lamarre and what he saw," interjected Robie.

Sonny put his hat back on and moved some strands of hair out of his face. "Did he say he saw it at my store? Because if he did, I can tell you he's a lying sack of shit."

"No, he didn't say that. We know he was the assistant manager here. At least that's what he told the drug rehab people on the intake form."

"He *was* the assistant manager. But that was only because *I'm* the manager and he was my only employee. He worked when I didn't and vice versa. I can't afford two people here at the same time, except on Fridays during football. Then me and Clément would work together. Place is open till two in the mornings on the weekends. During the week we open at six, close at ten. We'd split the shifts. Sometimes I'd do the mornings and then nights. Same for him."

"How long was he here?"

"About two years, I guess. Then he just stopped coming in. I mean, I kept his sorry ass on even after he stole from me, and look what that got me. Nothing. So I had to hire somebody else. Still have his last paycheck. But I deducted the cost of the crap he stole, including the Ho Hos." He paused. "Wait a minute. Why don't you just ask Clément about what he saw?"

"We'd love to. But he left rehab and then disappeared."

"Huh. That's strange. I always figured he'd come back here at least for his paycheck."

"Where did he live?"

"Well, sometimes he lived in the back room here on a cot. Other times there was a place about five miles from here off the main road. A house."

"Was it his house?"

"Shit, Clément never owned no house. He owned a piece-of-crap Datsun pickup that was older than he was. It was held together with duct tape and a Lord's Prayer a day."

"So whose house?"

"Some chick, I think. Give me a sec." He scratched his chin

and said, "Beverly something. Clément held an attraction to certain ladies. Till they realized he was a no-good SOB looking to take what he wanted, and then they'd kick him out."

"Can you give us the address?" asked Robie.

Sonny did so, writing it down on a piece of paper after consulting a record book under the counter. "He had to give me the address for payroll purposes. Don't know if he was living there when he stopped coming to work, but it's the only address I got for him."

He pulled a slip of paper from a file behind the counter and held it out to Reel.

"This is his last paycheck. If you see him, give it to him. He earned it."

"I hope we can," said Reel, taking the check.

They left the store while Sonny watched them from the door. Then they climbed into the truck and Robie started it up.

"You think he's on the up-and-up?" Reel asked.

"I assume guilty until proven otherwise. It just seems smarter in our line of work." He glanced at the check. "How much is it for?"

She looked at the slip of paper. "Two hundred bucks and change."

"You think that's for a full week's work?"

Reel studied the pay stub attached to the check. "That's what it says. Why?"

"That's about ten grand a year."

"Yeah. Some American dream."

"Right. I'd be pissed off, too."

As they pulled down the road Robie said, "You know you said the skinheads would be coming for us?"

"Yeah?"

He pointed behind them. "Well, you were right." He punched the gas.

30

Reel turned to see three pickup trucks behind them. There were three men in the cabs of each along with four men in the cargo holds.

She closed her eyes, and something popped into her head.

When Reel reopened her eyes, she was back in Iraq.

Robie glanced over at her then took a look in the rearview. "They're gaining. You want to do something about that?"

When she didn't respond, Robie said, "Jess?"

She blinked rapidly and shivered, like someone had dropped a bucket of ice on her head.

"Jess? You okay?"

Reel turned and looked at the men and the trucks again. In her mind's eye the skinheads turned darker and beards appeared on the fronts of their faces. They wore robes and head coverings. And in the bed of each truck was a .50-cal machine gun that was pointed directly at them.

"No, I'm not."

Robie gave her a searching glance. "Okay, slide over and take the wheel."

"What?" she said, her features confused.

"Take the wheel and just keep us pointed straight. I got this."

She undid her seat harness, as did Robie.

He had put the truck on cruise control, so his foot wasn't even on the gas.

"You go over, I'll go under," said Robie.

She put her hands on the wheel just as he let go.

The first shots fired from their pursuers impacted the rear glass of the Yukon, shattering it.

Reel stopped moving and ducked down.

"Come on, Jess, move your ass. Things are getting tight."

She regrouped and kept sliding, arching her back and legs in a yoga-like move to allow Robie to pass by underneath her. He slid into the passenger seat just as her butt hit the driver's-side seat and she focused on the road up ahead.

Robie slid over the front seat into the back. Staying low, he took out Reel's rifle and loaded it blind, keeping his gaze on the truck coming for them.

"They're getting ready to fire again," he warned. He glanced nervously back at Reel, hoping that whatever had gripped her wouldn't prevent her from keeping the truck on the road when the incoming fire occurred. "You can do this, Jess. I know you can do it and so do you."

The men in the truck beds opened fire, and Robie kept flattened in the back of the Yukon until the stream of bullets had passed.

The truck was holding straight and true, so Robie set up the rifle, took his sighting through the scope, and did what the idiots behind them should have already done.

He took out the front tires of the lead truck with two quick trigger pulls.

A vehicle moving that fast over uneven roads and losing its two front tires was not something that was going to end well.

Robie watched as the truck swerved to the right. The driver committed the cardinal error that had doomed so many others in the age of automobiles.

He overcorrected.

This sent the truck veering off at a sharp angle to the left. The tires left the asphalt, and then the point of no return had been reached.

The tires hit a soft spot in the dirt, dug in, and held.

And the truck flipped bow to aft. The men in the back were hurled out of the space, screaming and their limbs flailing, their guns falling from their grips, because they wouldn't be needing them anymore. They wouldn't be needing anything anymore.

They hit the dirt, rolled, and hit again.

The engine caught fire simultaneously with the cracked gas tank's vapor being released.

"It's going to blow," called out Robie to Reel.

And a second later the truck became a blast furnace, cremating the men still inside.

An errant shot popped out of the cab as superheated ammo went off without the aid of a finger pulling a trigger.

"Keep it steady, Jess."

There were two more trucks back there.

As Robie lined up his sights on the next truck, the skinheads finally wised up.

First the left rear tire was hit and then the right. The Yukon started to shake violently.

"Hold it steady, Jess," called out Robie.

Another bullet whizzed through the blown-out back glass, passed through the length of the truck, careened off a doorjamb, shot sideways, and took off a chunk of the steering wheel. The chunk flew back and hit Reel in the forehead, snapping her head backward against the seat, and then she was propelled forward, only coming to a halt when her harness engaged.

As she slipped into unconsciousness, she looked up ahead and saw the straight road. She also knew they had lost two tires.

Somewhere in the depths of her muscle memory a survival spark engaged.

She clamped her knees around the wheel and wedged her ankles against the console and the door.

Then, blood dripping down her face from where the chunk of hard rubber had collided with her head, Reel passed out.

"Jess? Jess, you okay?"

When Robie looked to the front of the Yukon he saw Reel slumped over. "Jess!"

The cruise control was still engaged.

They were still going at a high rate of speed.

But they had two blown-out rear tires.

And nobody was driving.

Robie had no choice. He abandoned his rifle and threw himself over the seat, even as the Yukon started to slide off the road as Reel's legs lost their rigidity.

Robie grabbed the wheel with one hand and fought to keep the Yukon steady and on the road. But they were vibrating so badly now that he knew that couldn't last.

A few seconds later a tire came off the rear rim, which made the truck lopsided. It pitched to the left like a boat in heavy seas.

Robie couldn't keep it on the road at this point.

He used a finger to punch off the cruise control.

This made the control situation better as their speed dropped.

He hit the gas with his foot to keep them moving forward.

He used his free hand to check Reel's pulse. It pumped strongly in her veins. He glanced down at the wound on her forehead. It was bloody but not deep. Her breathing was steady. He eyed where the missing chunk of steering wheel had been, and what had happened to her came into clearer focus.

He looked back and his features grew grim.

The trucks were right behind them and a dozen guns were pointed their way.

Robie cut the wheel to the right and the Yukon cleared the road and bumped over the uneven ground.

Robie hit the gas and then cut the wheel to the left, aiming for a stand of trees.

He reached it, slammed the truck into park, leapt back over the seat, and took up his sniper rifle once again.

The trucks pulled to a stop twenty yards away.

Robie placed his crosshairs on the driver in one of the trucks.

He didn't have enough ammo to take them all out, but he would take as many as he could with him. One less hatemonger alive was always a good thing.

His finger slipped to the trigger guard. His plan was simple.

Go down fighting.

The men climbed out of the truck beds. They had an assortment of shotguns, rifles, MP5s, pistols, and UMPs.

With all Robie had done over the years, all the dangerous countries where he could have died so many times, he had never imagined taking his last breath in rural Colorado.

But so be it, he thought.

At least Reel wouldn't see it coming. She would die peacefully.

He expected them to simply start shooting, engulfing the Yukon in fields of fire until a round found its mark or the gas tank exploded.

Instead, two men climbed out of the second truck.

And they were pulling someone along with them.

Holly Malloy's face was bruised and bloody. Her clothes were torn. She looked half dead on her feet.

One of the skins put a muzzle against her temple. "You put your fucking gun down and come out here or the bitch gets it right now. You got two seconds. One…"

31

ROBIE WAS SHACKLED and sitting next to Reel, who still had not regained consciousness, but sat slumped to the side.

On the other side of her was Holly, similarly shackled and also gagged.

They hadn't been able to talk at all after Robie had put down his weapon and the skins had hustled him out of the Yukon and carried the unconscious Reel behind him. They were now in a panel van that had driven up a few minutes after the battle had ended.

They were seated on the floor in the back with three skins across from them, pointing weapons at their heads.

Reel's head lolled around and came to rest against Robie's.

One of the skins grinned at him. "We're gonna so mess you up, asshole."

"Not the first time I've heard that."

The man sneered. "You and the bitch got lucky before. Now your luck's run out."

"Not the first time I've heard that either. You know we're federal agents. You want to bring that kind of attention down on you?"

"I see it as a bonus. Government's the enemy. And you're the fucking government in spades."

It seemed that they had been driving a long time before the van slowed, then stopped and then started up again, but only for a short distance. Robie thought he could hear some sort of machinery running.

The back doors of the van opened and more men appeared there. They were all skinheads, tatted with swastikas and other symbols of hate. They looked more like rabid animals than human beings, what with their malevolent eyes and bared teeth.

Reel moaned, twitched, and then opened her eyes.

She looked around, and as her thoughts passed from fuzzy to firm, she snapped back to her old self and her expression grew grim but focused.

She looked at Robie and whispered, "Sorry."

"No need," he whispered back. "Look to your left."

Reel turned and saw the bound and gagged Holly. "Shit," she muttered under her breath.

They were pulled up and hauled outside, their shoes hitting dirt a moment later. They were prodded and pushed toward a plywood-and-shingle building that was set inside a tall wire fence. The machinery sound that Robie had heard was the motorized gate, which had opened to allow them entry to the compound of twenty-first-century Hitler lovers.

"Déjà vu all over again," Reel hissed behind him.

He simply nodded at this and kept walking. Gun muzzles periodically poked him in the back, just because the armed men could do so without fear of attack.

Robie looked right and left and took in the entire compound, which looked like an Army outpost. Men in mismatched uniforms jeered at them. They carried rifles over their shoulders, and some had World War II–era Nazi caps and tunics with German medals on them. Some wore the black uniforms of the Gestapo. There were also 1940s-era military jeeps, half-tracks, and what looked like a small tank. For a moment Robie thought he had stepped back in time. But then he decided they had probably just bought the shit from some military surplus goods store.

Or maybe they got it online. You could buy anything on the web if you knew where to look.

One line of men stood by silently. They were all on aluminum crutches with their lower legs bandaged and their feet booted. These were the men that Reel had shot in downtown Grand when they had attacked Luke at the B&B.

The one man who had promised to watch Robie die grinned maliciously as they passed by, and then he flipped them off.

They reached a solid wood door, which was opened by a guard standing at attention there.

Robie, Reel, and Holly were pushed through this opening, and the door was closed behind them. The interior was dark, but only for a moment. Then they were hit with streams of lights from all corners of the room. They all blinked and averted their gazes from the harsh illumination.

"Welcome," said the voice.

Robie and Reel glanced in the direction of the words. Appearing from out of the darkness was a tall, overweight man with black hair and an unlined face.

Robie gauged his age at midthirties.

He was dressed in a loose-fitting green tunic and black slacks. On his head was a German officer's cap. He had a holstered sidearm, what looked to be a vintage Walther-designed P38.

"Christ," muttered Reel as she took in this spectacle.

The man took off his cap and set it down on a table. "My name is Dolph. Now to business."

Dolph opened a small notebook and scanned some pages. "You have, as of today, encountered my men in two separate engagements. You have cost me multiple ATVs and trucks. Five hundred rounds of ammo, sixteen weapons. Six men injured. Eight men dead. That is unacceptable."

Robie noted that the men killed were listed after the lost trucks, guns, and ammo. That clearly showed their leader's priorities.

Dolph closed the book and looked at them. "You of course must be punished for this. But I am a fair man and you will be able to defend your actions in a due legal proceeding."

"Really?" said Robie skeptically. "Do we get lawyers?"

"Of course. We will fly in the very best legal representation from Washington, DC. Perhaps the Justice Department? Or did you have someone else in mind?"

Robie didn't answer because he was unsure if the man was joking or simply insane.

Dolph snapped his fingers and one of the guards grabbed a chair and slid it under him right as he sat down.

Dolph took out a flat silver case, removed a cigarette, tapped it against the case, and one of his men used an old-fashioned lighter to light it.

Dolph took a long inhale and then let the smoke out in twin streams from his nose.

"I was, of course, not serious about the legal representation," said Dolph. "Or the fairness of due process. We are at war. During wartime, those elements are of no significance."

"Actually, some would argue that's when they're most important," volunteered Reel.

Dolph looked at her curiously, as though he was puzzled that a woman had chosen to speak in his presence.

"Identification," he said.

A guard moved forward and handed him the cred packs that had been taken from Robie and Reel.

Dolph viewed the documents.

"Very impressive," he said, his cigarette held between his teeth at a jaunty angle. "These of course confirm your guilt. You are spies. You must be executed."

"We're agents of the United States government," pointed out Robie. "And we're all standing in the United States right now. So there is no possibility of us being spies."

Dolph closed each of the cred packs and threw them at Robie. Even shackled Robie managed to catch them and thrust them into his pocket.

Dolph rose.

"An interesting argument, but you neglected one important fact, which is that the ground on which you stand is sovereign. It is not part of the United States. Therefore, your position is fatally flawed. I do not expect you to understand this, since you are woefully ignorant of all necessary facts and truths."

"And where might one find these necessary facts and truths?" asked Reel.

Dolph came to stand in front of her. He smiled disarmingly, but that only put Reel on higher alert. Her muscles tensed and then relaxed. She was ready to strike, even shackled.

"I will tell you," he replied. "For instance."

He snapped his fingers again and another guard came forward with a leather briefcase. Dolph set it down on a campaign desk in the center of the room and opened it. He took out several photographs.

"This is the punishment for spies."

He walked back over to the prisoners and held the photos up, splayed out like he was about to perform a card trick.

Holly gasped, her eyes fluttered, and she fell to the floor, unconscious.

Reel made a move to help her, but the guards gripped her arms and held her where she was.

Robie continued to stare at the three pictures. One was of Luke Miller alive and intact.

The second was Luke minus his head.

The third was Luke's head.

"So you murdered him?" said Robie stonily.

"I murder no one. He was executed for treason. He signed a sworn oath of allegiance. I have it here, in my pocket, if you would care to see it. He disobeyed that oath. He turned against us. The penalty for that is death. Nothing could be clearer. Nothing could be fairer. Strong leaders must be both clear and fair. And they must act with a firm hand when it is required. And I am a strong leader."

He glanced down at Holly. "Lift her," he commanded.

She was swiftly brought to her feet, though she was not yet conscious.

"Stimulate her," ordered Dolph.

Three hard slaps to the face and Holly came back to consciousness. Her gaze settled once more on the pictures and she started to scream. "You bastard! You murderer! I'll kill—"

Before Robie or Reel could even react, Dolph took out his P38, aimed it at Holly's head, and fired. The bullet burned a hole into her forehead, broke through her skull, and from there blasted into the soft tissue of her brain and stayed there.

Holly fell backward to the floor.

Reel and Robie stood there, covered in the dead woman's brains and blood.

Dolph looked at his pistol as though it were an affectionate pet. To add to this image he even stroked the heated barrel.

"And I am a strong leader," he said again.

He flicked a finger at Robie and Reel as though he were disposing of an irksome bug. Guards came forward and hustled the pair out.

32

"WHY ARE WE still alive?" Reel asked.

She and Robie had been thrown into a small wooden shack and the door padlocked behind them. It was already growing very warm, and Robie could feel the sweat on his face and under his armpits. They could hear the rustle of booted feet just outside, so they were keeping their voices low.

"Maybe the little son of a bitch only murders one person a day," said Robie grimly. He used his shirt to rub off blood and other matter from his face.

Reel did the same. "God, I feel like shit about Holly. And Luke. They beheaded him. They're no better than ISIS."

"I'd like to know how they got to them," said Robie. "They were supposed to be on a commercial bus headed to Denver. I didn't hear of any bus hijackings, did you?"

She shook her head. "Maybe they got to them after that."

"How would these pricks even know they were heading to Denver?" asked Robie. "We were the only ones who knew about that."

"Obviously not."

"You think they're behind the prisoners in the van? If so, maybe they got to Blue Man, too?"

Reel said, "If that prick killed Blue Man I will personally slit his throat."

Robie looked around the tight parameters of their cell. "We could easily break through the wood, but that doesn't get us anywhere with guards right outside."

"It's daylight now. We'll have to wait until nightfall."

"If we're still alive," he pointed out.

At half past seven the door was unlocked and a face appeared.

"Let's go," the guard said.

"Where?" asked Robie.

"Dinner."

Reel and Robie exchanged glances.

"Move it!" snapped the man, who looked like he wanted to just start shooting.

They were taken to a small outbuilding by a half-dozen guards and their shackles removed.

The lead guard said, "There's a shower in there. And there are clean clothes hanging on pegs inside."

"I'm fine with what I have on," said Reel.

"Well, *he's* not. So shower and change. You both stink. And you're covered in shit. And I've been ordered to shoot you right here if you don't comply."

Inside was a facility like a gym locker room. There was only one large communal shower with multiple shower heads.

"You can go first," Robie said. "I'll wait around the corner."

She rolled her eyes. "Robie, you've seen all of me there is to see."

They showered with Reel on one side of the shower and Robie on the other. He kept his gaze averted from her and thus didn't see Reel steal a glance at him. However, she was only checking out one part of his body.

"How's the arm, honestly?" she said, while soaping up.

Robie said, "Good as new. Your oblique?"

"You can see for yourself."

He flinched and then glanced quickly at her, to find Reel staring back at him. She pointed to the injured side. "All healed up. Even had plastic surgery to take care of the scarring."

His gaze dipped to the oblique and then slightly above and below before snapping back to her face.

"You look better than ever, Robie. Like you've been carved out of granite." She paused. "You seem uncomfortable."

"Mixed signals tend to do that to me."

She turned her back on him and continued cleaning up.

This time Robie let his gaze wander from the small, hard muscles in her back to the longer, ropier muscles in her delts and triceps. Then his gaze wandered lower, stopping at her feet before moving back up again.

"You look in great fighting shape, too, Jess."

"What every girl wants to hear."

"Is this change in attitude because you know we're going to die here?" he asked.

"Maybe a little. But only a little."

Robie was about to say something else, but finally just shook his head and rinsed off.

They dressed and were led to another building fronted by a pair of intricately carved double wooden doors. Inside was an elegant dining room.

The table looked antique. A square of Oriental rug was underneath. Cloth napkins were laid next to silverware and porcelain plates.

A chandelier with what looked to be real crystal pieces hung above the table.

A pair of sconces on one wall flickered with propane gas flames.

Reel touched the scratchy tunic she had been given to wear. It came down to the tops of her knees. Sandals were on her feet.

Robie was in medical scrubs a dull plum color. They had given him nothing for his feet. From the shadows of the room they could sense people watching.

Robie had given Reel her cred pack after getting it back from Dolph earlier. He'd slipped his inside the pocket of the scrub pants.

Another door inside the space opened, and a man wearing a white shirt and pants with black-and-white checks hurried in carrying two covered dishes. He set one down in front of one chair at the table, and the other in front of another chair. Then he disappeared back through the doorway.

Robie looked at Reel and shrugged. "Maybe we're eating alone," he said.

"No, you're not."

They turned to look in the direction from where the voice had come.

A high-backed leather chair swiveled around and there sat Dolph at a desk reading over some papers. He folded them over and placed them in a desk drawer. Then he stood, leaned behind a small book- case, and retrieved a rifle that had been set there against the wall. He held it up as he walked over to them.

"Yours, I believe," he said, indicating Reel.

Reel eyed the sniper rifle. "Yes. Can I have it back? Loaded?"

"Please, sit down and eat before it gets cold," said Dolph.

They sat and uncovered their dishes to see baked chicken, rice, and vegetables together with a small salad and bread.

Dolph took the seat at the head of the table.

As Robie took up his fork he said to Dolph, "You're not eating?"

Dolph waved this comment off as he continued to examine the ri- fle. He finally placed the weapon on the table. "My men tell me that you're both excellent shots."

Reel took a bite of salad and chewed it methodically, making him wait for her answer. "We're the best you'll ever see."

Dolph made no reaction to this bit of bravado.

"What's your real name?" Robie asked him.

"I already told you that," he said impatiently. He looked at them curiously. "How old do you think I am?"

Robie said, "Midthirties."

"I'm fifty-six."

Reel's eyes widened a bit. "So you've discovered the fountain of youth in eastern Colorado?"

"No, I discovered something far better. I discovered absolute power. It's wonderful for the complexion."

He sat forward and assumed a thoughtful expression. "I have so few people to share my philosophies with. My men, they're good and they work hard and they obey me. That last part is critical. But they don't think at the same level that I do. Now, you two are from Washington, DC. As barren as that place is, people do talk politics, competing philosophies."

"Your philosophies seem pretty clear," said Reel. "You're wearing them."

"No, no, disabuse yourself of that notion. I chose Nazi, but I could have chosen something else."

"I'm not following," said Reel.

"Hitler was only one of many. And, indeed, in terms of longevity, while he had perhaps the greatest impact on the world, he was not successful in maintaining what he had created. In fact, he was one of the worst."

"The Thousand Year Reich lasted, what, a couple decades?" said Robie.

"Precisely. I could name twenty others who did it longer and better than he did. But give the man credit. It took an entire world to bring him down."

"Well, the world was fighting Italy and Japan, too."

"Please, the Italians don't count. To a man they preferred wine and meatballs to fighting. The Japanese fought hard, I'll give you that. But they had a warrior tradition. The emperors of the Rising Sun ruled for centuries. The Chinese the same. The monarchies as well. And it all comes down to one thing."

Robie took a bite of chicken. "And what is that?"

"Democracies are clearly the weakest form of government there is."

"I don't think you'd find many free people to agree with that," said Reel.

Dolph looked disappointed by this comment. "I really had hoped for at least a bit of nuance." He sat back and puffed on his cigarette. "Yes, they're free. To live in chaos. Too many cooks in the kitchen. Too many people with a place at the table. Too many voices in the room. People are idiots. They don't know what they want other than to get as much as they can at the expense of their neighbor. You think that *Lord of the Flies* mentality happens only after a disaster? It happens every day, stopping just short of criminal action." Though his words seemed inspired by anger, Dolph suddenly laughed. "I'm sure you like facts. I will give some to you. America has the longest-running democracy in history. And what is it? About two and a half centuries old? In the timeline of history that's a rounding error. The most efficient, the longest-lasting form of government is, without debate, autocratic. One commands and others obey. People deride that as evil. I would say then the world dearly needs more evil."

"I think there's more than enough, actually," opined Reel.

Dolph did not seem to hear her. "You saw what happened when Saddam was toppled. Certainly he killed many of his own. Certainly he was cruel. But by taking him out of power, how many more have died? Ten times? A hundred times? I can give you example after example. People don't want freedom. People want to be safe. Democracies cannot provide that. But one person with the requisite power can. I am that person to my people. And I desperately want my *people* to greatly increase in number."

Reel had to use her hands to dig into the chicken since no knife had been provided, for obvious reasons. "So you're the leader who keeps your people safe?"

"I am not a joke, or a lunatic, since I know that is what you're thinking. I rule, but I do so benevolently."

"Like you did with Holly and Luke?" she said.

"Luke Miller broke his oath. This I have already explained to you. Holly was an example. This she brought upon herself when she formed her alliance with the traitor Luke. I must have rules. And those rules must be enforced. Otherwise, there is chaos. And chaos will bring down any regime. Even mine." He paused and stubbed out his cigarette on the tabletop. "Now, when you are trying to change things and your power is not yet at its height, you must use stealth. You work from the inside out. You turn people to your cause. Then before your opposition knows what is happening"— he stopped and, pulling a knife from a holder on his belt, drilled its point into the table—"*they* are the weaker ones and they can be vanquished."

"So that's your goal, overthrowing the United States."

Dolph pulled his knife free. "I don't have to overthrow the United States. I will never have the power to do that. But I just have to change the perspective of some in a few key places. That is all. People make it too complicated. I make it simple. And by making it simple my focus is complete and my odds of success are far greater. We are making terrific strides."

"'We'?"

"I'm affiliated with other organizations that share my core beliefs." He patted the stock of Reel's rifle. "We don't do it with this. We do it by raising dark money to fund policies and candidates that we like. We even help write legislation. We have infiltrated legitimate political organizations, or found those already inside those organizations who are sympathetic to our goals. It is a wonderful thing. To have friends in power."

He stopped and studied them. "You didn't expect some asshole simplistically labeled a neo-Nazi to talk about organizational infrastructure, policies, strategic legislative endeavors, and dark money funding, did you?"

"No, we didn't," admitted Robie.

"I don't go around screaming, 'Heil Hitler!' What would be the point? But by my playing dress-up and filling a cliché, as it were, people underestimate me. They put me in a little box and assume I will always be in that little box and not in the mainstream."

"And then before the mainstream figures it out, there you are with a lot more force behind you," said Robie.

Dolph nodded approvingly and pointed at Robie. "Now *there* is the nuance I was looking for. I take people underestimating me as a wonderful gift. Complacency by the masses is my greatest weapon. Did you know we have a very large social media platform? We have blogs and vlogs and online news organizations that communicate directly to our core population, which is growing exponentially every year. We get out the *facts* that need to be gotten out. Last week, our collective online clicks rivaled anything CNN or even Fox has been getting lately. It is tremendously exciting."

"I can see it probably gets you off," said Reel drily.

Before Dolph could respond, Robie said, "Global conquering aside, do you know Roger Walton?"

Dolph shook his head. "Who?"

"He disappeared from his cabin here about a week ago."

"And why is this of interest to me?"

"It's of interest to us."

"And why should you think that anything should be of interest to *you* now?"

Here we go, thought Robie.

"So when do we get a bullet in the head like Holly?" asked Reel.

"It is timely that you ask that," said Dolph. He hefted Reel's rifle. "You mentioned just now that you and your comrade are the best shots I will ever meet. I need good marksmen, excuse me, marks*people*."

"That's not going to happen," said Reel.

Dolph ignored her and said, "I'm going to give you a chance to prove yourself and perhaps save your life at the same time."

"How?" she asked.

In answer Dolph aimed the rifle at Robie. "A simple test. You shoot him, you live. You don't, you both die. And the test commences now."

He slammed his fist on the table.

The doors burst open and armed guards came in, seized Robie and Reel, and hauled them outside.

Dolph followed with the rifle.

33

THERE WAS NO blindfold.

There was no last cigarette.

There was no preacher with a Bible and a soothing scripture verse to give out to the condemned.

There *was* a concrete wall that Robie was hustled over to and made to stand in front of. He noted that it was splotched with blood and bullet pockmarks.

Every man in the place, including those on the watchtowers, was staring at the spectacle unfolding in front of them.

Fifty feet away Jessica Reel stood with Dolph next to her.

"I'm not going to shoot him," she said.

"I think you may come around to it."

"I won't. So you can just put a bullet in my head now."

He handed her the rifle and then placed the muzzle of his Walther against Reel's temple.

"Aim the weapon," he said.

Reel made no movement to do so.

Dolph pulled back the hammer on his pistol.

"Just pull it," said Reel. "And fuck you."

He called out to his men. "Shoot Mr. Robie first in the crotch. Then in the knee."

He looked at Reel. "We'll keep going, piece by piece, until he dies. Far better for you to just cleanly finish him off. And then you get to live."

Robie looked at Reel. "Just do it, Jess. Pull the trigger." He pointed to his heart. "Right here. No pain. Do it. Now. Better for me that way."

A tear trickled out from Reel's right eye. She lifted the rifle to her shoulder and sighted through the optics.

She placed her crosshairs on something she thought she never would.

Will Robie's chest.

Her finger wavered and did not venture to the trigger guard. The first stopping place for it before it descended to the trigger, and from there to the trigger pull.

"Do it, Jess," said Robie, as the moments trickled past.

"Two seconds," said Dolph.

Reel's finger touched the trigger guard and then dipped to the trigger.

"One second," said Dolph, as his finger went to the pistol's trigger.

The front gates of the compound exploded open.

And for a second time in recent memory, all hell broke loose in eastern Colorado.

The Hummer threw up dirt and gravel as it fishtailed into the interior court of the compound.

Two pickup trucks were right behind it. Bullets started flying from all three vehicles.

Reel had reacted the moment the doors had been knocked in.

She swung her rifle around and caught Dolph right in the gut. He dropped his weapon and bent over, gasping for air. She snapped the rifle straight up and the barrel caught him directly on the chin. This blow lifted him off his feet and he fell backward on his ass. A bare second passed before Reel had the weapon pointed right at his bleeding face. He looked up at her, his eyes pleading. She looked down at him, her gaze full of revulsion. Her finger swept to the trigger.

He shook his head. Tears filled his eyes.

He mouthed something that she couldn't hear clearly. It sort of sounded like *please.*

Yeah, right.

Her finger started to bear down on the trigger. Then she stopped, her finger barely a millimeter from the point of no return.

She took her foot and smashed it into his face, bouncing his head off the hard ground and knocking him out.

Meanwhile, Robie had rolled to the right and come up next to a guard who had ducked down when the Hummer had burst in.

It was the last thing the man would ever do.

Robie used the man's own knife to slit his throat. He seized the dead man's pistol and shot two men who were running toward him.

Reel dropped to one knee, aimed her rifle, and shot two guards off the watchtower.

Like a movie stunt scene they fell over the sides of the tower and plummeted thirty feet to the dirt. They felt no pain on impact, being already dead.

Robie raced toward the Hummer, which was spinning around while shooters inside were laying down fields of fire, keeping the skinheads running and ducking for cover. The pickup trucks were doing the same.

A door on the Hummer opened up and a man leaned out and beckoned to Robie.

"Get in!"

Robie didn't wait to be told a second time.

On the other side of the Hummer another man had opened his door and was calling out to Reel.

Keeping low, she sprinted hard toward the vehicle.

Rounds were flying through the air all around her.

One struck the butt of her rifle, shattering it. It knocked her off stride but she managed to hold on to it despite the shock wave of the impact.

She regained her balance and leapt toward the open door.

Strong hands snagged her and pulled her in. She sat up in the seat and slammed the door shut even as a bullet hit the window, shattering it.

They all ducked down.

A man yelled out, "Go, go!"

The driver put the Hummer in reverse, and the six-thousand-pound vehicle leapt backward, causing attacking skinheads to throw themselves out of the way.

The Hummer passed butt first through the gate, and then the driver put it into a one-eighty and pointed the nose toward open country.

Reel looked behind her and saw that the pickup trucks had done the same.

The three vehicles roared to safety as shots continued to chase them from the compound.

They reached the main road and headed west.

Reel and Robie looked around at the men in the Hummer.

Then the man in the passenger seat turned around to look at them.

It was Doctor King.

"What the hell?" began Robie.

"Hold that thought," said King.

He turned back around while Robie and Reel exchanged a confused glance.

Later, they pulled to a stop in the center of Grand.

King climbed out but the rest of his men stayed inside the vehicle.

Robie and Reel joined him. Reel still clutched her rifle.

King went to the back of the Hummer, opened the door, and said, "We got that from your truck."

It was the hard-sided case with their other weaponry.

He looked at Reel's damaged rifle. "Will it still shoot?" he asked.

She nodded. "So long as I have a target to aim at."

King pulled the case out and walked into their hotel. Robie and Reel, exchanging another glance, followed.

They went up to Robie's room, and when the door was closed King set the case down. "Your truck was pretty badly torn up. Don't think it's drivable. But we arranged for another truck for you to use. It's down on the street. Untraceable to us."

He tossed Robie a set of keys.

"Why are you doing this?" asked Reel.

"And how did you even know we'd been taken by the skinheads?" added Robie.

King sat down in a chair. He was dressed differently from before. Jeans, a dark shirt, a canvas vest, boots, and a ball cap.

He leaned forward. "To answer your second question first, I've got ears inside Dolph's place. That's how I knew. Glad we got there in time. The idiots on the watchtowers weren't even looking our way."

"They were watching us about to die," said Robie.

"And the answer to the first question?" said Reel.

King reached down to his boot, undid the heel, and pulled something out of the revealed compartment. When he held it up they could see it was a badge.

"FBI?" said Robie, looking stunned.

King nodded before putting the badge back in its hiding place. "Been out here for years. Undercover, of course."

"But why?"

"You just have to look around to answer that. There are more vigilante groups out here than you can imagine. There are pockets of them in lots of states, but they tend to gravitate to the great outdoors— translation being 'where law enforcement is spread very thin.'"

"But you started the King's Apostles?" said Reel.

"It was excellent cover. And a great source of information and interaction with some of the worst scum you've ever seen. I've been building cases against these assholes, like Dolph, all this time. I couldn't reveal myself to you initially, even though you were fellow Feds."

"No problem there," said Reel. "We don't reveal ourselves either if we can help it."

Robie said, "I had an encounter with one of your guys at the bar across the street. Bruce is his real name."

"No, his real name is Special Agent Todd Cummins. He told me about the encounter and that you helped him out big-time in front of the others. I appreciate that."

"So you got some backup here, that's good," said Robie.

"What's your actual name?" asked Reel.

"Special Agent Dwight Sanders."

"Well, you're doing a helluva job, Agent Sanders. And thanks for saving our butts."

Reel said, "So is that how your group is funded? With government dollars?"

"That's a big part of it. But you have to get in the dirt and muck around if you want to get to the really bad stuff. The Apostles are just young guys looking for direction. If I hadn't recruited them, Dolph or some others would have. We do a lot of good, but we do just enough bad for me to get what I need."

Robie nodded. "Sounds like a plan."

"So what were you doing at Dolph's compound?" Sanders asked.

"We didn't go voluntarily, they ambushed us," replied Reel.

Robie added, "Dolph had Luke Miller beheaded. And we saw him kill Holly Malloy right in front of us."

Sanders's jaw dropped. "Shit. You witnessed this?"

"We did Holly, and we saw pictures of Luke. So you can nail that prick for murder."

He gazed up at them. "I don't know much about you two. But I made some calls, and I know enough to understand that you didn't come here to be witnesses in a murder trial. You came here to find this Walton guy, who obviously is very important to this country."

"Correct," said Reel.

"Then I suggest you let me continue to build a case against Dolph and others. We'll nail the SOB. I go after just Dolph now, years of work goes down the drain. There're a lot more out there just like him. And I want them all."

Reel snapped, "No way! He killed Holly in cold blood. We can't just let this scum walk away. What if he's trying to get out of the country right now?"

"Like I said, I've got inside ears. I'd know."

"We should be calling the cops, the state police," persisted Reel.

"You do that, then a big part of my investigation goes to shit. And are you two willing to testify to what you saw? Because otherwise there is no case against Dolph."

Robie and Reel exchanged another glance.

Robie said, "That might be problematic for us."

"Yeah, I thought so. See, Dolph has lawyers. I know that for a fact. And they're good lawyers, so if we arrest him and try to bring a case, they're going to get their shot at you. And they may dig up stuff on you two that the government doesn't want dug up. And the reason why you're here in the first place to find Mr. Walton will also come out. They'll drag this thing out for a long, long time. I doubt your boss back in DC will be pleased by that."

"Shit," said Reel.

"We can't do that, Jess," said Robie.

"Let me handle this," said Sanders. "It's what I do for a living. When the time is right, the hammer will come down and he will stand trial for Holly's murder. I swear to you he will."

"But if we can't testify?"

"Were there other people in the room when he did it?"

"Yes, quite a few," said Robie.

"I'll have enough leverage over his stormtroopers by then that I'll get them to turn on him for a plea deal."

"Just keep eyes on him. He knows we're Feds. And he knows we saw what he did. He may make a run for it."

"If he does try to flee, we'll pick him up."

"But now that you rescued us, won't he be coming for the Apostles? He'll know it was you, right?"

"We've been at odds for a long time, and this was not our first skirmish. But you two being there complicates things for Dolph. He's not going to be worried about retaliating against me so much as he's going to be concerned with saving his own ass."

"What's the source of Dolph's funding?" asked Robie.

"Myriad. Gun running. Intimidation. Racketeering."

"Human trafficking?" asked Reel. "Drugs?"

"I've seen nothing linked to those." He stood. "I've got to get going. I'll try to have your backs when I can, but I can't promise I'll always be there." He passed Robie a slip of paper. "Here's a number where you can contact me if you need anything. If I'm still breathing, I'll get back to you."

Robie put out his hand. "Thanks, but you've done more than enough, Agent Sanders."

After shaking both their hands Sanders left. A minute later they heard vehicles driving away.

Robie put the slip of paper in his wallet and sat down on the bed.

"Well, that puts a whole new spin on things. So do we tell Sheriff Malloy that her sister is dead?"

Reel pondered this for a few moments. "I don't see how we can and not have her storm that place with her one deputy. With the result they both get killed."

"So we keep quiet?"

"Yeah."

"Okay, but I don't like it."

"I don't like anything about this damn place," replied Reel.

34

"I COULDN'T HAVE shot you."

Robie glanced over at her as the pair was driving toward La-marre's place. They had cleaned up and changed out of the clothes Dolph had made them wear. They were both gunned up and watch-ing their vehicle's mirrors carefully for any sign of pursuers.

It was now around nine at night and car lights could be easily seen. There were none back there.

"There was no reason for both of us to die," replied Robie.

She shook her head in disagreement. "You dead, me not, what would have been the point?"

"I don't get you sometimes. No, I don't get you *most* of the time."

She shrugged. "What can I say, Robie? It's a Mars-Venus thing."

"No, I don't think you're in the same *universe* as me, actually."

"On the other hand, I should have shot him."

"Who?"

"Dolph. I had him on the ground begging for his life. My muzzle was a foot from his chest. One pull, dead." She paused. "And I didn't do it."

"You couldn't kill the guy in cold blood, asshole or not."

"We kill in cold blood all the time, Robie."

"On orders. It's different when it's a personal thing."

"Doesn't matter. I still should have done it. I would have saved the world a ton of grief. I get a second chance, he's a dead man."

And Robie didn't argue the point.

The house where Lamarre had stayed, according to his boss, was a tumbledown bare-bones cottage, but despite its derelict appearance there was what looked to be a new car parked out front, and they could see lights on inside.

Robie stopped the truck about a hundred feet from the house and they got out, their hands on their backup guns, which had replaced the ones lost to Dolph's ambush.

"Think we're going to find a headless body inside?" Reel asked.

"I've found out here that anything is possible."

They approached the front of the house.

Robie touched the hood of the vehicle, a Toyota Land Cruiser.

"Cold," he said.

They stepped to the front porch. Reel stood to the right of the door, her gun ready, while Robie rapped on the wood and then stepped to the left.

They heard footsteps padding toward the door.

It opened and a young woman looked back at them.

She was about five four, in her thirties, with shoulder-length dirty blonde hair possessing dark roots. A nose ring hung from each nostril. She had on jeans with a tank top revealing a spread of tattoo that swept over her left shoulder and continued down to her wrist.

It looked to Robie like a woman being swept along by rough water.

"Can I help you?" she said, looking first at Robie and then Reel.

Robie said, "We're federal agents."

"Where are your badges?" she demanded.

They held out their creds.

"What do you want?"

"We're looking for Clément Lamarre. We understand he used to live here."

"'Used to' is right."

"What's your name?"

"Do I have to tell you?"

"You don't have to do anything. But we can take you in for questioning somewhere more formal. And I don't see how telling us your name is being too invasive."

"Beverly Drango."

"This your house?" asked Reel.

"It was my momma's, and she left it to me when she passed on."

"You know where Lamarre is?"

"No."

"When was he last here?" asked Robie.

"I can't remember."

"We have his last paycheck," Robie said. "Two hundred bucks."

Drango's eyes bulged. "In cash?"

"No, a check that he has to endorse on the back to cash."

Her eyes returned to normal. "Figures," she said disgustedly.

Robie said, "Sonny Driscoll said Lamarre never even showed up to get it."

"Sounds like Clém," said Drango bitterly. "He had no problem mooching off me, but God forbid he ever chipped in a dime. That money should be mine, plus a whole lot more."

"So if you help us, maybe we can work something out on that score," said Robie.

"Really?" she said eagerly.

"Can we come in?" asked Reel.

Drango looked nervous. "I don't usually have visitors. I mean, the place ain't too clean."

"I can guarantee you that I've seen worse," said Reel.

Drango held the door open and stepped back.

The room they walked into could accurately be described as a pigsty. Drango moved some junk off two chairs, and Robie and Reel sat down.

Robie pointed to her tat. "What does that mean? Someone being swept away?"

"Yeah, me. That's my life, out of control."

"Okay," said Robie.

"Why are Feds looking for Clém? Any illegal shit he does is definitely small potatoes."

"He ever talk to you about something he saw?" asked Robie.

"Saw? Like what?"

"Like people being held against their will?" said Reel.

"Against their will? Like prisoners?"

"In hoods and shackles," added Robie.

Drango didn't nod or shake her head. She just stood there looking down at them.

Reel looked over the woman's shoulder at the lighted backyard that held a rusted swing set and an assortment of faded toys. In a bookcase behind Drango were shelves of children's books.

"Where are your kids?"

"Don't have any."

"What are those for, then?" asked Reel, pointing out the window. "And those books?"

"I used to run a day care."

"Really?" said Reel, looking around at the trash pit that was the woman's home.

"When the kids were here this place was spic-and-span. Took good care of 'em. Fed 'em. Played with 'em." She plucked out a book from the shelf. "Read to 'em. Kids like books."

"What happened?"

"I . . . I made some bad decisions. I'm what you call a bum magnet. Moms didn't like their kids being around them."

"Okay, getting back to whether Lamarre talked to you about seeing these people?" prompted Robie.

Drango sighed, put the book back, and leaned against a bookcase. "You got to understand that probably half his life Clém was stoned, okay? He talked shit all the time. I never believed none of it."

"What kind of shit? Like seeing prisoners somewhere?"

"Are you telling me that he *did* see that?"

"We think he did. It might be the reason he's disappeared."

"Disappeared? Hell, he probably just run off. Boys like him do, you know. Going to get his honey from another hive, so to speak. I seen his kind all my damn life."

"Other people we think might have been involved in this *have* disappeared," said Reel. "Including one person we really need to find. So maybe 'Clém' didn't run off for fresh honey."

"But who would be keeping prisoners out here?" she asked.

"You know somebody named Dolph?"

Drango's top lip quivered just a bit. "No."

"You want to think about that and try again?" asked Robie.

Drango perched her butt on top of the bookcase. "Look, everybody around here knows *about* that psycho. But I don't *know* him."

"We've made his acquaintance," said Reel. "And I would affirm your description that he's a psycho. But are you saying he's not the sort to take prisoners?"

"I think he's the sort that would do whatever the hell he wanted."

Robie cocked his head and looked at her curiously. "You sound like you know more about him than you're letting on, Ms. Drango."

Drango fidgeted with one of her fingernails before saying, "I would not put it past those creeps to take prisoners. But I don't know if that's what Clém was talking about or not."

"The last time you saw him, was it before or after he left rehab?"

Drango hesitated.

"Just tell us the truth. You're not going to get in any trouble doing that," said Robie. "But if you lie to us, that's a whole other ballgame."

"After. He came back here one night. He looked clean. I mean really clean from drugs. I thought he'd just left me, and I was pissed. But then he told me he'd gone into rehab voluntarily. Gotten himself off the crap. He said he really wanted to get his act together." She stopped and rubbed at a sudden tear clinging to her right eye. "He said...he said maybe we should get married."

"So it sounds like he was planning on staying around," said Reel.

"Yeah, it *sounded* like it."

"When he came back from rehab did he have his belongings with him?" asked Robie.

"He had a suitcase with clothes and stuff. He had left a few things here before he went away."

"So did he take the suitcase with him when he left here?" he asked.

"Well, no, come to think. It's still in the closet in my bedroom."

"Can we see it?" asked Reel.

She led them back to a bedroom that, if anything, was more of a mess than the front room. She opened a closet door and pulled out a suitcase. "I haven't even opened the damn thing, I was so pissed."

"When exactly did he leave?" asked Robie.

"Let's see. I guess, yeah, it was over a week ago because I had just got home from a party I worked at over in Denver. I do private bartending and in-home casino work on the side. You know, pretend casino where you don't play with real money. Some rich asshole's birthday party. Paid me more to pour drinks and work a craps table in one night than I make waitressing in a week. Anyway, I'd called Clém and we were supposed to go out and get drinks and something to eat at this little place down the road called the Gold Coast. Don't know where they got that name. Sure as hell ain't no coast around here and no damn gold. He said that'd be cool. So when I got home I expected him to be here. Only he wasn't. I called and left voice mails. I texted and e-mailed and got zip. No Clém."

"We understand he had a vehicle?"

"A beat-to-shit Datsun pickup. That was gone too. I just figured he left his crap here because he didn't want to be bothered taking it with him. Then I quit caring. I just thought he got strung out again or something."

"But you said you talked to him that night, before you came home. Not enough time to get strung out, surely?" said Reel.

"With Clém and meth it only took one pop for him to be totally effed up."

"So one more time, Ms. Drango, did Lamarre tell you about seeing prisoners?"

She sighed and nodded. "Okay, look, it was before he went into rehab. He got home from work real late one night. I was just getting in bed after soaking my feet, which were swollen like watermelons from being on 'em all day. He walked into the bedroom looking like he'd seen a ghost."

"What did he say he'd seen?"

"A van pulled up to the store to get some gas. He said a dude got out but he had trouble with the pump. The reader thing wasn't recognizing the credit card or some such. Happens at the restaurant where I work, too. Anyway, there's a button you can press for assistance. So Clém came out of the cage behind the counter and went outside. He went armed, he said, because folks have tried to trick him before to get him out of the cage. But this guy was legit. The reader was screwed up."

"Okay," said Robie. "Then what?"

"So Clém is fiddling with the reader, trying to see what the problem was. While he was doing that the guy opens the driver's-side door to get something out. Clém said he saw a holstered weapon on the guy's belt when his jacket rode up. And the interior light comes on when the door opens. That's when Clém saw it."

"Saw what exactly?" asked Reel.

"In the rearview mirror. Clém said it was one of those panoramic ones. It showed into the back of the van. He said there were like six people back there shackled and hooded. They were alive, because he saw two of them move around a bit. A guy was guarding them."

"What did Clém do then?"

"Look, he's no hero, okay? Now, if somebody was coming after him or me, even Clém would fight you. But this wasn't his fight. He had no idea who those people were. When the guy got back out of the truck, Clém told him the reader wouldn't work but they could take cash. So the guy paid in cash, filled up his tank, and that was that. He drove off."

"And why didn't Lamarre call the cops?"

"Hell, I don't know. He said he'd half-convinced himself he'd imagined it all. Or that maybe the guys with guns were cops and the people in the back were prisoners. Maybe, you know terrorists. They use hoods on 'em. I seen pictures of them assholes at Gitmo."

"Gitmo is a long way from here," noted Robie.

"Hey, I don't know what to tell you. So he didn't call the cops. But I guess it kept bugging him. But why would he disappear? They didn't know he'd seen anything. If they did, wouldn't they've just shot him right there?"

"Maybe, maybe not," said Robie. "He didn't get a license plate number or anything?"

"If he did he didn't tell me. It was a white panel van. He did say it had Colorado plates."

"Well, that narrows it down to a few hundred thousand," said Reel sarcastically.

"I'm sorry, but that's all I know."

"We're going to take the suitcase," said Robie. "Anything else here of his?"

Drango looked around. "I don't think so."

"Did he have a phone or laptop?"

"He had a phone because I told you I called it. He didn't have no laptop."

"Okay, thanks. One last thing. Have you told anyone about what Lamarre told you?"

She hesitated. "No, not that I can remember. I mean, I thought it was horseshit, so why would I have?"

They left her standing by the front door looking as lost as the woman on the tattoo.

"Some life," said Robie.

"You think we have it any better?" replied Reel.

When they got back to the hotel in Grand, there was a package waiting for them.

"Bomb?" said Reel.

Robie opened the package. Inside were their pistols and phones.

"Where the hell did these come from?" asked Reel.

"There's a note."

Robie unfolded the slip of paper and read off it. "From a friend on the inside. Phones clean. Dolph laying low. DS."

"Dwight Sanders," said Reel. "He said he had someone on the inside with Dolph. They must have gotten our stuff back somehow."

"And Dolph is lying low. Well, that's something positive and might give us some breathing room," said Robie.

They finally hit the sack after what was, even for them, an eventful day.

CHAPTER

35

"THIS DOESN'T LOOK good," said Reel.

It was the next morning and they had just walked out of the hotel in Grand.

Valerie Malloy was climbing out of her Mustang. When the sheriff saw them she immediately rushed forward and confronted them.

"We found your truck shot to shit and you weren't inside it. Derrick happened on it a few hours ago and radioed it in. I've been calling your cells ever since."

"We had our phones turned off," said Robie.

Malloy got right in his face. "Cut the crap and tell me what's going on. This is my town and I'm responsible for what goes on."

"Okay, you want to discuss it here or back at the station?" said Robie.

In answer Malloy got in her cruiser and pulled out so fast Robie had to jump out of the way.

They followed on foot.

Inside the station they found Derrick Bender making some coffee.

"Glad to see you folks are okay," he said.

"Yeah, we are too," said Reel.

Malloy stepped out of her office. "In here. Let's have that pow-wow. You too, Derrick. And bring some coffee."

Reel and Robie followed Malloy back into her office. They stared at each other until Bender came in with four cups of coffee on a tray.

"Everybody okay with black?" he asked.

"Works for me," said Reel, and Robie nodded.

They all took sips and then Malloy pounced. "I thought we were going to be working this investigation together. But so far, you both have left us completely out of the loop."

"Not our intent, Sheriff," said Reel.

"It sure as hell is," countered Malloy. "Now, I need to know everything you've found out since we last spoke. And I mean everything. There's shit going on around here and I will not be left out of the loop."

Robie glanced at Reel and then looked back at Malloy. "Okay, we'll start from the beginning and go forward. How's that sound?"

"Don't leave anything out."

It took over thirty minutes, but between them Reel and Robie filled the pair in on what had happened. But they left out the part about Holly's and Luke's deaths and the FBI's being behind the King's Apostles.

"So they kidnapped you," said Malloy. "And tried to get Reel to murder you?"

"That's the gist of it," admitted Robie.

"Then we can nail those bastards," said Bender.

"With what?" asked Robie. "You and Bender and a few state cops who obviously want no part of those pricks? They've got over a hundred men there and they're loaded for bear. And they'll have gotten rid of any evidence, so it becomes our word against theirs."

"And nailing those bastards is not our job," added Reel. "Our job is to find Roger Walton. And our leads keep disappearing. Lamarre was our best shot and we have no idea where he is. So we're back at square one. We don't have time to be embroiled in a criminal trial."

"But it could be that Dolph and his skinheads took Walton," suggested Malloy.

"It could be, but we were there and saw no evidence of that. And like what happened with us, by now they would have covered any trace of that."

"If you broke out of his place, he's going to be coming for you."

"Maybe, maybe not," said Robie.

"And you can't guarantee our safety, we know," said Reel. "But we've got this."

"Look, you want to find Walton. I want to help you do that."

Reel said, "Okay, got any ideas on where we go from here?"

"Well, now that I have no idea where my sister is, I can focus my energies on coming up with some. I just hope to God she's safe."

At these words, Reel looked away.

Robie said, "A white panel van. It stopped at Clyde's for gas. Lamarre was working that night. He saw what he saw."

Bender said, "Well, if they stopped for gas, then I guess they were either starting out from here and going a long distance or else they were coming from somewhere and had to stop and fill up before they got there."

Reel looked impressed. "That's a good point."

He smiled shyly. "I have 'em on occasion."

Robie said, "So if the latter, where might that be?"

Malloy said, "I've never seen the skinheads in a white van. They favor pickup trucks. King's Apostles don't have any vans. They've got trucks and a Hummer."

"The white supremacists?" asked Reel.

Bender shook his head. "Harleys, Dodge Rams, Ford F150s. An old school bus and a couple of hearses."

"Hearses."

"They haul guns and ammo in them," said Bender.

"And where do they haul them?" asked Robie.

"Wherever they want to. No law against it."

"Sounds like your hands are tied," said Reel.

"I can get my sister Patti and her buddies to look for the van," said Bender. "They get around to places with their work that most around here don't get to."

"Okay," said Reel.

"There's something else," said Bender.

"What's that?" asked Reel.

"It has nothing to do with the investigation. But my mother has invited you two over for dinner tonight. Valerie's coming too. And Patti."

"I'm not sure we—" began Reel.

But Robie interrupted and said, "Sounds good. Thanks. Just tell us the time."

As they walked out of the sheriff's office a few minutes later Reel said, "What was that about? We have no leads on Blue Man. We've got some crazed Nazi gunning for us. The director is going to chew our asses out next time she talks to us, and we're going to dinner?"

"We have to eat. And maybe what we're missing on this case is some local color."

"What does that even mean?"

"It might mean finding Blue Man. And if it does, it's worth a dinner, Jess."

36

"You like Amarone, Will?"

Claire Bender was dressed in sandals, black slacks, and a white sleeveless blouse revealing long and wiry tanned arms. Her silvery blonde hair was pulled back in a bun and clipped in place. Her features were animated and a smile played over her lips.

He looked at the glass of red wine she was holding out. "I'm sure it'll be fine."

He took the wine from her and had a sip.

"It's better than fine," he commented.

Claire smiled. "I'm glad you like it. This is a beer-and-tequila sort of place. There aren't many people in Grand who would appreciate a good wine." She clinked her glass against his. "Roger loves Amarone." She stopped and looked down. "I'm sorry, I don't know where that came from. It was just automatic. We've shared many bottles of wine."

"I'm sure you did."

"Let me show you something."

She led him through to the rear of the house then out the back door. There was a detached six-car garage behind the main house.

She pulled a remote from her pocket and opened one of the doors. "What do you think?"

Revealed behind the door was a vintage burgundy Cadillac convertible with a pair of Texas longhorns mounted on the front.

"Impressive."

"I went to UT. Only time I really left Colorado. It just felt right at the time, but then I wanted to get back here. But I have a fondness in my heart for the Lone Star State. Go ahead and sit in it."

Robie opened the driver's door and slid into the front seat. The upholstery was white and in pristine shape.

Claire leaned against the front fender. "Took a year and more money than I want to think about to rehab this thing. It's a 1966 Cadillac DeVille convertible. It's got a 340-horsepower overhead cam V8. I think it actually gets minus miles to the gallon. It's eighteen and a half feet long, which makes it pretty much bigger than my first home here."

"They don't make them like this anymore."

"They don't make anything like they did anymore. Did you know Roger drove this car when he lived here?"

"No, I didn't."

"He earned the money for it working during the summers. When he left for college, he gave it to me. Lot of good memories in this pile of metal and vinyl."

Robie got out of the car and smiled. "I'm sure."

Her smile faded as she gripped his arm. "Find him, Will. Please."

"I'll do my best. That I promise."

Back inside Robie looked around and eyed Reel in conversation with Patti Bender. The woman had cleaned up from when they had seen her before. She wore a cream-colored skirt, an off-the-shoulder sweater, hoop earrings, and boots. Robie noted that she was not armed tonight. At least not visibly.

Her brother walked in a moment later with Malloy in tow. Derrick had changed into jeans, a white shirt worn untucked, his Stetson, and worn boots. His service piece rode in a holster on his hip.

Malloy had the most startling transformation. She was in a colorful sundress with strappy heels. Her hair was down around her shoulders and bounced a bit as she walked.

He felt a nudge on his arm. Claire said, "The sheriff looks mighty beautiful tonight, doesn't she?"

Robie nodded. "She cleans up well."

Claire smiled. "Yes, she does."

Then Claire turned serious. "So have you found out *anything* about Roger's disappearance?"

"I really can't discuss that with you."

"Oh come on. Do you think I'm going to go around telling everybody and maybe messing up your investigation? I want you to find Roger!"

"We're working on it, Claire. That's all I can say. And I meant what I said outside. I'm going to do all that I can to bring him back."

"I heard there was a disturbance yesterday."

"Where?"

"I can keep a secret, just like you."

With a triumphant smile, Claire moved off and worked the room playing the gracious host, pouring out wine and handing out beers and chatting everyone up.

Malloy found Robie in the corner.

He said, "Didn't expect to see you out of uniform."

"I'm always on duty but that doesn't mean I can't occasionally dress like a girl, Robie."

He lifted his glass. "I'm not saying otherwise. You look great."

"Thank you," she said primly.

A twinge of guilt hit Robie sharply enough to make him look away momentarily. He didn't like holding the truth of Holly's death from her sister, but they had made a deal with the FBI, and Robie couldn't jeopardize that investigation. Not even when his gut was telling him to pull Malloy into another room and tell her everything.

"You okay?" she asked.

He looked back at her. "Sorry, just preoccupied."

"I called a buddy of mine in New York. I told him about the creds you and your partner are carrying. You know what he said?"

"No, but I think you're going to tell me."

"He said that those sound like cred packs Feds use to cover up who they really are. And that people who do that are ones who have serious firepower back in DC."

"Okay."

"Is that an admission?"

"No, that was just me saying 'okay.'"

"Bender talked to Patti. She didn't have any insights on the white van. I mean we have them around here, but the ones I know about are used by contractors, subs…you know, plumbers and electricians. I know them all, and they're not going to be involved in human trafficking."

"So we really need to find Lamarre, if he's still alive."

"You really believe he saw what he said he did?"

"Why would he lie about something like that?"

"He probably wouldn't," she conceded.

"And the fact that he vanished right after telling his girlfriend he basically wanted to settle down with her and left his stuff behind?"

"You think whoever he saw got to him?"

"Sounds that way to me."

"So she said he disappeared around the same time that Roger Walton did?"

"A few days earlier than Walton."

"But he obviously saw the people in the van a while back. I mean he went into rehab in between that, when he talked to Holly."

"Yeah, that's true."

"So what happened to change the status of things?"

"You mean if he was safe for a while and then they snatched him, something changed. The people had to find out he knew something and needed to be taken care of."

"Right. And how would they have done that?"

"Well, he told his girlfriend about it. She might have told someone, although she denies that she did. He also told your sister about it. And we know she told JC Parry. And Parry probably told Walton. And they both disappeared."

"You mean all *three*. I've tried Holly's phone. I've e-mailed and texted and gotten nothing. Now, she's not the most communicative person in the world, but that's not like her."

"I imagine not, " said Robie.

"You think I'll hear from her at some point?"

Robie looked immensely uncomfortable. "I don't know."

Malloy sighed. "Family. I came all this way to help her and I don't think I helped her at all."

"Sometimes, people just need to help themselves, Sheriff."

"I'm off duty. So please, call me Valerie."

"Okay, Valerie."

He glanced over to see Reel in animated conversation with Derrick Bender, who, Robie thought, was standing a little too close to her, though Reel didn't seem to mind. She laughed at something he said.

The hairs on the back of Robie's neck rose a bit.

"You okay?"

He glanced back at Malloy and her empty glass. "You want a refill on that? Bar's this way."

A few minutes later Robie found himself talking to Patti Bender.

"We asked around but no one knows anything about Walton, or prisoners in a van," she said. "Or if they do they're not talking about it."

Robie sipped his wine and nodded slowly. "It may be a combination of ignorance and deceit."

"I know most of these people," said Patti. "I doubt they have it in them to keep something like that secret."

"I appreciate your asking around."

"Any word on Holly and Luke?"

"No," said Robie. "Nothing."

"Maybe they got out of here then," said Patti with a wistful look.

"Is that your goal? I thought you liked it here."

"I do. But the world's a big place. I'd like to see some of it before my time's up."

"You're still young, Patti."

"I'm not *that* young. I'll be forty soon. But around here, you always feel older than you really are."

"Your mom seems really cool."

"She is. And I'd miss seeing her."

"And your dad? Is he still around?"

"No," she said firmly. "He's not."

Robie was about to say something else when the door opened and a tall, lean man with a full head of silver hair walked in. He was dressed in a dark suit with a pocket kerchief and a white shirt, open at the collar. His face was deeply tanned. He looked to be in his late fifties.

"Roark," said Claire, going over to him and bussing his cheek with her lips.

"Claire, how do you manage to get younger and more gorgeous every time I see you?"

"I knew there was a reason I invited you tonight." To Robie and Reel, she said, "This is Roark Lambert."

Robie said, "You rented out the cabin to Roger Walton."

Lambert nodded. "Claire told me what had happened. I think one reason she invited me tonight was so you could ask me questions."

"We all want Roger back," said Claire. "And as quickly as possible."

They went in to dinner, which was served around a large table in the middle of what had to be the library, given the number of books on the shelves.

Lambert was seated in between Robie and Reel.

As the food was served and they began to eat, Robie said, "So Walton had rented from you before?"

"Several times. I own a number of cabins in the area. It's a nice business. Never going to get rich doing just that, but it's positive cash flow."

"Did you ever meet Walton?" asked Reel.

"A few times, yeah. Once here at Claire's. I'm from Denver and don't spend much time out here. He was tight-lipped about himself. I sensed he had some high-stress job and just liked to get away from it all. This is a good place to do that."

"How'd you end up owning rental cabins out here?" asked Robie.

"Well, Denver's not all that far away. And my father was born right across the border in Nebraska. When I was a kid, we would come through here on the way to visit his parents. There's not much out here, but it has its charms. And if you like to fish, bird-watch, take photos, or do some hunting, this isn't a bad place to be. I made some money in private equity and have now deployed it in real estate."

"So the rentals are your business?" asked Robie.

"Not my main business, no. Just a sideline. I've got my fingers in lots of pies. But what I'm focused on now is luxury prepping."

Robie and Reel looked at him strangely. Robie said, "I don't know what that means."

"You've heard of preppers, surely?"

Robie shook his head but Reel said, "You mean people getting ready for doomsday?"

"Well, at least for civil unrest and social upheaval," amended Lambert. "*Doomsday Preppers* is a show on the National Geographic Channel. Hell, it turned out to be the most popular show they ever had. So the interest in Armageddon is there. Some folks call it WROL, meaning Without Rule of Law. Others just call it SHTF." He grinned. "Shit Hitting the Fan. There are lots of problems out there. The social fabric is increasingly fragile. So people stock up on food, water, guns. They have survival shelters or plans when things go to hell. Some are just like cargo containers buried about twelve feet down with water and air capabilities. Nothing too fancy, but it's some protection."

"But you said 'luxury' preppers," pointed out Reel.

Lambert took a sip of his wine. "Right. There's no money in ordinary preppers. They get their stuff from the stores or online. But for those who can afford it, there are opportunities for profit. A lot of profit."

"How?" asked Robie.

Malloy, who was seated across from them and had been listening said, "Secure facilities when everything goes to hell."

"And where would that be?" asked Robie.

Lambert said, "In a former Atlas ballistic nuclear missile silo. I've finished two, one here in Colorado. I missed out on another one in the area. But I've got another silo done in Kansas. And I'm developing several more."

"Missile silos?" said Robie.

Lambert nodded. "They were decommissioned a long time ago and the government has been selling them off. At first you'd wonder what the hell to do with them. But then, when you combine the point one percenters' cash with the world looking increasingly shaky, you have a wonderful answer. You take an already hardened facility in the middle of nowhere and you turn it into luxury living. Then the very rich have a place to go to and be safe when everything goes to hell."

"And if it doesn't go to hell?" asked Reel.

Lambert shrugged. "Doesn't matter to these folks. They have homes all over the world. The silo condo—that's what they are, by the way, each floor is comprised of condos—is just insurance for them. They probably never want to use it because that means the civilized world is no more. And they're apt to lose a lot more of their wealth, if that's the case. You know, stock markets tank, gated communities and high-dollar properties are overrun by the masses. But at least if they come to the silo they'll get to live. Then when things quiet down, they can come out and pick up the pieces.'

"Sounds very egalitarian," noted Reel sarcastically.

"Hey, I grew up poor," said Lambert. "And while I make good money now, I'm not at the financial level of the people who have bought space in my silos. But there was a need in the market and I filled that need. Business one-oh-one."

"So those who can pay get to stay nice and cozy in the lap of luxury while the rest of us fight it out on the outside?" said Malloy.

Lambert eyed her. "Look, Valerie, you and I have had this discussion before. I don't make the rules. I don't want doomsday to happen. But if it does, I've provided a service for folks who can afford it. It's like catastrophic insurance."

"Not exactly," said Malloy, "but I won't push the point."

He raised his wineglass to her and smiled. "Appreciate it kindly, ma'am."

"So there are silos around here?" asked Reel.

"There are five former Atlas E missile sites in Colorado alone," replied Lambert. "They're in the northern plains, Larimer and Weld Counties. There are others scattered across the country. The ones here were decommissioned in the sixties and the missiles removed. Before they can be put up for sale they have to be investigated and cleared from an environmental perspective, of course. Some are being developed as luxury residences, some for commercial purposes, and some are still owned by the government. They can be used for storage or just sit there rusting away."

Claire joined them as Lambert finished speaking.

"I hope Roark isn't boring you to death about his doomsday business," she said brightly.

"It's actually quite fascinating," said Robie.

"Rich people escaping into their hidey-holes," retorted Claire.

"Now, Claire," began Lambert.

"Did he tell you about the billionaires building their own rockets and spaceships?" said Claire, her smile broadening. "They say it's to colonize Mars or charge people for a ride in space, but I have an alternative theory."

"Which is?" said Reel.

"Escaping into space, of course. No luxury bunker will do for them. They require an entirely new planet on which to ride out the chaos down here."

"Sounds like they're playing God," said Reel.

"There's no doubt about it," said Claire. "They *are* playing God. And they're quite comfortable doing so."

Robie turned to Lambert. "Where is the silo you've completed in Colorado?"

"About an hour's drive north of here. Would you like to see it?"

"I'm not sure we're going to have time," said Robie. "We're a little busy right now."

Lambert shrugged. "Suit yourself. I only offered because Claire told me about Roger Walton."

"I'm not getting the connection," said Reel.

"Well, I know the man has disappeared. But before he did he asked me to give him a tour of the silo. And I did."

Reel looked at Robie and then turned back to Lambert. "Did he say why he wanted a tour?"

"He said he'd been here when the Atlas was operational and had always wanted to go inside. Back then, of course, he couldn't."

"When exactly was this?" asked Robie.

Lambert told them.

Robie and Reel exchanged another look. It had been shortly before Blue Man had disappeared, and *after* he had visited Holly at rehab.

Reel said, "On second thought, we'd love to take a tour."

"Great. I'm not going back to Denver for a few days, so how about tomorrow?"

"Sounds good," said Reel.

"Count me in," said Malloy.

They all looked at her before Lambert glanced at Robie and Reel.

"Maybe you two would be interested in purchasing a condo. I've got two units left in the other silo I'm currently building out. The one I'll be showing you tomorrow is sold out."

An unsmiling Reel said, "I think we'll be part of the barbarians on the outside trying to get in."

"Well, good luck with that," said Lambert.

"It's never about luck," said Reel.

CHAPTER

37

"There has to be a connection," said Reel.

They were standing in the lobby of the hotel.

She continued. "Blue Man wouldn't just go on a tour of the silo after he'd heard what Holly had to say unless it was connected."

Robie slowly nodded. "I agree. Presumably Lambert has been working on this silo for years, and Blue Man has been coming back here all that time. So he could have gone to the silo lots of times. But he picked that time period to do it."

"What do you think he was looking for there?"

"I don't know. Maybe he knew more than we do. We'll just have to keep our eyes and ears open tomorrow."

"You have time for a drink?"

They turned to see Malloy walking into the lobby. She came to stand next to Robie. "Well?" she said, looking only at him.

Reel said, "I'm hitting the sack." She glanced at Robie. "Busy day tomorrow. We have to be at our best."

Malloy continued to stare at Robie. "How about you?"

When Robie didn't answer right away, Reel turned on her heel and headed for the stairs. Robie watched her go for a few seconds and then looked at Malloy.

"Okay," he said.

She said, "I don't mean to pry, but are you two more than professional colleagues?"

"Strictly business."

They walked across the street to the bar and sat at a table on one side of the room. The place was fairly full, though Robie didn't see one King's Apostle or a single skinhead.

"Not much else to do around here at night," explained Malloy. "That sort of place. Not like Manhattan," she added miserably.

"I guess not."

They ordered beers, and when their drinks came, Robie said, "So what's up?"

"I know you can't tell me who Mr. Walton really is."

"That would be an affirmative."

"And you can't tell me what you really do?"

Robie said, "I'm here to find him. Pretty simple."

"Right. But from what I've seen of you and your partner, finding people isn't all you do."

"Okay."

"Is that an affirmation?"

"It's whatever you want it to be. But if you tell anyone else, I'll deny it."

Malloy drank her beer but kept her gaze on him.

Robie ran his gaze around the room and then, for some reason he couldn't quite fathom, his eyes darted over Malloy, from her toes to her head.

Malloy didn't appear to notice this.

Robie blinked, sat back, and cradled his beer.

She said, "You must have some special skills if you escaped from Dolph."

"I've got some tricks up my sleeve. And Dolph got sloppy."

"I really want to nail that guy. It would go a long way toward making this area safer."

"So long as the bad guys outnumber the good guys you're fighting a losing battle. That's why people like Dolph come to places like this and set up shop. They can do their crap in the middle of nowhere without a SWAT team bringing the hammer down."

Malloy sighed and sat back. "I guess."

"You ever think of going back to New York?"

"Every day of my life."

"So will you?"

"Probably. But I need to make sure that Holly is safe first. I have to believe she's going to call me at some point. I mean, she always does."

Robie drank his beer down in three quick bursts.

"You in a hurry?" she said, watching him do this.

"Just thirsty."

His gaze once more involuntarily took her in. And this time Malloy did notice.

She slowly crossed her legs and sat forward. The sundress had a slit and the movement allowed him a glimpse of her thighs. "Are you married?"

"No."

"Ever been?"

He shook his head.

"Me neither. Got close once but that was it. Job always got in the way. Where'd you grow up?"

"Mississippi."

"Never would have guessed that. You don't have an accent."

"Lost it a long time ago."

"You travel a lot?"

"I've been around."

"Ever been overseas?" she asked.

"Yeah."

"I've always wanted to go to London."

"Nice place. I was just there."

"Was it fun?"

"It was business."

"Successful?"

"You could say that," replied Robie.

She leaned back. "I've never really been anywhere. Grew up in New York and then came here for Holly. That's it."

"You're young. You've got a lot of time to fix that."

"I wanted to have kids."

"You still can."

"I need a husband for that. I'm not even dating anyone," she added, shooting him a quick glance.

"How about Bender?"

She smiled. "He's not my type and I'm not his. Besides, it would be pretty awkward professionally."

"I guess so."

"You seeing anyone?"

"Like you, the job gets in the way."

"Jobs can suck," she lamented.

"Sometimes, yeah."

"But people still make do. Take advantage when they can. I've learned that. Don't let opportunities pass you by. You know what I mean?"

"I think so, yeah."

He felt her shoe flick against his ankle.

Yeah, I do know what you mean, thought Robie.

She finished her beer and set the glass down carefully on the coaster before looking up at him. The arc of her smile sent off clear signals.

"You up for a nightcap?" she asked slowly.

Robie tried to recall how many glasses of wine Malloy had had at dinner. And now the beer here. But he couldn't. Hell, he couldn't remember how much *he'd* had to drink. He was feeling a buzz for sure.

"We're going to the silo tomorrow."

"Just a nightcap, Agent Robie. That's all."

"Where?"

"I've got a bottle for special occasions at the office."

Now that the night's proposed agenda was fully out there, Robie had a decision to make.

His professional instincts were telling him very clearly what to do. Or rather what not to do. Another part of his thoughts drifted to the hotel across the street and to the room Reel was in.

He came back to Malloy when he felt her fingers touch his hand.

"Just a nightcap, Agent Robie. I think we deserve it. Never know when another *opportunity* will come up."

The rub of flesh on flesh did *not* decide the issue for him.

He thought back to the note left in his apartment by Reel.

It's complicated.

Well, tonight, right this minute, it's not. It's pretty simple, actually.

Robie put some money down on the table for the beers. They got up and walked out, her soft hip lightly bumping his as they made their way across the street.

In her office she retrieved the bottle of gin and a smaller bottle of tonic plus two glasses. Malloy took the glasses and mixed the drinks, giving generous pours of the gin for each. "I generally like mine on the rocks, but there you go," she said. "No ice here."

They drank their glasses down with her perched on the desk and Robie leaning against the wall and intently watching her.

He had to make an effort at professionalism, even if his heart wasn't in it. Even if he knew he was going to eventually succumb to the temptation presenting itself right in front of him.

He set his glass down. "I better get going. Thanks for the nightcap."

"I'll go with you."

"Where?"

"Next door."

"Next door?"

"Yes. Follow me."

When he made no movement, she edged closer to him.

"You want to say something?" she asked.

"You're a very attractive woman."

"That's very sweet of you to notice."

"So where does that leave us?" asked Robie.

She looked at him hungrily. "Let's go, Agent Robie. I know what I want and so do you."

They exited the station through a rear door and walked over to the B&B. She used a key to open the front door and they went inside.

As soon as the door closed behind them, Malloy turned to him and kissed him, her tongue flicking inside his mouth.

She tugged on his arm, pulling him down the hall and toward the stairs.

"You always this forward?" he said, stumbling after her.

"I'm from New York, so that would be a yes."

They walked down the hall and underfoot Robie heard the crunch of the glass shattered during the gunfight with the skinheads.

The windows had been boarded up with plywood, but Robie could see the bullet holes in the front door and walls.

They reached the upstairs and she led him into a room and shut the door.

She had put the gin, tonic, and glasses in a bag. She took them out and mixed fresh drinks. She handed him his and took a sip of hers. "Bombay Sapphire, only way to go with gin."

Robie's brain was seriously starting to wobble. He sipped his and said, "Nice."

"Oh, it's about to get much nicer," she said slyly.

She put her glass down and, steadying herself by gripping his shoulder, reached down and slipped off her heels. "I don't see how girls walk in these all day," she said, rubbing her foot and then dropping the shoes on the floor.

She unzipped her dress and stepped out of it.

No bra and a light blue thong.

Her breasts were full, her hips soft, and her backside—revealed as she did a slow pirouette for him—round and firm, the skin pale and smooth.

She took his glass away from him and set it down next to hers before turning back around and pushing up against him.

"You're a lot taller without my heels on," she said, grinning, her eyes half-lidded. She closed and opened them slowly. The look was making Robie even more light-headed.

"I g-guess so," said Robie, his voice cracking.

Malloy put her arms around his neck. "Not the official uniform, but I hope you like it anyway."

"I like it," said Robie quietly. "A lot."

She kissed him again, their tongues meeting. "I like you. A lot."

"You sure you're in complete possession of your faculties, Valerie? I don't want to take advantage."

"I know exactly what I'm doing, Agent Robie. There will be no regrets in the morning. At least on my end. I hope the same for you."

"You can call me Will."

"I will, Will."

She kissed him more deeply and ran her fingers through his hair, tugging gently on some strands. That simple maneuver sent shockwaves through Robie's body. He inhaled her scent, coconut shampoo from her hair, a delicate aroma of vanilla from her skin, the hard bite of gin from her lips.

Her fingers undid his shirt buttons, while his clenched her butt and pulled anxiously at the thong.

She kissed his chest and worked her way down. Her hand slipped lower and she gripped him. Next, she moved up to his belt and methodically worked it loose while his mouth dipped to her chest. He pulled her closer. She undid his zipper and the pants came down. He stepped out of his shoes and used one hand to wrench his trousers off.

Robie lifted her up and carried her over to the bed. He shed the rest of his clothes and then Malloy lifted her legs up, so he could relieve her of the thong.

Fully naked now, she lay back, reached up, and pulled him down on top of her.

The bed started to creak violently as the night carried on.

CHAPTER

38

THREE A.M.

Robie awoke and looked around.

The room was unfamiliar. The sounds the same.

The heat of the body next to him caused him to reach out and touch her.

Malloy mumbled something, moaned slightly, then turned on her side and fell back asleep.

Robie lifted the covers and looked down.

They were both still naked.

He lowered the covers and stared across at the window. He was cold sober now and was having a difficult time processing what he had done this night.

Robie rubbed his pounding temples.

Shit.

He looked over at Malloy. Her coil of hair was draped over one bare shoulder.

Images flashed through Robie's mind of two people smashing against each other under the sheets in what he could only describe as a fit of unrestrained libido.

Sometimes it really was just about the sex.

He rose, dressed, and softly closed the door behind him.

Malloy didn't make a sound as he did so.

As he walked down the stairs it occurred to him, and not for the first time tonight, that he was in the same place where he had first met Holly.

Dead Holly.

She was meeting up with her boyfriend and then on her way to a new life.

Only there would be no new life in California. Dolph had seen to that.

And the lady he'd slept with tonight didn't know about any of it.

I screwed Holly's sister and she has no idea that Holly is dead and that I know the truth. What does that make me?

Robie sat down on the bottom riser and put his head between his knees. It wasn't that he felt physically sick.

I just feel…empty.

This was not who he was. He didn't agree to keep secrets like that from someone. And he didn't sleep with people he didn't really know. Only that wasn't true. He had done that once over a year ago, and it had ended in disaster. He apparently had not learned his lesson. Still, he didn't recognize the person that he had been tonight.

Cool, under-control Will Robie. He had not been that way in coastal Mississippi, and it didn't appear that he was doing any better in rural Colorado.

By sleeping with Malloy he felt like he had cheated on Reel, but that was impossible because there was nothing between them. Well, again, that wasn't entirely true. There was nothing on her end.

But there is on mine.

And I just slept with another woman. And I enjoyed it. A lot.

He detected the scent of Malloy all over him. He took a deep breath and it was all he could do to stop himself from sprinting back up the steps, waking the woman, and doing it all over again.

He slowly rose and staggered to the door. A minute later he was back at the hotel.

As he passed Reel's room down the hall from his, he noted that there was no light coming from under the door. At three a.m. she was, like most people, asleep in her own bed.

Like I should have been for the last four hours.

He showered and lay down in the bed with just a pair of boxers on. He stared at the ceiling, hoping perhaps to find some answers to bewildering questions on the drywall up there.

It didn't work. There were no answers there or in his head.

He finally fell asleep and then rose when his phone alarm sounded. He dressed and went downstairs for breakfast.

He saw Reel had beaten him down. She was just finishing her meal at a corner table. She saw him and motioned him over. Robie squared his shoulders and marched toward her. He had more apprehension doing that than he'd had going into that home in London to battle seventeen armed terrorists.

Such was the unique effect that Jessica Reel had on him.

He sat down and ordered coffee from the waitress who hurried over to take his order. There weren't many people in the small restaurant, and she was probably happy to have something to do.

"You look tired," said Reel. "You didn't sleep well?"

"I'm fine. Maybe drank a little bit too much," he added in a low voice.

"Right. So what did Malloy want with her *nightcap*?"

Robie fiddled with his napkin. "Nothing much, but I'm getting fed up with not telling her about Holly."

"I told you how I feel about it, but I also see Agent Sanders's position. And we gave him our word."

"Yeah, well," said Robie, not finishing the thought.

His coffee came and he drank it down quickly.

Reel watched him and said, "You feel better?"

He nodded.

"You want something to eat?"

He shook his head. "So, luxury silos today?"

"Lambert texted me. He's going to come by around ten."

"Okay, but you really think there's a connection?"

"Blue Man toured the place right before he disappeared." countered Reel. "And you didn't have a problem last night with our checking it out."

"Fine," said Robie curtly.

"I think we just need to learn as much as we can about this place, Robie. The more we know, the chances increase we can find Blue Man. But if you have a better idea, I'm listening."

"I don't have a better idea," he said distractedly. "I don't have *any* ideas."

"Okay, so then we're on the same page."

They finished up and were waiting out front for Lambert when he pulled up in a Yukon at a few minutes past ten.

Robie watched dully as Malloy walked across the street, dressed in her uniform, at the same time Lambert arrived.

Shit.

He had forgotten that she was coming.

"Sheriff," said Reel as Malloy joined them.

Malloy nodded at her and then settled her gaze on Robie.

"Agent Robie," she said.

"Sheriff."

"That was great least night, wasn't it?" she said.

"What's that?" asked Robie nervously.

"The dinner at Claire's."

"Absolutely. She knows how to throw a party."

He didn't notice Reel glancing first at Malloy and then at him.

They all walked to the Yukon and climbed in. Reel took shotgun, and Robie and Malloy settled into the middle row.

Lambert said, "I brought donuts, if anyone's interested."

"I am," said Malloy, glancing at Robie. "I didn't get enough last night. I'm still *really* hungry."

Robie looked out the window, even as Reel glanced toward the back.

"Well, eat up," said Lambert.

Malloy took a donut and bit into it. "I plan to."

"Let's go," said Reel curtly.

39

"POLYCHLORINATED BIPHENYLS AND trichloroethylene were the two biggest issues for this site," said Lambert as they approached the former missile silo complex in his vehicle.

"See, the biphenyl got into the soil. And the trichloroethylene got into the groundwater. The missile crews used it to flush the fuel tanks after readiness tests."

"No problem with radiation?" asked Reel. "Didn't the Atlas missiles use plutonium for their core?"

"They did, but all warhead maintenance occurred at the manufacturing facility. Not here. Did you know a version of the Atlas was used to launch John Glenn into space as part of the Mercury program?" He smiled and slapped the steering wheel. "That's a part of American history for sure. Now, the truth is these missile silos had a short shelf life. They came online in 1961 and were put on high alert during the Cuban Missile Crisis. But then they were phased out in 1965 for lots of different reasons. Environmental remediation was complete around twelve years ago, and the site closure happened a couple years later. Then it went on the market. I bought it and developed it from there. Paid four hundred thou for the site and spent five years and about eighteen million dollars renovating it."

He pulled to a stop at a large steel link gate topped with concertina wire. There was a call box with a digital pad. Lambert rolled down his window, punched in a code, and a voice came through a speaker.

"Yes?"

Lambert waved at a camera mounted on a post. "It's me, Karl. With our guests."

"Yes sir, Mr. Lambert."

The gate swung open and Lambert drove through.

"The Army Corps of Engineers originally built the site," Lambert explained. "They picked the location too, and they picked well."

They navigated a long macadam road that meandered through open fields.

Lambert pointed to several tall posts along the way.

"State-of-the-art surveillance at regular intervals. We can see any-one coming from a long way away."

"And who exactly would be *coming*?" asked Reel.

Lambert shrugged. "In an apocalypse it's hard to say. Maybe ev-erybody who didn't plan ahead, I guess."

"You mean who didn't have the *money* to plan ahead?" countered Malloy.

"Well, that sort of goes without saying."

They finally pulled up to what looked like an enormous concrete dome with a large metal door.

"Blast door," said Lambert as he brought the SUV to a stop. "Sucker can withstand a nuclear strike. Concrete walls are nearly three meters thick. That dome can take five-hundred-mile-per-hour winds easy."

In front of the door was a parked Hummer that was decked out with a turret machine gun. Four men in cammies and bulletproof vests and carrying assault rifles were standing by the vehicle.

"So you have perimeter security as well," noted Robie.

"Absolutely, that's one of the chief selling points. In the event of an emergency the guards' families will be allowed in, of course."

"Of course," said Reel, the disgust clear on her features, though Lambert wasn't looking at her.

They climbed out of the truck and approached the door.

"So who buys these sorts of places?" asked Malloy.

"Wide spectrum of folks. I can't reveal any names of course, but we've got hedge fund managers, investment bankers, Silicon Valley people, you know, Facebook, Yahoo, Google. Captains of industry. Names you see in the *Wall Street Journal*. Got one professional ath-lete, a golfer."

"Silicon Valley, huh?" said Malloy. "Techies afraid of the apocalypse? I thought they believed technology was going to save the world."

"Hell, I met this one guy in the tech world. He's scared to death that people are going to be coming for him and other folks out there because this artificial intelligence stuff will be taking everybody's jobs away. He told me he had attended that fancy-ass economic forum they hold every year in Switzerland and all everybody was talking about over there was building hideaways. The rich are really running scared. And you've got to have serious money to buy at this level. Each full-floor condo in my silo will set you back about four million. And it's not like this is a residence used very often. So really you have to be worth well north of a hundred mill to make this work. We got a billionaire, too, although he hedges his bets even more."

"How so?" asked Malloy.

"Well, he has a place here. But he also has an island off the coast of New Zealand. New Zealand is real popular with rich people worried about global collapse. I guess they think it's far enough away not to be affected. But I'm like, well, you got poor people there, too. But hey, I figure if they're that rich they must know what they're doing. And it's not my place to second-guess somebody who made that much money. They must be smart, right?"

"Or they inherited it," pointed out Malloy.

"Or they get to operate on an uneven playing field because they paid off politicians to write the laws to favor them," added Reel.

"Well, there's some of that, sure," conceded Lambert in a half-hearted fashion. "Thing is, folks who buy here aren't getting a vacation home. They're purchasing an *insurance* policy so that if government and civilization go into a temporary tailspin, they'll be able to safely wait it out and come back to pick up the pieces."

"That's the theory anyway," said Robie.

"It's all theory when you think about it," added Lambert. "No way to really predict how it will all shake out. But these people are leaders in their business. Really smart folks, like I said. By talking to a lot of them who have bought units here, I can tell they believe they'll be able to bring civilization back online. So that's a good thing."

Malloy said, "But do they ever think that they might have helped contribute to society going to hell? You know, the haves and the have-nots?"

Lambert grinned. "Look, I try not to get into the middle of that argument. People can spout off facts on both sides and people believe what they want, and you're not going to change their minds. So it's a losing proposition. And I'm not an asshole. I'm not saying I particularly love any of this. You know, poor people beating on the door to get in and rich people saying, 'Hell no.' Fact is, it's their money, so they can spend it however they want. But I'm a businessman. There was a need for this and I'm filling that need. So long as people are willing to pay enough for me to earn a profit, then that's that. And I took a big risk with this project. The engineering was a bitch and the interior renovation was even more of a challenge. The day I closed on this sucker and we came and opened the door I thought I'd lost my mind and my money. I had to take out a big loan to do the work. And then I had to sell the units. I had to finish one model apartment before I could market it. Folks aren't gonna shell out millions based on a picture. But I found a strategy that worked."

"What was that?" asked Robie.

"I figured I'd go where the money is. I put ads in luxury yacht magazines and in private jet publications. I had my first customer within a month and then word spread fast. I mean the folks who can afford this place only move in pretty tight circles with other folks who have the money for a place like this. So I had the whole facility sold out in eighteen months. And there was no haggling over the price. People paid the asking. Everything was done high-end, and as you'll see we thought of pretty much everything. And I always made sure to have my biggest, baddest, and best-armed security out there when potential owners came to visit. They appreciated that fact, I can tell you."

"So do you have a place here?" asked Reel.

Lambert smiled. "Hell yes. I'm not going to be left outside. You can't spend your money if you're dead."

"I'm thinking that all the owners don't live around here, so how do they get here if there's an emergency?" asked Robie.

Lambert pointed towards the east. "We got a secure FAA-approved landing strip a quarter mile that way. It'll take jets all the way up to Triple Sevens. Folks fly in and then we motor them here to safety. See, that's the other reason you have to have serious money to make this work. You got to have your own jet. Folks won't have any way of getting here otherwise. If the world's gone to hell, it's not like you can just gas up your car and drive off down the interstate. It'll be packed with traffic, no gas available, people maybe shooting at each other from their cars. Now, as a last resort, we will take armored vehicles to Denver and pick up folks there, if that's the only way they can get here. But we do strongly encourage the private jet route."

"Well, that cuts down on the riffraff," opined Reel.

Lambert looked at her and smiled. "I'm not going to win you over on this, am I?"

"Doubtful, since I'm part of the riffraff."

Lambert shrugged. "Hey, I get it, but I don't make the rules. Anyway, we have room, you know, like servants' quarters, for their pilots and their families too, like our guards here. I mean you can't expect your pilots to fly you to safety and leave their families behind. We have that detail in our owner's manual so that people won't forget. Lot of details to keep straight. Hard to do in times of crisis."

"Yeah, families," said Robie, glancing at Reel, who now looked like she wanted to shoot Lambert.

He continued. "There are actually two underground complexes with the Atlas E facility. There's the missile launch and service building and the launch operations building. They're connected by a tunnel. The launch building is a huge storage facility, really. There was one missile to a facility. The Atlas was stored horizontally and then would be raised vertically so it could be fired out of the silo after the retractable roof was opened. The ops building was where the crew quarters were located along with launch control components and diesel-powered generators. You're talking about twenty-five acres total."

He led them over to the entrance door after speaking with one of the guards.

"I got friends who have motorcycles gassed up and ready at all times. They got their guns, ammo, some canned food, and bottled water that they'll carry in a little trailer as they head out of the nightmare. They got gold coins, too, and prearranged places where they'll meet up. Or maybe Bitcoins or cryptocurrency. Now, higher up on the scale are well-heeled executives who keep their choppers ready to go at all times and have a place somewhere remote with everything they need to stay alive, including air filtration. See, they figure if society collapses the worst stuff will happen in metro and suburban areas. You know, low-hanging fruit. Who wants to trek up a mountain to get to a rich person if they just have to turn the corner in Manhattan and throw a brick through a window and follow that with a gun or knife?"

"So people coming here will be escaping from big cities?" asked Robie.

"More than likely, yeah. I mean, that's where they make all their money, right? Hell, we're flyover country here."

"But I'm assuming there are rich people around here, too," said Reel.

"Sure, but most are still concentrated along the coasts and down in Texas with all the oil money. Stats on that are clear. And that's where most of my clients are from. And they know they can't go it alone. Not against a mob mentality. Not even with all their money. Money works only when you have laws and people to enforce those laws. So they need help. And we're that help."

Malloy said, "And where will the police be in all this?"

"No offense, Sheriff, but they're going to be part of the mob," replied Lambert promptly. "Cops don't make a lot of money. You know that firsthand. They're going to be out rioting along with everyone else unless they already cut a deal to act as security for the rich folks."

"Damn," said Malloy, shaking her head.

Reel looked at her. "Hey, maybe you hedge your bets and get your butt in here. I'm sure Lambert is always looking for an experienced gun for hire to show off to his rich clients."

Lambert smiled. "Sorry, Sheriff, I'd like to oblige, but we got sufficient security and we frankly don't have the room. Every square inch is spoken for."

"No problem. I'd prefer to take my chances on the outside with the *riffraff.*"

Lambert approached the door and pressed his thumb into a biometric reader. A control panel was revealed as a thick piece of metal slid upward. He keyed in a code and the hydraulic-powered door swung silently open surprisingly fast.

Lambert said, "The shield over the control panel will withstand pretty much anything you can throw at it. But even if it is disabled we have redundant controls inside. And that blast door can take a direct nuke hit, so forget about trying to get through it with conventional explosives. Isn't going to happen."

Robie looked over the width and depth of the gigantic door. "I can see that."

"Now, what you're about to see is the pinnacle response to prepping short of owning an island and employing your own army. I also refer to it as the extreme end of the survivalist's spectrum. On doomsday this is where you want to be."

He led them inside.

40

Lambert walked them over to a bank of elevators. "In the silo we've got a dozen floors and private apartments on each. Some are half-floor units that go for about two mill, but most of the owners have taken the whole floor for around four million."

"How many people total can you support in here?" asked Malloy.

"Around a hundred, but we're looking at ways to stretch that number a bit to allow some flexibility with staff and such."

"You mean pilots, guards, and their families," said Reel curtly.

"Well, yeah. *Immediate* families. I mean, we can't take cousins and nephews and in-laws. We just don't have the room. Now, we have enough food and fuel for five years, but we also have renewable energy capabilities that we keep improving upon, along with raising our own food, so we could possibly stay in here indefinitely."

"Who pays for all the guns and food, upkeep, security guards, the improvements you're talking about, and all that?"

"Monthly fee tacked onto the purchase price, like a condo fee. It's paid into an escrow starting from day one. So we have a nice buffer already built in. If doomsday happens and the monetary system goes down, well, we'll all be in survivalist mode. I don't think anyone will be worrying about a paycheck. They'll just want to stay in here and get by until it's okay to leave. But with that said, private security ain't cheap. Hell, none of this is cheap. That's sort of the point. Separating the wheat from the chaff."

"Or the clamshells from the pearls," amended Reel.

Lambert pointed at her and chuckled. "I might use that analogy in my future marketing materials."

"Was Walton interested in anything in particular here?" asked Robie.

"He asked questions about the silo's configuration, entry points, square footage, defensive mechanisms, even where I got the workers to do the job. Told him as much as I could."

"And where did you get the workers?" Reel wanted to know.

"Some local, some not. And no, I didn't use any illegals. This is specialized work. I needed trained folks who knew what they were doing."

"Illegal status doesn't mean they're untrained," pointed out Robie.

"Yeah, but you can get into a lot of legal hassles if you do use them, and I couldn't afford the headache."

They rode the elevator down to the bottom of the silo.

Getting off, Lambert said, "We'll work our way back up. In addition to the apartments we built out in the silo, we converted the launch operations area and part of the missile launch section into the public use areas. As you'll see, they're pretty extensive."

They climbed on a golf cart parked near a raised overhead door and Lambert drove them down a long tunnel that was well lighted and had a concrete floor. "This was the connecting tunnel I told you about." They arrived at the other end of the tunnel and climbed off the golf cart. Lambert led them into a space filled with raised wooden boxes with plants growing in them. Special lighting illuminated the room.

"Our hydroponic gardens. We grow vegetables with special lamps. We also will be raising fish for proteins. And we're thinking about having a chicken coop for eggs and the occasional white meat. No room for cattle down here," he added, grinning. "Behind those doors are our food storage areas. No perishables but nutritionally balanced provisions. We hired an expert to help us put the mix together. We also have state-of-the-art water, and NBC, or nuclear, biological, and chemical, air filtration systems. If the outside gets radiated, we'll be fine in here."

He led them through various other rooms containing a bowling alley, spa, gym, swimming pool, theater, and medical wing with a dentist chair and an operating room.

"Two of our owners are health-care execs and also doctors, so we lucked out there. They can perform any necessary medical procedures for the rest of the population."

He led them next to a wine cellar. "Some of our owners are collectors and they've brought some of their stock here. One of the perks of owning here. Some of the bottles in there are worth tens of thousands of dollars. Me, I'm a beer man, but I could be tempted."

"I'm sure you could," noted Reel.

He unlocked one room and they passed through.

"This is our armory."

On the walls and secured by chains and padlocks was an impressive arsenal of pistols, rifles, and submachine guns as well as grenades, RPG launchers, and boxes of ammo.

"Even though we have professional guards, you never know, so this is just in case we're breached or our guards go down during an assault. Each owner has been trained with these weapons. Next to the armory is a shooting range. One requirement of purchasing a property was that every adult had to be certified in weaponry."

Reel eyed the guns. "You're loaded for bear here."

"Well, bears might be coming," said Lambert quite seriously. "We've also got sniper posts outside in certain locations that I can't show you." He paused and added, "You can never be too careful around here."

"Have you had any threats?" asked Malloy.

Lambert seemed to choose his words carefully. "We have received some…communications from certain elements hereabouts that they'll be coming for us if the sky falls. Poor-versus-rich sort of thing."

"Are we talking the white supremacists, the motorcycle gangs, the Nazis, assorted others?" asked Malloy.

"Yes we are, but I can't elaborate further. But now you can see why we have the armory and the requirement that every owner here be willing to defend the silo. That's just the way it has to be. One for all and all for one."

"Did Walton ask you about that issue?" said Reel.

Lambert paused at the door and looked at her. "Am I missing something here? Why do you keep asking about what Walton wanted to know about this place?"

Malloy said, "Because maybe it had something to do with his disappearance."

"Now hold on, I had nothing to do with the man going missing."

Reel, scowling at Malloy, said, "We weren't suggesting that you did. We were just interested in why he wanted to see the silo at that exact moment in time. He must have had other opportunities."

"Well, I suppose he did. But he never asked before this trip out."

"How did he seem?" asked Robie.

"Tight-lipped, like I said before," replied Lambert. "Any conversation with that man you can guarantee that he found out more about you than you ever did about him. Except you had no idea he did until long after it happened."

Robie and Reel exchanged a brief smile. That description fit Blue Man perfectly.

The room next to the armory was padlocked.

"What's in there?" asked Malloy.

"Something you would be familiar with, Sheriff."

Lambert unlocked the door and they looked inside. There was a toilet, a shower, and a bed.

"It's a jail cell," said Malloy.

"We actually like to call it a chill-out room," amended Lambert.

"Who decides who goes in?" asked Reel.

"We have a governing body. They make the decisions while the silo is closed up. And in the event of a catastrophe, no one will be allowed to leave, because that might jeopardize the rest of us if that person were captured and revealed some intelligence about our systems, defenses, and such. Or they could be used as leverage against us."

"And if someone really wanted to leave?" asked Robie.

Lambert pointed at the tiny room. "They go there to chill out. This and all I'm going to show you is spelled out in the marketing materials and in the ownership documents that everyone has to sign. We didn't want anyone to be surprised." He wasn't smiling now.

"And if you have a mutiny?" asked Malloy.

"Well, let's hope it doesn't come to that. People who bought here are reasonable and think logically. I doubt they're going to lose their cool and spoil it all."

"That's the *theory*, anyway," said Reel.

Lambert stared at her for a moment before continuing. "And people will have chores to do. We rotate them so no cliques are formed. Four hours a day. Builds camaraderie and cuts down on boredom. We also have computer network technology tied to a satellite, data storage files, and a business center so that the owners can keep up to date on what's going on outside."

"If there's anyone left outside," noted Reel.

"Well, we need to stay positive," said Lambert curtly. "There's also a dog park because several owners have pets."

"You seem to have thought of everything," said Robie.

"We try. Now we can look at one of the apartments."

They drove back through the tunnel and rode the elevator up, stepping off on a floor that had a single door.

Lambert opened it.

Robie said, "Wait a minute, the apartments aren't locked?"

"No, we thought it best to have them unlocked in case of emergency. We have to have an element of trust here."

They stepped inside.

He pointed around the space. "It's about two thousand square feet. I know that sounds fairly large for an underground apartment, but keep in mind that the owners are used to living in mansions ten times that size, with full-time staffs, but there was no way we could duplicate that here. But we do try to make it as luxurious as possible, as you saw with the common areas. Now, we have nine-foot ceilings throughout, granite counters, Wolf and Sub-Zero appliances. This particular place is owned by an investment banker. His wife had her designer fly in to do the customized interior." He pointed to a window showing a scene with trees and a statue.

"That's Central Park," said Malloy.

Lambert nodded. "These are LED video screens. It's important when living underground that you have lots of light to stimulate people. You can customize them to whatever you want. There're also sounds associated with them, and the scenes are on a rotation so they change every few minutes. This couple is from Manhattan and wanted to replicate that experience. We've got another couple from Minnesota that prefers winter images. One guy from Hawaii likes waves and beaches. We have one guy who was born in England before moving to the U.S. as a teenager. He has an entire video wall in his bedroom with scenes from London. It's all in what you want the experience to be." He suddenly laughed. "In 1961 JFK called on all Americans to work together to build fallout shelters because of the Cold War. But somehow I don't think he had this in mind."

"No, I don't think he did," said Robie.

"But you look at Congress. They had that big underground shelter at the Greenbrier Resort in West Virginia. The press found out and they discontinued its use, but don't tell me they don't have other places to go in case the world goes to hell."

"Well, places like that are to ensure continuity of government," Reel pointed out.

"Well, places like this are to ensure that highly successful people survive and then come out and work to rebuild the world," said Lambert. "It's all in our marketing brochures. It's like we're doing a public service, really. These people are leaders. Frankly, I believe they're far better leaders than the do-nothings in Washington. How do you know a politician is lying? He has a pulse."

"That's one way to look at it," said Robie.

Lambert quickly eyed him. "Hey, I know you're with the Feds, and I got great respect for people putting their lives on the line for their country. I was in the Army for a while. Some of the best lessons I ever learned. My problem is with the empty suits spouting bullshit and not helping anybody. Maybe if they did their job we wouldn't have to build stuff like this." He grinned and rubbed the back of his head. "Sorry, I tend to get on my soapbox sometimes." He looked around at the space. "As elaborate as this is, there are other folks doing much bigger things."

"Such as?" asked Reel curiously.

"I hear they're developing a subterranean community near Dallas. Single-family homes, equestrian center, beaches, golf course, polo fields, zip lines. Three hundred million bucks or more it's costing, all underground, and all protected against an apocalypse. And there's a huge development of former military bunkers in South Dakota. That will house about five thousand people. And it's not just in the U.S. They're doing this at an old military bunker in Germany that'll have triple the number of residences that I have, and then there's the Oppidum in the Czech Republic. They're calling it the 'Billionaire's Bunker.' It has an aboveground estate and nearly eighty thousand square feet underground. Makes what I'm doing here seem like small potatoes."

"I hope no one ever considers something like this small potatoes," commented Robie.

"Anybody in residence now?" asked Reel. "Or do they just come when the nukes get dropped?"

"Most of the owners have come out and spent time here just to get a feel for what it's like. But they won't really know what it's like until there is a catastrophe. I mean, we don't put them to work or put them in the chill-out room now. That's only in the event of an emergency. There's a couple coming in tomorrow. They bought the last unit. He just turned thirty-eight, but he inherited a bazillion dollars from his old man. His wife was a model. Still could be. She's a knockout. They pretty much bought the unit sight unseen. Now they're coming to live here for a couple days to get a feel for it."

"Where's your apartment?" asked Robie.

"The bottom one," said Lambert.

"So they have to go through everybody else to get to you?" said Reel, staring at him with a knowing expression.

He grinned. "Nice observation. Hell, there's got to be some extra perk for the guy who built the damn place."

"And that's not in the marketing materials," said Reel.

"Must have left that one out," he said.

"Must have."

"So that's our little fallout shelter," said Lambert, making a mock bow.

"Well, let's hope you never have to use it for real," said Robie.

41

As THEY WERE leaving the silo, a stretch limo pulled up and the driver, a man in his sixties with curly gray hair and dressed in a chauffeur's uniform, quickly climbed out and opened the rear door.

Out stepped a tall, handsome, well-built man in his late thirties. He was dressed in corduroy pants and an ammo vest over a white shirt. What looked to be work boots right out of the box were on his feet. A compact nine-millimeter pistol rode in a hip holster.

He reached his hand back into the limo and helped out the woman. She was around thirty, with long dark hair that swirled around her shoulders. She was nearly as tall as the man and had the sort of long-limbed and narrow-hipped body that fashion designers craved for the catwalk. She had on faded jeans with a series of slashes at the knees and thighs. Her blouse bared both her tanned shoulders, and when she reached up to tousle her hair, the blouse pulled up to show rock-hard abs.

Lambert scurried forward to greet them as the woman checked her face in a mirror she pulled from the large Prada bag slung over her shoulder.

"How are you doing, Mr. and Mrs. Randall? I wasn't expecting you until tomorrow." He looked anxiously back at Robie, Reel, and Malloy.

"Change of plan. Suzy wants to go to our place in the Hamptons earlier than I thought. So let's hit this thing, Roark. I want to see what four mill bought me. And it better be damn good. Some of my friends are going the island route. I don't want to be left thinking I made the wrong decision. That's when the lawyers get involved."

"Absolutely, sure thing, I know you'll be pleased," said Lambert hastily. He called over his shoulder to the hulking guard standing next to the Hummer. "Hank, can you run these other folks back into town? You can take my truck. I'll be here for a while taking care of our clients here."

He tossed the truck keys to Hank.

Randall eyed Robie and then Reel and then said to Lambert, "Are they staff?"

"How do you know we're not owners?" said Reel.

Randall snorted. "Look, lady, I know what it costs to have a unit in this place. And I've been around big money all my life. I can smell the people who have it and I can definitely tell the people who don't have it. And you're definitely in the latter category. No offense, we can't all be rich, right? I mean, what fun would that be?"

"Well, you're right, actually, we're not owners. We're federal agents."

Randall eyed her and then looked at the uniformed Malloy and said to Lambert, "Why are Feds here checking out things? We don't have a legal problem, do we, Roark? That would definitely not make me happy."

His wife interjected, "Jesus, Scotty, can we just get this going? This wind is drying my hair out. I did not sign up for this shit. I mean, I didn't even know you could land a plane here. This is the part of the country you fly over, not come to."

"Just a minute, hon. I need to get to the bottom of this. Well, Roark, do we have a problem with the damn government?" he said, eyeing Reel suspiciously.

"No sir, not one bit. I was just showing them around. They are not here in their official capacity."

Randall hitched up his pants, placed his hand on the butt of his weapon, and said, "That's a good thing. I don't like legal problems. Got a whole army of lawyers to handle that crap."

"I'm sure you do," said Reel.

"So we'll just be going," added Robie.

"I don't like government folks," continued Randall. "They just get in the way of people that know what they're doing. They mess every damn thing up. It's like we're living in a communist country sometimes. I can take care of myself. I don't need the damn nanny state holding my hand while it sticks the other hand in my wallet."

"Okay, so when someone robs you, don't bother calling 911," snapped Reel. "Handle it on your own."

Randall patted his gun. "I got no problem with that, hon."

"Oh, I think you'd have a big problem with that. And don't pretend otherwise. I mean, isn't that why you bought your little insurance policy here? So they could protect you from the big, bad riffraff banging on the door to get in?"

His wife stepped forward. "Who the hell do you think you are? Do you know who he is? He could buy and sell you."

"Hank, why don't you go on and head out now while I show the Randalls to their quarters?" said Lambert quickly. "I just don't see the direction of this conversation as being productive."

The hulking Hank, an AR-15 slung over his shoulder, came forward. "Yes, sir, Mr. Lambert."

The chauffeur had popped the trunk and was pulling out massive pieces of luggage.

Reel eyed this and turned to the wife. They were about the same height. "Just a piece of advice, *hon*, in an apocalypse, no one is going to care what you're wearing."

Mrs. Randall glared at Reel. "You little bitch!"

Reel moved closer. "I'm someone with a badge, so lose the attitude and go check out your luxury digs while we get on with our petty little lives."

Reel had turned away when the woman grabbed Reel by the shoulder. "Hey, I'm not finished with you yet."

Reel moved so fast, it was hard to follow.

She pivoted, kicked out with her right leg, and took out the back of the woman's knees. Mrs. Randall cried out in pain and fell back on her butt. The next instant Reel was straddling her, pinning her arms to her side.

Randall leapt forward and grabbed Reel by the neck. But a moment later he was lying on his face with Robie's knee in his back and one hand on his neck, pinning him to the ground. When Randall reached for his gun, Robie blocked him and then leveled his own weapon against the man's temple.

"You and your wife just assaulted a federal agent. We could arrest you both for that right now. But in the spirit of generosity from the government you loathe, we'll let it pass. Don't let there be a second time, because this is your only 'get out of jail free' card."

Malloy squatted down next to Randall. "And that goes double from local law enforcement."

Reel rose off a gasping Mrs. Randall while Robie removed his knee from her husband's back. Randall scrambled to his feet while Lambert helped Mrs. Randall to hers. She staggered a bit and grabbed at her right leg.

"I'm gonna sue your ass off!" the woman screamed at Reel. "I think you tore something in my fucking knee."

"Well, we can always hope," said Reel.

"Please, everybody," said Lambert. "Let's just chill out here."

"Good idea, Lambert," said Robie. "Stick 'em both in the chill-out room. I think they could use it."

He glanced at Hank, who was standing there looking helpless.

"Let's hit the road," said Robie.

They all walked toward the SUV. When Robie looked back the Randalls were screaming at Lambert and pointing at Robie and Reel.

As Robie and Reel passed by the chauffeur, the man said under his breath, "You just made my day."

42

"SOMETHING GOING ON you want to tell me about?"

Reel was looking at Robie in the lobby of their hotel. Hank had just dropped them off. Malloy had walked across the street to the police station to make some calls and check on things.

"About what?" Robie asked.

"You tell me."

"I don't know what you're talking about," said Robie. "If I had something to tell you, I'd just tell you."

"Okay," said Reel, but she didn't look convinced.

Robie's phone buzzed and he groaned.

"What?" asked Reel.

"DCI's office. She wants another update tonight."

"Well, let's spend the day trying to get an update for her."

"Starting where exactly?" asked Robie.

"Everybody who knew about the prisoners in the van has disappeared: JC Parry, Clément Lamarre, and Blue Man."

"Holly Malloy was connected to that and she didn't disappear," pointed out Robie.

"That's true. But maybe they didn't know she knew. The others might have done something to show their hand. And maybe they *were* planning to get to her, but Dolph beat them to it."

"Okay, but where does that get us?"

In answer Reel pulled out her phone. "How about we get the Agency to dial up a satellite in this part of the sky to see if it saw the van that night and recorded something about it, the license plate, the direction it went, or even the destination?"

"Good idea," said Robie. "Let's do it."

They went up to Reel's room, where she made the call and laid out what she wanted.

She clicked off and said, "They're going to see what they can do."

"How long?"

"You heard me tell them to give it a top priority. I used the DCI update tonight as the stick."

Three hours later she received a call back. Her expression told Robie all he needed to know. When she clicked off he said, "They found nothing?"'

"They didn't have a bird pointed in that direction during the relevant time period. So there goes that."

Robie said, "Wait a minute, didn't Lambert say that they have a satellite-based network so they can monitor what's going on outside the silo?"

"Yeah, he did."

"You would think his bird would be pointed in the right direction. Meaning at the silo and the area around it. If memory serves me correctly, the silo's in the same general vicinity as Clyde's Stop-In."

"We'll need to get the details on the sat from Lambert in order to do that."

"Which would mean explaining to him why we want it. The fewer people we loop in on this the better."

Reel picked up her phone again. "Let's see what they can do with the information we do have."

She made the call and relayed what she wanted. Then Reel clicked off and looked at Robie. "They're working on it."

"Let's hope they work fast. I don't want to tell the DCI we have no progress to report."

"I don't care what she thinks," shot back Reel. "I just want to find Blue Man alive."

"So do I," said Robie.

"Good, I'm glad we're in agreement on that."

They walked downstairs to the hotel restaurant to grab some lunch.

Midway through their meal Roark Lambert walked in, spotted them, and hurried over. He grabbed a chair and sat down at their table.

"How're the Randalls?" asked Reel. "Still screaming?"

"Look, I'm sorry about that. I think I got them calmed down so they won't sue."

"I don't give a crap if they do. They assaulted me. They can go to a federal prison for that. So they should be thanking me for not arresting them, not feeling generous for not suing me!"

"I pointed that out to them seven ways from Sunday, but in case you hadn't noticed, they don't listen too well," Lambert retorted.

Reel said, "Piece of advice. If the world blows up and those two are in the silo, you might want to just put them in the chill-out room permanently, because I don't see either of them playing well with others."

Lambert nodded. "You're probably right about that. Just about all the other owners are as nice as they can be. I'm sorry you had to run into the Randalls. They are not representative of the other folks. I know rich people get a bad rap, but the other owners are really good people. Considerate and respectful and reasonable."

"I have no problem with rich people," said Robie. "I've met rich and poor and people in the middle of the pay scale who are great, and I've come across people along that same spectrum who are jerks."

Lambert said, "I think Randall's daddy spoiled him. And his wife just enables that crappy attitude because I think she's even worse than he is. I mean, she was screaming at *him* for not *shooting* you, Agent Reel. Slapping him in the face and everything. I finally had to hold her back. I mean, damn."

"If he had tried to shoot me, he'd be dead," said Reel. "I hope you know that."

"I have no doubt," said Lambert. "Anyway, they're in their quarters now. Her knee will be fine. She's got some ice on it."

"Trust me when I say I wasn't worried in the least about that," said Reel.

Lambert cracked a smile. "I wish you two could be in the bunker when things go to hell."

"*If* they go to hell," corrected Robie. "Remember, let's think positive."

With a hurried good-bye, Lambert rose and left them.

"I think he might be regretting this whole thing," said Robie.

"He made his bunker, now he has to sleep in it. Literally."

"So what do we do while we're waiting on the agency to see if they can access Lambert's satellite?"

Reel took a last sip of her iced tea. "Let's check Blue Man's cabin one more time."

"Why? There was nothing there."

"Blue Man is one of the most resourceful people either of us knows. There was no sign of a struggle at the cabin, so I don't think he was taken completely by surprise. He might have known they were coming. If so, he would also know that people from the Agency would be dispatched to find him."

"So you're saying he might have left a clue?" said Robie. "Something we missed earlier?"

"Let's hope to God he did."

43

SOMEONE WAS WAITING for them when they came out.

Malloy was leaning on the front fender of her patrol car.

"What's up?" asked Robie.

"What I was just about to ask you. After our little jaunt to the bunker, I figured you two would be heading out to do some investigating. So that's where I'm going too."

Reel said, "What we do is classified. We can't have conversations with you around. We can't examine information we have related to our investigation. So having you as a third wheel would pretty much make our work impossible."

"I thought you wanted to find this guy," said Malloy.

"We do," said Robie.

"Then it seems to me that you would use any tool at your disposal. I can be one of those tools."

Robie looked at Reel. She looked back at him with an expression akin to a fist coming right at him.

He turned back to Malloy and said, "We're going to search Walton's cabin again. If you want to follow us up there, fine."

He took his seat in the truck and started it up.

Reel slowly turned to look at Malloy.

"Just so we're clear—you die, it's not my responsibility." Then she climbed into the truck next to Robie.

Robie waited for Malloy to get in her cruiser and then pulled off down the road. They had driven for about five minutes before Reel broke the silence.

"You want to tell me what the hell is going on?"

Robie didn't look at her. "She's local law enforcement. She could be useful. And her sister's dead and we know it but she doesn't. I feel sorry for her."

"Feeling sorry for her does not justify letting her screw up our search for Blue Man."

"She's not going to screw it up. She's a trained professional."

"So you're really not going to tell me what's going on?" said Reel.

"There is nothing going on!" barked Robie.

Reel turned to look out the windshield.

When Robie glanced over at her a few moments later, he did not like what he saw.

They drove on.

*　*　*

"Someone's been here," said Reel.

They were standing outside of Blue Man's cabin. The door was still padlocked and the police tape was still up but there were fresh muddy boot prints on the porch. It had rained some the previous night.

Reel glanced at Malloy, who was looking at the prints. "I thought this was a crime scene. Shouldn't it have been secured?"

"Like I told you before, Agent Reel, we don't have the manpower for that," retorted Malloy. "And the door is still locked." She knelt down and studied the footprints. "They look familiar."

"You know people by their shoes?" quipped Reel.

"Some of them, yes," said Malloy, rising to her feet.

"So any idea who those belong to?" asked Robie.

"Working on it," she said evasively, a worried look on her face.

"Can you get this open?" Reel said, pointing at the door.

Malloy unlocked the padlock and opened the door.

Reel passed by her and went inside.

When Robie started to follow Malloy gripped his arm.

"I want to see you again," she said.

Robie shook his head. "Valerie, last night was a big mistake."

"Not for me it wasn't," she said sharply, as Robie kept shaking his head. "Are you telling me you didn't enjoy it?"

"That's not the point. It was a mistake. We're both working a case. We can't be personally involved."

She ran her hand down his arm and smiled. "I think that boat has sailed. We nearly broke the bed."

Robie was about to say something else when the front door swung open, revealing Reel.

"Are you coming?" she demanded, looking at each of them in turn.

Robie brushed past her on the way into the house.

Reel looked at Malloy. "What were you two doing out here?"

"Just talking shop."

"Right," replied Reel. She moved aside to let Malloy pass.

Inside, Robie was already looking around.

"You think Walton left something behind to help us find him?" said Malloy.

"That's the only reason we're here," replied Reel curtly.

The place was small enough that the search didn't take long. They regrouped in the front room.

Reel said, "We know his cell phone was missing, but it's been turned off or else it went dead, because it couldn't be tracked."

"Laptop?" asked Malloy. "There wasn't one found. I told you that before but you didn't comment on it."

"It's not been confirmed, but I doubt if he would have taken one with him," said Robie. "He wasn't working and he could be reached if need be, so having a computer was just something that could be lost or stolen."

"And I bet there are strict rules about that in whatever agency you work for," noted Malloy, gazing inquiringly at Robie.

"*All* federal agencies have strict rules about that," interjected Reel. "Even the Department of Agriculture."

"Okay, so where does that leave us?" asked Malloy. "We didn't find a clue that I could see."

Robie was looking at the fly-fishing tackle that was still lying on the table by the door. He picked up the rod and looked at it. "We messed up before about JC Parry. Walton didn't need a guide because he knew the rivers here well."

"Right, so?" said Malloy.

"So maybe we messed up about something else," opined Reel, staring at Robie. "Maybe we didn't see something else that's staring us in the face."

Malloy gazed around the room. "There's not much here. I mean he didn't leave much behind. His clothes and toiletries. His Glock ten-mil. Georgetown cap in the truck. His fishing gear."

"You said the Glock was taken in as evidence?" said Robie quickly.

"Yeah, I told you that when we came out here the first time."

"Where is it?"

"In our evidence room back at the station."

"Robie, what is it?" asked Reel.

He looked at her. "Someone I know once communicated something really important using a gun. I mean literally using the weapon to convey a really important message as to the person's *location*."

Reel flinched as though she'd been slapped. That person had been her.

Malloy looked between them. "Who the hell are you talking about?"

"Doesn't matter," said Reel quickly.

Robie said, "And it worked. It allowed me to find the person."

Reel said, "And did you tell Blu...Walton?"

"I did. He was quite impressed with the method. I'm sure he docketed it away like he did every other piece of information he ever received."

"Until maybe he needed to pull it out and use it," said Reel.

"Let's go find out," said Robie.

44

Piece by piece.

Both Reel and Robie had taken turns field-stripping the Glock. Fully assembled, it now lay on a cloth on Malloy's desk.

The three of them were staring down at it. They had found nothing of interest. No additions had been made. No deletions, either.

As they were standing there, Derrick Bender walked in and slapped his hat against his pants leg to knock off some dust.

"Who died?" he said jokingly, staring at their very serious faces.

Then he blanched when none of them cracked a smile. "Shit, don't tell me somebody *did* die?"

Malloy shook her head. "No, we were just hoping that this gun would give us a clue as to what happened to Mr. Walton."

Bender drew next to the desk and looked down at the Glock. "I'm not following. Why would it?"

"Just a long shot," said Reel.

"Well, that gun won't be any good for a long shot," said Bender, grinning. "Barrel's too short."

"Shit," said Reel.

"What?" snapped Robie.

In answer Reel hit the Glock's mag release and put the mag aside. Then she made sure the chamber was empty.

"You got a gun-cleaning kit around here?" she asked.

"Yeah," said Bender. He hurried over to a cabinet, opened the doors, and pulled out a box with a handle. He brought it over and gave it to Reel.

She opened it, found what she wanted, and took out the long, thin piece of metal.

"A bore brush?" said Robie.

She nodded and inserted it into the Glock's barrel. She moved it slowly and carefully into the barrel, then twisted the rod clockwise and counterclockwise before slowly pulling it free.

"What's that?" said Bender.

A bit of white had emerged at the muzzle.

Reel said, "You got tweezers?"

Malloy opened her desk drawer, rummaged around, and pulled out a tiny pair.

"Will this work?" she asked, handing them to Reel.

Reel gripped the tweezers and eased the ends onto the edge of white. She slowly pulled, and the white was revealed to be a piece of paper rolled up.

"Damn," exclaimed Bender. "How'd you think to look there?"

"When you said the barrel was too short for a long shot," replied Reel. "Thanks for the suggestion."

Bender grinned and squeezed Reel's shoulder. Reel patted his hand in return.

Robie observed this and once more felt the hair on his neck fire up. But then he glanced at Malloy and his anger quickly subsided.

Reel slowly unrolled the paper.

"Is anything written on it?" asked Malloy.

"No," said Reel, looking disappointed. "Just this."

She held up the paper for all to see.

It was a stick figure holding what looked to be a ball over its head.

"Anybody have a guess?" said Reel. "Walton obviously wasn't much of an artist."

"If he had an opportunity to put that in the gun for us to maybe find, why not just write out what he wanted to tell us," said Malloy.

"Maybe he didn't know enough to write it out. And it might have been discovered by someone else that he didn't want to let on about what he knew."

"So it's like a code?" said Bender.

"Sort of, probably," said Robie.

"Well, he outsmarted himself then," said Reel. "Because he stumped us too."

Robie took the paper from her and studied it. "This obviously means a person. Does it refer to him? To someone else?"

"I don't know how we answer that," interjected Malloy. "We don't know enough. Like why is he holding a ball? If that's what it is. It almost looks like he's about to shoot a basketball, and for the life of me I can't see how sports figures into this."

Robie said, "Walton played sports when he lived here."

Reel said, "But I thought we had decided his past didn't figure into his disappearance. It was tied to the prisoners in the van. If that's not the case anymore than we are right back at square one."

"I'm not saying that's the case," replied Robie. "But we at least know that Walton knew he was in danger and that he tried to leave us a clue. And while we may not know what it means now, we might figure it out at some point. In fact, we *have* to figure it out."

"Do you think it speaks to where he's been taken?" said Bender.

"Since he left the gun behind, how would he know where they were going to take him *before* they took him there?" said Reel.

"That's a good point," conceded Bender, a hopeless expression on his features.

"We have to figure out the clue," said Reel. "It's the only one we have."

Robie and Reel left Malloy and Bender at the station and made their way back to the hotel.

"We have to do something, Robie," said Reel as they entered the lobby. She looked at her watch. "We're going to be talking to the director in less than four hours. We have to have something to tell her."

Reel's phone buzzed. She answered, listened for two minutes, and then said curtly, "Thanks." She put her phone away and looked at Robie.

"Well?" he said.

"We might have another lead."

"Who was that?"

"The sat guys. They managed to break into Lambert's bird and see what it saw."

"And?" said Robie impatiently as she fell silent.

"They went back about a month focusing on the convenience store late at night. They saw the van at Clyde's. It all happened like Lamarre said. Van pulled in, trouble with the reader, and Lamarre came outside. And then the van drove off in the direction of Lambert's bunker."

"Did it actually go to the bunker?"

"They don't know. The bird swung away before that could be revealed. But it was damn close. Within a couple of miles, they said."

"A couple of miles out here is a lot of space to cover."

"But what else is out there other than Lambert's bunker, Robie? I doubt they were driving around in circles with prisoners in the back of the van. And Blue Man asked for a tour of the place. He was interested in it for some reason. And I'm thinking that interest stems from the prisoners in the van he was told about."

"Okay, but are you suggesting that Lambert is bringing prisoners to his bunker? For what reason? And if so, why would he have offered us a tour of the place, much less Blue Man?"

"Well, he sure as hell didn't show us the whole place," said Reel. "There must be lots of nooks and crannies down there to stash people."

"Granted, but for what purpose?" persisted Robie.

"Maybe we should take a ride and try to find out."

45

"Okay, I think I can see twenty miles ahead, and it looks exactly like the twenty miles we just passed," said Reel.

They had started at Clyde's Stop-In and left in the direction the Agency people had told them the van had taken.

"We just passed the road going to Lambert's bunker," said Robie.

"So that could be where the van went."

"If so, I don't see how we're going to get in there without Lambert knowing about it. You saw the security measures on the perimeter. And then how do we open the blast door? You got a nuke handy?"

Reel said, "And we don't even know for sure if the van is connected to Blue Man's disappearance."

"Damn, Jess, let's not keep turning the wheel back on that. Lamarre knew about the van. He told Holly who told JC Parry who told Blue Man. So Lamarre goes missing and so do Blue Man and Parry."

"And it seems that Lamarre was taken, too, because he left his suitcase behind," admitted Reel. "But what about Holly? How would anyone have known that Lamarre told Holly about the van while they were in rehab?"

"Well, like I just said, she told Parry. And Parry told Blue Man."

"Right, but Holly didn't expressly say that she told Parry or Blue Man about where she'd gotten the information from."

"That's true," said Robie. "Though she might have."

"Let's assume that she didn't. How would someone have found out Lamarre was the source?"

"He told his girlfriend, Beverly Drango," pointed out Robie.

"And she said she told no one. And she hasn't disappeared."

"Well, she hadn't when we saw her."

"But isn't it odd that they would snatch Lamarre from her house and not take her too?" said Reel. "I mean why wouldn't they assume that he had told her about what he saw?"

Robie thought for a few moments. "They would have had to assume that he would tell her. But maybe she wasn't there at the time."

"They could have gone back when she was there. Or put eyes on the place so they'd know when she did come home. And yet there she still was when we went to her house."

"Maybe we need to talk to her again."

"Maybe we do."

As they drove along Robie said slowly, "That was a good deduction you had about the gun based on what Bender said. You two seem to feed off each other well."

"Yeah, there seems to be a lot of that going on around here," Reel shot back.

Robie glanced away, whatever he was about to say forgotten in the wake of Reel's not-so-subtle reply.

After a few moments of silence he said, "Patti told me that their father's been gone I guess for a while. But she didn't say what happened to him."

Reel looked at him. "He died in a car accident twelve years ago. Drunk driver killed him. Derrick told me at the party at his mom's house."

"That must have been tough."

"Life is tough, Robie. But you just have to keep slogging through."

* * *

Later, they were approaching the house when Robie slowed and then stopped.

"What?" said Reel, scanning ahead.

"No Land Cruiser."

"She's probably at work. It's not quite five o'clock."

"The front door is open."

Reel slipped her gun from its holster. "You take the front, I'll hit the back."

Robie parked the car and they climbed out. Reel immediately darted to her right, went around the detached garage, and flitted to the back of the property.

In his mind's eye, Robie, who knew her so well, could visualize every tactical movement his partner would make on her way to the house.

Robie shifted from cover point to cover point until he reached the front door. Standing to the side, he called out, "Ms. Drango? Agents Robie and Reel. We need to ask you some more questions."

There was no answer, not that Robie was expecting one.

He used his foot to nudge the door fully open. "Ms. Drango, are you in there? If so, please call out and reveal yourself."

No calling out and no revealing.

Again, he wasn't surprised. He was just wondering where they would find the body.

And maybe her killer.

He entered the house and immediately moved to his left and took up cover behind a ragged couch. He peered over the top of the furniture in time to see Reel's face peeking out from the doorway into the kitchen.

"Clear here," said Reel.

"Bedroom," replied Robie.

The door was nudged open and it took all of ten seconds to search the room.

"Clothes gone," said Reel, examining the empty closet as Robie pulled open the empty bureau drawers. "She's run for it. Question is, because she was scared or because she was in on it?"

"We can have the Agency try to track her down," suggested Robie. He got on his phone and relayed the woman's personal information, description, and what vehicle she might be driving.

"Long shot," said Reel, peering around until her gaze was riveted on something on the bureau.

She picked up the pack of cards. "Drango said the night she was expecting to meet Lamarre she was doing some casino work at a birthday party in Denver."

"That's right. Some rich a-hole, she said."

"Roark Lambert lives in Denver. And I guess he qualifies as rich. And he's as capable of being an a-hole as the next person. Maybe she worked the party at his house." She paused. "What do you think?"

"I think it's worth checking out," replied Robie. "But how do we do that?"

"She must work for some company that does stuff like that. We'll need to get the name somehow. Maybe Malloy or Bender would know. Small town where everybody knows everybody else's business."

"So maybe we can find out whether Lambert had a birthday party in Denver recently."

"Well, we can certainly find out when his birthday is."

Robie pulled out his phone and did a search. He read through some screens. "Okay, this is him and they have his bio." He read down the screen. "And his birthday was…five months ago."

"Shit, there goes that theory."

Robie was looking at a pile of papers on the bureau next to where the pack of cards had been.

He started going through them.

After about a minute he held one up. "Colorado Casino Fun and Games. Located in Denver. Looks like a notice they sent out to her. It has the company's phone number."

"Well, what are you waiting for?"

Robie called the number and a person answered on the second ring. "I was trying to locate one of your employees, Beverly Drango," he said.

The woman on the line said, "Beverly's not an employee. She's an independent contractor."

"Oh, sorry. I just arrived here in Colorado and was looking her up. I know she worked a party in Denver about a week ago."

"What's this about?"

"I'm a friend of hers. We grew up together before I left the area.

We were supposed to get together when I came back for a visit. But she didn't show up. Have you heard from her?"

"No. But she's supposed to work a job for us tomorrow night."

"Well, I'm at her house right now and it looks like she's gone. I was worried about her and then found your number with some of her papers."

"Do you think something happened to her?"

"I don't know. I do know that she phoned me recently and said something weird had happened at the party she was working in Denver."

"Weird how?" the woman said sharply.

"That's just the thing. She wouldn't tell me, but she said it had left a bad impression on her mind. Do you have any idea what she might be talking about?"

"No, she never reported anything like that to us."

"Do you know where the party was held? She said it was a birthday party."

The woman said, "It was at a hotel. I can't provide the details of who it was for. That's a client confidence. If you think something has happened to Beverly you should call the police. And I should find a replacement for her for tomorrow night."

"The police will at least want to know which hotel," Robie persisted. "It might be connected to whatever's happened to her."

"I told you that—"

"The name of the person might be confidential, but surely the venue can't be. Not if it's a public place like a hotel. I'm not asking for someone's private address."

He heard the woman sigh. "Okay, it was the Lancaster. It's a new luxury hotel downtown."

"The Lancaster Hotel. Thank you very much."

"I hope Beverly is okay."

"Me too." Robie clicked off and looked at Reel.

She said, "I guess we're going to Denver."

46

THE LANCASTER WAS a ten-story hotel with a granite hide and a long green awning out front, guarded by a liveried doorman in a top hat. Robie and Reel parked in the underground garage and took an elevator to the main lobby.

It was large, and meticulously designed and decorated. The men and women traversing the lobby looked far more affluent than the average citizen.

"I wonder what rooms cost here?" asked Reel.

"More than we can afford on a government per diem, that's for damn sure," replied Robie.

They approached the front desk, where Robie showed his credentials.

The young woman looked like she'd been jolted by electricity. "How can I help you?" she said nervously.

"We understand there was a birthday party here about a week ago, complete with a casino theme?"

"I don't have personal knowledge of that."

Robie pointed at her computer. "Well, maybe that thing does."

"Should I get a manager?"

"Not if you can hit the right keys on the computer. It's a national security interest case," he added.

The woman gulped. "Do you mean terrorists?"

"I can't get into that, but it's really important that we know about this party."

She clicked some keys and said, "Okay, that's right. Eight days ago there was a casino-themed birthday party in the main ballroom."

"Can you tell us who threw the party?" asked Reel.

The woman clicked some more keys. "It appears that a Roark Lambert paid for it."

"But his birthday was five months ago," said Robie.

"I don't know about that. But he clearly paid for the party."

"Do you know the name of the person who the party was for?" asked Reel.

"That's not on this information sheet."

"Is there another way to look it up?" persisted Reel.

"I'm not sure what a birthday party has to do with national security," the woman said suspiciously.

"Do you at least have someone here who worked the party that we can talk to?"

The woman scanned the screen. "I think Jerry, one of the waiters, is in today. He was working the party." She picked up a phone, dialed a number, and spoke into it.

After a few moments she put down the phone and said, "He'll be here in a minute or so."

"Thank you very much," said Robie.

They moved off to a corner of the lobby.

Reel said, "Something is bugging me."

"Like what?"

"Something someone said to us."

"Who?"

"That's what I'm trying to think of."

As a young man dressed in a hotel uniform came out from a back hall and looked around curiously, Reel said, "Got it."

"What?"

She hurried over to the young man. "Are you Jerry?" she asked, as Robie joined her.

He nodded. "This is about some party I worked here?"

Reel said, "Was it a birthday party for someone named Randall?"

"Yeah, that's right. Scott Randall. Some really rich guy. Got a supermodel wife. It was a really wild party."

"Did you see any of the casino folks that were hired to work the party?"

"Yeah. I met a couple of them. A guy named Barry and a woman. I don't really remember her name."

"Beverly Drango?" suggested Reel.

He snapped his fingers. "That's right. She had a name clip with Beverly on it. She worked the craps table."

"Did you see her interact much with Randall? Or the guy who threw the party, Roark Lambert?"

"Not really. It was pretty crazy. Lots of people and I was hustling drinks all night. It was free booze courtesy of the host. And there were a lot of really good-looking women. I think they might have been like, you know, escorts or something that were hired to attend. Some of the guys were getting really looped and copping feels all over the place. But the ladies didn't seem to mind, which is why I think they were paid to be here. And some of the guys left with some of those women and went upstairs. For dessert, I guess," he added with a grin.

"Anything else strike you as out of the ordinary?" asked Robie.

"Not really. Just lots of money, lots of booze, and people having a good time. I remember thinking that there'd be a lot of guys who'd want to be Scott Randall. He's not that much older than me. Money, gorgeous wife. I heard somebody say he played college football. He's a big, strong guy. Good-looking. And somebody said he's got his own jet."

"Makes you feel any better, he inherited it all from his dad."

"Damn, some people have all the luck."

"Yeah, well if I were you, I'd aim higher than Scott Randall," said Reel before walking away.

Barry looked at Robie. "What'd she mean by that? I don't see any private jets or supermodels in my future."

"Are you an asshole?" asked Robie.

"What? No, I mean, no, I'm not. I may not be rich but I'm a nice guy. Ask anybody."

"Then that's what she means by aiming higher."

Robie caught up to Reel at the elevator banks. "How'd you figure Randall in this?" he asked.

"I remembered what Lambert said to us. He told us that Randall had recently turned thirty-eight."

"That's right. But why would Lambert foot the bill for the birthday party?"

"Because Randall had just dropped four million on an apartment in the bunker. I guess the profit margin allowed Lambert to throw the guy a party."

"Never would have occurred to me. Guess that's why I'm not a businessman."

"Guess so."

They rode the elevator down to their truck and drove out of the garage.

Robie said, "So Drango worked a party thrown for Scott Randall and paid for by Roark Lambert. Which rich a-hole was she referring to?"

"Maybe both."

"But how does that help us?"

"It could be a coincidence that Drango worked that party. But if Lambert or Randall was involved with the people in the van, Drango might have overheard something at the party."

"But she said that Lamarre had already told her about the van."

"Right. So if she did hear something suspicious at the party she would have been able to tie it to the van *because* she knew about it."

"That makes sense." He smiled. "You have the makings of a good detective."

She didn't return the smile. "And my *detective* skills are telling me something is off with you and Malloy. And I'd like to know what it is."

Robie's grin faded and he focused on his driving.

47

"You think Blue Man found out about these prisoners in the van and then was taken?"

Robie and Reel were in his hotel room staring at the laptop screen where DCI Rachel Cassidy was staring back at them. She looked tired, her eyes heavy and reddened and her posture reduced to a slouch. Behind her Robie thought he could see a glass with some amber liquid in it.

If this job didn't drive you to drink, no job could, he thought.

"We think it's possible, Director," said Reel. "He was clearly investigating what had happened. And everyone else who was in that line of disclosure from Clément Lamarre has either disappeared or is dead, in the case of Holly Malloy."

"But she was killed by this Dolph person, for unrelated reasons," pointed out Cassidy.

"We're not sure they're unrelated. Dolph said he killed Luke Miller because he was disloyal and was trying to escape the neo-Nazi way of life. Holly was connected to Luke and knew that Dolph had killed him. So she had to die. But he could have been jacking us around. Which means he could also be connected to the prisoners in the van."

"You said you got some sat feedback from the Agency?" said Cassidy.

Robie said, "They hacked into Roark Lambert's satellite. But they could only follow the van's path in the direction of the bunker before the sat turned away. We can't prove that the van went there."

"Where else might it have been going?"

"There's really nothing else out there," remarked Reel. "Just open land. We searched the immediate area and didn't find anything helpful."

Cassidy sighed and sank farther back in her chair. "I don't have to tell either of you that that is not good. We need Blue Man back. We can't discount the possibility—in spite of whatever connection you think there is to the van—that his disappearance is tied to enemies of this country. He has a lot of institutional knowledge and there are ways to get even someone as tough as Blue Man to break."

"We're aware of that, Director," said Reel. "We're doing all we can, and we have some fresh leads and we will follow them up as fast as we can."

"In the interests of full disclosure, there have been noises from the FBI," said Cassidy, the bags under her eyes seeming to swell as she spoke. "They know things are not going well. My counterpart has suggested that perhaps assistance is in order. I do not want to go down that road yet. I'm counting on you two to get this done. Faster than your current pace! Or it will be out of my hands."

The screen went blank.

Robie looked at Reel. "Well, that wasn't particularly helpful."

"She looks like she's about to crack under the strain."

"Cassidy is tough, but she's new to the role and she doesn't want a cock-up in her first few months in the job. Losing Blue Man would be catastrophic. Her detractors will be armchairing that all day long. Why he didn't have security when he came out here, stuff like that."

"Scott Randall," mused Reel. "If he's involved somehow, I would be more than willing to cut his nuts off. After I strangle his wife," she added.

"Lambert threw him the birthday party probably as a thank-you for purchasing a doomsday condo. Beverly Drango worked the party, and then she comes home from it to find Lamarre has disappeared. Coincidence or not?"

"Wait a minute, Robie. That's what she *told* us. She's the only one we have who can vouch for when he disappeared. What if he'd already been taken and she just fed us a lot of shit about the timing?"

"Okay, now I know it's how she earns extra money. But how likely is it she would be working a craps table at a birthday party for Scott Randall paid for by Lambert? Coincidence?"

"Maybe she helped them somehow and her being there wasn't a coincidence. And I can think of one reason why she might want to be in the same room with either or both men if she had helped them somehow."

"To get paid off for whatever it was that she did," said Robie.

Reel nodded. "You wouldn't want any money trail to follow. But if she surreptitiously got paid off in cash while working at a birthday party? Who would be the wiser?"

"But what would she have done for them?"

"Lamarre told her about the van with the prisoners in the back."

"And you think she told Randall or Lambert? But why would she know they might be connected to that?"

"That's the piece I don't know. But she might have put two and two together, somehow. So she contacts one or both and tells them what Lamarre told her. He might have also told her that he had let it slip to Holly in rehab. They could have found out the same thing we did: that Holly called JC Parry and then Blue Man came to visit her. They might assume it had to do with what Lamarre told her."

"That seems to add up," agreed Robie.

"Or it could be all wrong," conceded Reel.

"Well, we figured out what happened in Mississippi with my family. So we can solve this. I mean, in Mississippi and right after, anything seemed possible. Right?"

Reel turned away from the blank screen to find his gaze fully on her.

"I thought we had put this behind us," she said.

"*We've* done nothing. It takes at least two to be a 'we.'"

"What's going on with you and Malloy?"

He blurted out, "I slept with her. Okay?"

There was a long moment of silence as Reel stared at Robie and Robie stared right back at her. It was impossible to tell which one was more surprised by his admission.

"We're on a mission, Robie," she said tersely. "And you just broke a cardinal rule."

"And can you point to anything that I've done or haven't done to prove that I'm not doing my job to the best of my abilities? Because I can point to at least one time where you screwed up and almost got us killed."

She seemed taken aback by this. "I...I don't know what you're talking about."

"You froze. When Dolph's boys were bearing down on us, you froze."

She looked away, her distress evident on her features.

"I know what that's like, Jess. I froze in the middle of a mission too. Right in the middle of a damn shot. I put someone in the crosshairs who was simply not there. He was in my head, but he wasn't in the line of my shot. And I screwed up."

She looked back at him. "You can't compare the two," she said dully.

"I *am* comparing the two," he retorted.

"No, I mean mine was much worse."

Now Robie looked taken aback.

Reel rose and started to head to the door.

"Jess, can you at least tell me what changed between the time we got back from Mississippi and right now? Things...things seemed so...perfect. For the first time in my life. And I thought it was the same for you. I thought that—"

"What? What did you think?"

He glanced up at her. "That I wouldn't have to be alone anymore."

She looked away from him. "That was an illusion, Will. That wasn't real."

"No, Jess, it was. It was real. We were both there for each other."

She shook her head. "Have fun with Malloy. Let's find Blue Man. And then we can get the hell out of here."

"And then what?"

"You go back to being Will Robie. And I go back to being Jessica Reel. Because, at the end of the day, that's all either of us has."

IT WAS MIDNIGHT when the knock on the door came.

Robie was up in an instant, the pistol held loosely in his right hand.

He approached the door of his room and, standing to the side of it, said, "Who is it?"

"Valerie."

Robie silently groaned. "Is something wrong?"

"Can I come in?"

He opened the door, expecting to see her dressed in some sexy number and holding a bottle of gin.

She was still in uniform.

"What's up?" asked Robie, as he stepped aside to allow her to pass into the room. He closed the door and turned to her.

The pistol was pointed at his chest.

"Is there a problem?" Robie said calmly, even as he thought about how he would disarm her.

She pulled a piece of paper from her pocket and handed it across to him.

He reached out for the paper, gripped her wrist instead, spun her around, ripped the gun from her other hand, and deftly pushed her back on the bed.

He slipped the gun into his waistband and held up the paper.

"What the hell are you doing?" he said quietly.

"Read the paper, you bastard. And tell me if it's true or not."

He could see tears sliding down her cheeks. He glanced at the paper, already fairly confident about what would be on it.

He unfolded it and read, *Your sister is dead. Ask the Feds. They were there.*

He folded the paper and put it in his pocket.

Malloy sat up on the bed. "Is it true?"

Robie didn't answer.

She stood. "Is it true?" she said in a louder voice.

Robie still didn't answer.

"So it *is* true," said Malloy, her voice smaller, weaker.

She sat back down on the bed and looked at the floor.

Robie pulled up a chair and sat across from her.

He leaned in and said, "Dolph killed Luke. And he killed your sister. And we were there, as Dolph's prisoners."

"But you escaped. Why didn't you tell anyone? Why didn't you tell *me*?"

Robie sat back. "It wouldn't have changed what happened to Holly. And we're going to get Dolph for this."

"How? He's probably out of the country by now."

"He's not out of the country, although he's lying low. He knows that we have him for murder. But we have eyes on him, Valerie. He's not going to get away."

"What eyes?"

"You have to trust me on that one."

"Trust you! You've done nothing but lie to me."

"I've told you everything I could tell you."

"We slept together, Will. And you screwed me knowing that my sister was dead. Knowing that I was worried about her? You let me believe she was okay."

"That was not how I wanted to handle it, trust me. But it was very complicated. We were caught between a rock and a hard place and we had to make a decision. And maybe we made the wrong one. I'm sorry. I never wanted this to happen."

She gave a hollow laugh. "Oh, great, that makes everything just fine."

"I know you're upset and you have every right to be. But this was the only way we could play this out. Or at least we thought it was."

"Play it out? So my sister being murdered by that dick is just a game to you?"

"None of this is a game. You know that. We've been nearly killed a handful of times since we've been here. Hell, it was safer in Iraq."

She started to say something and then paused. "You were in Iraq?"

"I've been in a lot of places."

She slowly nodded. "How did she die? How did Dolph kill my sister?"

"I can't think of one good reason for you to know the particulars."

"Tell me, Robie. You at least owe me that."

He drew a long breath and said tersely, "Gunshot to the head. She died instantly."

Malloy suddenly turned green. "Oh, God, I'm going to be sick."

He helped her up and half-carried her to the bathroom. He shut the door and heard her vomiting.

He sat back down in the chair and waited, his mind reeling with all that had happened in the last five minutes.

Robie was good at many things.

But I'm not good at this. Lying to people who don't deserve it. Trying to comfort people when I've spent most of my adult life training hard and planning meticulously to take the lives of others.

"Shit," he muttered, putting his face in his hands and rocking back and forth in the chair.

Five minutes later he heard the toilet flush and the sink tap turn on.

He sat up and wiped his face and tried to clear his mind.

A couple minutes after that the door opened and Malloy walked unsteadily out. She sat heavily down on the bed and wouldn't look at him.

"Who sent you the note?" asked Robie.

"I don't know. It was shoved under the door to the station. Why?"

"I'd just like to know."

"I thought Holly and Luke were on their way out of the state," she finally said. "You said you put them on a bus."

"We thought we did too. She had it all planned out. Reel and I were helping them, like we told you."

"Why?"

Robie didn't answer right away. "Everybody deserves a second chance."

She looked up at him. "I think you're telling the truth for once."

"But later we got ambushed again by Dolph's goons. And they had Holly. They used her as a bargaining chip to make us come quietly. They took us to Dolph's compound. There they showed us a picture of Luke, minus his head."

"Omigod."

Malloy looked like she might be sick again.

Robie jumped up, ran into the bathroom, soaked a washcloth in cold water, and brought it out to her. She accepted it without a word and swabbed her face with it.

"And…and then he shot Holly?"

"Yes."

"But why?"

"Luke loved her. Luke was leaving Dolph's group because of her, and the little prick couldn't stand that."

"And then he tried to kill you. But you two got away. Only you never said exactly how. You just said you broke out."

"And that's all I can say on the subject, for now."

"I want to go and find Dolph and put a bullet in his head."

"You'd just be pissing your life away. I told you that we're going to get him, Valerie."

"And so I should just accept that as gospel and sit on my ass and do nothing to avenge my sister?"

"Holly would not want that asshole to get a shot at killing you, too."

"Holly never even liked me. I was the bossy older sister."

"Yeah, she said you were bossy. But if you don't think she cared about you, then you're wrong."

"How would you know?"

"She talked to me about you. She said she was jealous of you. How you wore the uniform and put your life on the line. She never thought she could measure up to that."

"You're just saying that."

"I would have no reason to. She said the problem was hers, not yours. And that you'd been supportive of her even with all her mistakes. And before we parted ways at the bus station, she told me that she knew you loved her and that she loved you. She had every intention of calling you and making amends. I think she knew it was because of you that she had this shot at getting her life back on track."

Malloy was now quietly sobbing into her hands.

Robie rose, went back into the bathroom, and came out with a roll of toilet paper and handed it to her.

She used it to wipe her eyes and blow her nose.

Robie handed her back her weapon.

"I loved her too," said Malloy.

"No doubt about that."

"I can't believe that she's really gone."

"I'm sorry, Valerie, I really am so sorry."

"She was my only sibling. We were never that close growing up. She was super smart and I was the athlete in the family. We traveled in different circles, but I was as proud of her as a sister could be."

"I'm sure. Family is tough. And complicated."

"Do you have family?"

"My dad and a much younger half brother."

"Do you see them much?"

"Not until recently. But I plan to see them more. They're the only family I have."

Malloy let out a long breath. "I can't stay in this place much longer. I feel like I'm suffocating. I need to get back to my family. The family I have left."

"I understand. You should."

"Do you…do you know what they did with her body?"

"No, I don't. I'm sorry. All hell broke loose and we barely got out alive."

She rose and walked over to him.

Robie stood.

"About last night," she began.

"I think we both needed something last night. And we got it."

She slowly nodded. "I think you're right about that." She fell silent for a moment. "And Mr. Walton?"

"We might have a lead."

"Tell me."

"Are you sure? It's not like you don't have enough going on."

"It takes my mind off."

"Beverly Drango was Clément Lamarre's girlfriend."

Robie went on to tell Malloy all that he had learned and suspected about Drango's connection to either or both Lambert and Scott Randall.

She said, "I met Randall once before. This was while Lambert was building out the silo and Scott Randall came into town to meet with him. Private jet, stretch limo. His bitch of a wife wasn't with him, but he was plenty all by himself. I've never met a more self-centered, egotistical creep in my life."

"I've found that guys who inherit like that often have a chip on their shoulder. The man brags too much about how successful he is. Somebody who'd earned it probably wouldn't feel the need. You don't see Warren Buffett telling everybody how brilliant he is at business. His actions speak for him."

"But why would they be involved with prisoners in a van?" wondered Malloy.

"I've got no idea. There may be no connection, but it's still odd that Drango worked a party for Lambert to celebrate Randall's birthday, and her boyfriend is the one who saw the prisoners in the van and told her about it."

"And now you say she's disappeared?"

"Whether against her will or not, we don't know. But her clothes were cleaned out and her car was gone."

Malloy shook her head. "This is getting really muddy."

"In my mind it's been muddy for a long time."

"I better get going. It's late. I'm... I'm sorry I pulled my gun on you."

"If it were me, I would've done the same and maybe more."

She kissed him on the cheek.

He took her hand and said, "Whatever happens, I give you my

word that I will get Dolph. He's going to pay for what he did. You have to trust me on that."

She stroked his cheek. "I do, Will. I do."

He shut the door behind her, fell back on the bed, and closed his eyes.

Part of him wished he were back in London about to walk into a house with seventeen terrorists and a nuke.

It had to be easier than this.

49

"WHO SENT HER the note?"

It was the next morning and Reel stared at Robie across the width of the table in the hotel restaurant. Robie had told Reel about the prior night's encounter with Malloy.

"I don't know. She said someone slipped it under the door to the station."

"Do you think it was Agent Sanders?"

"No. He would never divulge that, because it could torpedo his investigation. And it mentioned that we were there and Valerie should talk to us about it. Again, Sanders wouldn't do that because it could tank what he's trying to do."

"But lots of people were there, Robie. It could be one of Dolph's guys. They could have done it on his orders."

"That's more likely. But why would they want her to know?"

"To turn her against us?"

"Why would that matter to a guy like Dolph?"

"I don't know." She peered at him over her coffee cup. "When did Malloy tell you about this?"

"Late last night. She came to my room."

"Oh, she did? Did you have sex before she told you? Or after?"

There was a long moment of silence as they stared at each other.

When Robie spoke, his tone was stiff. "You think she'd want to have sex with me after finding out I hadn't told her that her sister had been murdered?"

Reel looked away. "I guess that would be pretty screwed up. But then so is everything we're in the middle of here. Screwed up."

"Some of it is our own doing."

"No argument there." Reel put down her cup. "We need to do something."

"What?"

"If I knew that I'd be doing it," she snapped.

"If we can get to Drango things might clear up."

"Might. We need more than that."

"I think she lied to us. She must know something."

"So it could be Lambert and/or Randall and prisoners for some reason," noted Reel.

"But prisoners for what purpose?"

"We answer that, we answer everything."

"Drango could give us that answer," Robie pointed out.

"But she's on the run. We put the info on her out there and got zip. So how do we get any answers from her?" Reel retorted.

In answer Robie made a call. Into the phone he said, "Yes, we spoke yesterday about Beverly Drango? Right. Have you heard from her? Will she be showing up for work tonight?" Robie stiffened and glanced at Reel. "So she will be coming to work tonight. That's great. I'm so relieved. I'd love to surprise her. Could you give me the address and time?"

He clicked off and stared at her. "How does that make sense? Drango clearly was on the run. But she's pulling her gig tonight?"

"Where?"

"Same place. Lancaster Hotel in Denver."

"I guess that's where we'll be tonight, then."

"Guess so."

* * *

Robie and Reel walked into the lobby of the Lancaster at six o'clock that night. The event Drango would be working was posted on a marquee board next to the check-in desk. It said it would start at six thirty. It was a retirement party for someone named Jorge Schindler in the lower-level ballroom.

"She's probably already here doing setup," noted Reel.

"Probably."

"How do you want to do this?"

"With as little fuss as possible. I don't want to drag her out of here, but I will if I have to."

"The stairs to the lower level are over there," said Reel.

They walked down them and hit the main corridor on the lower level. People were rushing around, obviously finishing up last-minute tasks to get the event ready for the guests.

Robie poked his head inside the ballroom and noted the casino set-up. Craps table, blackjack, a roulette wheel, and a row of slot machines.

Robie turned to Reel. "Drango works the craps table."

"You see anyone there?"

"No one who looks like her."

Reel checked her watch. "I see other people dressed up like they're working in a casino."

"Let's ask."

They approached one man who was fiddling with one of the slot machines. He was in his fifties and paunchy with a pinched face.

Robie said, "We're looking for Beverly Drango. We're old friends from out of town. Your office said she was working here tonight."

The man looked irritably at them. "I'm the owner. She *should* be working tonight. She called and said she was on her way. That was two hours ago. But I haven't seen her yet. She was supposed to be here for setup an hour ago. I've called her cell phone five times. Nothing."

"Can you give me her cell phone number?"

The man did so. "If you find her tell her she's persona non grata with me."

He left them to continue prepping for the night's event.

Robie took out his phone and made the call. He gave the Agency person the cell phone number. "We need a fix on her location ASAP. I'll hold."

Two minutes went by and then the voice came back on. Robie listened and said, "Thanks." He clicked off.

"He's sending me her coordinates."

A beep on his phone came and he looked at the screen.

"Shit, she's right nearby. Come on."

Following the map on his phone, Robie and Reel left the hotel and turned left. Robie spotted the alleyway about fifty feet down from the hotel entrance.

"It says she's right down there."

"This isn't looking good, Robie."

She pulled her gun. Robie did the same.

They walked to the alley and turned down it. "This is the right side of the hotel," noted Robie.

They approached the truck parked there. Its back roll-up door was still open. A door to the building was standing open.

Inside the truck was a slot machine. "This must be where they were unloading their stuff for the event," said Reel.

"There are two other cars here, neither of them Drango's."

"Maybe she came in another car," suggested Reel.

"It's possible." He looked at his phone. "The signal from her phone shows it's farther down the alley."

They walked past the truck and the two parked cars after peering into them to make sure they were empty. They continued on until they were very near the end of the alley.

"Robie!" said Reel.

He had already spotted what she had.

The Dumpster against the wall. There was a phone lying in front of it.

Robie raced forward and picked it up. "I'm guessing this is hers. But where is Drango?" He glanced at the Dumpster.

Reel had joined him by then and took a peek inside the Dumpster. She moved aside some trash and took a closer look.

"Well, Beverly Drango won't be working any more casino gigs."

And that was when the bullet hit the Dumpster an inch from her face.

50

ROBIE PUSHED REEL down right before another round struck directly where she had been standing.

They slid along the asphalt, then Robie gained traction with his feet and pulled Reel behind the Dumpster.

"Shot came two clicks to the left," said Robie, as Reel righted herself and peered around the corner of the metal container.

"Thanks for the assist." She paused. "I can't seem to get out of my own way lately."

Robie realized how hard this was for her to admit, but now was not the time to discuss the point with his partner.

"You think they're still out there?" she said.

"If they are, we can take care of that."

He pulled his phone, punched in 911, and reported shots fired and a body in a Dumpster at their location.

Only a minute passed before they heard the sirens.

That was followed by feet rushing away.

"More than one," noted Reel.

"Go, go," urged Robie.

They leapt up and ran down the alley after the sounds of the retreating shooters.

They emerged from the alley and looked around.

"There," said Reel.

A van was accelerating down the street away from them.

"Shit," exclaimed Robie as the van turned a corner and disappeared from sight.

"Move it," said Reel as the sirens grew closer.

They turned in the other direction and were soon back at their SUV.

"License plate on the van?" said Robie.

"It didn't have one. At least on the rear."

Robie started the vehicle and they pulled out onto the street as a police car flashed past to stop next to another cruiser that was parked at the opening of the alley. He turned in the opposite direction and sped up. They were soon on their way out of Denver and back to Grand.

"So there goes Beverly Drango," said Robie. "You sure it was her?"

Reel hiked her eyebrows and Robie said, "Okay. So there goes our last lead."

"Well, somebody keeps killing them," replied Reel.

"And they tried to kill us too. And now I'm thinking this whole thing was a setup."

"They knew we were coming to see Drango tonight. They killed her and waited around to kill us. When we went looking for her and slipped down the alley, it was perfect for them."

"Only they missed," said Robie.

"But they wouldn't have the second time, so I'd be dead but for you," replied Reel slowly, her gaze rigid as she looked out the windshield. "I froze again."

"It happens."

"No, it doesn't. At least not to me. But it keeps happening. To me. And one time you're not going to be there, Robie. Or you will be and I'll be the reason you get killed. I can't let that happen."

"I don't see it that way."

"There's no other way to see it!" she barked.

He slowed the truck and then pulled off the road. He turned to her. "What happened in Iraq?"

"I'm not lying on a couch and you're not my shrink."

"But like you just said, I have a vested interest in you not freezing again, right? Because then maybe I'm dead too."

Reel clearly had no logical response to his words and her subdued expression evidenced this.

She leaned back in her seat. "Keep driving. This might take a while."

Robie pulled back onto the road.

Reel was silent for a few moments as though collecting her thoughts. "Until that night things had been going okay, but then it all went to hell in a minute." She described the events of that night in a detached fashion, but the hollow tone of her words and haunted look evidenced that Jessica Reel was barely keeping it together.

"I was the only survivor. The rest of the team was either blown up, burned up, or lying around without their heads. And I just kept shooting. I used my main gun with incendiary rounds to take out the trucks and the fifty-cals, then my backup gun with the Raufoss round. Found the soft spot on the ASV and that was…that. The SEALs came back for me and…"

As her voice trailed off, Reel looked out the window, where a steady drizzle had commenced.

"I'm sorry, Jess. But you've got to realize that you did everything by the book. Combat is totally indiscriminate. It kills those who are incompetent and those who are unlucky. And everyone in between. You've got survivor's guilt. You know that."

"I know a lot of things, Robie. I know that when we were being chased by Dolph's assholes, my mind flashed back to Iraq and suddenly I couldn't do my job." She shot him a glance. "And you almost died because I didn't do my job."

Robie slowed the truck. "Maybe we're getting too old for this, Jess. I'm seeing people in my crosshairs who aren't even there. I'm freezing up and can't do *my* job."

"You had family issues," she reminded him.

"I don't think it matters what causes it," he replied. "So long as you address it. You helped me face my past in Mississippi. I can help you address your issues. If you'll let me."

She glanced at him, and her eyes were so full of pain and hurt and some things Robe couldn't readily identify that he could hardly believe the person next to him was the indomitable Jessica Reel. The person who had killed more people, survived more hellish situations, overcome more obstacles than anyone alive.

Except possibly for me.

"I don't think you can help me, Robie. But thanks for the offer."

"Is that what you meant by 'It's complicated'?"

She looked away. "I wrote that because it is...complicated."

He attempted a smile. "More complicated than a messed-up kid from Mississippi with daddy issues who was seeing nonexistent people?"

She slowly nodded. "I think so, yeah."

His grin faded. "Can you at least tell me why? I'm a good listener. I'll listen as long as you want me to."

"It won't take long, Robie, to tell you."

"Then tell me."

He seemed to sense the monumental moment that was fast approaching, so Robie pulled off the road again. The only sounds were those of the engine and the wipers flicking off the rain.

He turned to her.

Reel turned to him.

"The problem is...I love you, Will Robie. More than I've loved anyone. And that's why you'll never be able to help me through this."

51

ROBIE SAT ON his bed in the hotel in Grand.

His face was pointed directly at the floor.

And though his feet were firmly planted on the carpet, his thoughts were in another galaxy.

The drizzle had opened up into a hail of rain that pounded the single window in his room. Streaks of lightning popped and faded, as thunder rumbled consistently after each slash of light.

It was good to be indoors on such a night. And yet Robie was oblivious to the unruly elements.

The problem is…I love you, Will Robie. More than I've loved anyone. And that's why you'll never be able to help me through this.

It made no sense. It was a complete contradiction. But Reel had said it with total conviction, and Robie understood that there was nothing he could do to change her mind.

They had driven back in silence, as the weather and their moods had worsened.

She had gone to her room and he to his.

When he felt his hands shaking, Robie stood, went into the bathroom, and ran cold water over his face. When he looked up from the sink he caught his reflection staring back at him in the mirror.

He looked ten years older, he thought, than when he had started the day.

He gripped both sides of the sink and willed himself not to throw up, or pull his gun and go looking for something, someone to kill. Right now, it would have been too easy.

He looked to his left toward Reel's room.

Is she as miserable as I am? But then again, she did say she loved me. More than anyone else.

Robie's momentary flicker of hope was extinguished just as quickly.

He well knew that there was a steely resolve in the woman that even Robie could not match. If she had truly made up her mind, then that was that, whether she loved him or not.

So why am I still screwing around? Forget it. Forget her. I need to move on.

And Robie was going to start that journey right now.

He went downstairs and then outside. He glanced down the street.

Malloy's police cruiser wasn't there. She had probably gone to her house, wherever that was.

He pulled out his phone and called her. She answered on the second ring.

"You want some company?" he asked.

She gave him her address. It was about twenty minutes outside of town, tucked away off some little back road.

That's all there seemed to be out here, he thought.

Back roads.

To nowhere.

Houses tucked away.

In nowhere.

The rain had slackened to a steady drizzle. He had just about reached his truck when Patti Bender appeared out of the darkness. She was dressed in the same odd assortment of work clothes she was wearing when they first met her. And a pistol was in a holster on her hip.

"What are you doing out this late?" he said, stopping with his hand on the truck door.

"I'm too old for curfews, Will," she said with a smile. "You look troubled."

"Story of my life, I guess."

"Any word on Mr. Walton?"

"Nothing. But we have some leads."

"Well, that's better than nothing."

"We went back to the cabin where Walton was staying. Malloy thought she recognized a boot print there. She's going to follow it up."

"She's a good cop, and that's not an easy thing to be out here."

"How about your brother? Is he a good cop?"

"I was surprised, to tell the truth, when he put on the badge. He was a hellion as a teenager. More likely to be arrested than arrest somebody else."

"Maybe he just grew up," said Robie.

She looked at him strangely. "Do boys ever really grow up, Will?"

"I'm not sure I can answer that."

"Where are you off to now, more investigating?"

He looked down. "No, just getting some fresh air."

"Well, we have an abundance of that here. Your partner not going with you?"

"No…she's tired."

"Aren't we all? Well, I won't keep you."

He watched her walk off and then climbed into the truck.

He got there in fifteen minutes, driving at a rate of speed that was above reckless on such an inclement night.

Maybe a part of him was hoping he wouldn't reach the place at all. Too fast around a curve, an animal jumps out of the darkness directly in his path, then it would be over.

He would be over.

He pulled into the driveway of a neat story-and-a-half bungalow painted blue.

The skies opened up again and the rain poured down.

Malloy's police cruiser was under a carport. A potted plant was on the front stoop, the flowers drooping under the barrage of rain.

She was waiting at the front door with a drink in hand. He took it.

And then up the stairs the pair went, undressing each other along the way.

By the time they got to the bedroom, they were both naked.

They hit the mattress hard and Robie used up every last bit of energy he had pleasing her, pleasing someone, letting her rising moans and groans and the prodding of her fingers against his body guide where she wanted him to go.

He increased his intensity of motion to the point where the bed was in peril of collapsing under them. Seeming to sense this, Malloy locked her legs around his torso. Right on cue, he lifted her off the bed and pushed her against the wall.

In his mind Robie sought to drive the both of them right through the drywall and out into the storm, to just let the rain engulf them. Wash everything he was feeling away. Gone.

For good. Never to return.

Climaxing simultaneously, she screamed and ripped at his hair and he cried out as though in pain, though he was feeling the exact opposite.

Totally spent, he carried her back to the bed and collapsed on top of her. Still gasping, she gently stroked the back of his head. Though the room was as cool as the outside, they were both drenched in sweat with their commingled efforts.

He could feel the smacks of her heart against his heaving chest and she could no doubt feel his as well.

Robie felt like he had just run a marathon, every nerve and muscle twitching.

He also somehow sensed that he had not yet finished the race. That he would never reach the finish line.

Robie finally rolled off her and put an arm over his eyes, blocking everything out.

"My God," she whispered breathlessly into his ear. She slipped her leg on top of his stomach and lay curled tight to him. "My God," she said again. "That was intense, Will."

He nodded his head, trying to silently tell her that it was the same for him.

Though he had just finished having sex with a very lovely woman, the only image in Robie's head right now was of another woman.

A woman who had this night, for the first time in her life, told Robie that she loved him. And then in the next breath, she had destroyed that astonishing admission before he even had a chance to react.

Or to tell her that I felt the same way about her.

"What are you thinking, Will?"

Robie blinked, came back to the room he was in, and turned sideways to stare at her.

I'm thinking about the woman I wish were here with me.

Of course he couldn't say that, and he didn't.

Guilt and shame were added to the swell of other emotions he was already feeling.

Guilt, shame, whatever you wanted to call it. The precise name didn't matter. It was all bad.

"Nothing," he said.

He could feel her relaxed body tense just a bit and then that tension was released.

Malloy replied, "You can talk to me, you know."

"I'm fine. It was great. It was beyond great. Thank you. I...Thank you."

His words rang hollow even to him.

He turned away from her and fell asleep on his side.

She lay there for a bit watching the sharp edges of his muscular back before she turned in the opposite direction and eventually fell asleep.

Robie did not slumber long. He woke thirty minutes later. He was dressed, out the door, and back on the road two minutes after that.

He saw the headlights behind him about ten miles outside of Grand. They stayed with him the whole way, never speeding up, although he gave the vehicle several chances to pass him.

When the bullet cracked the rear glass of his truck, he smiled. That was all the confirmation he needed.

God help you, whoever you are.

52

Jᴇssɪᴄᴀ Rᴇᴇʟ ʜᴀᴅ watched from her window as Robie drove off into the night after speaking with Patti Bender.

Part of her wanted to run down the stairs and stop him. Not only because she thought she knew where he was going, but because people had been trying to kill them ever since they had set foot in Grand.

But she had not run down the stairs. She had not tried to stop him.

She had sat like a slug at the window watching him go off.

She had seen him glance toward the sheriff's station, where the police cruiser was not parked. The thoughts in his mind had been easy enough to decipher. As was the identity of the person he had phoned as she again watched from the window.

Valerie Malloy.

She shifted her position and looked across at the bar. It was ten o'clock now and it seemed like the place was just getting going.

And Jessica Reel, ever the woman of action, decided she needed to get going, too. She was tired of sitting here doing nothing.

She gunned up, left the hotel, and walked across the street. She spotted the stretch limo and wondered for a moment if the Randalls were at the bar. It seemed unlikely. She doubted the couple would stoop to drinking beer with the great unwashed.

She entered the bar and took a few moments to look around.

In one corner were a half-dozen Apostles, though she didn't see Dwight Sanders among them.

In another corner were several burly men wearing Confederate caps and do-rags and others with T-shirts that said DON'T TREAD ON ME.

Someone had put money in a jukebox, and a few couples were doing their best drunken moves on the small dance floor set up on the right side of the bar.

Sitting at the bar was the limo driver she had seen out at the bunker. The one who had thanked them for taking the Randalls down a peg. That explained the stretch parked outside.

She walked over to the bar and sat down next to him. He glanced up from his beer and flinched.

"So how are the Randalls?" said Reel.

He smiled and swallowed some of his beer.

"Who gives a shit? He don't even tip. Punk's got more money than God and he can't even slip me a fiver? And she just sits there either checking her phone or fixing her makeup. Oh, and I've been 'instructed' to not make eye contact with her."

"Well, that might be a good thing. You look at Medusa, you get frozen."

He laughed. "Can I buy you a beer?"

"Why not."

He ordered and then held out his hand. "We were never formerly introduced. Tommy Page."

"Jessica Reel," she replied, shaking his hand.

Her beer came and they tapped bottles. Page ran a hand through his thick gray hair.

Reel took a swallow of her beer and said, "So you been driving limos long? Doesn't seem like there would be much demand out here."

He shrugged. "I used to work at an ore plant that went out of business. Then I worked on an assembly line for a car parts company that went under too when Detroit and the Big Three cratered. Then I got a job at a grocery store stocking shelves. Got downsized from there and went to a McDonald's flipping burgers. My paycheck kept shrinking and my back kept getting sorer and sorer. Finally, got old enough for Social Security. I inherited the limo from my old man. He had a funeral home business. I kept it in the garage.

Then when this Uber thing took off, I was like, what the hell. I can put on a suit and drive a fucking car. Did some weddings and proms. And I got some gigs taking people to Denver and back. Parties and crap like that. And I knew Roark Lambert from way back. He hires me to bring his rich clients to the bunker. The pay's okay. And I can't sit around and do nothing. I ain't dead yet. Right?"

"Right," replied Reel, sipping her beer.

He grinned. "You two really shook those assholes up. They were screaming about what they were going to do to you."

"You took them back today? To their jet?"

"Yep. I don't think she liked the bunker much. All she was talking about was jetting off to the Hamptons. That's in New York somewhere, right?"

"Long Island. Very wealthy. On the water. Homes there go for like forty million."

"Are you shitting me? Forty million bucks for something you live in?"

"Yep. And for a lot of those folks it's their second or third home."

"Damn. Might as well be on another planet far as I'm concerned." He paused. "I've worked since I was sixteen with some unemployment here and there. I'm sixty-six now. That's fifty years. One night I added up all the money I've made. Want to know how much?"

"Sure, why not?"

"Nine hundred and fifty thousand dollars. Sounds like a lot. But not over fifty years. Comes out to less than twenty grand a year. Thing is, I know folks who made even less than that. Look, I made shitty choices, I know. Dropped out of high school. But my dad died so I had to help out, you know. Maybe I should have joined the military, learned a trade. Too late now." He gave her a sideways glance. "So you're a Fed from DC?"

"That's right."

"I bet you make good money."

"I guess."

"You look like you could handle yourself in a fight."

"I've been in a few."

"Ever killed anybody?"

She stared at him. "Now, is that a proper question to ask a lady?"

He looked sheepish. "No, sorry. I ain't thinking straight. No offense."

"So was that the first time you'd driven the Randalls out to the bunker? Lambert told us this was the first time they were coming to actually stay there."

"First time for the lady. I've driven Randall around before. And Mrs. Randall had her 'designer' come out and oversee the work. So I took the designer lady out too. She was nice. Nothing like her boss."

"What do you think about the whole luxury bunker thing?"

"Hell, it's their money. If they want to do it, more power to 'em. My take, though, is that if things are so bad they got to run off to some nuke-proof bunker, they're going to be living there the rest of their lives because what happened up top has got to be way past fixing, right?"

"One would think."

Page had raised his hand for another beer when Reel thought of it.

"What do you mean you've driven Randall around before? I thought that was the first time they've been to the bunker."

"It was, at least as far as I know."

"So where else did you take him?"

"Oh, that. Well, he would jet in to another private strip about an hour from here. I'd pick him up and take him to a cabin. Sometimes he'd have some buddies with him."

"Where exactly is the cabin?"

"I got it on the GPS in my limo. Bluff Point Road. It's pretty far as the crow flies."

"What did they fly in to do?"

"Don't know. Not my place to ask. Then a couple days later I'd take 'em back to the jet."

"A couple of days? What could they do in a couple of days?"

"Beats me."

"How many times did you do this?"

"Maybe a half dozen. Maybe more."

"Did they bring anything with them?"

"Some duffels. Maybe they were fishing."

"He didn't strike me as the fishing type."

"Don't know what to tell you."

"These buddies? What were they like?"

He grinned at her. "Hey, now, why the third degree?"

"I'm here trying to find someone. And Randall is an asshole. Wouldn't it be great if I could pin something on him?"

Page's eyes lighted up. "Damn, wouldn't it?"

"So the other guys?"

Page thought about this for a moment. "They weren't like him. I mean he's a big, strong guy but he's soft too. I mean you can just tell. Punch him in the nose and he'll go crying to his momma. These guys, well, they were serious dudes, if you get my drift. They didn't talk much. But I wouldn't want to get on the wrong side of them either. I'm not even sure they were American." He glanced at her again. "Why, you really think Randall is up to something?"

"If he is, I'll be sure to send him your best right after I bust him."

Page lifted his glass. "Amen to that."

Reel walked out.

53

CHICKEN.

As a teenager Robie had played the game on the narrow back roads of coastal Mississippi.

As a man he had played the same game on five continents.

He was about to do it again. But in a slightly different way.

As a teenager he had used a car when playing the game.

As a man he had used mostly guns as his weapon of choice when doing so.

Tonight, he would use both.

As another shot rang out and missed his vehicle completely, Robie looked down at his speedometer. He was clocking seventy. He punched the gas and clicked that quickly up to ninety. Then he was at triple digits.

He checked his rearview.

The car had mirrored his acceleration.

Robie pushed the gas down even more.

One-ten came and went.

The truck had a monster V-8 power plant, but it was not designed to go that fast on slicked roads.

Robie knew this. And he also knew he was going to push it even more.

He clicked up to one-fifteen. There wasn't much room for the speedometer arrow to go farther.

The car behind him did the same. And they were no longer shooting at him. No doubt they were too busy white-knuckling their seats while going this fast in a storm.

Robie made sure his seat belt was secure. He checked the mirror one more time.

Then he crushed the brakes.

Smoke blew out from the rear tires as he laid rubber down the road.

He kept his hands firmly on the wheel. When the truck started to shake and edge to the right, he guided it back to the center with slight maneuvers of the wheel.

He didn't brace himself.

He relaxed.

He looked in the mirror.

The car had gone out of control as it sharply decelerated. It had turned to the left, but its forward momentum was carrying it right toward the truck.

Three…two…one.

Robie smoothly steered the truck to the left, and the out-of-control car flew past him on the right. He could see the panicked faces of the three men inside as it sailed by. And then it rolled twice before coming to rest back on its wheels.

Robie slowed, then stopped and slammed the truck into park. He ripped off the seat belt and came out of the truck charging forward with his pistol aimed directly at the driver. Robie's laser sight was on the man's chest.

The second man was in the passenger seat, and the third in the rear. They all looked knocked out amid a sea of deployed air bags.

As he approached, Robie recognized one of them in the illumination of his truck lights.

He'd seen him at Dolph's compound.

He hoped one of them was still alive. He needed information.

Robie pulled open the driver's door, pushed aside the air bag, and checked the man's pulse.

Dead.

He pulled open the rear door and did the same to the man slumped over there.

He had a pulse.

Robie slapped him in the face. The man groaned. Robie slapped him even harder.

The man's eyes slowly opened.

Robie gripped the man's chin and pointed it upward so he was looking directly at Robie.

"Where is Dolph?" he asked.

The man's head listed to one side. Robie pulled him back up straight.

"Dolph!"

The man shook his head.

In the front passenger seat the man there stirred and caught sight of Robie in the rearview. His hand slowly went down to his gun.

"Dolph!" said Robie again.

"I…I don't…"

Robie shook the other man. "Where is Dolph?"

"Bu-bunk…"

"In the bunker? In Lambert's bunker?"

"G-God, I'm h-hurting s-so bad."

"Answer my question and I'll end your pain right here and now."

The man didn't answer and Robie shook him again.

The man in the front seat edged his pistol over the vinyl and fired.

The round hit the other man in the forehead.

Without missing a beat Robie pointed his gun to the side and peeled off a shot, hitting the shooter in the hand. He screamed and dropped his gun.

Robie let go of the dead man and pointed his gun at his colleague, who was whimpering in the front seat while holding his wounded hand. Robie placed the muzzle of his pistol against the man's left temple.

"You got three seconds to tell me where Dolph is."

"Fuck you!"

"Two seconds."

"I don't know."

"One second."

The man screamed, "The silo! He's in the damn silo."

"Lambert's?"

The man's hand flew to his fallen gun.

Robie fired before he could even pick it up.

He looked around the car's interior. Three fewer hate-filled assholes in the world. Nothing wrong with that.

But Dolph in the bunker? What was that about? Did that mean that Roark Lambert was somehow working with Dolph? That didn't make sense, at least with what Robie knew about Lambert. But the fact was, he didn't know that much about the man.

He walked back to his truck and pulled out his phone.

She answered on the third ring.

It was Malloy.

"I thought you were still here," she said groggily.

In clipped sentences he said what he needed to say.

He could envision her sitting up naked in bed and struggling to come to grips with what he had just said: shots, a chase, three men dead.

He had not told her what the man had said about the silo. Right now he didn't trust anybody in this damn place.

"Are...are you serious?" she stammered.

"Serious as shit. You want to get out here, or you want to call in Bender?"

"I'm getting dressed. And I'm calling him. You stay right there."

"No, I've got places to go."

He clicked off before she had a chance to respond.

He set out flares so no one coming along here would slam into the car, which was still partially on the road.

He climbed back into his truck and drove off in the direction of the silo.

CHAPTER

54

REEL HAD HOT-WIRED the old limo's engine and was now twenty minutes outside of town. Tommy Page would surely be pissed when he got outside only to find his ride gone, but she figured he was probably too drunk to drive anyway.

His portable GPS was on a carrier suction-cupped to the dashboard. She had punched "previous destinations" and the address for the cabin on Bluff Point Road had popped up. She'd clicked on it, and the device was telling her she had about another twenty minutes of driving to get to it.

The rain had picked up again as she drove along. The sky was so overcast that not a single star was visible. The land was flat for as far as her headlights would show. If there had been sand outside instead of dirt, Reel could have believed she was in the Middle East.

Right now she didn't know which was more dangerous, Iraq or eastern Colorado.

Next, her thoughts, despite her best efforts, turned to Robie.

She was sure that he had gone off to see Malloy tonight. And Reel also was certain that she had driven him to do that. In fact, her words had practically demanded that he do so.

And why had she said to him what she had?

Part of her didn't know.

Part of her thought she did, but the confidence level was ebbing.

She blinked, and with a swipe of the windshield wipers her mind also skipped to another train of thought. She was entering Robie's apartment while he was gone and placing the note on his bed. She had gotten a week's leave from the Middle East deployment. And she had flown directly back to the United States mainly to do what she had, after confirming that Robie was out of the country on assignment.

Essentially, fearless Jessica Reel didn't have the courage to face the man over it.

But it had been six months since Mississippi, and she had returned none of his calls, none of his texts or e-mails. She had purposely avoided him at every turn, until he had simply given up.

She had volunteered for the most dangerous duty she could think of, and it had very nearly ended up killing her.

And for what reason?

What was the end game here?

You were always supposed to have one. You never started a mission without a concrete goal firmly in mind.

But Will Robie and I are not like a mission. We're not even close to it. We're something "else" that maybe neither one of us is prepared for.

Which was why she had written the note that she had.

It's complicated.

No shit.

So she had taken sniping in Iraq over trying to find common ground with the only man she had ever felt anything for.

Sniping was easy. Sniping was something she knew how to do, excelled at. She feared nothing when she was behind the scope and trigger.

But this other stuff?

I'm clueless. And it scares the hell out of me.

With another whisk of the wipers, her mind returned to where she was going tonight. The minutes ticked by and she finally saw the bent signpost for Bluff Point Road.

She turned down the road, after cutting her lights.

According to Page, the Randalls had flown out to their Hampton digs. But that didn't mean that the other guys with him on these "other" trips weren't still in residence.

She passed four dark and what appeared to be empty structures.

The cabin was up ahead. She came to a rolling stop and looked over the place. It was dark, but that meant nothing. It was late and those inside might be asleep.

She got out, made sure she had a round chambered, and checked her ankle holster for her backup.

A Ka-Bar knife rode in a sheath on her right hip.

Serious dudes was how Page had described Randall's companions. She wondered what serious dudes were doing around here with the rich, spoiled brat. She didn't think *fishing* was foremost on their to-do list. So what then?

They had found no connection between Randall and the prisoners in a van. But she didn't know they weren't connected, either. And she had to believe that if they found out the truth behind the prisoners, they would find out what had happened to Blue Man.

She moved forward, keeping low and staying in one place only long enough to check for any signs of activity from within the cabin.

Ignoring the front door, she went around to the back. There were no vehicles parked at the place, but that could also mean nothing.

She reached the back door, and after listening for a bit she took out two slender instruments and efficiently picked the lock.

The door didn't squeak as she opened it, for which Reel was immensely grateful. She stepped inside and quietly closed the door behind her.

Reel looked around the room and nothing jumped out at her, figuratively or literally.

She searched the rooms on the first floor. There was a half floor above reached by a set of stairs. The place was pretty rustic, and Reel couldn't see rich boy Randall spending much time here. And she doubted that his wife knew anything about it, or if she did, she would never choose to set one foot inside a place that was about as far away from the Hamptons as one could get.

But according to Page, Randall came here often, and he must have a reason for doing so. The fact that he chose this place over his luxury doomsday bunker was puzzling. Reel assumed there must also be a good reason for that. And also a compelling purpose for needing the serious dudes along for the ride.

In an upstairs closet Reel finally discovered some things, although she couldn't make sense of any of the items.

A pair of work boots covered in dirt and grime and smelling of chemicals.

An old map of an area she didn't recognize, though it could have been somewhere in eastern Colorado.

A box of ammo. Forty-five-caliber ACPs.

But with one important difference.

Reel slid one of the cartridges out and looked at it. Her mouth dropped open in surprise.

They're blanks.

CHAPTER

55

Robie slowed the truck about two hundred yards from the bunker's outer perimeter fence.

He pulled off the road and parked behind a copse of trees, cut the engine, grabbed a pair of night optics from the duffel in the rear, and climbed out. He squatted on his haunches and surveyed the flat ground in front of him.

The dying guy had said *the silo*.

Were the prisoners in there somewhere?

But how could that be? Why would Roark Lambert have led them on a tour of a place that held people against their will?

Yet as Reel had pointed out, surely they had not seen every inch of the bunker. And for all Robie knew there were secret compartments in there that none of the other owners might know about. In fact, they were almost never here. And the prisoners could easily be gotten out of the way when owners showed up. So prisoners could be kept in there and no one would know about it.

Robie, however, had no way to get in. The bunker was closely guarded, and even if he managed to somehow evade all the security, he had no way to defeat the blast door.

But he would watch the place tonight and see if anyone went in or out, including a white van with prisoners in the back.

An hour passed and he had a thought after mulling over another question of his.

He took out his phone and texted a message to the number that Dwight Sanders had left them.

Ten minutes passed and then the answer dropped into his in-box.

Others have left Dolph. I don't think he cares. There will always be others.

That answer was puzzling.

The sole reason that Dolph had given for his going after Luke and Holly was that Luke was planning to leave the skinheads and Dolph blamed Holly's influence on that. But according to Sanders, other followers had left Dolph and the man had done nothing.

There could be only one answer to that, Robie knew.

Dolph had gone after and killed Luke and Holly because he knew that Holly was aware of the prisoners in the van. And Dolph had to assume that Holly had told Luke about it.

So they had to be killed.

Robie stiffened and sank deeper into the shadows as a car passed by on the road heading to the bunker.

As it passed by he saw that it was not a white van.

It was Roark Lambert in a Range Rover.

Through his optics Robie watched the vehicle pull up to the gate. His window came down, and Robie assumed he was speaking into the voice box as he had done on their previous trip to the bunker. The gate opened and he pulled through. After a bit, Robie lost sight of the Rover.

He looked at his watch. A bit late to be heading to the bunker. But then again, he was staying overnight, so it made sense that he would sleep at the bunker.

More time passed and no other car came down the road. At first, Robie had thought that Lambert might be meeting someone here, but that apparently wasn't the case.

Robie waited a bit more, then climbed into his truck and headed back to town.

His phone buzzed along the way.

It was Malloy.

"Well, you left a shit storm behind," she said.

"Sorry, but they brought it on themselves."

"They are with Dolph's group. Even without the uniforms, I recognized two of them."

"Right."

"Where are you now?"

"Heading back to town."

"Heading back from where?"

"Someplace."

He heard her sigh.

She said, "You have no problem coming to my home tonight and having sex with me, but you still can't give me straight answers? How messed up is that?"

"One is completely different from the other. I wall them off."

"Well, thanks for walling me off right now. But I need you to meet me at the police station and give a statement. If you don't," she added quickly, "I'll have no choice but to get an arrest warrant issued. You *did* leave the scene of a crime. And I only have your word for it that these guys attacked you."

"I've got rounds from their guns embedded in my truck."

"Great, I look forward to seeing it."

"Where's Bender?"

"Processing the scene. I didn't mention your involvement to him."

"Why not?"

"I wanted to talk to you first."

"Okay."

"Robie, just so we're clear, I need you to meet me at the station in one hour."

"I can make that."

He heard her let out another sigh, this time perhaps one of relief at his acquiescence to her request. "Great. Do you have any idea why they came after you?"

"Because they wanted to do me harm."

"Yeah, that one I already figured out on my own. I mean why tonight in particular?"

"I don't know, Valerie. I really don't. Unless it was for revenge because of what we did to Dolph."

"I guess that would be a good motive. I'll see you at the station in one hour."

He clicked off and kept driving.

Nearly fifty minutes later he arrived at the police station. Malloy's car was parked out front.

He went inside, preparing in his head what his "statement" might consist of.

The overturned chair got his attention first.

Then the smashed glass on the floor.

And some blood on the floor by her desk.

He pulled his gun and quickly searched the space.

He reached the rear of the building and saw the door standing open.

Outside, he saw tire tracks.

Malloy was gone.

And it clearly wasn't voluntary.

56

REEL PULLED THE stretch limo back in front of the bar and, despite the late hour, noted that things were still going strong inside the place.

She had taken photos of the map and the ammo box and had used a cloth she found in the cabin to take samples of the dirt and other grime from the boots. If they could get it analyzed, it might provide an answer as to where the boots had been.

She climbed out of the limo and walked over to the bar and peered through the front window.

Tommy Page was still at the bar and he was still sipping on a beer. How many he had drunk since she had left and taken his car, she didn't know. And really didn't care.

She looked around the space and saw that some of the Apostles were still there. As were some of the burly guys wearing Confederate caps. The same couples were on the dance floor doing the same moves.

But there were others there now who hadn't been there before.

Claire and Patti Bender were sitting at a table off to the side. Claire was dressed elegantly if simply in black slacks, a white blouse, and high heels. Her daughter had on cammie pants, an Army green T-shirt, and work boots.

Somewhat in keeping with their dress, Claire was sipping on a glass of white wine while Patti had her fingers curled around the neck of a beer.

Reel walked over to them. "Having a nightcap?" she asked.

Claire smiled up at her. "Actually, we're just getting started. Care to join? Women out here are outnumbered and I haven't had a real girls' night out in ages."

Reel sat and ordered a beer. When it arrived she took a swig and studied the other two women. They could not have been more dissimilar in appearance.

She set the bottle down and looked around. "Place is hopping."

"What else is out here?" said Patti. "You want another drinking hole you have to drive a long way. Might as well go to Denver."

"How's your investigation coming?" asked Claire, her features turning serious.

"It's a puzzler," admitted Reel. "I'm not sure we're much further along than when we started."

"Did you speak to the skinheads?" asked Claire. "They're disgusting people. If anyone had something to do with Roger's disappearance I have to believe it was them."

"We did interact with them," said Reel slowly. "And I agree that they could have had something to do with whatever happened. Apparently, Dolph has gone underground."

"If you mean underground as in dead, that would be wonderful news," said Claire.

Patti cracked a smile at this.

Reel said, "I wish I could tell you that was so, but what I meant was he's lying low."

Claire took another sip of wine and eyed her appraisingly. "Is that because of your *interaction*?"

"Can neither confirm nor deny," said Reel, but a smile played over her lips.

"Well, then I hope you get to interact with him again soon," said Claire.

"Where's Will?" asked Patti. "I saw him driving off tonight."

"He was running down some things," Reel replied quickly.

"Really? He told me was just getting some fresh air."

"He keeps things close to the vest."

"I guess you have to," noted Claire.

"So how's the medical marijuana business?" said Reel.

Claire lifted her glass. "Better than ever. I'm trying to get my daughter here to join the cause. Lead it into the future. But she wants to keep playing tomboy."

"I'm not cut out to sit behind a desk," said Patti. "And are you surprised? Look where I grew up. In the great outdoors. I never even went to college."

"You could have," said Claire pointedly. She looked at Reel. "In high school she was a straight-A student. National Honor Society and everything. One of her teachers said he'd never seen a more talented student." She looked back at her daughter. "You could have been a great scientist or something. Or a writer."

"College wasn't my thing."

Claire said, "Okay, but you don't have to have a sheepskin to run a business. Look at Bill Gates. He dropped out of Harvard. I've built up a great company. Your brother has no interest in it. I'd like at least one of you to take it over."

Patti glanced at Reel. "Mom rarely accepts defeat in any argument."

"I wasn't aware that we were arguing," said Claire, her tone turning a bit icy.

"Actually, we're not, since my decision has already been made. And I wouldn't call it being a tomboy. I just like my guns, the country, and being my own boss. And I'm not that much into weed, really."

Claire smiled, but it didn't reach her eyes. "Well, you can't blame a mother for trying."

They both fell silent. Reel finally said, "Do either of you know Scott Randall?"

Claire looked at her curiously. "He bought one of Roark's places in the bunker, right? Roark mentioned him to me before."

"He's the one whose daddy left him a ton of money and he runs around with that bitch of a wife," observed Patti.

Reel looked at her. "How do you know that?"

"They came into town a while back. I think when they were first purchasing the unit. They came into the bar. You could tell that he thought he was the cock of the walk and he just wanted to show off his wife. She wiped the chair before she sat down and refused to drink anything here. She thought it was all cheap shit."

"Well, I ran into the lady too, and I have to agree with your assessment," said Reel.

"Why do you ask about Randall?" said Claire.

"I found out that he comes back here from time to time, but he doesn't go to the silo. He stays in a cabin a ways from here. And he goes there with folks who have been described to me as serious dudes." She looked at both of them. "You two know anything about any of that?"

Claire shook her head. "I have no idea. Unless he was hunting or fishing."

Reel focused on Patti. "How about you? You get around, see things. Maybe Randall without his wife?"

Patti shrugged. "Yeah. I saw Randall around here a few times. I didn't see these other people you're talking about."

"What was he doing when you saw him?" asked Claire curiously.

"One time he was driving. Another time he was walking."

"Was he armed?" asked Reel.

"Not that I could see."

"Where was he walking?"

"Bluff Point Road. Around there."

"That's where his cabin is."

"Didn't know that," said Patti.

"You think that Roger is dead, don't you?" Claire asked Reel abruptly.

They both looked at her.

"Why do you ask that?" said Reel.

"Because I'm not stupid. I know that when someone goes missing this long and it wasn't voluntary that chances are not good that they're still alive."

"We're working on the assumption that he is still alive. He's a resourceful person, more so than the average person."

"I'm well aware of Roger's capabilities," Claire said bluntly. "But I also know that the fact that he is still missing and has not communicated with you does not bode well for his safe return."

"I'm not going to give you false hope, Claire. Things do not look good. But I'm doing my job and I'm going to keep doing my job until we find him."

"Dead or alive?" she replied.

"We're going to find him," Reel said again.

Claire finished her wine. "Good, because I've been thinking about what you said about regrets. Maybe Roger and I should have another go at it."

Patti set her beer down. "What, you're going to get married?"

"I didn't say that. But what if we did? I'm not getting any younger and neither is he."

"You're assuming that he wants to," said Patti.

"We've had talks," answered her mother. "I'm not sure we're all that far off in our opinion of the future we might have. Together."

"Well, this is the first I've heard of it," exclaimed Patti.

"I haven't really talked about it," replied Claire.

Patti was about to say something in return when the door to the bar opened and there stood Robie.

He saw them and hustled over to their table.

"What's up?" asked Reel coldly, no doubt thinking of where he had just come from.

"We've got a big problem," answered Robie.

57

Reel couldn't take her eyes off the bloodstain.

Valerie Malloy's blood presumably.

Robie stood to her right, staring at the same spot on the floor.

Derrick Bender was on her left. He was on the phone talking to the state police.

He clicked off and looked at them. His face was weary and when he spoke, his voice was scratchy.

"They're putting out BOLOs, and they're sending in a forensics team to go over this place." He looked around. "I can't believe it. Who the hell would have done this? She's the sheriff."

"Do we know her movements?" asked Reel. She was looking at Robie.

"She called me tonight. She wanted to meet."

"About what?"

"About my run-in with some of Dolph's guys."

"What!" exclaimed Bender. "I was out there processing the scene."

Robie took a couple minutes to explain what had happened.

Bender said, "She didn't tell me you were involved in that. What were you doing out there at that time of night?"

"Just driving," answered Robie, still staring at the blood. "Before he died one of the guys said something about the silo. I had asked him where Dolph was and he said in the bunker. I called Malloy and told her about all this. She came to investigate."

"So you saw her then?" said Bender.

"No, before she got there I went over to the bunker to check things out, see what I could see. Malloy called me while I was there and asked me to meet her here. I did, only she wasn't here."

"Did she call you from here?" asked Reel.

"No, she was on her way back. I was about another fifty minutes out, so that's the time window we're dealing with for when she was taken."

"So you didn't see Malloy at all tonight then?"

This came from Reel.

He looked up from the blood. "No," he said curtly.

She looked at Bender. "When will the state cops be here?"

"It's going to take them about two hours."

"Great. Based on what the dead guy said, can we get a warrant for the bunker?"

Bender said, "I don't know. I'll have to make some calls. But it'll have to wait until the morning. The closest judge is a hundred miles away."

"Great again," said an exasperated Reel. "I'm sure if Dolph is at the bunker he'll just stay right there until we execute the warrant and come and get him."

"Lambert could get us in there," noted Robie. "He's there right now. I saw him drive into the bunker while I had it under surveillance."

"And if he is housing Dolph there why would he do that?" countered Reel.

"Maybe he knows nothing about it."

"And maybe I'm a Martian," snapped Reel.

"It might be worth a shot. Otherwise, we're not getting in there anytime soon."

Reel shook her head stubbornly. "But if he lets us in that either means he's not in on it, or he'll have Dolph hidden away from us somewhere in there. And if he's *not* in on it there has to be someone on the inside who is, otherwise Dolph would never have gotten in there. Maybe it's one or more of the guards. And they'll alert Dolph that we're coming."

Robie leaned on Malloy's desk and rubbed his temples. "So what do we do?"

Bender said, "Why would they have targeted the sheriff?"

"Because she's been helping us investigate this case," said Reel.

"Right, but she's been doing that for a while."

"So you're saying something might have changed?" said Robie.

"It's possible. I mean they came for her right here. They attacked her judging by the bloodstain and the knocked-over furniture. I'm surprised no one heard anything."

"Everybody in town at this hour is at the bar," Reel pointed out. "And there was so much noise in there you could barely hear yourself, much less something down here."

"Maybe she saw something out where the guys died," said Bender. "That's why she wanted to meet with you."

"She said she just wanted my statement," replied Robie.

"She might not have wanted to mention it over the phone," persisted Bender.

"You were out there, too," said Reel. "Did you see anything? Or did she say anything to you that might explain what happened to her?"

"No, nothing. It was pretty straightforward. A wrecked car and three dead guys. One from the trauma from the crash and two from gunshot wounds."

"How would whoever took her have found out about something she had discovered?" asked Robie.

"Maybe she let it slip to someone she shouldn't have," said Reel. "We might check her phone log to see who else she might have talked to tonight."

Bender said, "We got ways to check that."

He walked into another room and they heard him clicking away on a computer.

"There's something else," Robie said to Reel in a low voice so Bender couldn't possibly overhear. "I spoke with Dwight Sanders. He told me that other skinheads have dropped out on Dolph and he never went after them."

"So why target Holly and Luke?"

"Because Holly knew about the prisoners, and they must have assumed she told Luke about it. That's why they were trying to kill them, not because Luke was leaving. It was because of what Holly knew. And that follows the same pattern as the others. Everyone in the loop on the prisoners has disappeared."

Reel drew closer to him. "You lied to Bender."

He stared at her impassively. "How so?"

"You *saw* Malloy tonight."

"And how do you know that?"

"I watched you drive off after you spoke with Patti Bender."

"I went for a drive."

She looked at him curiously for a long moment and then glanced away.

"I took a drive too," said Reel.

He said sharply, "Where?"

She told him what she had discovered from the limo driver and her trip out to Bluff Point Road.

She pulled out the cloth that she had used to collect the stains from the boots back at Randall's cabin, and showed him the pictures on her phone.

"Blank forty-five rounds, a map, and dirty work boots," said Robie.

He eyed the picture of the map. "Any idea where that is?"

"No. But I was going to compare it to a larger map of the area to see if that would tell us anything."

Robie sniffed the rag. "I smell oil...and some other chemical. Not sure what."

"Why blank rounds?" asked Reel.

"I can't think of a reason why someone out here would want ammo that can't hit anything. Most folks are gunned up all the time."

"But it has to mean something," said Reel. "A map and dirty boots and blank rounds at a cabin used by Randall and his cronies."

"Lambert never mentioned that Randall came here other than for the bunker."

"Well, his wife clearly would prefer not to come here even for the bunker."

"If doomsday comes, something tells me she'll be first in line to get in."

"But Randall is up to something."

"And maybe the Agency can help us with that," said Robie.

He pulled out his phone and made the call, speaking for a couple of minutes. When he clicked off he said, "They're going over Randall's past with a fine-tooth comb and will get back to us."

"In the meantime we've got a long list of missing persons."

"We do. But something tells me they all went to the same place."

"Lambert's bunker?"

"The dying guy said Dolph was there. He didn't mention any others. But for me it's the most obvious place."

"If that's the case Lambert has to be in on it. And all the guards would have to be in on it too."

"Agreed."

"So what now?"

"I don't see anything for us to do right now other than catch some sleep."

Robie called out to Bender that they would be at the hotel.

As they walked out, Reel said, "Are you and Malloy...?"

"No, we're not. But I still want to find her."

"I want that too," said Reel. "Very much."

He glanced at her. "Why?"

"If you have to ask, you wouldn't understand."

She walked ahead of him out into the night. Robie slowly followed.

58

WHEN ROBIE CAME downstairs the next morning Bender was waiting for him in the lobby.

"Any news?" Robie asked.

"The BOLO produced nothing. The state police team came and went over the crime scene. It's human blood. But they didn't find much else."

Bender drew a step closer to Robie. "Now I have to ask you something."

Reel came down the stairs at just that moment.

"Ask away," said Robie.

"I checked her phone records. We saw the call you made to her after your run-in with Dolph's guys. And we saw the call she made to you presumably about coming to meet her at the station. But you made an earlier call to her."

"I did," said Robie.

"What was it about?"

"It was about me going over to see her, which I did."

"You went to her home?"

Reel joined them at this point.

"Yes, I went to her home."

"Why?" demanded Bender.

"I wanted to see her. It was personal. Nothing to do with the investigation."

"And you just forgot to mention that last night? In fact, you lied to me because you said you hadn't seen her. That's a crime right there."

Robie shrugged. "Like I said, it had nothing to do with the investigation."

"So you say," shot back Bender.

"What, do you really think I had something to do with her disappearance?"

"Hell, now I know you were the last one to see her," Bender snapped.

"Other than the people who took her. And if I did anything to her, why would I have called you in? I almost got killed last night by Dolph's clowns. Why not go talk to the ones who are still alive?"

"I don't have to. They already came to me."

"Excuse me?" said Robie.

"They came to me and said that you attacked their guys and murdered them."

"They attacked me and I defended myself. It's not my fault they don't know how to drive."

"I examined the bodies. Like I told you last night, two of them had been shot."

"I shot one of them."

"Are you confessing to murdering the guy?"

"Self-defense. And the other guy was shot by his buddy."

"Why would he do that?"

Robie shrugged. "Maybe he didn't like him,"

"You never should have left the scene."

"I had somewhere to go. The bunker. I already told you that."

"And Valerie conveniently goes missing."

Robie took a step forward. "You don't want to go there, Bender. You really *don't*."

Bender put his hand on his sidearm.

Robie moved so quickly Bender had no time to react. His left hand had gripped Bender's and his right hand held a knife an inch from Bender's throat.

"Don't be stupid, Bender, you're out of your league."

Reel stepped between them and pushed them away from each other.

"Don't be idiots," she barked. She looked at Robie. "Put the knife away and just shut up for a minute."

She turned to Bender, who looked shaken by Robie's actions. She said, "We need to go over to the station and we need to tell you something about Dolph."

"Reel!" began Robie.

She shot him a scathing look. "What part of 'shut up' don't you get? Now let's go!"

She marched out.

Bender and Robie glared at each other and then followed her out.

* * *

At the sheriff's station Reel faced off with both of them.

"Holly Malloy and her boyfriend, Luke, are dead. Dolph had Luke killed and he shot Holly in front of us." She glanced at Robie. "And Valerie knew."

Bender grabbed the side of the desk to steady himself. "Wh- what?"

"They're dead. Murdered."

"But you said you were there. With Dolph!"

"He kidnapped us. He was going to kill us. But we escaped. But before we did, he murdered Holly."

Bender's face flushed crimson. "Then why the hell didn't you go back there and arrest his ass! You're fucking Feds."

"It's more complicated than that," said Reel. "Besides we had no proof other than our word. And we're here on assignment. We can't get mixed up in that."

Now Bender turned his fury on her. "*Mixed up?* People were murdered!"

Reel said, "And they're going to pay for what they did, Bender. I promise you that."

"How? How the hell can I believe you?"

"We're not walking away from this. He tried to kill us, too. If you knew what we really are, you'd understand that nobody does that to us and gets away with it."

"Wait a minute, you said, *what* we are. What does that mean?"

"It means we go into a situation and we make it right. And if bad guys get in the way, it never ends well for them. We've already taken out a slew of Dolph's guys. I mean taken out in a way that means they are no longer breathing. And I'm not just talking about the guys last night."

Bender looked over at Robie, who nodded and said, "That was the reason he came after us. We were helping Holly and Luke to get out of here, and we killed a bunch of his men."

Reel added, "So we're going to finish the job, Bender. I promise. But what we told you about Holly and Luke you can't tell anyone else."

"I'm a cop! You just told me about two murders."

"And if you tell anyone else it could very well mean that Dolph and his people will never be punished for what they did."

Bender sat back on the desk and slowly took all this in. "There has to be another way. All my cop instincts are telling me to go get this asshole right now."

"So are mine, but sometimes your instincts are wrong," said Robie. "We've thought this through every way you can. And this is the only way, Bender. Otherwise, Dolph wins."

Bender gave a resigned sigh. "Okay, okay," he finally said. "So what do we do right now?"

Robie said, "I have to think that Valerie was taken by Dolph and others who are working with him. One of Dolph's guys said that he was at the bunker. We think maybe these prisoners might be there too. And Parry, Lamarre, and Walton."

"But why at the bunker?" asked Bender. "What does that have to do with prisoners and missing people?"

"I don't know. But if you were going to stash people somewhere, that would be a good place to do it."

"But didn't Roark Lambert take you on a tour of the place?"

Reel said, "He just showed us a slice. That place is so big, there could be a lot of people in there and we'd never know it."

"But I know some of the guards out there. They're good guys. They'd never be party to shit like that. And they'd have to know, wouldn't they?"

"Not necessarily, at least not all of them," replied Robie.

"But why?" asked Bender. "It's a survival bunker for rich people. Why would they take people prisoner? I remember Lambert telling me at my mom's dinner that there was barely enough room and food in there for the people who pay millions for the space."

Reel said, "That may be true, but it might be that these prisoners won't be there when doomsday comes. But they might be there now for a completely different reason."

"Like what?" asked Bender.

"Right now I have no idea," admitted Reel. "But if we don't figure it out fast, we might never see any of the missing people again." She stared at Robie. "Including Roger Walton." She looked at Bender. "And Valerie Malloy."

59

"I'M NOT USED to this, Robie."

It was the next day and Reel was by the window of her hotel room looking out while Robie sat in a chair staring at the floor.

"Not used to what?"

She turned to him as he looked up. "Being helpless. I hate it."

He shrugged. "I'm not too fond of it myself, so I took a snapshot of the map and sent it to the Agency. They might be able to get us something on that."

Someone knocked on the door. Reel crossed the room and looked through the peephole.

She opened the door to reveal Claire Bender standing there.

She was dressed casually in jeans and a light blue sweater. Her long silver hair was tied back.

"I heard about Valerie," she said, stepping into the room.

Reel shut the door behind her as Robie rose from his chair.

"Has there been any word?" Claire asked.

"Nothing so far. There were signs of a struggle at the station and some blood."

Claire turned a bit pale, and Robie helped her sit down in the chair.

She gasped. "I can't believe what's happening here. A little over a week ago everything was as right as rain. And now?"

"Have you spoken to your son?" asked Reel.

She nodded. "Derrick was the one who told me about Valerie. He's very worried. I don't think I've ever seen him like this."

"Was that all he told you?" asked Robie, his gaze fixed on her.

She looked up at him. "Isn't that enough?"

"I suppose it is," agreed Robie, who shot a quick glance at Reel.

"But while we're discussing communications, I have to admit that I didn't tell you everything," Claire said slowly. "It's the reason I came by."

Both Robie and Reel tensed. "Meaning what?" asked Robie.

"Meaning that Roger and I were a bit closer than I led you to believe."

Reel said, "You were engaged to be married. That's pretty close."

Claire pulled a tissue and dabbed at her eyes. "Roger came back here after he finished graduate school. We were both still in our twenties, with our lives ahead of us. He wanted to make a go of it again, I mean with us as a couple. He wanted me to move with him to Washington. I loved Roger, but I just couldn't bring myself to do that." She paused, and glanced at each of them in turn. "But we parted on a very amicable note."

"How so?" asked Reel, studying the woman's features.

Claire let out a breath. "I've never really talked about this before, but what the hell. I ended up pregnant."

"Are you saying that Patti—" began Robie.

Claire nodded. "She's Roger's daughter, yes."

"Does he know?" asked Reel.

Claire shook her head. "The next time Roger came back here I was married. I got walked down the aisle about six months after Roger left that last time. Patti was four years old but he didn't know her exact age. So he had no way of knowing that Patti was not the product of my first marriage. And I never told him. I . . . I just didn't see the point."

"How many times have you been married?" asked Robie.

"Three. Roy Bender was my first. Derrick is Roy's son. And Roy always treated Patti as his own, even though he knew he wasn't the father. And he never knew that Roger was Patti's dad. After Roy died I got hitched twice after that, but only because I was bored. And lonely. Neither lasted all that long."

"And Walton?"

"Roger continued to come back here. But there was no more talk of us getting *together*. That time had passed, I guess. And there was no more, well, sex." She sighed. "It was stupid, I know. Roger had a right to know about his child."

"You may be the reason he kept coming back here," pointed out Robie.

"You might be right about that. I used to just think it was because it was his home. But it wasn't like he was particularly happy here, especially after his parents died. But still, who knows how much time we have left. Maybe I should have told him how I really feel when he was here this time."

"I hope you get a chance to tell him," said Reel earnestly. "And you might be surprised at what he has to say to you."

Robie glanced at her with a quizzical look but said nothing.

"But you have to find him first," Claire pointed out.

"Can you think of nothing to help us?" said Robie.

"I've been wracking my brain trying to come up with something. But I haven't. Look, we have bad types around here. I can only think that Roger might have stumbled onto something and these folks found out and..." Her voice trailed off and she dabbed at her eyes with the tissue again.

"I ran into one of Dolph's guys," said Robie. "Did Derrick tell you about that?"

"No. He's very professional and keeps police business close to the vest."

"The guy told me that Dolph might be at the bunker."

She looked puzzled. "At Roark's silo?"

"I guess."

"I don't see how that's possible. I doubt that Roark even knows Dolph. It's not like they moved in the same circles. And why would he be at the silo?"

"Hiding out?" suggested Reel.

"Why would he be hiding out?" asked Claire.

"I can't get into that," said Reel.

Robie took out his phone and showed Claire the photo of the

map Reel had found at Randall's cabin. "Do you recognize this?" he asked.

She put on her glasses while Robie magnified the image. "Well, if I had to guess, I'd say that was southeast of here. You see that name there, that's what makes me think that. I actually drove over there a few years ago with Roark."

"Why did you do that?" asked Robie.

"Well, he was thinking about buying that second missile silo site, but for some reason it didn't work out. That's where the site's located."

Reel and Robie looked at each other.

He exclaimed, "A *second* missile site!"

"Shit, Robie," said Reel. "That's right. Lambert mentioned that to us at the dinner party at Claire's. He said he missed out on another site around here."

"Yes," said Claire. "Another old Atlas missile site. That's the one I'm talking about."

Robie thought about this for a moment. "One of Dolph's guys said he was at the bunker. Then the other guy shot him before he could tell me anything else. Then the guy who shot him told me Dolph was at the silo, meaning Lambert's silo."

Reel said, "*Silo* versus *bunker*. Different terminology because they were talking about two different places."

"And the second guy shot the first guy before he could tell me anything else. And then he tried to throw me off by saying Dolph was at the silo."

"Why wasn't Lambert able to buy it?" Reel asked Claire.

"I don't know for certain, but I would suppose it was because somebody else beat him to it."

Robie and Reel exchanged a quick glance.

"Any idea who?" he asked.

She shook her head. "Roark might know."

"We'll be sure to ask him," said Robie.

Reel said, "Claire, can you tell us how to get to this other silo?"

"I think so but it might be better if I write it down." She took a sheet of notepaper from the top of the desk, picked up a pen lying beside it, and took a few minutes to slowly write out the directions.

She handed it to Reel. "This is as about as much as I can remember. You should see a sign for the road to turn at. It's in the middle of nowhere, which I guess was the point when they picked the site."

"So unlike Lambert, whoever might own this hasn't started trying to turn it into a luxury bunker?" Reel said.

"Not that I'm aware. And I would be. Hell, the whole town would. When Roark was building his out, he had an army of guys, including a bunch of locals. They came to Grand to eat and drink and some stayed here at the hotel, others at a bunch of mobile trailers Roark set up out on-site and powered with diesel generators. You can't hide all those workers. It takes a lot of manpower to overhaul a missile site and turn it into a place people will plunk down millions for."

Reel looked down at the directions and said, "So whoever bought the silo might have purchased it for another reason."

"Or maybe they're trying to get financing," said Claire. "I know Roark took out loans to do his work. It took a while for the banks to see the potential."

"That's possible," said Reel, who was looking at Robie.

"I need to get going," said Claire, rising from the chair. "With all this going on, I'm going to make Derrick and Patti dinner. At least then I can keep an eye on them."

After she left Robie pulled out his pistol. Reel looked at him strangely.

"Thinking of shooting someone?" she asked.

With his other hand Robie pulled out a slip of paper. It was the one with the drawing of the stick figure holding the ball that Blue Man had left behind.

Robie said quietly, "I think Blue Man was being quite literal."

"What do you mean?" asked Reel.

"There were actually *two* clues here," replied Robie. "And they both were trying to tell us the same thing."

He rolled the paper up and partially slid it inside his gun muzzle.

"A man in a silo." He pulled the paper back out. "And I'm thinking that's not a basketball he's holding. It's supposed to be the world. He's holding up the *world*."

Reel gaped. "Like Atlas. The Atlas silo."

"Right," said Robie.

60

THEY WAITED UNTIL it was dark to head to the second silo site. Reel's phone buzzed. Reel answered.

It was the Agency. She put the call on speaker.

A man's voice said, "We found out some things about Scott Randall that might be helpful. His father made a fortune in the oil exploration business and then he and his wife died in a house fire. Scott was the only child and inherited everything. All told it came to nearly a hundred million net after estate and other taxes."

"Convenient house fire," said Reel. "From what we've seen of the guy the police might want to look into that a little more."

"But the son was not his father's equal in business. Not even close. He lost a lot of the money in several stupid deals where he was apparently in way over his head. Then he tried to build his fortune back up by going to Vegas and trying to become a professional gambler."

"I wouldn't think the odds of doing that were too high," noted Robie.

"They're not. He lost what little he had. He came out of that pretty much penniless and without many prospects."

"But the guy has a jet and a place in the Hamptons and a multi-million-dollar luxury doomsday bunker," said Robie. "And that's just what we know of. So he's not penniless anymore."

"Plus a wife that I seriously doubt would have married him if he wasn't rolling in dough," added Reel.

"We took a look at some of his recent financials and they do show that he has come into a lot of wealth lately. But it's tied to shell companies and offshore accounts, and it's hard to see what the source of the money is."

"You think he's laundering money for a criminal enterprise or foreign interest through some of these companies?" suggested Reel.

"It's possible. One other thing, he renounced his U.S. citizenship and is now a citizen of Ireland. Thus his time in this country is restricted and access to his financial data by us is limited. He pays his taxes in Ireland unless any is due in this country."

"We know he owns properties here," said Robie.

"There's nothing against the law about that," said the man. "But fuller details of his wealth and what taxes he pays would have to be gotten from Ireland."

"We don't have time to do that," said Robie. "But one more thing. There's an old Atlas missile site in southeastern Colorado. We know of one that was sold and developed by a guy named Roark Lambert into luxury condos. But we need to know who bought the other one. Can you dig that up?"

"Purchasers of Atlas missile sites should be easy enough to track down. I'll get right on it and call you back."

"Thanks."

"And good luck. We all want Blue Man back."

"Roger that," said Reel, who then clicked off and looked at Robie. "So Rich Boy blew Daddy's money but then got the dollars back somehow."

"Do you think he's the one who bought the second missile site?"

"Well, we have the map from the cabin he was staying at. And the boots I found, with all the grime and chemical smells on them? I bet a missile site that hasn't been renovated would have all kinds of yuck down there."

"And Blue Man's drawing and leaving it in the muzzle of his gun," added Robie.

"All points to *a* silo. We just thought it was Lambert's but maybe it's this one. It would make a lot more sense and also it would explain away the problem of having so many people in on it, including Lambert and the guards at his silo."

"So if he's not building something, what could Randall be doing there?"

"Holding prisoners, maybe."

"For what reason?" said Robie. "We were thinking human trafficking, but Agent Sanders said he had heard nothing about that."

"That's why we're heading there now. To find out."

"So this might be the 'bunker' the skinhead said Dolph could be hiding in. If Randall does own this place, he might be involved with Dolph somehow."

They had driven another twenty minutes when the phone rang again.

It was the same man from the Agency. He told them that he had completed a quick down-and-dirty on the sale of the Atlas site by the federal government.

"It was purchased several years ago by a company based in Jamaica. There's very little information about it. No listing of Scott Randall anywhere, but he could be using that as a subterfuge to hide his involvement. It's a pretty common tactic."

Reel said, "Do we have an approximate date on when Randall's financial fortunes started to turn? Like when he bought the jet and all that? That would be very helpful if we could pinpoint when his money issues started to turn around."

"FYI, he doesn't own the jet. It's leased, although it still costs a pretty penny. That lease was signed two years ago. The house in the Hamptons was purchased eighteen months ago. The luxury condo you mentioned was bought by him about a year ago."

"So maybe all the money and properties came in *after* he bought the silo," said Robie. "Or *if* he bought the silo, since you can't confirm that."

"And he got married twelve months ago. I dug into that, too. His wife was a lingerie model before their marriage, with a reputation for being very difficult to work with."

"What a shock," said Reel.

"So maybe the silo is his financial golden goose somehow," said Robie.

"Well, it would have to be a pretty big goose," said the man. "The house in the Hamptons has a twelve-million-dollar mortgage on it. The plane lease is millions more. He must have had sound financial resources for the bank and aircraft lessor to do those deals."

"Plus he laid out about four million for the luxury condo," said Reel. "And I think his wife will end up being his most expensive purchase. What was the purchase price for the other site?"

"Eight hundred thousand."

"That's double what Roark paid for his," noted Reel.

"That's a lot of money for basically a hole in the ground that has no use unless you pour millions of dollars into it," said Robie. "There aren't many people competing to buy these suckers."

"That's true," said the agency man. "But someone wanted this site. I looked at other places in the Midwest and this fetched one of the highest prices."

"We're going to have to find out why that is," said Reel grimly.

She clicked off.

Robie said, "We'll have to recon the site first, size up the security overlays."

"If this place has a blast door like Lambert's I don't see how we get in."

"Maybe if we're patient enough someone will let us in."

She shook her head. "I don't think we're that lucky."

"I didn't think luck had anything to do with it."

"I think now it does."

"Well, then we'll make our own."

61

THERE COULDN'T HAVE been a greater contrast between the second silo site and the one Lambert had turned into luxury condos. There *was* an old chain-link fence, but there was no perimeter security. The road into the site was barely graveled and in poor condition. From here they couldn't even see the entrance to the silo.

There was no sign that anyone was around.

"Could the residue you saw on those work boots be from that gravel?" asked Robie.

"Pull up a little bit," said Reel.

He did so, and she climbed out of the car with the rag she had used to take a sample from the boots.

She knelt down over the gravel and dabbed it with the cloth. She climbed back into the car and used her phone light to compare the marks.

"It's sort of gravelly but it's not the same, Robie." She sniffed the fresh sample. "And there's no chemical smell."

"Where would there be gravel with a chemical smell around here?"

"I don't know. Let's park the truck behind those trees and have a look around."

After leaving the truck hidden, they scaled the fence and dropped down onto the other side.

There were no sounds, no lights, no one.

They skittered forward, keeping low to the ground.

"Why would you pay eight hundred thousand for this place and do nothing with it?" asked Robie.

"When Lambert paid half that for his site and did something with it to make money," added Reel.

They made their way forward staying parallel to the gravel road, and about a quarter of a mile later they crossed a small knoll and there it was.

"Blast door straight ahead," whispered Reel.

Robie stopped and nodded. He slipped his night optics out and took in a full view of the area in front of them.

"Looks deserted," he said. "The gravel hasn't been disrupted. I don't think a vehicle's been along here."

"Then why buy it in the first place?" said Reel. "If not to use it somehow. And if you're going to rehab it, you have to go inside."

"And there would be lots of evidence of that sort of activity."

"Maybe there's another way into the place."

He looked at her incredulously. "Another way into an Atlas missile site? Doesn't that sort of defeat the purpose?"

"I didn't say it had always been there. Maybe whoever bought it made another entrance somehow," pointed out Reel.

Robie pulled out his phone.

"What are you doing?" asked Reel.

"Trying to find a back door."

He phoned the Agency again and made his request.

When he clicked off Reel said, "You think another entrance is possible then?"

He looked around. "I think anything in this godforsaken place is possible."

Ten minutes later his phone buzzed. Robie listened, asked a few questions, and then clicked off. He turned to Reel. "Let's go find Blue Man."

62

"An abandoned rock quarry?" said Reel. "I didn't know they even quarried rock here."

They were hunched down in the darkness, staring at the quarry on the west side of the former Atlas missile site perhaps owned by Scott Randall. Reel had her sniper rifle slung over one shoulder and a small duffel over the other.

Robie said, "The Rockies aren't that far away. And while this area is pretty flat, there are elevated portions. We passed that ridge right before we got there. So there's got to be lots of deposits of rock around here. That quarry is really deep, but there's an access road around its top lip and also a road to get there. Let's go."

They made their way toward the top edge of the quarry site and looked around.

"Lots of 'no trespassing' signs," said Robie.

"Not that anyone would want to come up here."

"Which probably makes it ideal if you're doing something illegal."

"How do we tell if this is the right place?" asked Reel.

In answer, Robie stooped, rubbed his hand across the rocky ground, and then sniffed it. He held it up for Reel to smell.

"Same chemical odor," she observed. "Must be from whatever they were using here at the quarry."

"Look at your shoes."

He hit her shoes with his flashlight.

"Like the residue I took from the boots at Randall's place."

Robie nodded and rose. "So that means those guys came here. The Agency satellite zoomed in on this place as a possibility when

I told them about the chemical smell and the sort of soil residue we were talking about. The quarry was the only place in the area that might fit that criteria, they concluded."

"But they couldn't find an entrance?"

"No. But it would be well hidden, since that's the whole point."

"What do you think they're doing in there?"

"I have no idea, but I intend to find out."

He pulled out his gun, and using a flashlight he'd taken from the truck, he moved forward with Reel on his right flank.

The darkness was made complete by low-level clouds, which managed to fully obscure a three-quarter moon.

They had moved about fifty yards forward when Robie's light hit on something. "There have been vehicles over here," he said, pointing down at the slight ruts in the dirt.

"Well, they must be heading somewhere then," replied Reel.

They followed the ruts past a small stand of trees.

"Robie, somebody's cleared this area enough to run this 'road' through here."

Robie nodded and looked around. "And I doubt anyone would even notice, because there's no reason to come here."

Another hundred feet in they cleared the trees, stopped, and knelt down. Robie powered up his optics and took a look around. A few moments later he said, "Son of a bitch."

"What is it?"

He pointed into the darkness. "There's a rock wall a hundred feet down there. And there's a damn door built right into it."

"Let me have a look."

He slipped her the optics and she saw what he had.

Robie said, "This is the other end of that ridge we passed. Most of this area is flat, but they have these elevated portions, too." He shined his light on the ground. "And the vehicle tracks run all the way here."

Reel added, "Okay, if my geography is right this ridge backs onto the eastern edge of the Atlas silo facility."

"I think you're spot-on."

"That door has to be really secure, Robie. And maybe monitored."

"They might already know someone is here," he said.

"So do we stealth it or do a bull run?"

Robie said firmly, "I don't like bull runs."

"Well, neither do I. I like as much intel as possible before I commit myself."

"So where do we get intel from? Unless the Agency's satellite can look through rock I don't think they'll be much help."

"What about Derrick Bender?" said Reel.

"You think he knows something about this?"

"If he knows about the door he might be in on whatever's going on in there. But I don't think he is. He was genuinely pissed about what happened to Malloy. And he seemed totally surprised when we told him what had happened to Luke and Holly."

"But how can he help us?" said Robie.

"He gives us a third gun and the weight of the law."

"The weight of the law apparently means jack shit here."

"And he can give us some local information. Maybe about how this door can hook up with the Atlas missile site."

Robie thought about this in silence for a few long moments. "But just him. We don't need the state police charging up here. For all we know they'll screw everything up or else get us all killed."

"And their response time in the past hasn't been exactly stellar. By the time they got here, we might be ready for retirement."

"You want to call him?"

"No, you do it," replied Robie.

"Why me?"

"He likes you better."

"Okay, but just so you know, I haven't slept with the guy."

63

To his credit Bender didn't ask many questions when Reel called him on his cell phone. He said he would be on his way in a few minutes after Reel told him exactly where they were located.

Robie kept a watch on the door with his optics while Reel went back down the road to await Bender's arrival.

One hour later Robie heard someone coming. As they rounded a slight bend and came into full view, Robie relaxed the grip on his gun. He stepped out so Bender and Reel could see him, noting that Bender had a shotgun with him along with his sidearm.

"So what do you think we got here?" he asked as they walked up to Robie.

"You tell us. Who owns this quarry?"

Bender looked around. "Long time ago it was a company based in Nebraska. Then whatever stone they were hunting for here ran out."

"So no one's been working it for a while?" said Reel.

Bender shook his head. "Hell, it's probably been decades."

"It backs up to the second Atlas silo site. A *second* site!" Robie added for emphasis. "Why didn't you tell us about it? Did you know even about it?"

"Yeah, most folks around here do. But I didn't think it was relevant to anything. It was just an abandoned government site."

Robie said, "Why would somebody want to buy the site? And pay double what Lambert paid for the one he developed?"

"I don't know," said Bender. "I didn't even know somebody *had* bought it. But why are you so interested in it?"

"There's a door built into the rock wall about a hundred yards down that path. You can see where there's a road cut through the trees."

"Hell, they cut roads all over the place up here when they were doing the quarrying. And I know the door you're talking about."

"You do?" said Reel.

Bender nodded. "When I was a kid me and my buddies would come up here. We weren't stupid enough to dive down into the water at the bottom. There's crap and stone and everything in there. That would be suicide. But we'd ride our dirt bikes up here."

"And the door?" persisted Robie.

"There's an old storage room in there."

"So you've seen it?" asked Reel.

"When I was a kid, yeah."

"What was in there?"

"Just crap. Old boxes, broken tools."

"How'd you get in?"

"There was just an old padlock on it. We used a crowbar to pop it."

Robie handed him the night optics. "Come on. I think somebody might have upgraded security."

Robie led them back down the road and through the trees, drawing to a stop a hundred feet from the door.

"Take a look and tell me if it's changed from when you were a kid."

Bender put on the night optics and Robie powered them up.

"Well?"

"That door's metal. The one when I was a kid was wood. And that lock looks pretty new."

"And pretty secure," said Robie. "I recognize the lock on that door because my Agency uses something similar to secure its facilities. You're not popping it with a crowbar or a stick of dynamite."

"So what does that mean?"

"It means the purpose of that room has changed," said Reel. "Tell us about the adjacent missile site."

"I don't know much about it. It's been abandoned forever. But nobody ever went near it. When we were kids we heard it was contaminated. You know, radiation. We didn't want to start glowing in the dark. It wasn't until after Roark built his out that anybody thought differently. And even then, we knew he'd spent a fortune cleaning the place up."

"Is there any way someone could have connected up that second missile site with whatever's behind that door?" asked Robie.

Bender rubbed his chin as he thought about that question. "Now that I think about it I remember Roark talking at a get-together at my mom's about this site. He said he actually preferred it to the one he developed."

"Why?" asked Reel quickly.

"It had more acreage for one thing. And he said it had more buildable space underground. So he could maybe sell more of those units."

"So more underground space presumably might mean that the site extends close to the ridge."

"Or, Robie, maybe it goes *into* the ridge," suggested Reel.

Bender said, "You know, that's possible. And I remember that storage room from when I was a kid. It went really far back, but we never went that far in. No lights and too spooky."

"So it could be that with a little work a tunnel could have been dug connecting the two," reasoned Robie.

"What for?" asked Bender. "I mean if you bought the missile site you could use that door. Why mess with the hassle of connecting up with this place?"

"The site is sort of out in the open. So you'd do that if you didn't want anyone to know you were accessing the missile site. You'd come in this way instead and no one would be the wiser."

"But why all the secrecy?" asked Bender.

Reel answered. "Well, if you're bringing prisoners in here you wouldn't want anyone to know."

"Wait a minute, you think those prisoners are being held in the missile silo?"

"It would make sense of the drawing Walton left behind in the muzzle of his gun," said Robie. "He obviously wanted to draw our attention to it."

"But, Robie, he asked to take a tour of *Lambert's* silo," Reel pointed out. "Not this one."

"He may not have known at which place they were being held. But if it were Lambert's there would have to be a lot of people in on it, and that sort of widespread conspiracy just becomes too unrealistic. But that's not the case with this Atlas site."

"And it could be that if he was brought here the other missing people were, too," added Reel.

Bender glanced in the direction of the door. "So what do we do? Get a warrant and search the place?"

Robie shook his head. "That'll take too long, and tongues seem to wag here, so word might get out and the prisoners, if they are in there, might get moved. Besides, I don't even know if we have enough probable cause to get a warrant. What do you think, Bender?"

The deputy looked uncertain. "Well, I've found judges around here aren't too fond of the Fourth Amendment. They like people to be able to keep their property free from unnecessary searches. And I saw all the NO TRESPASSING signs when I was coming up here. That's technically what we're doing, trespassing."

"Well, that answers that," said Reel.

"Can you open that door?" asked Bender.

Robie looked at Reel. She patted the duffel she had taken from the truck and said, "I brought some stuff that will handle it. The question is are we prepared for what might be on the other side of that door?"

"We're going to have to be," said Robie. "Because the only other way in is through a blast door, and I don't think you have anything in your duffel that will crack that one."

She looked at him. "So what about not liking bull runs?"

"I think time is running out for Blue Man."

"Who?" said Bender.

"Never mind," said Reel, keeping her gaze on Robie.

He held out his hand for the duffel and added, "And sometimes people are worth dying for."

Reel and Robie held gazes for a moment longer before she broke it off and handed him the duffel.

"So let's run with the bulls," she said with finality.

CHAPTER

64

Robie held point.

Bender had his right flank.

Reel covered them both with her long gun as they approached the door.

Robie knelt in front of the lock and took out a small bag. He inserted the squirt end of a bottle into the lock and squeezed the plastic. Some liquid from the bottle was injected into the lock. He next ran a length of fuse into the lock and unspooled it onto the ground. He struck a match, lit the twine, and moved back as the fire moved along the fuse toward the lock. When it reached the lock, there was a flash of fire and a puff of bright, white light. A smoldering smell reached their noses.

Robie crept forward, waited about sixty seconds, and, being careful not to touch the doorknob, inserted a tool into the lock and cranked it to the right. The doorknob turned easily.

Bender joined him. "What was that stuff?"

"A mixture of magnesium and some other elements. It burns at such a high heat, over five thousand degrees, that it's melted the inner workings of the lock."

"Damn. You guys have lots of tricks like that, I would imagine."

"I think we might need a few extra tonight."

Robie opened the door fully and shined his light inside, while keeping his gun trained in front of him.

Bender did the same.

Reel moved up to within a dozen yards of them, her gun making sweeps left and right.

Robie and Bender stepped into the room and peered around.

Bender had pulled out a powerful mag light and was making sweeps with it, too.

The space was full of stuff, old boxes, crates, and rusted tools.

"Looks like it did when I was a kid," said Bender. "Are you sure you're on the right track here?"

"Keeping it the same here is intentional. It dissuades anybody with enough balls to breach that lock from thinking that anything has really changed. But they couldn't hide the fact of the new door and the fancy lock. Nobody would go to that trouble to keep this crap secure."

"Down that way," Bender said. "The room continues."

They made their way down a long, dark corridor. Unlike the room, this space was clear of debris.

The walls were stone and had been smoothed out by whoever and whatever had managed to dig this tunnel.

Reel had followed them in and was using her optics to see past the area of light.

"There's a door down there," she said. "At the end. Rest of the way is clear."

They picked up their pace and reached it about ten seconds later.

"It's got mag locks," said Robie, studying the metal door's exterior. "I don't see any surveillance cameras. I'm not sure why not. If I'd gone to the trouble of securing this tunnel like they had, I'd have some type of monitoring in place so I'd know if the place had been breached or not."

Bender looked around and said quietly, "Do you think there's something else they're using? Trip beams, maybe? We could have already triggered one of them."

"We could have," said Robie. "Which means they may already know that we're here. So let's keep moving forward."

"Use the magnesium," said Reel. "To breach the door. The magnesium solution should work."

Robie pulled out the squirt bottle, matches, and a length of fuse. He used the same process as before, then stepped back as the fire wound its way into the lock.

The puff of brilliant white smoke occurred a few moments later.

Robie used the same tool to open the door. A long, darkened tunnel confronted them.

"It's running right towards the missile site," observed Robie.

"You think it connects up?" said Bender.

"I'm about to bet my life that it does," replied Robie. He looked back toward Reel. "Things are probably going to start getting dicey at this point."

She nodded. "I expect they will."

The three of them started to move forward. The tunnel began to narrow substantially so that they had to walk single file along it.

"Stay alert," he whispered to Bender. He didn't feel the need to tell Reel that.

Bender nodded and gripped his pistol more tightly.

They had traveled what seemed to Robie to be about a quarter mile when they came to yet another door.

"Shit," muttered Robie.

There was no doorknob, only an electronic pad.

"It's a biometric reader," he observed. "Like the one that Lambert uses to access his silo."

Reel drew closer and looked at it as Bender took a step back so he was behind the both of them.

"Our magnesium brew won't work on that," noted Reel.

"No, it won't." Robie felt the door. "Solid metal. I'm guessing three or four inches thick, steel hinges set right into the rock. We'd need an RPG round to make a dent."

"We've got one back in the truck," said Reel.

She looked back at Bender, who was staring at her, his gun pointed in front of him.

"No!" screamed Reel, when she saw the red dot flicking around him. She launched herself but it was too late.

The round slammed into the back of Bender's head and stayed there.

He stood there teetering in his boots for a second before toppling forward face-first, his pistol dropping from his dead hand.

The door they were going to break into swung open, and ten guns were pointed at them along with blinding lights.

Dolph emerged from behind the armed men.

He smoothed down his uniform jacket and said, "I think this is where you lay your weapons down. Or we'd be perfectly fine with shooting you right here."

Robie and Reel laid their weapons on the ground.

From down the tunnel they heard footsteps approaching.

Out of the darkness a silhouette appeared.

And then it emerged into a fuller, more solid form.

Yet it was only when the person used a flashlight to illuminate her features that she became recognizable. The rifle with the laser scope and heated barrel from the just-fired round was held in her other hand. It had been the red dot from the scope that Reel had seen.

Reel gasped, "You just killed your brother."

Patti Bender looked down at the body and said, "Actually, my half brother. So it really doesn't count, does it?"

65

THE AIR WAS stale and warm, with a chemical odor permeating throughout.

Robie and Reel sat in a small concrete block room behind a barred door. They had been stripped down to their underclothes, searched, and shackled. Their phones and weapons had been confiscated.

"I'm sorry, Robie."

Robie glanced at her. "For what?"

"I didn't secure our rear flank."

"Well, considering we had about a dozen guns on our *forward* flank, I don't think it mattered. If it's anyone's fault it's mine. I did a bull run and screwed us."

"You didn't have much choice."

"People always have choices. I made the wrong one. And now Bender is dead."

"I didn't see Patti being in on this."

"Neither did I. But maybe it's starting to make sense."

"How so?"

Before he could answer, someone appeared at the doorway. It was Dolph.

Robie looked up at him.

Dolph said, "Well, there is justice after all, even for people like me. I had you as prisoners before and I do again. This time the result will be very different. There will be no Apostles to aid you."

Reel said, "So what's the game, Dolph? Hiding out in an abandoned missile silo? Afraid to come to the surface and fight it out mano a mano? Going for the angle of the cowardly Nazi?"

Dolph pursed his lips. "I don't think you've quite grasped the enormity of what's going on here."

"So enlighten us," interjected Robie.

"I'll be right back," said Dolph. "Don't go anywhere," he added with a smirk.

A few minutes later someone approached the cell door once more. It was a man neither of them recognized. He was in his thirties and skinny with thick bushy hair.

"Who the hell are you?" demanded Reel.

"My real name is Arthur Fitzsimmons." When he next spoke his voice was one that they both instantly recognized. "But you might also know me as Dolph."

Both Robie and Reel gaped.

"God, that feels so good," Fitzsimmons said, running a hand through his hair. "That latex head mask is a real bitch to wear. And the fat suit! Well, even in the cool weather it's a bitch. Now I can understand what actors feel like."

"Why the alter ego?" asked Reel.

Fitzsimmons used a sanitary wipe pulled from his pocket to clean some sticky gum from his face. "Well, I didn't want anyone to know who I really was, of course. If things went to hell the police would be looking for a pudgy guy named Dolph who was in his fifties. I actually have a Ph.D. in chemistry from Caltech. And I'm not a Nazi, in any sense of the word. My great-grandmother was an Orthodox Jew, which means my mother was Jewish, and thus so am I. Though my mother never practiced her religion after her marriage. My father never converted. I was raised as a Catholic."

Reel said, "So the commandment about 'Thou shalt not kill' never really sunk in with you, did it?"

"So why the neo-Nazi subterfuge, then?" asked Robie.

"It was a good cover for what we were doing here."

"Like being a murderer?" said Reel.

Fitzsimmons smiled a bit embarrassedly. "I have to admit, that was quite an adrenaline ride. I never got that rush poring over the periodic table, I can tell you that."

"You killed Holly in cold blood," said Robie.

"You pushed my hand. Of course, I never expected you to escape, either. Scared the crap out of me. It's why I had to lie low here."

Reel said, "How did you get to them? They were on a bus heading to Denver and then on to California."

"They never got on the bus. We tracked them to the bus station via Luke's cell phone. He'd thrown it away, but he did so at the bus station. They were about to board the bus when my men showed up. They came with no problem because we told them if they made any trouble we'd shoot everyone in the station dead."

"You bastard!" said Reel.

Fitzsimmons performed a mock bow. "I'll take that as a compliment. But I couldn't very well let them go, could I?"

"And Beverly Drango?" said Robie. "You couldn't let her go either?"

"She was stupid. We knew she lived with Lamarre. We were going to take her out along with the others, but she was smarter than Lamarre. She had learned some things through her job with the casino company. She put two and two together. And tried to blackmail us. Well, we paid her. You might have noticed that she lived in a dump yet she had a new car. But it apparently wasn't enough. So we had to tie up that loose end."

"And I'm assuming that under the guise of it being Roger Walton, you paid Zeke Donovan to try to scare us off," said Reel.

"I should have paid him and his idiot nephew to put the bullets through your head, not the windshield. But hindsight is twenty-twenty."

"So what's really going on here?" asked Robie. "What's the point of all this?"

Fitzsimmons stared at him. "How about I *show* you?"

A few minutes later, wearing yellow jumpsuits but still shackled, Robie and Reel were led out of the cell and down a long corridor where a golf cart awaited them.

They climbed onto the cart along with three guards, Fitzsimmons driving.

"Lambert has a golf cart to get around his missile site too," observed Robie.

"It's where I got the idea," admitted Fitzsimmons.

"So Lambert is involved in this?" said Reel.

"Hell no. He's a legit guy, which means I have no use for him. And he's also a drunk. Loose lips sink ships, as they used to say."

Fitzsimmons started the cart and drove down a long tunnel with dim lights that appeared to be battery powered. After a ten-minute ride Fitzsimmons stopped the cart, and they all climbed off.

He unlocked a door that had a biometric reader similar to the one they had seen right before Bender had been murdered. They passed through the door, and Robie and Reel had to blink their eyes rapidly to adjust to the heightened level of light.

The room they were in was large, with numerous stainless steel workbenches and sophisticated automated equipment and machinery neatly arrayed around the space. There was also a conveyor belt assembly line down which packages and plastic trays were moving. The place was spanking clean. The tiled floor looked as though you could eat off it. The air was pure with no residual chemical smell and the temperature was comfortable.

Robie counted twenty workers dressed in blue scrubs with masks over their mouths, goggles over their eyes, and latex gloves on their hands. This was obviously a manufacturing line of some sort.

Reel's observations had gone even further. She said, "You're making drugs."

Fitzsimmons glanced over at her and smiled encouragingly. "That's exactly what we're doing, and on a grand scale if I might say so."

"What sort of drugs?" asked Robie.

In answer Fitzsimmons strode over to a bench and picked up two plastic bottles and a small baggie. He carried them back over and held them up.

"We have a diversified product line. Just like Apple, you have to have many things to entice your customers." He indicated one of the plastic bottles. "Oxycodone, as fine a quality as anything manufactured by Big Pharma." He indicated the other bottle. "Fentanyl. Some really powerful shit. The plastic bag, on the other hand, contains meth, but of a quality that is light-years ahead of the typical product you can buy on the street. And for that we charge a premium." He swept a hand over the workspace. "We have four rooms just like this one sprawled across the missile complex. And living quarters for the staff, as well as other essentials."

"How does a Caltech chemist end up doing this?" asked Robie.

Fitzsimmons looked sheepish. "I have to admit, I was a huge fan of *Breaking Bad*. And I thought, why not? I'm a smart guy with special skills. I was making peanuts at my old job. Why not go for the brass ring? I just decided to do it on a much bigger scale."

"How did you manage to build out all this without anyone noticing you rehabbing the space?" asked Reel.

"Oh, we didn't do it on the scale that Roark Lambert did. We weren't building out luxury condos, after all. So we used the tunnel from the quarry to bring in all the equipment and other materials. And we did it all at night. We actually didn't have far to go. Some research showed us that the Army Corps of Engineers had tunneled pretty far into that ridge to increase the amount of usable space for their operations. So we just connected up on the other side." His gaze swept over some of the workers in blue scrubs.

Robie noted that not one of them had looked up from their tasks when he and the similarly shackled Reel were led into the room. Also arrayed around the space were men with guns.

Fitzsimmons followed Robie's gaze. "We take security very seriously."

"I can see that."

"We also brought sophisticated business, manufacturing, and distribution protocols to the illicit drug market. There's too much crap out there. It can kill you. There's this stuff going around now, heroin laced with carfentanil, or elephant tranquilizer. It's lethal if you smoke it, swallow it, or even inhale it. Hell, it can make you really sick if you just touch it. And then there's this shit called gray death, which is just a mixture of crap that'll be the last hit you take. You got all these idiots trying to mix anything with stuff like fentanyl to give the big bang and they don't know what they're doing and they end up snuffing people left and right. And what business survives by killing its clients?"

"Ask Big Tobacco about that," retorted Reel.

"Anyway, you have all these drug sites on the Dark Web. Remember Silk Road? They took that down years ago, but it was small potatoes compared to what's out there now. There are hundreds of sites up now that are far bigger and trade only in synthetic drugs. Although the South American cartels are catching on to it, most are manufactured in China, shipped through to Hong Kong, and then mailed to the U.S."

"Mailed?" said Robie incredulously.

Fitzsimmons smiled. "Heroin, coke, and pills are bulky. And easily tracked. Fentanyl on the other hand? You can ship enough Fentanyl to OD a hundred thousand people in a manila envelope. Two flakes of the stuff are lethal to an adult. But the thing is, the Feds are onto the Dark Web stuff and the use of the postal service. And they're looking hard at shipments coming in from overseas. That gives homegrown manufacturers like us a huge leg up. American made, right? People want manufacturing jobs to come back here, right? Well, baby, here we are."

"I don't think they had what you do in mind," pointed out Reel.

Fitzsimmons shrugged. "We can give people the same big pop much more safely with our crossover synthetics. And our drugs are made to exacting standards. Our facility is maintained to Big Pharma production standards. We actually have clean rooms where some of our most delicate processing takes place. We make custom products to order, too. We're even thinking about using drones to deliver some of the stuff. You know, taking a page from Amazon. People do that right now to get stuff into prisons all over the country."

"But it's all illegal drugs," pointed out Reel.

"I know all sides of the argument," said a smiling Fitzsimmons, as he put the bottles and plastic bag back where he had gotten them. "People are going to use drugs regardless of what the law is, right? So we're giving them a pure, safe product for their doping pleasure. And it's not just druggies. Oxycodone is a *painkiller*. Do you know how much pharmaceuticals charge for it? It's a disgrace. We're actually making it affordable for people. I consider it a public service."

"You mean servicing their addiction," said Robie.

"We can mince words all day," said Fitzsimmons amiably.

"How much money are we talking about?" asked Reel.

"Last year was our best, but this year I think we're going to top it. Well into the nine figures," he said. "Who knows, some day we might top a billion a year. And that's with gross profit margins of nearly seventy percent."

"Is that because your labor costs are so cheap?" said Robie. "I mean it's not like you're paying these people, right?" He nodded toward the blue-scrubbed workers.

"Well, we do have to feed and house them, if for a limited time."

"So they're not permanent workers?" said Reel.

"Nothing in life is permanent. Only death is permanent."

"Very philosophical of you."

Fitzsimmons smiled. "I actually studied philosophy in college. It balanced out the science part of my brain."

"And what does Scott Randall do for the 'business'?"

"He has his uses. He gets his healthy cut plus other things. That's all I'll really say on the subject."

"And Patti Bender?"

Fitzsimmons smiled again. "She's a free spirit. I met her when she came out to California for a few months. We really hit it off. We could see that our strengths and ambitions played well together. I let her know what I was thinking and she said she thought she could help. This operation was actually her idea. She knew about this silo. She also had a relationship with Scott Randall. She'd done some guide work for him. I just supplied the science. So I came out here as Dolph because she thought it would be good cover. And she said there were lots of 'alternative' groups in this part of Colorado. What was one more? I set up my neo-Nazi operation. In the background she actually helped with recruitment. There are a lot of lost souls around here looking for answers. For structure. Looking to belong to something. And I became their answer. But it was all just a sideshow for this operation, although it did help me meet people who provided excellent distribution for our product. We even ship internationally."

"So Patti really came up with this whole idea?" said Reel.

"I think she got the concept from her mother's marijuana business, which is a very nice, profitable, and legitimate business. But Patti wanted more than that. And to tell the truth, I think she loves the risk."

"When I first met her she just seemed like a relatively simple person who was independent and liked the outdoors," said Robie.

"She is that, plus a lot more. There are several more layers to the woman. I'm not sure I've seen them all, actually."

"But what does she do with the money she makes? She certainly doesn't dress like she's rich. And she and her buddies go off acting as guides."

"Oh, she likes the money. And I can tell you that she has a beautiful hideaway on an island in the Caribbean. I think she may end up there one day permanently."

"So she goes off to the Caribbean and her mother and brother have no clue?"

"She disappears for weeks at a time," said Fitzsimmons. "It's the nature of who she is. Her mother and brother are well accustomed to that."

"She killed a police officer who happened to be her *brother*," said Robie.

"Well, the way I see it, she had no choice. She was actually quite fond of Derrick. And she blames you for his death. Had you not involved him, he never would have come here and he'd still be alive."

"That's one way of looking at it," said Robie.

"How *exactly* do you distribute the drugs?" asked Reel.

He wheeled around on her. "Why? So you can go and tell a certain Apostle all about it?"

Reel said nothing, her features inscrutable, but Fitzsimmons still smiled.

"I saw through that a long time ago. And when he 'rescued' you, my suspicions were confirmed. But he's not a real concern. He thinks I'm into guns and other stuff, not drugs. As to our distribution, it's a trade secret and not something you need be concerned with."

"So where are they?" asked Robie.

"Who is that?" said Fitzsimmons as he watched the workers.

"Roger Walton, Valerie Malloy, JC Parry, and Clément Lamarre."

"Well, we'll have to see. But don't you want to ask about our workers here? You already commented on our not paying them."

"They're the prisoners, right?" Reel said.

"We needed people to help connect up that quarry room with our facility. Fortunately, we were also able to do the work at night and dump the debris into the quarry." He added with a smile, "Along with the workers, of course. Then, we needed to have people on the manufacturing line."

"And of course you didn't want to hire them and actually have to pay them," said Robie.

"Well, there's that and also the fact that there are too many damn undercover cops around. If they infiltrated our operation? Well, that would be problematic. Thus, we made an executive decision to utilize 'disposable' workers."

Robie and Reel looked at each other. Reel said, "So you just kill them?"

Fitzsimmons said quietly, "We terminate their work status at the appropriate time."

"And exactly how do you do that?" asked Robie.

"I invite you to use your imagination," replied Fitzsimmons. "But I can show you one method. Two birds with one stone, you see. And I'm the sort of person who always goes for the shortcut."

Reel studied him. "And the fact that you're telling us all this means that you don't expect us to be able to tell anyone else?"

Fitzsimmons smiled, but it never reached his eyes. "I thought that went without saying."

66

THEY REVERSED COURSE on the golf cart and soon found themselves back where they had started, at the quarry.

"We've gotten rid of your truck and Bender's police car, of course," said Fitzsimmons. "No one will know where you've gotten to."

"You have to know that an army of police and Feds are going to descend on this place like locusts, don't you?" said Robie.

Fitzsimmons said, "I quite understand that your Mr. Walton is a VIP in DC. And that you two are also highly valuable. Now, with the entire police force of Grand, Colorado, missing, the locusts, as you say, *will* descend. So that means we have to move our operation. And we're going to do it very quickly, starting tonight." He suddenly scowled. "You know, in an ideal world an idiot like Clément Lamarre would not be allowed to bring down an operation like this."

"In an ideal world scum like you wouldn't have the opportunity to build an operation like this," retorted Reel.

Fitzsimmons ignored this and continued. "We traced every person he could have told, from Holly to your Mr. Walton. Patti knew he was well connected. When he started snooping around, asking questions, getting a guided tour of Roark's facility, that concerned us."

"So you knew about that?" said Robie.

Fitzsimmons gave him a condescending look. "I know about everything. I just couldn't figure out how you two came to learn about this place."

"It helps if you know your Greek mythology," said Robie.

"Come again?"

"It doesn't matter."

"You're right. Nothing matters for either of you anymore."

He led them to the edge of the quarry. There was something large lying on the ground with a tarp over it.

Fitzsimmons lifted the tarp to reveal Bender's body perched on what looked like a seesaw. They noted there were chains and weights wrapped around the corpse.

"Now, the disposal method. I think you'll find it relatively straightforward."

"Wait!"

They all turned to see Patti Bender striding toward them.

She didn't look at Fitzsimmons, Robie, or Reel as she passed by.

She knelt down next to her dead half brother. "Give me some privacy," she said quietly.

Fitzsimmons nodded at the guards, who grabbed Robie and Reel and hustled them away. Fitzsimmons slowly followed, glancing back twice at Patti.

From a distance Robie and Reel watched as Patti gently touched Bender's face and crossed herself. Robie could see her lips moving but couldn't hear what she was saying.

She finally rose and walked over to them. She had on dirty jeans, a compression Under Armour shirt, and a parka. A Glock rode in a holster on her hip. Her boots were dusty. Her hair was tied back with a rubber band.

She studied the ground for a few moments before looking up at Robie.

"I will never forgive you for this," she said. She glanced at Reel. "Both of you."

Reel said, "I didn't shoot your brother, so I don't think forgiveness is my problem. I think it's yours."

She slipped a knife out of a holder on the back of her belt and held it against Reel's throat.

Reel looked down at her, her features relaxed. "That's the easy way, Patti. I would expect better from you after coming up with your drug empire."

"We *did* have a plan, Patti," said Fitzsimmons nervously. "And I think we should carry it out."

Patti put her hand up to Fitzsimmons and he instantly fell silent.

Robie noted that the two guards had stepped back and would not make eye contact with the woman. It was clear to Robie that Patti Bender and not Fitzsimmons was running the show and had the respect of the guards.

Patti slid the blade along Reel's throat, drawing a bubble of blood a centimeter from where Reel's carotid wobbled at the surface.

She smeared the drop of blood along Reel's throat before putting the blade away.

"You came here for the truth?" she said.

"Only reason we came to this place," said Reel.

"You won't find it. Truth doesn't exist."

"Your partner here has already tried to wax philosophical with us. But we're blue-collar types doing a job. No ivory towers need apply."

"I didn't mean that," said Patti. "When I say truth doesn't exist, it's a fact, not a theory."

"So does this mean you've been sampling some of your product, because I'm not following," said Reel.

"I loved Derrick even though we had different fathers."

"I really can't believe that, since you murdered him."

"The moment you brought him here you killed him. My brother was the law. This place is not about the law."

"Meaning he would have exposed you and sent you to prison. You killed him to avoid that happening. Doesn't sound like love to me. Sounds like every selfish crook I've ever come across."

"I did what I did so he wouldn't find out what I'd done. I don't care about prison. I've been living in one all my life. But I didn't want Derrick to know this about me. I couldn't have lived with that."

"Well, you made damn sure that he couldn't live with that, either."

"Where are the others?" said Robie. "Walton and the others?"

"They're here," said Patti. "They're waiting."

"Waiting for what?"

"For you, of course."

With that she turned and walked back into the tunnel.

Fitzsimmons stirred and said, "Well, now you know. You *will* meet up with your friend, Mr. Walton."

"He's Patti's father, did you know that?" said Reel.

"Perhaps I did and perhaps I didn't."

"Is that what this is all about?" said Robie. "She has daddy issues?"

"I'm a chemist, not a psychologist. And I don't really care." He shook his head and grimaced. "To think that all of this started because that idiot Lamarre saw something in the back of a van that he shouldn't have seen and then started blabbing. Every day it seemed like we had one more person we had to silence. It was like a virus mutating."

"Well, sometimes the virus wins," said Reel.

"And sometimes it doesn't," replied Fitzsimmons. "The key is quarantine. And then finding a way to kill the contagion."

Fitzsimmons motioned to two of the guards, who came forward and lifted up one end of the seesaw. Now Robie and Reel could see that it was actually being used as a slide.

Bender's body zipped right down the board and then off it.

They watched it fall over two hundred feet, where it hit the mucky water and then slipped under the surface.

Fitzsimmons explained, "We always slit the lungs so they won't inflate when the gas builds up as a result of decomposition. And of course the weights and chains serve to keep the body at the bottom. It's quite deep down there. And impossible to see anything in the depths."

"Why do I think that's not the first time you've done that?" said Reel. It was clear from the revulsion on her features that if she could have gotten to Fitzsimmons, he would be a dead man.

"Well, it's not."

"And I guess that's where we'll be ending up," said Robie.

"I normally leave that up to Patti. But be warned, though I can kill in cold blood, I'm actually simply a humble chemist and genuinely a nice person. She's far more dangerous than she appears."

"So are we," Reel muttered under her breath. "So are we."

67

"Do you think Blue Man is dead?"

Robie didn't answer Reel's query right away.

They were back in the same cell.

"I don't think so. Patti said they were waiting for us. Not that I have any reason to believe her."

"So she figured we'd end up here as prisoners, too?"

"She seems to be a long-range planner," replied Robie.

"Where do you think those prisoners are coming in from?"

"From the little I could see behind the blue scrubs, they looked to be young and mostly Hispanic."

"Are they snatching them from their hometowns?"

"Maybe they're runaways or they came into the country illegally. That might make more sense. You start snatching kids from homes, there're going to be a lot of questions and people looking for them."

"You're probably right."

"They might have sold them a story of good-paying jobs and a new life before putting bags over their heads."

"Some life."

Robie leaned back against the cinderblock wall. "I'm not sure how good our lives are looking right now."

"Well, I don't see too many options."

He said, "We have to wait. And adapt."

"Story of our lives. What's Patti's motivation, do you think? It's not like she's living this rich lifestyle. She's still here in her dirty jeans and boots."

Robie shrugged. "I mentioned she might have daddy issues. Maybe that's it."

"Blue Man didn't even know he had a daughter."

"That's what Claire told us. Maybe she told Patti something else. Or she might have discovered it on her own."

"But that couldn't be why she went into a business like this," pointed out Reel.

"Like Dolph—or Fitzsimmons—said, I'm not a shrink. I don't know. All I do know is that we're in a tight spot with very few options."

"They're not going to let us sit here long. We'll be reported as missing at some point."

Robie said sharply, "By who? Both of the cops in this jurisdiction are out of commission."

"The Agency. When we don't get back to them."

"We can't count on *that* saving our lives."

"I've never counted on anyone else saving my life," retorted Reel.

Footsteps along the corridor alerted them that someone was coming. They both sat up straighter and stared expectantly at the barred cell door.

Patti Bender appeared there. They both noted that her fingers were tapping the butt of her holstered Glock. Then she reached her hand out of sight and jerked on something.

A moment later Blue Man was standing in front of them.

His clothes were dirty, his hair unkempt, and his face unshaven. Yet his eyes were clear and alert and his manner calm and unflustered. Like them, he was shackled.

Both Robie and Reel stood.

Blue Man said, "It's good to see you're both still alive."

"I was about to say the same to you," said Reel.

"Stop talking, please," Patti said quietly.

Blue Man glanced at her, and Robie noted something in his eyes that he never thought he would see in his superior.

Fear.

Patti nodded at something out of their line of sight, and a guard appeared. He unlocked the door and Patti pushed Blue Man forward, causing him to stumble as he crossed the threshold. The door was locked after him.

"It won't be long now," Patti said ominously. Then she disappeared.

Blue Man wearily sat on the cot against the wall while Robie and Reel hovered in front of him.

He looked up at them. "I trust London and Iraq went according to plan?"

"Not precisely according to plan, at least for me," said Reel. "But the mission was accomplished."

"We found your drawing in the gun muzzle," said Robie. "Atlas. We were just a little slow on getting to your actual meaning."

Blue Man nodded. "I knew that was a long shot, but I didn't have much time to consider alternatives."

"How did you figure out what was going on?"

"I didn't figure it all out—only enough pieces, I guess, to make people nervous."

"We know you spoke with JC Parry and Holly Malloy."

"JC is a good man, who knows a bit of my history. He came to me with this most incredible story of prisoners in hoods. That's what started all of this."

"How did you get onto the silo?" asked Reel. "I mean this one, the second silo?"

"I knew about the Atlas missile sites from growing up here. I knew there were two in the vicinity. By coming back here over the years, I knew that Roark Lambert had turned one into a doomsday safe haven for the affluent. But the other one had lain fallow all this time. But when Holly told me what Lamarre had told her, I started doing some digging. Where could you hide prisoners here? I knew of the neo-Nazis and white supremacists in the area. I knew of the Apostles, although they struck me as being rather innocuous."

Reel looked at Robie but neither of them spoke about King's actually being an FBI undercover agent. They didn't know if the cell they were in was being bugged or not.

Blue Man continued, "But I couldn't think of a reason why any of them would be bringing in prisoners. And they really didn't have the facilities to discreetly keep a group of people against their will. Word would have eventually gotten out." He paused. "But I had something else working to my advantage that perhaps others here didn't. I knew from reports that had crossed my desk that somewhere in this general vicinity it was suspected that there was a large-scale illicit drug-manufacturing center. Both DEA and ICE had internally reported on it to us. Though we can't operate domestically, the Agency still conducts joint task forces with our sister agencies. And there seemed to be an international element to this operation, which did bring it within our purview. But no one had been able to pinpoint the location in this country besides believing it was in a general six-state quadrant. That was far too large an area to do any type of concentrated search or investigation."

"Yes it is," agreed Robie.

"But one day I was taking a drive towards the old rock quarry. There are some good streams to fish in nearby. The quarry was in operation when I was growing up here, though it closed a long time ago now. But I had passed the second silo site on my drive, and it occurred to me for the first time how close the two sites were. I don't know why I had never noticed that before, but now I did."

"It took us a while to make the connection too," admitted Reel.

"I had the benefit of having toured this facility several times on some of my trips back many years ago. It's quite the labyrinth."

"We know you also toured Lambert's place," said Reel.

Blue Man nodded. "I wasn't sure what was going on or who was behind all this. I felt I had to look at all possible options. I knew Lambert through Claire. I got the tour so I could see the lay of the land. See if it was possible for them to be holding prisoners here. But it would have been problematic for Lambert to have prisoners at his silo. Too many people would know. This place is different. Thus, it didn't take a great deal of conjecture to come up with a possible solution to the problem of where one keeps prisoners clandestinely."

"Did you know they were going to take you here when you left the clue in your gun?" asked Reel.

"When I heard them coming, I thought they were going to either kill me or kidnap me."

"Have you seen the others? Lamarre or Parry? Valerie Malloy?"

"The sheriff? She was taken?"

"Just recently."

Blue Man shook his head. "I haven't seen anyone. They've kept me in a cell by myself."

"Patti Bender shot and killed her half brother," said Reel.

Blue Man looked deeply shaken at her words. "Derrick is dead? Does...does Claire know?"

"I doubt it. It just happened. They dumped his body in the quarry."

Reel looked closely at Blue Man. "Claire talked to us...about Patti. That she's...she's your daughter."

Neither one of them had ever seen Blue Man dumbstruck before. Neither had seen him out of control.

Until now.

He slumped over and put his head in his hands. A quiet sob escaped from his lips. "I never knew," he said hoarsely. "Oh my God. Patti."

Reel sat down next to him and placed a supportive hand on his quivering shoulder. "That's what Claire told us. And I don't think Claire knows anything about what's going on here."

Robie stared down at him. "We all have family issues, sir. You know that about us better than most."

Reel nodded as Blue Man slowly regained his composure and his gaze rose to meet Robie's. "We do, some perhaps more than others." He paused and took a deep breath and rubbed at his eyes. When he looked up the calm that they both had always associated with the man had returned. And his features seemed resolute. "I suppose you were sent out here to find me?"

Reel nodded. "The Agency can't lose you."

"Well, the Agency can't lose you both, either. More so than me, actually. And so I'm very sorry that you two had to be brought into this." He looked around at the cell and then down at his shackles. "They're very well organized."

"Which means it won't be easy," replied Reel, reading his thoughts.

"Did they show you what they're doing here?" asked Robie.

Blue Man shook his head. "I wasn't given the grand tour. But I had my suspicions because of the briefings I received. It's drugs, correct?"

"On a big scale. Dolph the neo-Nazi is actually a chemist geek named Arthur Fitzsimmons from Caltech doing his very best impression of Walter White from *Breaking Bad*. He and Patti are in this together."

Blue Man frowned. "Claire will be devastated by all this. Devastated." He slowly shook his head.

Reel said, "Fitzsimmons said they're closing up shop here and moving somewhere else. They know with all of us disappearing that an army of Feds are going to be converging on this place."

She fell silent as footsteps approached once more.

Patti reappeared at the door. "It's time," she said.

68

THEY WERE TAKEN down a series of stairways until it seemed to Robie that they had reached the lowest level of the silo. It was dark, the air dank, but warm. It was hard to breathe down here and he suspected that the air filtration was not really working at this level. There were flickering lights overhead but they gave, at best, a meager portion of light. And farther down the long corridor Robie could see that the light kept diminishing until, at one point, it receded to total darkness.

They neared a doorway when Patti, who had led the group to this point, stopped.

The armed men with them immediately pointed their weapons at the prisoners. Robie glanced at Reel and their looks said it all.

Is this it? The point of our execution?

But no one opened fire, even as a door in the wall opened and Robie, Reel, and Blue Man looked on, surprised, as another group of people joined them.

Three of them were in blue scrubs. Two were male, and the other was a petite woman. All three were Hispanic and they looked terrified.

A fourth person shuffled forward. He was tall and lean with a trim white beard.

Robie recognized him from a photo as JC Parry, the one who had told Blue Man about what Lamarre had seen. Then the man himself stepped out.

Clément Lamarre.

He was thin, with lank hair and a scraggly beard. Both men

looked dirty and weak, and Lamarre's face showed evidence of physical abuse.

Blue Man said, "JC?" He made a move to step forward, but one of the guards thrust a gun muzzle in his face and Blue Man quickly stepped back.

Patti faced off with her father.

"You're finally reunited with your old friend," she said, her gaze roaming over his face.

Blue Man stared back at her, a mixture of emotions fighting for supremacy on his features until one finally won out.

Empathy.

"Your mother never told me," said Blue Man. "I had no idea about…us. I'm sorry."

Her gaze now held firm on his. "But you're a very smart man, Mr. Walton. You could have easily figured it out. If you had wanted to. Which you obviously didn't. So I can't really accept your apology. Nor do I."

"I can understand that," said Blue Man.

"I don't really care if you do or not."

Robie interjected, "Where is Valerie Malloy?"

Reel glanced at him and then back at Patti.

Patti said, "Maybe she's dead. Maybe I shot the sheriff *and* the deputy."

Robie appraised her. "No, I don't think you did. So where is she?"

"I'm here, Robie."

Malloy appeared from around the corner being pulled along by another guard. She was shackled, and her face was bruised and cut in several places.

She was jerked within a foot of Robie and looked at him. "Good to see you." Her eyes were watery and unfocused, as though she might have been drugged.

Robie shot Patti a glance. "Why did you take her?"

When Patti said nothing Malloy said slowly, "The boot print at Walton's cabin. I finally recognized it."

"It was mine," said Patti. "Luckily, she told my brother first and he came to me. He just thought I'd been out there looking around after the fact and wanted to confirm that, which I did."

"Was that the other reason you killed him?" asked Reel.

"What!" barked Malloy, no longer looking unfocused. "You killed Derrick?" She tried to lunge at Patti but the guard held her back.

Reel said to Patti, "What happens now?"

Patti didn't even look at her. She spoke directly to Blue Man.

"I've hunted all of my life. I do it fairly. With respect. Sometimes I win, sometimes the thing I'm hunting does."

"I'm not following you," said Robie.

"It doesn't matter," said Patti, wiping a bit of dirt off her face. "And I won't be the one doing the hunting tonight."

"So does that mean we're the prey?" asked Reel. "We're the ones who are going to be hunted?"

She looked at Reel. "I had no beef with you, not really. I sort of liked you. Even admired you. But then you came here. Then you made me kill Derrick."

"We didn't make you do anything," retorted Reel. "You pulled the trigger."

Patti didn't even seem to hear her. She looked back at Blue Man. "You'll have a chance, not much of one I'll admit. But it's more than what I had in life. I got stuck in this place. I got stuck with…this."

"You don't have to do this, Patti," said Blue Man. "There are other options available to you."

She smiled. It made her look vulnerable and even lovely somehow.

And then she slammed her fist into his face. Blue Man staggered back as Robie and Reel moved forward, only to be met by gun muzzles and fingers pulsing on triggers.

As Patti rubbed her injured hand, Blue Man slowly straightened. There was blood pouring down his face from his broken nose.

"I suppose I deserved that," he said.

"So what?" said Patti. "But it's what I wanted to do. And so I did it. It's just how I'm wired."

She nodded to one of the guards.

And then Patti Bender turned and walked back in the direction from which they'd come. Soon she was out of sight.

Robie looked at the guard expectantly. "She said she hunts fair."

The guard cracked a smile. "Well, she's not hunting tonight, like the lady told you."

"So who is?" asked Robie.

"That would be me."

They all turned as the man came out of the shadows.

It was Scott Randall.

69

Randall stepped forward. He was wearing cammie gear, jump boots, and a pair of NVGs on his head, though they were tilted upward.

He was also carrying a Remington rifle with an infrared scope, both Robie and Reel noted.

And he was sporting a malicious grin.

"I was hoping we would hook up again at some point," he said. "We left things...incomplete last time."

"I thought the outcome was pretty straightforward," countered Reel. "You and your wife were lying on the dirt with your tails tucked between your legs."

Randall's grin faded. He shook his head. "You were maybe going to get a little bit of sympathy from me, lady. But that just went out the door."

"I don't need sympathy, certainly not from a dick like you."

"You need to learn how to keep your fucking mouth shut," shouted Randall.

Robie said, "Patti mentioned something about being fair?"

Randall turned to him and chuckled. "You'll be armed. You'll get a head start. Maybe you'll pull off a miracle. But I wouldn't bet the farm on it."

"Do we get NV optics?" asked Reel.

"That would be a negative," said Randall. "And just so you know, I won't be alone." He called over his shoulder. "Hey, guys, don't be shy. Come out and show yourselves."

From the shadows, seven men appeared. They were all tall and muscular with shaved heads and hardened countenances. They did not appear to share Randall's cavalier attitude toward what was happening. They said nothing. They held their weapons professionally and stood in the manner of men with military training.

Robie studied them. He assumed these must be the "badasses," and they looked it. They were completely focused. On the mission.

Killing us.

He said, "You guys look like the real deal. So I can't believe you're good with this idiot being your leader. He could lead you right to an early death."

"Shut up," snapped Randall. "The only ones dying tonight will be all of you. Especially you and the bitch."

Robie kept his gaze on the men. "You didn't answer my question." He glanced at Randall. "But maybe they already know the answer."

Randall pointed a finger at him. "I was an ROTC commander in college."

"Yeah, where I'm sure you killed quite a few kegs of beer," said Reel.

Blue Man stepped forward. "In the interests of not prolonging whatever this is, how exactly is it going to work?"

Randall focused on him. "It's a classic thing, really. You run and we hunt you down. We kill you or you kill us. It's even, right down to the numbers."

Parry looked around and said, "But there are nine of us and eight of you."

In answer to this, Randall pulled a pistol from his holster and shot one of the blue scrubs in the head. The man fell where he stood.

The man and woman in the blue scrubs leapt back. The woman started to sob.

"Thanks for reminding me," said Randall. "Almost missed that one. Never was good at math." He grinned.

Robie stared down at the body for a moment and then looked at Randall and said, "You mentioned that we'd be armed?"

In answer Randall pointed to a doorway in the wall. "In there. Guns for everyone. You arm up, you get five minutes to run, and then we come and find you. Kill or be killed."

Reel noted his optics. "But you'll have the clear advantage with those."

"Hey, *home field* advantage, way I see it. But you guys are Feds. You're supposed to be good."

"And how many times have you done this thing down here? Enough times that you know the lay of the land like the back of your hand?"

Randall shrugged this off. "Again, home field advantage. Gotta love it."

"And why are you doing this?" asked Blue Man. He looked at the hardened men behind Randall. "I mean if you're going to kill us, why go through something this melodramatic?"

Randall patted his rifle. "It's got a real purpose. It's honing our skills for when the apocalypse comes." He pointed upward. "When it hits, you're going to have all sorts of shit going on up there. And the little people are going to want to get in where we are. And despite all the stuff that Roark Lambert built into his site, some ass-wipes are going to get in. And then it'll come down to mano a mano. We've been training a while now."

"You mean killing all those enslaved drug workers?" said Reel. "Like that guy?" She looked down at the dead man.

"Hey, it serves a dual purpose. We don't like to keep them around too long. It's sort of like culling vermin, you know, that get in your house. And we have to practice our hunting skills, so we always need fresh meat. Win-win."

Reel continued to stare down at the dead man. "Not sure he'd see it that way."

"Who gives a shit?" said Randall.

"So the drug op was a way for you to fill your coffers back up?" said Robie. "After you went through your old man's fortune because you didn't know what you were doing?"

Randall said defensively, "I'm a good businessman. But people cheated me."

"Yeah, right."

"Enough jawing. We need to get going." He took a key from his pocket and tossed it to one of his men. "Take off the shackles."

The man handed his rifle to his colleague and came forward to do this.

Randall held up a stopwatch. "Once you're unshackled, you get five minutes. You can grab the weapons behind that door." He added with a grin, "And come up with a plan to survive. There's another door on the far side of the room. You go through there." He paused as the grin widened. "And then you run like hell."

Once the chains were off her, Reel rubbed her wrists and said, "Just to be clear, when we kill all of you, we're home free, right?"

Randall laughed, but Reel's expression didn't change. She gazed at each of the other men, lingering on their features, sizing them up. Then she returned to Randall.

"Is that right?"

"I'm not sure you have to worry about that."

"Is that right?"

"Yeah, it's fucking right, okay," snapped Randall impatiently.

"Thank you," said Reel. "I'll be sure to notify your wife of your passing."

Randall smirked at her. "You're living in an alternate reality."

"You have no clue to the reality I live in. But you're going to find out tonight."

She walked through the door to get her weapons. Robie and the others followed her.

70

"Do you speak English?" Blue Man asked the two people in scrubs, as Robie and Reel quickly looked over the weapons stacked on a shelf in the room.

The woman wiped her eyes and nodded. "Yes."

"What are your names?"

"I am Camilla and he is Mateo."

"Do you have any experience with guns?"

Camilla shook her head but Mateo said, "I have fired a pistol. My father's."

Robie hefted a rifle and looked at Reel, who was sliding a nine-mil into her waistband. She tossed one to him. He automatically checked the action and popped the mag to make sure there was ammo loaded in.

That was tough to do because it was so dark he could barely see the guns.

JC Parry walked over to them and said, "I can shoot either a rifle or a pistol."

Reel handed him a pistol and an extra mag.

Parry took it and said, "These are some sick sons of bitches."

"Let's just focus on turning them into *dead* sons of bitches." She glanced over at Lamarre. "What do you want, pistol or rifle?"

When he didn't answer Reel snapped, "We've got maybe thirty seconds. Which one?"

"Pistol, I guess."

"You ever fired one?"

"No. But I carried one at my old job."

She quickly showed him what to do.

Robie said, "I've been counting clicks. We've got sixty seconds."

Reel handed Blue Man a pistol and an extra mag. Robie passed a pistol to Mateo and shoved another pistol into his waistband.

He looked up as Malloy came over to him and put a hand on his shoulder. "I can't believe it's come to this."

"I can't believe a lot of things about this place."

"If we get out of here alive, I'm going back to New York."

"Sounds like a good plan." He handed her a nine-mil and gave her a reassuring smile. "For what it's worth, Jess and I are pretty good in situations like this."

She returned his smile. "Something I already know."

Reel called out, "What's our ammo count?"

"All told we've got a few hundred rounds," Robie answered.

"Roger that."

She walked over and eyed the door they had used to enter the room. She hurried over to the shelf, ripped off a metal slat, placed one end on the concrete floor, and jammed the other end against the doorknob.

"Good thinking," said Blue Man.

"Every second counts. Robie, any lights?"

He had just opened a box and held up two plastic flashlights. When he turned them on they emitted weak streams of light.

"They're not NVGs but they're better than nothing."

Parry said, "Hell, they'll give them a direct line to shoot us, even without the damn goggles."

"That's why we're going to use them in a different way," said Robie in a low voice.

Blue Man said, "I can help tactically."

Robie and Reel stared at him expectantly.

Blue Man continued, "Years ago, because of my professional status and due to some national security issues, I toured the silo and was even given some blueprints of the facility, which I kept in my cabin. I studied them when I realized that this place might be the center of what was going on." He pointed toward the far door. "Once we leave this room there's a long corridor to the right. The second door on the left will take us through a series of other doors and passages, to what was the maintenance wing of the complex. That's also where crew quarters are located. It's a rabbit's warren of spaces, which might give us some tactical cover."

Reel looked at Robie. "And also the possibility of ambush."

"Right." He looked at Blue Man.

"Ready?" said Reel. "Let's go."

She took point, opened the door, and slipped through it. The others followed in single file, with Robie bringing up the rear.

"They're gonna kill us all," said Lamarre. "You know that."

Robie, who was directly behind him, gripped his shoulder and said, "Just so you know, they killed Beverly Drango. Shot her and threw her body in a Dumpster in an alley in Denver."

Lamarre whirled around. "They...they killed Bev."

"Yeah. So start thinking about how you're going to kill them back."

Reel called out, "Robie, you want to test this thing?"

"Just thinking the same thing."

Parry looked at Blue Man, who was walking beside him.

"What are they talking about, Roger?"

"I'm not entirely sure, but I would rather have them with me right now than an entire Army brigade."

"Works for me."

Robie dropped back after telling Lamarre to keep going.

Malloy went with him even though he shook his head and pointed for her to continue on with the others.

"No," she said firmly.

He used the flashlight to briefly illuminate where they had come from. Then he balanced the light on a broken piece of brick on the wall so that it was about eye height, with the weak beam pointed in the direction of where they had come.

He stepped back and took aim with his pistol after motioning to Malloy to get down on her knees.

He heard banging.

They were breaking through the jammed door.

Robie counted to five as he envisioned them crossing the room and then opening the door.

He heard the squeak and waited a few more seconds, allowing them to recon the situation and conclude that it was safe to step out.

But they didn't wait. They stepped right out. That surprised him.

He could see their silhouettes, darker against the dark.

Robie opened fire, placing his rounds into legs, torso, and head. Ejected rounds from his pistol hit the floor.

Not a single one of the men he had shot at fell. Instead, they opened fire. The light shattered as they focused on that target.

But Robie knew with their optics that his hiding place would soon be uncovered. He did the only thing he could do. He grabbed up Malloy and they ran.

Shots hit all around them, pinging off the walls and ricocheting like pinballs.

"Robie!" she gasped.

"Keep going."

Robie knew that this was a shit show with a survivability rate hovering near zero. They were in a dark, narrow tunnel, and the people shooting at them had night optics.

There were several outcomes to this, and most if not all were bad.

Keeping a tight grip on Malloy's hand, he banged off one side of the wall and then careened into the other. He followed no pattern because he knew the shooters behind him were looking for that.

He let go of Malloy's hand. "Forward roll, now!"

As he came out of the roll, he felt the burn on his right calf and a similar sensation on his left shoulder.

He'd been lucky.

The bullets had grazed rather than entered his body.

When he looked at Malloy he realized she wasn't so lucky. Her left arm was dangling.

"In and out," she said between clenched teeth.

He saw the blood flowing down her limb. He gripped her right hand and pulled her along. With his other hand he pulled his pistol and emptied his mag behind them.

He was immediately answered with more rounds zinging his way. He slipped the pistol into his waistband and tightened his grip on Malloy's hand.

They passed one door on the right, then another on his left.

Right before a barrage of bullets blasted down the tunnel, he pulled Malloy forward and down as the rounds passed overhead.

They hit the floor and slid. Robie hooked the second doorway with his left hand, cantilevered his body around, and flung himself and Malloy through the open doorway.

A hand reached down and grabbed his, pulling him up.

Reel and Robie were eye to eye.

Robie helped Malloy to her feet.

"She's hit," he said.

"What the hell happened?" she said. "Did you take some of them out?"

Robie shook his head. "We're screwed."

71

ROBIE PUT HIS finger in the muzzle and spun his digit around. Slowly something came out of the muzzle. He held it up as Reel shined her light on it.

She muttered a curse under her breath. "Restrictor plug."

Robie nodded. "That explains the box of blanks you found at Randall's cabin. The restrictor caused just enough blowback to make the slider functional and enable the ejector to kick the bullets out. That's what confused me. I hit three of them with no result."

He popped the mag and pulled out a bullet. The end was crimped.

"Gunpowder but no bullet," said Reel.

Robie rolled Malloy's sleeve up and examined her wound. "You were right, in and out."

He tore a strip of cloth off his sleeve and used it to stanch Malloy's wound and then wrap it.

When he looked up Robie could see Blue Man and the others huddled near a doorway across the room.

Blue Man approached. "Status?"

In answer Reel raised her pistol and fired at the ceiling. Everyone jumped but when no bullet impacted the concrete ceiling Blue Man's features indicated he understood immediately. "So much for a fair fight," he said. "So what do we do now?"

"We keep moving," said Reel. "And we find or make weapons we can use against them."

"Let's go," said Robie. "I hear them coming."

They rushed out through the other door and Blue Man led them through a labyrinth of passages until they reached a steel door. They opened it and moved through.

"These are the crew quarters," said Blue Man as they looked around the dimly lit space. There were metal beds, some with rotted mattresses. Gunmetal-gray desks and shelving were aligned in another room they could glimpse through an opening. Cabinets were built into the walls.

"They must have a generator down here," observed JC Parry. "To make the lights work."

Robie and Reel weren't listening. Reel was collecting all of the ammo from their guns.

Lamarre said, "Why are you taking those? Guns are worth shit if you don't have bullets."

"Don't you get it?" replied Reel. "They're blanks."

"Blanks! We're in a shootout and we got blanks?"

Reel didn't answer. She took the mags over to a desk, set them down, and started searching drawers and cabinets. Blue Man helped her.

"What are we looking for?" he asked.

"Anything. Don't care what it is, just anything," she said tersely. "And look for a first aid kit. The medicine in there might not be any good, but there might be bandages for Malloy's arm." She called over her shoulder. "Robie, this is going to take time. We need to secure our flanks."

Robie nodded and said to Blue Man. "Is there any other way in here, other than through that door?"

Blue Man paused in his search and said, "Down that hall and to the left. It's the space where the missile would be stored before it would be raised up to fire. There's another door down that corridor coming off a hallway that runs perpendicular to this space."

Parry said, "Raised up? I thought there was a silo that the missile was lowered into."

"There is a firing silo, but the missile was kept on its side and then raised up into the silo for firing," explained Blue Man.

"Which doesn't really matter right now, guys," pointed out Reel as she grabbed things out of the drawers and piled them on the desk.

Robie motioned to Camilla and Mateo. "Camilla, you help them look for stuff we can use. Mateo, we need to find things to secure the two doors, okay?"

Mateo looked frightened but nodded.

Robie looked over some of the things that Reel and Blue Man had pulled from the drawers and cabinets. An old first aid kit was in there. Blue Man took some of the gauze and a roll of tape over to Malloy, who was sitting on one of the beds looking pale and sick.

Robie grabbed a roll of gray duct tape, then snagged some wooden boards that had formed the shelves of a storage unit against one wall.

He broke two boards in half, leaving jagged edges on each one.

He handed them to Mateo.

Next, Robie stepped to the door they had come through. He listened at the metal and then cautiously opened it and did a quick turkey peek. If there was someone out there he couldn't see or hear them.

He wrapped the outside doorknob over and over with the duct tape. Then Robie closed the door and took a board from Mateo. He jammed it under the door's bottom edge on the right side. He inserted the other board into the doorjamb and wedged the other end against the floor. He unlocked the door and tried to pull it open. It didn't budge.

He locked the door.

"Okay, that'll have to do. Let's go take a look at the other door."

As they passed by Reel, Robie could see that she had taken Parry's and Blue Man's glasses and had broken the plastic lenses and filed them to a jagged edge.

"Give me some of that duct tape, Robie," she said.

He did so and watched as she used the tape to secure a shard of the plastic to the end of a rifle barrel from which she had broken off the wooden stock. She handed it to Robie.

"Best I can do right now. I hope to have more soon."

He nodded, and he and Mateo headed off.

When they reached the second door into the space, Mateo said, "If we block off both doors, doesn't that trap us in here?"

"It could. But until we can equal the playing field we have to secure our flanks first. I'm hoping we get the chance to attack these suckers, but we're not there yet. So we make them come get us."

Robie did another quick turkey peek out the door.

This time the result was totally different.

Robie's hand moved faster than the eye could follow. It did so after years of training and fieldwork that demanded that he be able to do this or else die.

The shard of eyeglass lens cut right across the throat of the man who was standing on the right side of the door.

Blood spurted out from the man's slashed throat. His hands went up to his neck and his rifle dropped to the floor. Before it could hit, Robie caught the rifle and with his other hand he grabbed the man's collar and jerked him through the open doorway.

He kicked the door closed as bullets slammed into it.

Robie laid the man on the floor as he called out to Mateo to wedge the boards under the door and lock it.

Mateo rushed forward to do so.

Robie knelt next to the man, who was gurgling with blood in his throat. The man stared up at Robie, panic in his eyes, but also an emerging resignation.

Robie took the man's sidearm and held it against his temple. But he didn't pull the trigger. He didn't have to. The man's eyes became fixed and his mouth sagged as he finished bleeding out.

Robie looked back over his shoulder and saw Mateo frantically wedging the boards under the door and into the doorjamb.

Robie took the man's night optics, rifle, and spare ammo. He also took a sheathed knife from the dead man's belt.

"We're starting to even the playing field," said Robie.

"He's…he's dead?" asked Mateo, slowly straightening.

Robie headed off without answering. Mateo followed more slowly after giving a backward glance at the dead man.

72

Reel and the others had been busy.

Blue Man had fashioned a makeshift knife using a piece of wood, duct tape, and a long sliver of jagged metal he had found in an old toolbox.

Reel had used a pair of rusty pliers and an old vise bolted to the top of a worktable to extract all the gunpowder from the blanks. She had placed half the powder into a canvas bag they had found under one of the beds. The other half she had put in an empty paint can. She then added to each some nails, screws, and other bits of jagged metal that they had found in some of the cabinets.

When she saw Robie with the weapons and the NV goggles, she said, "How'd you score that?"

"Just lucky timing. What do we got?" he said, looking at the paint can.

"I'm taking a page from our 'friends' in the Middle East and making a couple of IEDs."

He checked on Malloy. Blue Man had dressed her wound as best he could.

"I can still fight," she said. "I'm right-handed, so make sure I have something to fight with."

Robie nodded and walked over to the table and picked up what had been the barrel of one of the rifles, which had also been removed from its stock. Duct-taped to the muzzle was a very sharp-edged piece of metal.

Reel called out, "So there are seven of them left?"

Robie nodded. "But don't put it past them to add reinforcements.

Remember that Dolph and Patti and some of their cronies might still be here."

"Let's focus on getting the seven first," replied Reel. "Especially Randall."

"They're going to have both doors covered," said Lamarre.

"Which means they had to split their force, three and four," said Robie.

"But if we open one of those doors they're going to open fire and we're dead," rejoined Lamarre.

"My, my what an optimist you are," said Reel.

"So what are we going to do?" asked Mateo.

"We need to create a diversion," answered Robie.

"With what?" snapped Lamarre. "Using one of us? Well, I'm not sacrificing myself."

"Well, that's a good thing, because we don't need you to. We have someone else to play that role," said Robie.

He walked out of the room and a minute later came back carrying the dead man over his shoulder.

"Holy shit!" exclaimed Lamarre. "What happened to him?"

Robie set the body down. "I killed him before he killed me." He examined Lamarre. "You're about his height. Switch clothes and put his ball cap on."

"What?"

"Take your clothes off and put his on."

"But they're covered in blood."

Reel stepped forward after hefting the piece of glass attached to the metal gun barrel. "Either switch clothes or I gut you right here. And then you'll be covered in blood. *Yours.*"

Lamarre looked at her incredulously. "You can't be se—"

Reel placed the glass right against his neck.

Blue Man said, "Based on experience I can tell you that she is *dead* serious."

Lamarre started quickly stripping off his clothes. While that was happening, Robie and Mateo had found an old push broom. After they had put Lamarre's clothes on the dead body, they used duct tape to secure the body to the broom and positioned him standing up. Reel used the tape to stick one of the nine-millimeter pistols to the dead man's hand and then taped it to his side so it looked like he was pointing it.

They moved the body over to the door they had come through.

Robie said to Reel, "We'll do the positioning, you take the rifle and goggles." He explained the plan to the others and put his hand on the door.

Lamarre said, "If they've got this night-vision shit, won't they know it's a dead guy? Their own dead guy?"

"Night optics aren't like looking at a high-def TV," pointed out Robie. "And they're going to have maybe a split second to decide to fire. But if you have a better idea, I'd be glad to hear it."

In response, Lamarre looked down at the floor.

Robie glanced back at Reel. She had on the optics, and the rifle was pointed toward the door.

"We can't tell which way," he noted.

"As you know, I can always be flexible," she replied, swinging the rifle to the left and then the right.

He looked at Blue Man and Parry, who had hold of the upright corpse.

"Move him closer to the door," he said.

They did so and then Robie glanced at the others. "Get out of the line of fire and stay down."

Malloy, Mateo, Camilla, and Lamarre backed away and knelt down.

"On the count of three," said Robie. He performed the countdown and then wrenched open the door.

Blue Man and Parry pushed the corpse forward and out into the corridor and then dropped to the floor.

Barely a heartbeat of time passed before the shots rang out, hitting the dead man in the head and chest but, of course, failing to kill him a second time.

Another second passed, then Reel's rifle fired three times.

They heard one scream and then two bodies hit the floor down the corridor and to the left. They heard feet running away.

"Three down, four to go," said Reel.

"And now they know we're armed," said Blue Man.

Robie said to Reel, "Let's go get some more real guns and level the playing field."

They sprinted out into the darkened hall, with Reel covering Robie.

Robie reached the dead men. Neither was Scott Randall.

Reel noted this and said, "Good. I want to kill him up close and personal."

Within thirty seconds they had two rifles, two pistols, a load of spare ammo, and another pair of night optics.

And something else of immense value that Robie quickly pocketed.

They ran back to the group and distributed the weaponry.

Robie put the night optics on and looked through them.

He noted the bullet hole through the right lens and glanced at Reel.

"Nice shooting."

"Do they still work?" she said.

"Better than what we had."

Reel said to the others, "Okay, now we outnumber them. We're going to go on the offensive and get the hell out of here."

Robie added, "We'll split up into two groups. Jess will go with one group and I'll go with the other. The third guy ran away to the right. We'll go that way. Jess and the others will go to the left."

"But how will we communicate, Robie?" asked Blue Man.

In answer Robie held up the other things of value he had found on the corpses.

Two communication packs complete with headsets.

"They're going to know that we took out two more guys and they'll have to assume that we got these. They'll change their radio frequency so we won't be able to get any intel from that. We'll change our frequency, too, and communicate that way."

They geared up and started to divvy up their forces.

Malloy stepped toward Robie and said, "I'd like to go with you."

Reel glanced at Robie but made no comment.

"Okay," he said. Looking at Blue Man he said, "Sir, you go with Jess, Mateo, and Lamarre. Parry and Camilla can come with me."

They split up into these groups.

Robie looked at Reel. "Good hunting."

"Same to you."

"Feel better about our odds?" he asked.

"I never doubted them. Even with fake bullets."

"You know they're going to bring reinforcements."

"God, I hope they do."

She turned and led her ragtag band away into the darkness.

73

Fuzzy green on black with constrained depth perception. Like being underwater with one eye closed.

That was the best way Robie could describe the world he was seeing now through his damaged optics.

His rifle was pointed out in front of him.

Behind him were Parry, Malloy, and Camilla. They were each armed, but they were counting on him to see what was coming.

Parry whispered hoarsely, "Getting hard to breathe."

Robie nodded. He had noted that, too. "They've probably cut whatever air filtration they have down here."

Camilla said fearfully, "So they're going to try to what, smother us?"

"Something like that."

It was also getting hot.

Malloy rubbed the sweat off her face. "Feels like a sauna down here."

"Yes, it does," said Robie.

She looked at him. "You're not even perspiring."

"I've been in dry heat before. I guess you get used to it."

"Dry heat? Arizona?"

"Try Fallujah. But when it's a hundred and thirty in the shade, it doesn't really matter whether it's a dry heat or not. It's just hot."

He paused and held a hand up. He motioned to Parry to kneel on his right and Camilla on his left. He tapped Malloy on the shoulder and indicated for her to follow him.

Then Robie saw it, but too late to do anything about it. The round zipped right past his waist.

He heard it impact something. That something grunted and then pitched forward.

Camilla cried out. "Omigod!"

Robie said nothing. He calmly aimed right above the muzzle flash he had just seen. His rifle barked twice. Malloy fired rounds from her pistol.

The shots went where they were supposed to and another man died.

Robie sprinted forward, keeping his rifle aimed in front of him. Malloy was right behind him, her pistol at the ready.

"Down!" Robie snapped.

They both hit the floor on their bellies as a hail of gunfire zipped right above them.

Robie returned fire, as did Malloy.

"Give me some cover," he told her. "Five shots and then stand down."

She slipped in a new mag and awaited his signal.

"Now."

She sprayed five shots at the other end of the hall.

Robie readied the canvas bag that Reel had given him. She had inserted a fuse through the bottom of the bag and run it into the pile of gunpowder inside.

He lit the fuse and looked at Malloy. "On the count of three, five more shots, direct them down the right side of the hall."

She nodded as he got to his knees and looked up ahead to see where his target was.

"One...two...three."

Malloy fired five rounds down the right side as Robie launched himself down the left side.

Come on, come on.

When Malloy's last round fired, he crouched down but kept moving forward.

Then he saw it. Two men, ten yards away on the left, preparing to fire.

He lit the fuse, let it burn to the side of the canvas, then swung the bag back and then hurled it forward. He looked like he had just launched a bowling ball. The bag slid along the floor.

He knew his IED didn't have a lot of range. He would have to get it close for it to do any good at all.

The men lined up their shots.

Robie could see this through the one good eye of his optics. He sprawled on his stomach, his hands over his ears and his eyes closed.

The canvas bag slid within six inches of the men when the flame hit the nail-and-screw-infused powder. There was a boom and a flash and then heavy smoke.

When it cleared Robie saw the two men. Or what was left of them.

Jessica Reel obviously knew how to build an improvised explosive.

He hustled over to the dead men. Though the bomb had done considerable damage, he could see that neither was Scott Randall. He had already seen through his optics that the man he had gunned down wasn't Randall, either.

Okay, five down, three to go.

Robie felt like he was back in London.

Malloy looked in the direction of the explosion and said, "Are we good?"

Robie looked behind him at the body of JC Parry.

Camilla was standing helplessly over it with tears in her eyes. "He…he must have seen something. He threw himself in front of me. He saved my life. And lost…his."

Malloy crossed herself and said quietly, "JC's a hero."

"Yeah, he is," said Robie. "And it's our job not to let him die in vain."

Malloy drew closer to Robie, rubbing her injured arm. "This is a nightmare."

"No, a nightmare is what's coming for the rest of these assholes."

74

SHARP AND CLEAR.

The dark passage was bright as day in Jessica Reel's optic-powered universe.

She was point with Blue Man behind and on her right.

Mateo was on her left looking determined.

Lamarre was bringing up the rear looking terrified.

"Can you tell where we are?" Reel asked Blue Man.

He looked around and nodded. "The passage bleeding off the secondary hall to the missile room. Up ahead is a door on the left that will access that space."

"And beyond that? How do we get back to the surface?"

"Through the missile room there are stairs leading up."

Reel's comm crackled.

It was Robie. "Three down and done," he reported.

"Casualties?"

"Parry."

"Randall?"

"Negative. He must be on your end."

Reel smiled grimly. "Give me your nine."

He told her his location. She relayed this to Blue Man, who then took the comm and told Robie how to get to the surface before passing the headset back to Reel.

Reel said into the headset, "I'll nail the three if they're still down here. Then we need to hook up at the point Blue Man just relayed to you. From there we can fight our way out."

"Roger that. On our way."

Reel's headset went silent. She turned to Blue Man. "Parry's dead."

Blue Man looked at her grimly. "JC was a good man who got caught up in something while trying to do the right thing."

"The same could be said for you," Reel pointed out.

Lamarre said from the rear, "Hey, do we have any idea what the hell we're doing?"

The bullet caught him in the back of the head and ended the need for any answer to his query.

Mateo screamed and threw himself down on the floor as Reel and Blue Man turned.

Reel dropped to the floor, sighted through her optics, and fired three shots. She only had one image in her scope but she wanted to be sure.

The dead man hadn't hit the floor yet before she had found and acquired another target. This time she only pulled the trigger once.

It was enough, as the round tattooed a black hole on the man's forehead.

Another shot rang out, and Reel heard a grunt behind her.

Even as feet ran away down the hall, she turned and rose up in time to stop Blue Man from falling.

"Where?" she said.

His face gray and his breathing labored, he pointed to his right shoulder.

She felt the front of his shoulder and found the entry wound. She felt the back of his shoulder and found nothing. The round was still in him. It might have banged around inside her boss and done far more damage than was readily apparent.

She muttered a silent curse.

"Mateo!" No answer. "Mateo!"

"Y-yes."

"Are you hurt?"

"N-no."

"Then I need your help."

Mateo rose and took Blue Man's right arm, helping to hold him up.

Reel checked Lamarre, but it only took a glance to see that he was dead. The rifle round had gone through the back of his head and stayed in his brain, because there was no exit wound in the front. That sort of shot was fatal ten times out of ten, because all the bullet's kinetic energy stayed inside the brain.

Hard metal against soft tissue was no contest at all.

She took the paint can with the IED that Lamarre had been carrying and hooked it to her belt.

Reel had brought some first aid supplies. With Mateo's assistance they cleaned and bandaged Blue Man's wound as best they could.

The man showed his grit by not making a sound as they worked around the wound.

Then Reel got on her comm and explained the situation to Robie. "How bad is he?"

"Bad enough. We have to get out of here pronto."

"We're double-timing it."

After that they slowly moved down the passage heading toward the door that Blue Man had mentioned. It was bothering Reel that the remaining shooter—she didn't know if it was Randall or not—had been running in the opposite direction from the passage leading up. But maybe there was another route. She would have liked to ask Blue Man, but he was in no condition to answer.

They reached the doorway, and after Reel made sure it was clear, they passed through.

Or so she thought.

The bullet barrage hit them at their most vulnerable.

It couldn't be just one person, Reel knew. Because she was hearing different types of weapons firing.

She dropped to the floor and returned fire.

When she looked to her left, she saw Blue Man lying there breathing heavily.

On top of him was Mateo.

Where his left eye should have been was a gaping hole.

Shit.

Reel grabbed Blue Man by the back of the shirt and dragged him behind a stack of metal bars situated near a wall.

She said, "Are you hit again?"

"No. Mateo?"

"Dead."

Reel peered over the stack of bars and nearly got her head blown off for the effort.

They were pinned down. She got on her comm pack and relayed their situation to Robie.

"Two minutes away," he replied.

As the line went dead Reel knew she didn't have two minutes.

Blue Man was bleeding. They were pinned down. If Robie and the others tried to come though that door they would get slaughtered.

She took the scope off her rifle and managed to work it between two of the bars on top of the stack.

She saw three men parked at the top of the short stack of stairs that led through a door and then up several more flights of stairs to the surface. They had high ground, good cover, and thus the clear tactical advantage. That also meant that reinforcements had joined the battle.

She was never going to get off enough shots to take these guys out without exposing herself to return fire. And if she went down it was all over.

She gauged the distance between her and them.

Thirty feet.

It might be possible.

But she needed a diversion. And they had no handy corpse on a stick.

She got back on her comm and explained her plan to Robie.

"Roger that. One minute."

"Give me a five-click warning," she said.

"Done."

She told Blue Man what she was about to do.

"You going to wish me luck?" she said.

Holding his shoulder he managed a weak smile and shook his head.

"I know," said Reel. "It's never about luck."

She put the scope back on her rifle's rail, ran through the plan in her mind, and judged it to be good enough. She eyed the top of the metal stack and the trajectory there to her intended target.

Then she loosened up her right throwing arm. This was far more intense than throwing out the first pitch on opening day. If she didn't toss a strike, they were dead.

She positioned her rifle barrel on top of the metal stack, making sure to keep her head below the barrier.

She got the five-click warning from Robie.

What she was about to attempt was the mother of all multitasking.

You can do this, Jessica. This isn't as hard as what you did back in Iraq. Nothing is as hard as what you did back in Iraq.

The door burst open and shots were fired through it.

As Reel expected, her adversaries pointed their weapons that way and returned fire.

She stood with the paint can in her right hand. She swung it around to gain momentum and force and then heaved it at the stairs.

As soon as it left her hand and arced toward the target she dropped to the floor and sighted through her rifle as the paint can began its descent.

She waited...waited.

Her aim with the can had been good enough.

Her focus was complete. There was nothing else on earth right now, other than her and that can.

Like shooting clay pigeons.

She fired.

The round punctured the can and the heat from the bullet did what the match and fuse would have accomplished.

She ducked down right before the explosion.

After the smoke cleared she sighted through her optics.

Her pitch had been long and loopy, but ultimately right down the middle of the plate.

A few moments later Robie was next to her.

"It worked," he said. "But we lost Camilla. She caught a round in the chest."

He turned to Malloy. "You're going to stay here with Walton. Watch his bleeding and do whatever you can to comfort him. I don't think there are any of them left down here, but be on guard."

Malloy didn't look pleased by this plan at all. "I can fight," she said.

"I have no doubt of that," said Robie. "But Jess and I will be better off without anyone."

"You think I'm going to hold you back. I can take care of myself."

"And you think leaving a wounded man alone makes sense?" said Reel.

Malloy hesitated and then said resignedly, "Okay. But what are you going to do?"

"We're going to finish this," said Reel.

75

"Déjà vu all over again," whispered Reel as they moved along. "We're hunting in pairs."

"If it ain't broke, don't fix it," replied Robie.

Reel glanced sharply at him, but he wasn't looking at her.

He had snagged an undamaged pair of optics off one of the dead men and took a long look around.

There was a door up ahead, at the top of the stairs. They reasoned that just beyond it was the level on which they had entered the silo. They needed to get help. They were well aware that Blue Man could not survive much longer in his condition.

They were also under no delusions that there would be no one on the other side of that door waiting to kill them.

"If Randall is still here, leave him to me," Reel said.

"You really hate the guy."

"*Hate* doesn't really cut it."

They reached the door and Robie put his ear against it, listening intently.

He nodded and Reel cautiously opened the door as they each peeled off to either side of the portal.

They both recognized the staccato burst of an MP5 emptying dual mags.

"Me high, you low," said Robie.

Sixty rounds later Reel and Robie pointed their rifles through the doorway and sprayed their rounds in a one-eighty arc, top to bottom.

They caught the man reloading the MP5. One of Reel's rounds

tore into his thigh while two of Robie's bullets hit the man in the head and chest, respectively.

They burst into the room and Reel grabbed the MP5 from the dying man's grip, while Robie pulled free two full mags from holders on the man's pants.

"Good lesson in keeping some of your powder dry, *moron*," said Reel to the dying man.

"This is the JV team," said Robie. "We left the varsity down below."

Reel slammed the mags in and gripped the weapon as she looked ahead. "I recognize this hall."

"I do too. The manufacturing area Fitzsimmons showed us is that way," said Robie, pointing to his left. "So that means the long passage where we took the golf cart ride to see Bender's body dumped is beyond that."

"And the exit door out of this hellhole."

He stooped over the dead man, searched his pockets, and pulled out a phone. "It's passcode-protected," he said, tossing it down as the phone's owner breathed one last time before expiring.

"How many you think are left?"

"Considering they only had one guy waiting to greet us here, I think their numbers are limited."

"Or maybe some of the guards up here have jumped ship."

Robie nodded. "I don't know what they're getting paid, but it's probably not enough to die for."

"Fitzsimmons's Nazi guys?"

"I can't believe they recruited any of them for this. He'd want to keep his identity separate. But Patti probably has stuff in reserve. And then there's Randall."

They passed through another doorway and moved down the well-lighted hall.

"I don't like this," said Robie.

"Too easy," added Reel.

"In here," said Robie.

They slowly opened the door and found themselves in the drug-manufacturing area they had seen previously.

But unlike before, it was totally empty. The work areas looked like they had been deserted recently. Chemicals were still bubbling, computers were still working, and they could see half-finished projects all around. But the motorized assembly line had been shut down.

"You think they cleared out?" asked Robie.

"Well, Fitzsimmons said they were moving their operations beginning tonight. Maybe they started with getting the workers out of here."

Reel nodded, her gaze reaching out to all corners of the room. "So let's go find them before they find us."

Robie peeled off his comm pack. "How about a little misdirection first?"

He turned the frequency back to the original one. He adjusted his headset, then held it away from himself and started speaking. "You're wounded and you've got no way to get out of here. Just contact Patti and the others and tell them it's over. Do it now. It's your only chance to survive this."

Silence of course followed, and Reel said in a loud voice, "Just kill him, Robie."

"We kill him, we're not going to be able to find our way out."

Reel waited a moment and said, "I know where we are. We're ten minutes from the manufacturing area we were in. I can get us out of here once we reach it."

Robie said, "Then we don't need this guy after all." He deliberately pulled back the hammer on his weapon.

Reel said, "Don't use the gun. Too much noise. Slit his throat."

Robie pushed some stuff off a workbench and then made other scuffling noises followed by a scream and a gurgling sound. Then he pushed a box off a shelf to create a thudding noise, as though a body had just hit the floor.

Robie turned off the comm pack.

"You think they bought it?" she asked.

"I think we're going to find out."

76

THEY DIDN'T HAVE to wait long.

The door to the area they were in burst open two minutes later and four men hurtled through the opening.

Scott Randall was one of them.

Three trigger pulls by Robie and Reel later, and Randall was the only one left alive.

Randall threw himself behind a cabinet and shouted, "I'm going to kill you fuckers dead!"

Reel cast an amused glance at Robie. "And how are you going to manage that, Scotty?" she said.

She followed this up by placing a round right through the cabinet. Randall screamed and sprawled on the floor in plain sight.

Reel pointed her rifle at his head.

He had a pistol in his hand.

"Go ahead, Scotty. Kill me dead."

"You'll shoot me before I can."

"Boy, aren't you the smart one."

He let go of the pistol, pushed it away with his elbow, slowly stood, and raised his hands. In a sneering voice he said, "You think you've got me? You've got shit."

"A little remorse goes a long way," said Reel.

"Remorse for what? I've done nothing wrong."

"You call drug trafficking and murder right?" said Robie.

"I've got nothing to do with the drugs."

"So you're just doing this out of the goodness of your heart?"

"I get paid a fee for professional services."

"And the killing of innocent people?"

"They're nobodies. Who cares? It's not like I'm killing people who matter."

Reel glanced at Robie. "You know, just when you think someone couldn't go any lower."

Robie said to Randall, "You're going down for all of this. I don't care how much you have in your bank account."

The man shook his head. "None of this is my fault. I've done nothing wrong. It's everybody else's problem. Go after them." He pointed a finger at them. "Listen up, I'm somebody. I have incredible value to the world."

"What you have is a classic narcissistic personality," said Reel. "On top of being an asshole."

Randall's sneer deepened. "You know what else I've got? The best lawyers money can buy. They'll make mincemeat out of you. He said, she said. I won't spend one day in jail, guaranteed."

"You think so?" said Reel.

"I *know* so, bitch."

"You know what, I think you may be right. I mean whoever heard of a millionaire on death row, right? It's all about the high-priced lawyers. You buy justice in this country. Right?"

"Got that right, sweet cheeks. Maybe you got a brain after all."

"But that only happens if there's a trial."

"Everybody's entitled to a trial."

"Not everybody."

Randall looked incredulous. "It's in the Constitution, you dumbass. And you call yourself a Fed. Jesus."

"Yeah, but you have to be alive, right? No dead guys go on trial. I mean, what would be the point?"

Randall looked puzzled. "What the hell are you..." Then realization spread over him.

"Exactly," said Reel, right before she pulled the trigger.

As he fell dead to the floor with a hole in his face, Reel looked over at Robie. "You have a problem with that?"

"Problem with what?" replied Robie evenly.

"Some ways it's good not to be a cop. All that 'you have the right to remain silent' bullshit."

Robie looked down at Randall. "Well, he's definitely silent now."

She lowered the rifle. "Just saving the public the expense of a trial. The government doesn't have a lot of spare cash."

"Works for me. But we have to get Blue Man out of here fast, or he's not going to make it."

They both looked at the door through which Randall and the others had charged.

Reel said, "What do you think? Patti's still out there. And our fake Nazi friend."

"Actually, I'm right here."

Robie and Reel whirled to look behind them.

Patti Bender was standing there with a gun held to the temple of Blue Man.

He said weakly. "There was another way down there, apparently. It wasn't on the original plans."

"That's because we put it in ourselves," said Patti.

"Where's Malloy?" said Robie.

Patti studied him. "You liked her, didn't you?"

"Is she dead?"

"Not yet."

"What does that mean?"

"It doesn't really matter." She pushed the gun muzzle tighter into Blue Man's skin.

"He needs a doctor," said Reel.

"No he doesn't," replied Patti. "He doesn't need anything."

"You can't kill all of us," said Reel, her grip tightening on her gun. "You drop him, you're dead."

"It's my preferred way," she said calmly.

"So you're suicidal?" said Robie. "Is that your way out?"

"You have no idea what you're talking about."

"Sure I do. I know exactly what you're going through, actually. Daddy issues."

Patti shook her head. "If you think all this is about my 'father' here, you're about as wrong as you can possibly be. I don't care one way or another. I had a dad growing up until he got killed. He wasn't great, but he wasn't bad either. If Walton hadn't started digging into what was going on around here, I'd have no problem with him."

"Then you just like killing people?" said Reel.

Patti looked at her. "Don't you?"

"It's my job."

"Well, it's part of my business, so I guess we're more alike than not."

"And the drugs?" said Robie. "Hooking up with Fitzsimmons?"

Patti shrugged. "I grew up with nothing in the middle of nowhere. I've always had a chip on my shoulder, and the years only made it grow bigger. My mom started making money later in life but it's not mine. I didn't earn it. I wasn't going to piggyback on what she did. And a legal pot business? Anybody can do that. I wanted to do something that was far more challenging."

"So it is just about the money," said Robie. "Your island in the Caribbean?"

"I can't say it sucks, because it doesn't. I had wanted to move there permanently, someday. But I guess that's not going to happen now."

"Patti, please don't do this," said Blue Man.

"I *am* going to do this and there's nothing you can do about it. Father or not."

"I'm asking you for the last time," said Blue Man.

"And I'm telling you to shut up and die like a man. I'll be right behind you. Who knows, if I get lucky I might take one of your friends with me."

Blue Man jerked his arm and there was a thudding sound.

Patti looked down to see the makeshift knife that Blue Man had fashioned earlier sticking out of the center of her chest.

For one long second father and daughter stared at each other. Then the blood started to ooze from Patti's mouth and she fell forward. Despite his injury Blue Man grabbed his daughter and gently laid her down on the floor.

He knelt beside her and held her hand as her breaths starting coming faster and her chest began to heave.

"I'm sorry," said Blue Man. "I'm sorry I didn't know. Things might have been different if I had."

Patti gazed at him for a moment longer. She started to say something but then her eyes glazed over and her body went limp as she died.

Blue Man reached over and closed her eyes.

Reel and Robie stepped forward, as one, and each put a hand on Blue Man's shoulder.

"I'm so sorry, sir," said Reel.

Blue Man slowly rose with their assistance.

When his gaze fell on Robie he said shakily, "I now know how your father felt. And I..." His voice trailed off and he could only slowly shake his head.

"Yes sir," said Robie.

The next second, the explosion rocked the room, pitching them head over heels.

CHAPTER

77

Dɪʀᴛ, ᴅᴜsᴛ, ᴏᴍɪɴᴏᴜs creaks of support beams.

Then part of the roof caved in, making a thunderous noise and filling the room with more smoke, dust, and debris.

Robie opened one eye and looked around at a world that seemed turned upside down. Something heavy was on top of him. When he struggled to turn on his side the weight lessened and then fell away altogether.

He was looking at the body of Patti Bender. The explosion must have thrown them together, with her body landing on top of him.

Robie slowly regained his footing and looked around at the devastated space.

The bomb must have been in the room somewhere.

As his reason returned he became panicked.

Reel?

Blue Man?

He heard a moan and raced toward it.

Under a desk and a metal file cabinet he found Reel, bruised and bloody but alive.

"Blue Man?" she said as she got to her feet with his assistance.

"Don't know."

They frantically searched the room until they found him.

He was alive, but the gray tinge on his features told him that it would not be for long.

And then they heard another sound and looked up.

Fresh cracks were appearing in the ceiling. In other spots where the ceiling had already given in, they could see rock behind it.

"The whole thing's starting to cave in," said Reel. "When they said they were moving their operation, I didn't take it to mean they were going to bury what was here."

Robie helped Blue Man to his feet.

"Take him out of here, quick as you can."

"Me? Where are you going?"

"Malloy," he said, before turning away and hurtling over debris toward the door they had come through.

"Robie!" cried out Reel, but he had already passed through the door.

Reel turned, and with Blue Man leaning on her made her way to the exit door.

Robie double-timed it down several flights of stairs even as the facility shuddered and creaked around him. Breathing hard, he burst into the room where they had left Malloy.

It didn't take him long to find her. She was lying on the floor behind the pile of metal Reel had used as a shield. She was bound hand and foot with a cloth over her nose and mouth.

Robie knelt down next to her and took off the cloth. He saw blood on her neck. When he examined it more closely he saw the cut there. He instantly knew what Patti had done.

She's nicked the carotid. Slow death.

Malloy was not conscious. Robie lifted her off the floor and carried her up the stairs. As soon as he cleared them, the space gave a long shudder and a section of the stairs fell away.

He redoubled his efforts, racing up the next two flights of stairs and down the long hall until he reentered the space where the drugs had been manufactured.

He carried Malloy over to the door.

"R-Robie?"

He looked down. Malloy was awake now and staring up at him.

"Just stay quiet. We're getting out of here."

Her face was deathly pale.

Robie had used the cloth to wrap the wound, but she needed medical attention or she was going to die.

And even if they got out of here it was a long way to a hospital.

Blue Man and Malloy were probably going to expire before they could get help. And there was nothing he could do about it.

But he was still going to try.

He edged open the door and slipped through.

"Get on!"

It was Reel. She had loaded Blue Man onto the golf cart.

Robie ran forward and sat down in the rear-facing seat while still holding Malloy.

"I told you to get out of here," Robie snapped.

"And I decided on a different course," she snapped right back. "How's Malloy?"

"Not good. Patti cut into her carotid."

"Shit!"

Reel punched the accelerator and they rocketed forward.

The tunnel fortunately did not collapse on them. At the other end they got off and hustled as fast as they could to the exit door. From the inside it only required the turning of a crank.

After hurrying down the passage they were out in the open air.

"They said they got rid of the vehicles," called out Reel, who was supporting Robie. "Can we find some way to call for help?"

"What the hell is that?" said Robie.

They heard the *whump-whump*, and then felt the prop wash as the large chopper descended.

They backed away to allow the skids to hit the dirt. The door to the aircraft opened.

"Agent Sanders?" cried out Reel.

It was indeed FBI Special Agent Dwight Sanders. He was dressed in cammies with a bulletproof vest.

He grinned at them, but that grin quickly faded when he saw Blue Man and Malloy.

"They need medical attention, fast!" screamed Robie.

Sanders and two other men jumped out and raced over. They carried Blue Man into the chopper while Robie hustled over to it, still carrying Malloy.

"Got room for all of us in this bird?" shouted Reel over the roar of the chopper's blades.

"You bet we do," Sanders shouted back.

They loaded everyone into the chopper.

Sanders called out to the pilot, "We got two badly wounded. Hit it fast to the hospital. I'll call ahead. We can land right on the roof."

They lifted off and the chopper turned around and hurtled across the dark sky.

"Wait a minute," barked Robie. "Hit that with your light." He pointed down at a vehicle that was moving fast around the far lip of the quarry and had nearly reached the road leading down.

One of the crewmen activated a spotlight and shined it on the vehicle as they swept lower.

"It's Dolph!" exclaimed Reel. "Or Fitzsimmons, or whatever the hell his real name is."

It was indeed the man driving in an open-top jeep.

Robie grabbed his rifle with the scope and said, "Take me down lower. I'm going to jump for it."

Reel grabbed his arm. "What the hell are you talking about?"

Robie glanced over at Malloy, where the EMTs were working frantically on both her and Blue Man.

He said to Reel, "I made a promise. I gave my word."

Reel looked over at the unconscious Malloy and slowly removed her hand.

The chopper dropped lower as Robie opened the door and climbed out onto the skid.

He called out to Sanders, "Once I'm clear hit it to the hospital."

"But what about you?" asked Sanders.

"I'll find my way back."

When the chopper was about six feet off the ground Robie leapt, landed, rolled, and came up in a crouch.

The chopper immediately rose, banked, and soared away in the opposite direction.

Robie sprinted forward about ten yards, keeping the jeep in sight the whole time. Then he dropped to the dirt, lay prone, and took aim through his scope.

It would have been difficult to say who was the better shot, Robie or Reel. It might have depended on the day in question.

But this day, not one sniper in the world had more motivation to bring down his target than Will Robie.

He fired.

His first round tore into the left rear tire. The jeep went sideways off the road and plowed into a mound of dirt.

Robie rose and sprinted forward.

A panicked Fitzsimmons looked behind and saw what was coming. He put the jeep in reverse and backed it out. He got it back on the road and hit the gas. But with the bum tire the jeep couldn't go very fast.

Behind him Robie picked up his pace. He had never run this swiftly in his life. Yet even with the bad tire, he would not be able to catch Fitzsimmons.

He dropped to the ground again, took aim, and shredded the other rear tire.

The jeep went off the road onto the other side. Fitzsimmons fought to get it back on the road, but the tire unraveled and came off the rim.

Fitzsimmons leapt out of the jeep, wildly fired a few shots in Robie's general direction, and ran for it.

But now, with its being a footrace, the conclusion was foregone.

Robie hit him low and hard, and both men tumbled to the dirt. Robie landed on top of Fitzsimmons and immediately cranked his right hand out and back, then levered the forearm at a backward angle until it shattered.

Fitzsimmons screamed, but Robie flipped him over, struck him with his elbow directly in the face, and crushed the man's nose.

Robie raised his fist again with the intent of driving it right through the man's skull when he paused.

The bloody Fitzsimmons stared up at him.

"Do it. Kill me. Do it."

Robie could easily have done it. He had killed many men who were far superior fighters. Instead, he lowered his fist, took out the duct tape he had kept in his pocket, and secured Fitzsimmons's arms and legs. He rose.

Fitzsimmons gazed furiously up at him. "What are you doing?"

"Colorado doesn't have the death penalty. So you get life without parole. But I'm thinking that you're a terrorist. So maybe you go to Gitmo, or another place not in this country. Where there are no rules, and where your jailers may not even be American."

"I'm an American citizen," sputtered Fitzsimmons. "You can't do that!"

"No, you're Dolph on your very own patch of sovereign soil. American laws don't apply to you. You told me so yourself. So maybe we'll send you to the Israelis. They know how to deal with Nazis."

"You can't do that!" Fitzsimmons screamed.

Robie knelt next to him and placed his face an inch from Fitzsimmons's. "You're going to find out that I can do *anything*."

He rose and started to walk away.

"Where are you going?" screamed Fitzsimmons.

"To find us a ride."

"You can't leave me here. There are…animals."

"I'm sure there'll be enough of you left to send to prison."

Fitzsimmons kept screaming.

And Robie kept walking.

CHAPTER

78

"YOU HAVE DONE a great service to your country."

Rachel Cassidy finished speaking and sat back in her office at Langley.

Robie and Reel sat opposite the director.

"We wouldn't be here without your intervention, Director," pointed out Reel. "Agent Sanders told me that you dialed up the FBI director and that he sent Sanders looking for us. Luckily, they spotted Fitzsimmons's jeep near the door into the silo and came in for a closer look. If you hadn't done that, there was no way Blue Man was going to make it."

"But he did make it. And so did Sheriff Malloy."

Robie looked at her. "And Fitzsimmons?"

"Need to know, Robie," she said, her eyes twinkling. "I do have a status report on Fitzsimmons. Do you by chance read Hebrew? I know you've been to *Israel* quite often." Her eyes twinkled even more.

"No, I don't, Director, but I think you answered my question."

Her gaze swept over them. "So another mission successfully accomplished. After completing arduous missions before that." She tapped her fingertips together.

Robie glanced at Reel, but by her look she was as puzzled by the director's words as was Robie.

"I think you two need a little time off, but I have a suggestion as to where you should go."

"Where?" said Reel warily.

"I'd like you to accompany an old friend to eastern Colorado."

"Blue Man wants to go back?" said Robie incredulously. "There?"

"Well, it *is* his hometown. And there is someone there he needs to talk to. About something important. Will you go with him?"

Robie and Reel didn't need to look at each other.

They both said "Yes" at the same time.

* * *

"It was so good of you both to come."

Blue Man was thin and drawn. It was the result of being in a hospital for nearly a month recovering from his various wounds. He was sitting across a table from Robie and Reel.

As the Agency jet descended into the airspace over Colorado, Blue Man's hand flicked to his necktie. He was dressed as he always had been at the Agency: conservative dark suit, striped tie, and crisp white shirt, along with black wingtips. He next moved a strand of hair back into place.

"You look very handsome," said Reel as she observed his movements.

He seemed embarrassed by her comment, turning slightly red. "Being shot does not do much for one's appearance."

"What are you going to say to her?" asked Reel.

"I've been thinking about it every day. And I'm still not sure. I've never been this indecisive in my life. If I did my work with this much uncertainty, I wouldn't last a minute in the job."

"This is different," Robie pointed out. "This isn't a job."

Reel said, "We went by your old home. We know what happened there and were puzzled that you decided to keep it."

Blue Man nodded. "I was perhaps puzzled myself. But in the end it came down to this: I had many happy memories there, and one single awful memory can't be allowed to erase that from my life. Keeping the house and some of my old memorabilia there was a way for me to remember it."

The plane landed, and an SUV was waiting for them.

As soon as they stepped into the vehicle and buckled up, the driver set off. He apparently knew the address, because he asked for no instructions.

When they arrived at the house, Blue Man said, "It might be better if you wait out here."

"Are you sure?" asked Reel.

"No, but I still think I need to do this alone."

"Are you going to tell her…about what happened to Patti?" asked Robie.

"I think now is the time to tell the absolute truth," replied Blue Man.

He closed the door behind him and walked slowly up the drive to Claire Bender's home.

They watched as he knocked. A few moments later the door opened and there was Claire.

Even from this distance Robie and Reel could see that the woman looked like she had aged ten years.

She stepped back for Blue Man to enter and shut the door behind them.

She had glanced once in the direction of the SUV, but the tinted windows prevented her from seeing inside.

Robie said, "You want to take a stroll?"

They crossed the road and walked across a field. The air was nippy and Reel stuck her hands in her jacket pockets.

"What's up?" she asked.

"I met with Malloy."

Reel looked taken aback for a moment. "Where?"

"Brooklyn. She moved back there after she got out of the hospital."

"I can understand that. No reason for her to come back here."

"None," said Robie. "I did tell her that I got Fitzsimmons. I sent her a picture of him all duct-taped."

"I'm sure she appreciated what you did, Robie, but I wish they could have found her sister's body."

"They did."

Reel gave him a sharp glance. "What?"

"It was in the same place they found Derrick Bender's. The quarry. They drained it two weeks ago. It was a graveyard. They're still counting corpses."

Reel stopped walking. "Jesus."

She looked at the dirt.

He drew closer to her but kept a bit of space between them.

"It can end any minute. We know that better than most."

She glanced up at him, her brow furrowed. "I think I know that better than you."

"Come again?"

"It *will* end for us, Robie. Maybe not tomorrow, or the next day. But it will. With a bullet to the head. Or a knife to the gut."

"So that's that, then?"

"What else? We have occupations where the survival rate is pretty damn low. Do you really want to commit to a person doing that? I'm not sure I do. Do you understand how badly it will hurt?"

"I understand how badly it hurts now," replied Robie.

"We're not cut out for each other, Robie. We're just not. We've made our beds. We have to sleep in them. Separately," she added with firmness. "I almost died in Iraq. I *should* have died there. I didn't care about the men I lost over there nearly as much as I care about you, and that loss is still eating me up inside."

"And anybody can get hit by a bus or die in a terrorist attack or get cancer. And people all over the world still choose to be together."

"It's not the same."

"Because you say it isn't."

"Because it's *true*."

"So you're saying that you won't feel bad if I die, because we're no longer together?"

She looked confused by this. "No, of course not. I would feel bad."

"So what's the issue here? If you're going to feel bad anyway, why not be together while we can?"

She snapped, "I'm not going to your funeral, and I don't want you coming to mine."

"You're way overthinking this, Jess."

"I'm not going to debate this with you." She paused. "And you have Malloy. She would obviously say yes to whatever you asked her."

"She probably would. But it does take two, Jess. "

"I know that."

"We could leave the service."

She said, "And do what? What else do we know how to do other than *this*?"

"So where does that leave us, Jess?"

Without another word, Reel turned and walked back to the SUV.

They sat silently in the truck until Blue Man came out.

He opened and closed the door to the house himself. They didn't see Claire at all this time.

When he climbed back into the truck he told the driver, "Back to the plane, please."

As they pulled off Robie said, "How did it go, sir?"

Blue Man kept his gaze directly out the window. "Much as I expected it would."

"Is that a good or bad thing?" asked Reel.

"Much as I expected it would and yet hoped that it wouldn't. She just lost both her children. One by my hand."

"So you really told her about that?" said Reel.

"When I said the truth, I meant it," replied Blue Man. "She deserved to know, no matter how much I didn't want to tell her."

"That must have been hard," said Robie.

"The truth is hard, Will. Far harder than a lie."

"How did you leave it with her?" asked Robie, his choice of words drawing a quick stare from Reel.

"I have no clue, Robie. And for someone in the intelligence field, that is never a good thing."

Don't I know it, thought Robie as he looked out the window at the gathering dusk.

"I asked her to marry me," said Blue Man abruptly.

"What?" exclaimed Reel. "Isn't that sort of sudden?"

"It's actually many decades overdue."

"But after everything that's happened," said Reel. "What you told her about Patti."

"I had to try. I had to."

"Why was that?" asked Reel.

"Because I love her. Sometimes it's just as simple as that. And if someone can't act on love, then what does anything else really matter?"

Robie hadn't really reacted to any of this. He just stared out the window, his mood growing fouler by the moment.

Until he felt it.

He looked down.

Reel's steely fingers had closed around his.

When he looked up, she was gazing straight ahead.

Yet he thought he saw the barest glimmer of a smile on her face.

And a solitary tear clutching at her right eye.

Robie gripped her hand back.

The truck drove as the night enveloped them.

Yet perhaps for Will Robie and Jessica Reel there was now a seam of light somewhere inside the darkness.

ACKNOWLEDGMENTS

To Michelle: Remember when we weren't sure if there'd ever be more than one book?

To Michael Pietsch, for always having my back.

To Lindsey Rose, Andy Dodds, Brian McLendon, Ben Sevier, Karen Kosztolnyik, Beth deGuzman, Brigid Pearson, Bob Castillo, Anthony Goff, Michele McGonigle, Andrew Duncan, Joseph Benincase, Tiffany Sanchez, Stephanie Sirabian, Oscar Stern, Matthew Ballast, Jordan Rubinstein, Dave Epstein, Rachel Hairston, Karen Torres, Christopher Murphy, Ali Cutrone, Tracy Dowd, Lukas Fauset, Thomas Louie, Laura Eisenhard, Anne Twomey, Flamur Tonuzi, Blanca Aulet, Mary Urban, Barbara Slavin, and everyone at Grand Central Publishing, for being a terrific partner all these years.

To Aaron and Arleen Priest, Lucy Childs Baker, Lisa Erbach Vance, Mitch Hoffman (and thanks for another fine editing job), Frances Jalet-Miller, John Richmond, and Rachael Burlette, for being great friends and advocates.

To Anthony Forbes Watson, Jeremy Trevathan, Trisha Jackson, Katie James, Alex Saunders, Sara Lloyd, Amy Lines, Stuart Dwyer, Geoff Duffield, Jonathan Atkins, Anna Bond, Sarah Willcox, Leanne Williams, Sarah McLean, Charlotte Williams, and Neil Lang at Pan Macmillan, for continuing to build me to lofty heights around the world.

To Praveen Naidoo and his team at Pan Macmillan in Australia, for topping themselves with each book.

To Caspian Dennis and Sandy Violette, for being both great drinking partners and top-notch literary agents!

To Kyf Brewer and Orlagh Cassidy, for your astounding audio performances.

To Steven Maat and the entire Bruna team, for doing a wonderful job.

To auction winners Brenda Fishbaugh, Clément Lamarre, Roark Lambert, and JC Parry, I hope you enjoyed your characters. Thank you for supporting such wonderful organizations.

And to Kristen White and Michelle Butler, for keeping Columbus Rose going strong!